Also by Karen Eisenbrey

Daughter of Magic

Wizard Girl

Strongly Worded Women: The Best of the Year of Publishing Women - An Anthology

The

Gospel

According to

St. Rage

by

Karen Eisenbrey

First edition published by Pankhearst in 2016
Reissued by Not a Pipe Publishing in 2019

Published in the United States by
Not a Pipe Publishing, Independence, Oregon.
www.NotAPipePublishing.com

Paperback Edition
Cover designed by Evangeline Jennings and Benjamin Gorman

ISBN-13: 978-1-948120-38-8

Dedication

For Mom,
who was never invisible,
wore a good hat,
and believed in grace and second chances.

The
Gospel
According to
St. Rage

1

INVISIBLE GIRL

Long ago but not at all far away, I met a wicked witch with blue eyes and golden hair. We had one thing in common: we were eight years old. For reasons I will never understand, she waved her wand, and I went invisible.

No, not literally. Duh. It's a figure of speech. The wand, I mean. But she was a witch. I'd spell it differently today, but still ...

Her name was Storm.

Seriously. Storm. I wish I had a name half as cool. Not a designer name — I'm not a designer girl — but maybe something vintage — Emma, Olivia, Rose. But no. My parents called me Barbara. That's not vintage. That's just old.

Although looking back, maybe Barbara's not so bad. Not compared to the magic nickname Storm gave me.

Picture this: I'm on the playground at recess, watching ants crawling in and out of a crack in the asphalt. Let's assume some kind of smudge on my shirt, another on my face, at least one Band-Aid, and wild hair that won't hold a curl and refuses to lie smooth no matter what I do. Because I'm concentrating on the ants, it's safe to say I'm nibbling my fingernails, a lifelong habit when I'm thinking or nervous or bored. Hey, it's a free country.

A shadow darkens the ant parade. It's Storm, a Pretty Little Girl straight out of Central Casting, with her gang of hangers-on. They're all cute, too, but Storm is the star. She wears name-brand clothes that never get dirty or ripped. Her shoes have sequins and lights. And her perfect hair always follows orders. She has a sweet voice and the most beautiful handwriting even though no one uses cursive anymore. She can cartwheel and do backbends. I can't even touch my toes. I hate her and I want to be her and I never have any reason to have anything to do with her at all. Why is she here?

"Ew, Barbara's eating boogers!"

Her giggling followers respond with a chorus of, "Ew!"

"No, see, it's fingernails." Like anyone's even listening. "I know, it's a bad habit. I should — "

"Barbara Booger! Barbara Booger!" Storm chants.

Then she stamps on my ants with a glittering, light-up shoe and prances away.

I hope, I pray it's over, but somehow she finds me to repeat her incantation, day after day after day. It never occurs to me to tell an adult. They'll tell me not to be so sensitive. They'll point out that if I didn't bite my nails, there'd be nothing to talk about in the first place. They'll blame me. Because Storm is perfect.

I guess I should be grateful. Storm had a gift for humiliation, but word in the halls was her big sister used fists. Heather was older and I never met her, but she was kind of a legend; probably still is. Whatever — I'd had enough attention of any kind, and I got busy trying to be inconspicuous. I stopped joining playground games. I didn't try for a swing. I no longer raised my hand in class — not easy when I usually knew the answer. I learned to be on time and always have my stuff ready so I wouldn't have to fumble around. By sixth grade, I was tracking my assignments in a spreadsheet rather than risk missing a deadline. I never dressed up for school, not even on the first day, which I've since learned is kind of cool, but in those days it was nothing but self-defense. I spoke as little as possible and tried not to move. And it worked! After a while, it was like Storm couldn't see me anymore.

Unfortunately, neither could anyone else.

OK, not entirely true. My parents see me, of course. Through parent-colored glasses. Mom tells me I'm beautiful in my own way and I just need to believe in myself. Thanks, Mom; I'll get right on that.

Dad has typical clueless dad-like advice: "Stay in school, don't do drugs, don't get pregnant." But he's also my music buddy. He tells me what he's listening to, asks what I'm listening to, and actually checks it out. That's cool, I guess. No one else seems to care.

Oh, yeah — the choir ladies at church. They can see me. They adore me because I bring down the average — I'm the youngest member of the choir by, like, ninety years. (But they say the same thing to my mom. Weird.) Singing is the thing I enjoy most, and the ladies have names like mine — Molly, Wendy, Betty, Kathy. Even another Barbara. We don't have enough teenagers for a youth group, so choir's my church group. Probably a better fit for me, anyway.

Storm and I went to different middle schools. I thought about trying to be more visible, but middle school is such an awkward time for everybody, passing unnoticed wasn't so bad. High school was going to be my coming out, the debut of a brand new me.

But —

Yeah, you guessed it. I show up the first day, all set to join clubs, audition for concert choir, try out for plays or sports or something ... and there's Storm, taller and blonder but unmistakable, somehow already running the show even as a ninth grader. Maybe she's only running it for the ninth graders — what do I know? — but that kind of squashes my plans. I fade back into the bulletin boards before she sees me, and that's where I've stayed.

So here I am — a junior in high school still trying to break Storm's third-grade spell. I'm tired of it, but I don't remember how to be seen.

Somewhere in the middle of all this invisibility, when I was twelve or so, my dad put on one of his records (which is the coolest thing people my parents' age have going for them: huge collections of amazing old vinyl) and I started screaming and jumping up and down. We differ in our recollection of which song it was. I say it was the Velvet Underground, "Rock & Roll;" Dad is sure it was the Ramones, "Rockaway Beach." For all I know, we're both wrong and it was Iggy and The Stooges. Whatever it was, I had found my thing.

Dad started taking me to shows — a couple of big stadium concerts, but mostly we prefer smaller theaters, little clubs, the minor stages at outdoor festivals. We've seen big names from decades past and up-and-coming local acts. It was good father-daughter bonding time, but last year, I persuaded him to let me go to some shows by myself in the hopes of maybe meeting other like-minded kids.

Here's my dream: I go to a show at VERA or some other all-ages club. Between bands a group of kids sits near me, and they're talking about starting a band, too. I say, "I've been writing songs," and they say, "Cool, you should be in our band." What actually happens is I go to shows and don't exchange words with anyone besides the door guy and the concession people. I stake out a spot near the stage, but wherever I choose to stand turns out to be in a major passage to the restrooms. Everybody has to walk where I'm standing. Everybody except this one huge guy — there's always this one huge guy — who plants himself right in front of me. Or worse, starts moshing wildly. I end up at the back out of self-preservation. I can't see much, but the bands are killing it. The music is loud and astringent and worth all the trouble, so I keep going. And I notice two things. The so-called cool kids don't form bands, and the people having the most fun are all up on the stage.

2

THE MAGIC HAT

The part of the daydream where I say I write songs? That's true. I don't play an instrument, but I had enough piano lessons to learn to read and write music. Mom says I always used to make up little songs while I played in my room with dolls and trains and blocks. She probably doesn't know I'm still using the toy keyboard I got for Christmas when I was six. I haven't told her that when I outgrew the rest of my toys I replaced them with a notebook full of lyrics and enough notation so I can remember the tunes ... you know, in case anyone ever does invite me to join their band.

I've been thinking I might reinvent myself as that

off-beat girl who gets her clothes from the thrift store and puts together her own quirky look and plays guitar on the front steps of the school. OK, we already have one of those off-beat girls, I don't actually play guitar, and she has a nose stud, which is further than I'm willing to go. But God knows I could use a new look, if what I have now even qualifies as a look. I'm so over my collection of T-shirts from summer camps and PTA fundraisers.

So on a blah Saturday in the middle of January when I have had it with Old Me, I take the bus to the nearest Value Village, where I quickly discover I have no idea how to put together a look. Where do I even start?

Maybe with the opposite of what I already have. I start looking for crazy stuff. Fake-fur vest? Yuck. Real-fur vest? Double yuck. Brown leather trench coat? Over-the-top awesome, but too nice to leave in my locker and too heavy to wear indoors all day. Funky hat? No, I don't wear hats. Sparkly purple minidress? About as far from school clothes as you could get. I throw it in my basket anyway, because it's only eight bucks and who knows? If anyone asks me to be their backup singer, I'm all set.

I've always secretly wanted to be one of those girls who wears cute shoes, so I take a chance and wander into the Shoes and Boots section. I can't believe my luck. There should be a bright light and a choir of angels, because my quest leads me to the Boots of Destiny. Purple suede with decorative fringe. I love fringe, and the color matches my backup-singer dress. No way they'll zip over my non-skinny jeans, though. I get a dressing room, take off my pants, and try on the boots. They zip, they fit, and they look kind of comic-book fabulous with my underwear. (If superheroes wore fringe. They totally should.) They're great with the glittery dress, too, though now it's even less of a school outfit. I'm thinking I might have to look for some skinny jeans, but when I take a step, I wobble and totter and almost break an ankle. I've spent years training my klutzy body not to trip or bang into things; that's a sure way to attract the wrong kind of attention. I just say no to heels. No great loss — I like my jeans comfy.

In the end, I grab a lime-green T-shirt from someone else's family reunion in 2006, and a tie-dye T-shirt from a fun run I didn't run in, which seems sort of vaguely quirky. I'm on my way to check out when I notice a green and orange flannel shirt that kind of goes with the family reunion shirt. There's also a blue and gray one that looks really soft, and a red and black plaid. In this climate, flannel's practical three seasons of the year — four, some years.

I grab all three of them. If I can't change my look, I can at least add a layer.

The school lunchroom is a huge time suck. You end up waiting in line for two-thirds of the lunch period and then inhaling whatever's on your tray in order to get to class on time. I bring my lunch from home and eat outside when the weather's nice, or in a classroom when it's gross. You learn which teachers are cool about it (and to stay out of the chemistry lab). When you're quiet and punctual and pass all your tests, you can get away with a lot. That's one theory. The other is I really am invisible. Whichever, I can read my book, enjoy my lunch, and still have a leisurely fifteen minutes to get to algebra. Which is a good thing, because it's way the heck on the other side of the building.

I like to take the back hallway. It's not a shortcut, so no good for the usual five-minute passing period, but I prefer it to the crowded main hall. There aren't lockers or a lot of classrooms down there — just the band room and storage closets for drama stuff. Some people think it's sketchy, but I don't usually see anybody except sometimes orchestra kids, drama kids, or the occasional stoner sneaking back in from the parking lot. They're all right. I don't bother them and they don't bother me. Because, you know, I'm invisible.

So I'm down there and when I come to the storage closets, one of them is open and the light's on. Well, what would you do? I slow down to take a peek, and somebody says, "Here, hold this," and plops a hat on my head.

"Excuse me?"

The guy turns around, and OMG, it's Jackson Durand.

I know, right? *Jackson.* Other people get all the good names.

He looks at me and instead of saying, "Sorry, I thought you were somebody else" (or more likely, "Sorry, I thought you were somebody"), he says, "Darling, that hat is *you!*"

OK, I know how that sounds. Jackson can get away with more flamboyance than most people because he's out and proud, not to mention talented, and the most gorgeous guy in school. Inventory: tall but not too tall; a streamlined swimmer's build; big, dark-chocolate eyes; black hair long enough to hang around his face in perfect little curls; cheekbones you could shelve books on; and precisely the right amount of stubble. At seventeen. I swear, for a second, I'm thinking I should have been a guy.

Anyway, I come back with a brilliant, "What?"

"That hat loves you, girl. I might have to let you keep it."

"I don't wear hats."

"Now you do. There's a mirror there — check it out."

I step into the storage room. It's crammed with racks of costumes. The walls are lined with shelves of hats and props, jumbled every which way. "What are you doing in here?"

"Organizing hats and costumes by decade."

"During lunch? 'Cause it looks like it'll take a while."

"I have a free period after this."

Like that'll be enough, but maybe he has superspeed. I find the mirror and take a look. There's a simple green tweed cap on my head, and I have to admit, it does in fact seem to love my face or my head or whatever it is hats love. I smile at my reflection, and my reflection smiles back. "I don't know ... "

"Well, here, try this one."

Jackson whips the cap off and replaces it with a bowl-shaped straw hat with a wide ribbon band. It looks good, too, in a different way.

"Maybe I do wear hats. What I mean is, I can't take

a drama department hat. That's, like, stealing."

"That cloche is a drama department hat, but the green one isn't. Not yet. I was about to donate it." Jackson swaps the hats and looks me over again. He sees me. "We should totally go hat shopping. What's your name?"

"Barbara."

"Lucky, you got a first name that's actually a first name. And it's my mom's name — easy to remember." He pulls a little case out of his pocket and extracts a plain white card:

Jackson Durand
Fashion Advice,
Sassy Commentary,
Unfiltered Opinions

What kind of high schooler carries business cards? Well, obviously, the kind with loads more style than me, so maybe I should pay attention here. It lists all his contact information. Wait, he wants *me* to call *him*?

He's studying me again, a thoughtful little frown creasing his forehead. "I should know you."

"Why would you?"

"Why wouldn't I? I mean I do know you from somewhere, but not school. Why haven't I seen you here?"

"Because I'm, like, invisible?"

"Obviously not."

"Must be the hat, then." I take it off.

Jackson's still watching me. "Nope, still visible.

Although, yeah, not as much. Could be the hat."

I grin and put it back on. "Magic hat."

"Magic or not, I think I can guarantee if you wear a hat around school, people will notice."

"They'll notice the hat."

"They'll notice you wearing the hat."

"I'm willing to risk it. If I don't want to be seen, I'll take it off."

"Oh, so now you have superpowers?" Jackson smiles and shakes his head. "I still think I've seen you somewhere. Hey, do you sing?"

"Uh ... yeah. In a church choir."

He snaps his fingers. "That's it! At the big brick one by the university? With the huge tower?"

I nod. Where's he going with this? "That's the one."

"Yeah, I thought so. It's hard to miss the one young person in that sea of gray hair. You even had a solo one time."

He heard me sing a solo? Part of me wants to crawl in a hole; the rest of me wants to squeal and faint. I somehow manage to keep my cool. "I haven't seen you there." I take a brimless pink hat off the shelf and try it on.

Jackson gives me the thumbs down. "Nope, pillbox doesn't work for you. Here, try this fedora." He sets a gray hat on my head and tilts it just so. "And you're not supposed to see me. I slip in and sit in the back to hear the organ and choir. Pretty great music for free."

"The sound's better in the middle." I check the mirror. The fedora has transformed me into an old-time movie star. Well, no. I don't have the hair, makeup or lighting. But the change is so dramatic, I can barely breathe. I return the fedora to the shelf. I'm not ready to be that visible. The green cap is a better way to ease into it.

"I wouldn't want to disrupt anything when I sneak out after the anthem. I'm only there for the music."

"Then you shouldn't leave! Sometimes we sing again at the offering, and the postlude is like a mini-recital." I can't believe I'm telling Jackson Durand what to do. The hat is kind of going to my head.

"Not sure it's worth it if I have to hear about Hell or Super Jesus doing magic tricks. I'm not even sure there's a God."

"And yet you go to the trouble of dragging yourself to some random church on Sunday morning." Yeah, this hat is definitely affecting me; that thought wasn't supposed to make it out of my head.

"Not so random. Like I said, I go for the music. I don't need to go to church to hear a rock band, but what you guys are doing, I can't find that just anywhere."

"Yeah, sometimes music is why I'm there, too. And outside of my family, it's the only group I have."

"We'll need to work on that." Jackson smiles in a thoughtful way. "So you don't believe in a magic man in the sky?"

Oh, great. Like I always spend my lunch period talking theology in a closet. But for that smile ... "I believe there's *something*. Not in the sky, and for sure not a man."

He laughs. "Oh, a magic woman, then?"

"Let's leave gender out of it. I don't know about magic, but something ... *more*. I call him or her or it

'God' because that's easier than making up a whole new name."

"That's refreshing, I guess. So you don't believe in miracles?"

"Well, not literally. I love those stories, but they're not so easy to take when you've had a few science classes."

"Exactly! How can you trust your book when it's full of impossible stuff?"

"I'm probably not the best person to ask — I've been questioning everything lately. But you can take what Jesus taught, without the miracles, and still have somebody worth following. I mean, wouldn't it be great if people actually lived that way, treated each other how he said?"

"You're making it sound a little more appealing. But it's hard to believe I'd be welcome."

"Come and see; we're not all like that. And if you sat in the middle, you'd be able to hear the music better."

"No promises, but I'll think about it. How come you don't sing at school?"

"I'm allergic to auditions."

"Try it sometime. They get easier. But you don't have to audition for the chorus in the spring musical. Just sign up."

I wave my hands to put a stop to that line of thinking. "Not really my thing."

"What is your thing? Grand opera?"

"I don't know, maybe. No! More like ... garage?"

"Seriously? You mean garage bands?"

"Yeah, that whole DIY, unprocessed sound — love it. It makes high school ... go away."

Jackson laughs, a big, unrestrained guffaw. "I never heard anybody put it that way, but I completely agree. And I should've guessed — you're rockin' that grunge look, Church Girl."

"I'm really not."

"You totally are. Though I'm not sure how often lime green was part of it. But I hear the nineties are back, so you're all set. Do you get to many shows?"

"Not as many as I'd like. A couple a month if I'm lucky."

"Me, too. How come I haven't seen you anywhere?"

"Invisible, remember?"

Jackson laughs. "Fine, you win. Don't rule out the musical, though. Speaking parts have already been cast, but chorus sign-ups go through next week."

"I'll ... think about it." I don't want to promise anything, but it could be a way to be more visible. "Hey, if you like garage bands — my dad took me to hear a band from way back. I thought they'd be lame, but they were amazing. Have you heard the Sonics?"

"Oh my God, those guys are so sick!"

And right there, he starts to sing "The Witch." I'm laughing my head off because this totally cool dude knows this totally cool old song that's kind of a classic but also kind of obscure. And even a capella, he's putting it across pretty well. Maybe when he's finished, I'll request "Cinderella."

I happen to glance into the hall, and wouldn't you know it, speak of the devil, while Jackson Durand is singing her song, here comes the infamous Storm Skye. I remove the green cap and prepare to disappear.

Jackson cuts off mid-line. Storm strides in on

stratospheric-heeled boots, dressed in a floaty, layered tunic that looks sheer but only reveals more layers, over jeans so skinny they must be tattooed on. Give the girl credit — she has a look and can walk in heels like it's her superpower. She gives Jackson a gigawatt smile and me a dismissive glance. She makes a shooing motion with her fingers. "Run along. I need to talk to Jackson."

I take a step toward the door, but Jackson waves me back.

"We're almost finished. Storm, have you met Barbara?"

Another quick glance, accompanied by a fake smile. "I don't think so. Hi, I'm Storm."

"Hi." This is probably the closest I've been to Storm in eight years, and my heart hits speed-metal tempos. But it's like she's already forgotten I'm there.

Jackson scrutinizes her face and frowns. "That looks bad. Heather do that?"

"What do you think?" Storm spits back. She turns from him in a way I'd call self-conscious if it were anyone but her. Now I can see the discoloration that mars the otherwise flawless makeup on her left cheek.

Jackson moves in for a closer look. "That's new; she never used to go for the face. Are you going to report it?"

"Oh, and make things worse?"

"Well, you should talk to someone."

"I'm talking to you."

"So you're talking to a gay teenager inside an actual closet. The metaphors write themselves."

This is weirding me out. Storm is shrinking before

my eyes, melting down to a human being with troubles of her own. I probably shouldn't be hearing what I'm hearing, but she's standing in the doorway. This'll be awkward whether I stay or go. I try to sidle out.

"Put the hat back, Barbara. It's not yours."

My sympathy evaporates. I start to put the hat on a shelf, but Jackson interrupts. "Actually, that one is."

And then it hits me. Storm can see me. And she doesn't know me. She has no idea who I am. For a nanosecond, I'm mad enough to tell her. How many years have I wasted? But why go there? Her power is broken.

Jackson lets her cool her stilettos a while longer. He turns to me. "Text me before Saturday, and we'll set something up. You've got my card."

Storm looks at me with more respect. "Ooh, can I have your card, Jackson?"

"Honey, you need a completely different one. Did you eat today?"

She scowls. "Yes, *Mom*. A granola bar and a yogurt."

"That's something."

OK, this has officially moved beyond awkward. "I'll be in touch." I turn to Storm with what I hope is a sympathetic smile. Maybe I'll give her another chance. Yeah, right, like she needs anything from me. But who knows? She might want invisibility lessons.

I head out and get about one step into the hall when I think of something. I turn back so fast I almost lose a shoe. "Hey, Jackson — what's the name of that girl who plays guitar on the front steps?" I probably knew it once upon a time, but this is a big school and I don't talk to a lot of people. Obviously. But Jackson knows everyone.

He grins. "Carol Anne Cochran. Why?"

"No reason."

Carol Anne. With a name like that, she has to be my people, right? She'll probably be able to see me. I might be able to talk to her. And she's in my algebra class.

I have to hurry, but I'm not late yet. I still can't believe I'm going hat shopping with Jackson Durand on Saturday. And tomorrow, maybe I'll sign up for the musical.

But today, I'll introduce myself to Carol Anne and ask her to be in my band. I don't know what I'll do if she says no.

3

HUGE GUY IN THE MOSH PIT

CAROL ANNE

I scoot into algebra exactly thirty seconds before the bell. I was sure I'd be late. I was playing down in the Commons, like I do when it's gross outside, and Marina showed up with requests. Anybody else would ask for Beatles songs, Led Zeppelin, Ramones, Nirvana. Not a problem; I can play those. Marina asked for folk songs, labor songs, standards ... things Grandad taught me. Holy Joe Hill. No surprise I lost track of time.

I'm still catching my breath when a girl I don't know slides into the seat in front of mine and turns around to face me.

"I'm starting a band. Wanna be in it?"

"Um, what?" I've never seen this girl before. I'd remember that hat.

"Sorry, sorry, sorry." She shakes her head. "You're Carol Anne, right? You play guitar?"

"Yeah, but — "

"OK. I'm Barbara. I write songs and I'm starting a band but I don't play anything ... so you wanna be in it?"

Do I? I love playing music. In theory, I like playing music with other people. In reality, I mostly play by myself. Not that I'm secretive about it. If I'm not playing at home, I'm out on the front steps of the school, or as I said, down in the Commons. People hang around and listen from a distance, sometimes shout out requests, make me late for class. If I play a familiar tune, some kids will even sing along. Marina says she doesn't sing outside the shower (which would ruin my guitar) but she knows a lot of songs. Jackson Durand will actually sit down next to me and sing harmony.

Everybody knows me because I'm a *quirky character*. Nobody has ever asked me to be in their band. Until now.

There's nothing remarkable about Barbara. Brown hair, brown eyes, neither tall nor short, fat nor thin. She dresses like a teenage boy from the nineties, if he liked bright colors. (I'm one to talk, with my cardigan, crinolines, and a chiffon scarf in my hair. And a nose stud, for a twist.) Barbara's look kind of works for her, though, especially with that cute military cap. Maybe it's Barbara that's cute. She's got a gleam in her eye like she's been to the mountaintop and come back with good news.

Before I can give her an answer, our algebra teacher calls us to order. I'll have to do this the old-fashioned way, since I don't have Barbara's number. I rip a scrap of paper from my notebook and write:

BAND = YES!!! TALK AFTER.

I fold it up into a tiny wad and toss it onto Barbara's textbook. She stares at it like no one's ever passed her a note before. When she finally unfolds it (under her desk, in the most obvious way possible) and reads it, her neck goes pink.

After algebra, we exchange numbers so we can make plans and then end up walking to history together. Apparently, we have the same schedule.

"So, Barbara, are you new here? I don't think I've seen you before."

"Nope, nobody has. I've been ... I mean, I had a — " She adjusts her cap. "I'm trying to be more visible. That's why I want to start a band."

"Why with me?"

"Why not with you? I've heard you play, and you've got that pretty Martin." Barbara gestures toward my guitar case.

So she knows instruments, at least a little. And it is a pretty Martin. It's too valuable to leave anywhere, so I have special permission to keep it with me during the school day. Part of being a quirky character. "I've got electrics at home — a Strat, and a Daisyrock twelve-string I got for Christmas."

"I knew I came to the right person! I had a feeling as soon as Jackson said your name."

"What about my name?" But if Jackson Durand is involved, it's probably OK. He knows everyone and is a good judge of character.

"Well, Carol Anne isn't exactly a fad name in our age group, is it? Almost as bad as Barbara." She makes a barf face, but it doesn't last. "I was named for my mom's college roommate. How 'bout you?"

"My father's sister Carol and my mother's sister Anne."

"What I would give to be called Olivia or Rain or, or, or ... "

"Storm?"

Barbara goes pale. "No, not Storm."

"OK, we'll keep our names. What about the band — what's the name of the band?"

"Don't we need more people first?"

"Who else is in it?"

"Just us so far. Do you know any drummers?"

"We should get Whitney."

"Which one?"

Fair question. There are at least five of them in our grade alone. "Whitney P — she's good, and I don't think she's in a group right now."

Barbara beams. "An all-girl band! I like the sound of that."

So do I, Barbara. So do I.

Who had the bright idea to schedule history class in the afternoon? Ten minutes in, we're all half-asleep. Things liven up when Oakley, our resident history-nerd, gets the teacher off on a tangent about Jackie Kennedy's pink pillbox hat. His theory seems to be that the shooter was aiming for the hat and missed.

My phone vibrates in my pocket. I pull it out and check it under the desk (not at all obviously) — a text from Barbara: hat like that in drama closet. didn't work for me

What is she talking about? Still, I tap out: **good thing, oakley'd see a conspiracy!**

I'm more awake now, but I'm glad it's the last period of the day. Barbara and I still have a lot to talk about. We end up at my house after school because it's closer than hers.

Mom's in the kitchen with her afternoon cup of coffee. It'll keep her up tonight, but I guess she'd rather complain than give up caffeine. Before I can even introduce Barbara, Mom looks up and says, "Leave your door open, remember?"

"Yeah, sure." We hustle up the stairs.

"What was that about the door? She doesn't think I'm a boy, does she?"

"Oh, no, it's about ... heat. The furnace works better with the doors open."

Barbara's jaw drops when we get to my room. I've totally papered it with posters of my sheroes and role models: Nina Simone, Mary Paul, the Wilson sisters, and ...

"Sleater-Kinney! Nice. So glad they got back together." Barbara walks up close to that poster. "Ooh, and Mo Tucker. I love the Velvets. Who's this?" She's looking at the only man on the wall, a framed photo of a smiling, silver-haired gentleman.

"My first guitar teacher — my grandfather. The Martin was his."

"He gave it to you? That's very cool."

"Well, he *left* it to me. In his will."

"Oh. It's still cool, but bummer that he died. I'm sorry."

She has no idea. I'm the youngest of twenty grandkids, and he specifically left his valuable guitar to me. I needed it, too. I grieved by playing it constantly. Grandad passed away a couple of weeks before the start of freshman year, and I literally could not get through the day without that guitar. That's the other reason I have special permission to carry it with me. I don't need it like that anymore, but it's a comfort I don't intend to give up. "It's been a few years now, but I still miss him."

"I like him," Barbara declares. "He looks very ... understanding."

"Yeah, he was. I could tell him things, and he didn't have to try to fix it, or get overinvolved. It was just ... OK."

Barbara moves on to a newer picture. "She looks familiar."

"That's Mary Lambert. You know, she did that song with Macklemore?"

"Oh, right." Barbara looks between me and the poster. "You could be her slimmer little sister."

Slimmer? Not an adjective my curves hear very often. "Keep talking."

"Well, you have a similar look, except for your glasses. Your hair's a darker red, but the lipstick's the same. How do you do that? Or eyeliner. When I try to do makeup I look like a clown! So I gave it up."

"You don't really need it, Barbara."

"Yeah, nobody looks at me anyway." That's not

what I meant, but I let it go. She checks out the guitars on their stands. "You've got all this gear, so why aren't you already in a band?"

"No one asked me."

"Nope, sorry, that was my excuse. You gotta come up with your own."

"Fine. Nobody's good enough to play with me." Wow, did I say that aloud?

Barbara gnaws a thumbnail. "Now I'm intimidated. What makes you think I might be?"

"Nothing yet. Just sing me a song already."

"OK, but it's hard if you're looking at me." Barbara goes and faces the corner, under my Patti Smith poster. Like *that's* not intimidating? She pulls a small notebook from her pack and flips through it. "OK, here's one that's not too embarrassing. This is 'Huge Guy in the Mosh Pit.'"

The song is short, fast, and funny. I like that; so many teenage songs are all angsty or soppy. Her voice is higher and purer than you usually get in a punk song, too.

I keep quiet while she's singing, but when she's finished, I can't contain myself. "Sweet mother of Gershwin!"

She turns around, wide-eyed. "Um, what?"

"Sorry; something Grandad used to say when I played especially well. Do you have any more like that?"

"Not really. Now that I look at them, most of these songs are pretty silly."

As if "Huge Guy" isn't silly, but I hold that thought. "Come on, let me see. You don't have to sing if you don't want to."

We sit next to each other on the floor by the bed. She holds the notebook so we can both see and starts flipping pages. They're not bad lyrics, but she's right. They trend young, with topics like gym class and field trips and pets. Still, a few of them have me laughing out loud.

"Maybe we can make a children's album someday. I like this one about the cat, and the squirrel one is hilarious."

"You think so? I like those, too, but they're not very garage-y."

"Too true. 'The Art Museum Hurts My Eyes' seems kind of punk, but the rest of them, probably not. What key is 'Huge Guy' in?"

"I don't know. I sing where it's comfortable."

"So that's the first thing to figure out." I get the guitar out and noodle around until I've come up with some basic chords. "I think it needs a rave-up after the first verse, don't you? Because it sounds like a classic garage-rock song."

"Does it? That's what I was hoping. Play me what you're thinking."

So I do, and pretty soon, we have a rough arrangement. "We're doing this, Barbara. Let me text Whitney, see if she's in."

"So she's good enough?"

"Yeah, but she was never available before. Now that Plague of Turtles is over — "

"Plague of Turtles?! Wow, I heard them at a talent show in eighth grade. They were great — why'd they break up?"

"Creative differences. So we must have gone to the same middle school. How come I never saw you before today?"

"Nobody saw me before today."

"Uh-huh." I text Whitney: wanna be in a band with me & barbara?

She answers within seconds: so long as I don't have to lead it. who's barbara?

writes songs. you'll like her.

"Whitney's in. Can you practice on Saturday?"

"I can't this Saturday. I'm going shopping with Jackson Durand, and then there's a Ne'erdowells show at VERA I want to catch."

"Shopping with Jackson? Lucky you. I didn't realize you guys were close."

"I never talked to him before today, when he put this hat on me. Next thing I know, he's offering to take me shopping. No way I'm turning that down." She flops back and gazes at the ceiling. "He is soooo cute!"

I nod. "Not my type, but definitely a good-looking specimen. You do know you're completely out of luck, right?"

She sighs. "Yeah. Probably just as well; if he was straight, he wouldn't even notice me."

"OK, knock it off! Straight boys are dumb, but they're not that dumb."

Barbara sits up, pink in the face; yeah, they'll notice her, all right. "Maybe you're right. I mean, nobody had a chance to notice me, right? Now, they'll at least see the hat."

I'm not sure what she's talking about; I wave it off. "Back to the topic at hand: if we're starting this band, we should find a time to practice."

"I don't have a lot going on. I can't do Wednesday nights — that's choir practice."

Which explains the sweet voice. "What kind of choir?"

"Church — me and my mom and a bunch of old folks." She frowns. "That didn't come out right. We sound a lot better than we should — the weekly miracle."

I laugh with her, but now I'm worried. A church girl. That might pose a problem. "You're not thinking of this as a Christian band, are you?"

"Ew, no. But ... all music is sacred, right?"

I kind of like that thought. Maybe it'll be OK. "So who all is going to this show on Saturday?"

"Just me. Ooh, do you wanna come along?"

"Yeah, I haven't been to a live show in ages. I don't feel comfortable going by myself. Don't guys hassle you?"

"That's the advantage of being invisible. I might get stepped on, but I've never been harassed."

"I find that hard to believe."

"You'll see. We'll pick you up at eight o'clock."

Right at eight on Saturday, the doorbell rings. I figured Barbara would text me from the car and I'd dash out, but OK. I'm ready to go, even though I changed outfits four times and ended up back at my first choice. I'll run down and ... Mom gets to the door first, which means everybody gets asked in and introduced. We need to get out of here before she goes full hostess.

"Mr. Bernsen, it's so nice of you to give the girls a ride."

"Please, call me Steve."

"I'm Nancy, and this is my husband, Mike. Would you like some tea before you go? Oh, here's Carol Anne now."

Barbara's dad gives me a wave. "Hi, Carol Anne, nice to meet you. See, Barbara? It wouldn't kill you to put on a dress when you go out."

"Dad, we're going to a punk rock show. Besides, that's not just a dress — that's a period costume. Which looks great, by the way. Where do you find such cool old stuff?"

"This was my Aunt Anne's. Vintage works better for me than new." The *costume* is a blue and silver lamè minidress and white go-go boots, which looks fab with my cat-eye glasses. There's even a shoulder bag that matches the boots. Aunt Anne was built like me, the opposite of long and lean, but it didn't stop her from having great style. (Mom, in grade school at the time, got the matching Barbie doll.)

Barbara's not dressed any different than she was at school: jeans, T-shirt, flannel. These jeans are black, and so is the T-shirt, except for a red band logo. The flannel is a black and red plaid. She's got an oversized bag with fringe on the flap, but she's not wearing her cute cap. She pouts. "I was gonna ask what you thought of my new duds, but now I feel scruffy."

"You're fine — much better for the occasion." I put on my coat and join her by the door. "I can't believe Jackson Durand picked those out, though."

"Nope, this is all me. Isn't this fringe-y bag

amazing?"

"It's totally you." It doesn't go with the rest of her outfit, to be honest. But anything that makes a person smile like that will always be in style.

Barbara's dad gestures toward the bronzy-orange PT Cruiser parked out front. "Ladies, your carriage awaits."

Good, Mom didn't have a chance to put the kettle on. We escape down the front walk to the car.

"Anyway, wait and see," Barbara says. "Jackson came through for me big time. I'm never going shopping without him, if I can help it."

I figure she'll call shotgun, but we both get into the back. When her dad gets in, Barbara taps the back of his seat and says haughtily, "Drive, Steve," like it's *Downton Abbey* and he's the chauffeur. And we crack up. We're so immature.

Barbara's dad drops us off at The VERA Project, a tiny all-ages club. (Of course, it would have to be all-ages. With a fake ID, I might be able to pass for twenty-one, but I'm not sure Barbara could even pass for sixteen.) The non-profit that runs it also offers classes to teens interested in music and music production. I've been meaning to get down here more, but so far, I've only been to one show, back when Plague of Turtles was a thing.

We pay the door guy our seven bucks each and head down the stairs, through the little art gallery, and into the club. We pile our coats in a booth in back with everyone else's. The opening act has already started, but it's not crowded yet. We're able to get right up close to watch this pretty girl play her pretty Gibson (but not as pretty as my Martin). She's all right — plays well enough, strong voice, but the songs are too mopey for my taste.

The crowd is thicker by the time the set ends, a mix of teens, parents, and twenty-somethings. I'm thinking we're the only ones from school, but then I see the back of a head that looks familiar, heading out of the club. "I'm gonna hit the restroom. You?"

Barbara shakes her head. "I'm OK. I'll hold our places here if you'll bring back some water."

I didn't notice inside, but as I make my way out, there they are: elevator eyes, all around me. I kind of regret my choice of a short, fitted dress. On the other hand, screw 'em. I love this dress. At least nobody says anything. Must be because of all the moms in the room.

In line for the restroom, I spot the familiar face I'm looking for. "Marina! Enjoying the show?"

When she turns and smiles at me, her dimples go up to eleven. Her short hair is dyed black, and if anyone could teach Barbara about eyeliner, it's Marina. She's wearing cut-offs and lace tights, a great look for her. "Hey, Carol Anne. Yeah, the opening singer is my cousin Rebecca. She was nervous, so Mom and I came out to support her."

"Cool! She was ... good. I couldn't tell she was nervous. Nice guitar, too. Are you staying?"

"No, I can't this time — the maternal unit doesn't like loud music. But, hey, I'm glad I ran into you. It's my birthday next Friday — sweet-sixteen-never-been-kissed." She grins and winks at her own dumb joke. "That's what my step-dad calls it. Wanna come?"

Now I'm glad we haven't made solid band plans.

"Sounds fun. Big party?"

"A few friends. As for a kiss ... maybe it'll be my lucky night."

"Someone special gonna be there?"

Her eyebrows flick up and her smile turns wicked. "I hope so. Give me your number, I'll text you the details."

"Cool." We swap numbers, and then a couple of stalls open up. When I come out, she's gone. It was nice of her to invite me, but I don't know. It'd be different if we were besties, but if her crush shows up, a casual acquaintance like me will only be in the way.

I stop by the concession stand for two bottles of water, then head back in. I can't find Barbara at first, though she hasn't moved. There are guys all around, but they don't seem to notice her — or me, now. I hand her a water.

"Thanks!" She takes a swig. "I've heard this next group once before. They might get loud — want some earplugs?" She digs into her bag and passes me a package, so we're both ready when the Ne'erdowells take the stage.

They're a trio of boys about our age, and they play straight up garage punk. During their set, I notice another familiar face from school: Oakley, standing alone off to the side. He's got his arms wrapped tight around himself and he's intent on the floor as he listens. I'm glad he's not looking at me. He doesn't do elevator eyes; that dude never even blinks.

I can't have heard the name right for the next act. I think he said Your Mother Should Know, which sounds like a Beatles tribute band. This isn't that. They're a two-piece sibling act — brother on guitar, sister on drums — and roughly my parents' age. What they lack in youth they make up with musical intelligence and well-crafted pop songs. The headliner is Dead Bars, a five-piece pop-punk act who sound like they're inventing the genre in the moment. Their songs remind me of Barbara's, goofy observations of whatever happens to be going on. They're even louder than the previous bands, so I appreciate the earplugs. The energy in the room is amazing. The kids from the Ne'erdowells and the guy from the middle-aged duo are slamming each other like old friends. Barbara and I are singing along at the top of our lungs to songs we're hearing for the first time. It helps that they have a lot of lah-lahs and woah-woahs.

Then a guy the size of Sasquatch parks himself right in front of us, completely blocking our view of the stage. To make matters worse, he starts moshing wildly. I move back a couple of steps, but he steps right on Barbara's foot. She shoves him off, but then he's right back practically on top of her. I brace myself to catch her if she falls. She doesn't. She rears back and kicks him right in the butt. Are you kidding me? She must be a lot stronger than she looks, too, because the kick launches him into two of his buds. All three of them land in a heap in front of the stage. He jumps up and looks around, right over or past or through but not at Barbara, or me standing behind her. I guess we're not likely-looking suspects, but c'mon — I'm wearing a silver dress, and he can't see me? What the hell is going on?

Laughing hysterically, Barbara drags me back to the

booth with all the coats. We shove a few over and plop onto the benches. "One at every show!" she yells. She extends a foot — she's wearing combat boots. "Genuine Doc Martens! Jackson found them for me — $10 and practically new! And check this." She reaches into her bag and pulls out a red newsboy cap, even cuter than the green one. She puts it on and her whole outfit pops to life.

It's getting warm in here with so many people thrashing around in a small space. The band pauses between songs to joke about the absence of beer, and Barbara takes her hat off. The band starts up again. Across the room, Oakley claps his hands over his ears.

"That poor guy!" Barbara yells. "Be right back."

She dodges around the crowd, taps Oakley on the shoulder, and offers him one of her earplugs. Huh. Does she know that weirdo? I lose sight of them as the crowd shifts. Then a guy I don't know sits down across from me. He's looking me right in the chest.

"Hey, babe, you here by yourself?"

Before I can answer, Barbara slides in next to me and puts her hat back on. She drapes her arm around my shoulders. "No, she's here with me."

After the show, we wait outside for Barbara's dad. I'm still jazzed from the high-energy music. I definitely need to get out to more shows. Or play in some. "Did you notice that out of eleven performers total, only two were women?"

"Yeah, it's usually kind of lopsided."

"We have to do our band. For the greater good."

Barbara laughs and nods in agreement. She's

bouncing up and down to keep warm. "I love these boots! I can't believe I kicked that guy!"

"I know, that was nuts! And what was up with giving that guy your earplug? But, you know, that other thing you said — 'She's here with me'? — Some people might take that the wrong way."

"Wrong way how?"

"They might think you're a lesbian."

She considers this. "Could be worse. Up to now, nobody's thought I was anything."

"But you're not, are you?"

She kicks at the concrete with the toe of her boot. "Probably not."

I take a deep breath and dive. "I, um, probably am."

"Yeah, I wondered."

"You did? What gave it away?"

"Uh, maybe the Mary Lambert poster? It kind of clicked with what your mom said about the door. You out to her?"

"Yeah, but not to my dad."

"Oh. Awkward."

"We're going to talk to him together. Soon, I hope."

"Is your mom OK with it?"

"She's ... trying to be OK. It's an alien planet for them, you know?"

"Wow, yeah, I guess it would be. What about your grandad?"

"I never got to tell him. I think he would have been supportive, though. That's how he was." I don't want to ask, but I have to. "It's not a problem for you?"

"No, why would it be?"

"Church people can be weird about things like

that." Which is why I quietly stopped going after confirmation. A lot of kids leave then; I never even had to come out.

"Then they're doing it wrong. My church is trying to do it right. Besides, as of now, all my friends are gay — what am I supposed to do?"

I laugh at that. I'm feeling better about things.

Barbara bounces a little more, then shoots me a sly grin. "So you know my crush. Who's yours?"

Hoo-boy. Well, why not dive deeper? "A sophomore named Marina."

"Marina? Oh, yeah, I think I know who she is. She signed up for the spring musical the same time I did. She's got those cute dimples? Kind of goth, but too smiley to pull it off?"

I have to chuckle at the description. "That's the one. But the musical? She doesn't even sing."

"I think she was signing up for stage crew. S'pose she plays bass?"

"I ... don't think so."

"Bummer. Think she knows you like her?"

I shrug — who can tell? "She invited me to her birthday party. I want to go, but ... she hinted there might be someone special there. I don't think I could take watching her make out with some guy."

"What if the someone special is you?"

I hadn't thought of that, but she did seem happy to see me ... "OK, maybe I will go to the party."

"You should sign up for the musical, too. Good excuse to hang out."

"I might — what's the show?"

"*Anything Goes.*"

Wow, it's like a sign. And Cole Porter, to boot. Grandad would be pleased. "OK, I'm in. Just not sure I'm all the way out."

She nods and bounces a few more times. "Hey, I'm making a resolution. Wanna hear it?"

"Barbara, it's February."

"So I'm slow; eventually I get there. Here it is: I resolve to no longer give a shit what other people think." She covers her mouth and giggles like a fourth-grader. "I said shit!"

"It's a word. People say it."

"Not me. Must be the hat. Or the boots. Anyway — the resolution. It might be easier if I'm not keeping it by myself."

"In theory, I like the idea. But is it safe?"

"You should be able to be who you are." She crosses her arms and puts on a fierce face. "Anybody wants to give you trouble will have to go through me."

The ferocity lasts about a second and then dissolves in our giggles. I mean, Barbara's maybe an inch taller than I am and twenty or thirty pounds lighter. She's no hero, no matter how many huge guys she kicks. But for that second, I could almost see a cape and high-heeled boots.

"Barbara, whatever happens, we will have the most kickass band in the universe."

"Yeah. With or without a bass player."

4

LOST CHILDREN

WHITNEY

Fuck, is it only Thursday? This week, this year (while we're at it, high school) can't end fucking soon enough. Dad stays late on Thursdays, so I'm riding the bus home after school — the four sideways seats in the middle, my preference. Sitting there even with three strangers feels more like riding by myself than sitting with only one in the regular seats. Although you run the risk of ending up across from a weirdo, like that stoner Oakley.

Anyway, I'm on my way home and I get a text from

Carol Anne Cochran, of all people.

wanna be in a band with me & barbara?

What the actual fuck? I mean, I know who Carol Anne is; everybody does. We kind of connected at a music thing last year and exchanged numbers, but we don't hang out or text. She's, like, vintage clothes, vintage guitar, folk songs and oldies; I'm black leather, spiked hair, lip ring and punk rock. But what the hell? She sure as fuck can play. Besides, I miss the band energy since Plague of Turtles broke up. Which was *my* band to begin with, but I made the mistake of forming it with shithead boys, one in particular, but we don't talk about that. This looks like a girl group, which is more my style.

I text back: **so long as I don't have to lead it. who's barbara?**

writes songs. you'll like her.

Sounds promising. I put my phone away and look up to find Oakley staring at me.

"Take a picture, asshole, it'll last longer."

He twitches and blinks. "I ... um ... sorry, I — " Rather than finish that articulate thought, he leaps from his seat and flees to the back of the bus. Weirdo.

Hard to believe I used to hang out with him and his stoner buddies back in ninth grade. That was a rough year. I wanted to go to the arty alternative school; my parents insisted I go to the big conventional school where Dad teaches. My best friend Storm was going there, too, but then I almost never saw her. On top of that, my band was in conflict and I had boyfriend troubles. It felt good to rebel in the mellow company of the stoners out by the parking lot. By the time the fun wore off, I'd wasted almost the whole year. Summer school got me back on track, a pretty steep price for a backfired rebellion. I never went back to the parking lot, and I don't care to acknowledge those guys when we meet, say, on the bus. But also — Oakley's a capital W Weirdo.

I go looking for Carol Anne during lunch on Friday. She's easy enough to find — she's the one in the Commons playing guitar. What's different is, I don't recognize the tune. I don't recognize the shaggy-haired dude next to her on the couch, either.

"Hey, the nineties called — they want their flannel shirt back." The kid looks up and he's a she, giving me a look of complete panic.

Carol Anne stops playing. "Whitney, say hello to Barbara."

"Oh, shit, I'm sorry. Don't mind me. I've got a mouth with a mind of its own. Doesn't know when to quit."

Barbara starts breathing again. "Oh, hey, Whitney. That's OK; my mouth usually doesn't know when to start. So, Carol Anne says you want to be in our band."

"Well, I'm open to the idea. What kind of music do you play?"

Carol Anne grins and starts over on the tune I didn't know. This time, Barbara sings a short, funny punk song about an experience I know too well. There's always this one huge guy. I'm laughing out loud by the end of the song.

"Barbara, if you've got a few more like that, I am in. Who else do we have? Bass, keys?"

Carol Anne shakes her head. "I've been asking

around, but nobody has time for another project."

"Fuck 'em. We'll do it as a three-piece. We got a name yet?"

"Not yet. Or a practice time or practice space."

"You guys free on Thursdays after school? We might be able to practice here. Dad stays late to work with the chamber ensembles. If we could use the band room, I wouldn't have to move my kit."

Barbara presses her hands to her head like her hat might fly off. "Mr. P is your dad? How dumb am I that I didn't know that?"

"Why would you? Aren't you new here?"

Barbara grins. "I don't blame you for thinking so, but we've been in classes together off and on since sixth grade."

Carol Anne grabs Barbara's hat. "Barbara's had a minor visibility problem; this band oughta fix that."

Barbara snags the hat back and settles it on her head. "It's just, you don't look much like your dad."

Understatement of the year — Dad's a skinny little black guy in a bowtie and glasses, while I'm a half-black, half-Asian chick with spiky green hair and a bunch of facial piercings. When people see the punk surface first, they're less likely to ask, "What are you?"

"Thursdays are good for me," Carol Anne says. "But calling us a chamber ensemble is a stretch."

"A garage is a chamber." Barbara says this with such sincerity that I'm not sure she's joking, until she snorts.

I think we'll get along fine. "Anyway, it's just a technicality so we can use the room."

Carol Anne stows her guitar in its case. "We're

going to a show at VERA tomorrow. Wanna come?"

"Wish I could, but the 'rents are going out to the symphony. I have to keep an eye on my bro."

Which I really thought I wouldn't have to do anymore. I mean, Hideo's twelve and bigger than I am now — he should be able to stay by himself for a few hours. But because he and his worthless friends seem to get into trouble whenever they're left on their own, I have to play warden.

And here I am, ten o'clock on a Saturday night, already in my sweatpants and the ratty old Ramones shirt I wear to bed. And Storm's hand-me-down Uggs, which are not my style at all but I'll admit they're cozy to wear around the house in winter. I've washed my face, so I'm in for the night, voice-chatting with Storm while I succumb to clickbait on the Internet. Lamer than lame, but we're having a good time reading each other celebrity gossip and taking stupid quizzes. "I know why I'm in the convent. What's your excuse?"

It takes Storm a moment to answer. "Going out takes energy I don't care to spend."

"Thought you were feeling better."

"I am, some. This week didn't start out so great. Shit, have you even seen me? You should see this."

We switch to video. Whoa, I haven't seen Storm without makeup or contacts since probably sixth grade. She'll always be beautiful, but that bruise gets in the way. Even the hipster glasses can't hide it.

"What. The. Fuck."

"Heather found out I dropped Cheer, and you know how she gets when I try to run my own life."

"That was before Christmas, when you had mono, right?"

"I was pretty sick. Heather's been distracted, so I managed to keep it from her till now. She's got a serious boyfriend, and she's trying to finally graduate."

"Does the boyfriend know about her temper?"

"You think I'm gonna warn him?" She gingerly touches the bruise. "She'd kill me."

"Shit, I'm sorry. I wish I coulda helped somehow."

"No, it's OK. Jackson worked his usual magic, got things headed in the right direction. I don't think I've ever seen my dad so pissed — as of last night, Heather is O.U.T. out."

"Out of the house? About fuckin' time." She should be in jail, in my opinion, but it's their family.

"And ... I plan to start seeing someone."

"Like, a guy? That's nothing new."

"No, like a therapist. Once Dad figured out how much he'd missed, he jumped in to fix everything. Mom's going to rehab, too."

I thought I knew Storm pretty well, but an awful lot of this is news to me. What do I have to offer? Then Storm hands me a perfect opening.

"Girl, I'm tired of the pity party. We should do something fun."

"What, this isn't fun?" I laugh at us in our sweats, hanging out online. "You're right. But not shopping. I'm sick of the mall." I had a job there over the holidays. Retail will never be the same.

"Never thought I'd say it, but me, too. I'm thinking something ... different. Something Heather would hate."

"Well, then, I have the perfect thing. Some of us are starting an all-girl punk band. You wanna be in it?"

"Wow. Heather would absolutely hate that. But I don't play anything."

"You could sing backup, play tambourine. Just dance or something. It'd be good for you."

"Good for me how? Like kale?"

"What the fuck does kale have to do with it? I just think it'd do you good to have some fun with a different group of people. Like a cultural exchange."

"I'll think about it. Maybe I could — "

I hear the front door open and close. "Oh, shit, he's making a break for it. Seeya!"

I shove my phone into my pocket and race through the house. I make the porch in time to see my brother tearing ass down the street. Moron — he left his skateboard. I pull on my biker jacket, grab the board, and roll off in pursuit.

I haven't been on a board in years and the sidewalk's pretty gnarly. A teeth-rattling sidewalk hump catches the front trucks and stops the board cold. Because fucking inertia is a fucking property of fucking matter (thanks, Science Guy), I, the object in motion, stay in motion. All that gymnastics training finally pays off, though. I manage to turn the fall into the world's shittiest handspring. What, I should stick the landing and go ta-da? I'm happy to land on my feet instead of my head. My palms sting; I don't recommend handsprings on concrete, but it beats a face plant. I pat my pockets to make sure I've still got my wallet and keys, then jump on the board again.

I'm gaining on him. A bus rumbles past me when

I'm half a block from catching up. Shit, the kid's at a bus stop and dives on as soon as the doors open. I pound the side of the bus so it won't pull away, jump off the board and scoop it up. The doors open again and I climb up, tap my wallet against the sensor, and follow my dumb brother to the back of an almost empty bus. When he sits, I plop down next to him.

"So, Dee, what's the plan?" I put an arm around him and hold him down in case he's thinking of jumping off at the next stop.

"Fuck you, Nee. I don't need a babysitter."

"Tell Mom and Dad. I didn't ask for this gig."

"So let me go. Tell 'em I snuck out."

"Too late for that." I pull out my phone and call the landline at home. It goes to voicemail. "Hey, it's Whitney. We decided to go out. Hope that's OK. We'll probably be kinda late. Seeya!"

Dee stares at me, wide-eyed. "You didn't tell on me."

"No. I didn't. Now can you trust me enough to clue me in?"

He slouches in the seat. "A bunch of guys were gonna sleep over at Logan's tonight, maybe go do something fun. Mom wouldn't let me go."

"No shit! Remember what happened last time you stayed over at Logan's? You vandalized your school!"

"It was a blank concrete wall. Our graffiti improved it."

"If you'd painted a mural or tagged it, I'd agree. But no, you little assholes spray-painted four-letter words and cartoon penises all over it. It was so obviously the work of middle schoolers. And that other time—you shoplifted Doritos and Mountain Dew from 7-11."

"Only the Doritos; we paid for the pop."

"Oh, well, then ... " I'm about to say something cutting, but the kid's near tears. "Seriously, dude, what is up?"

"Why am I the one in jail? The rest of the guys were grounded for, like, a day or two. They get to hang out, go places without a nanny. Why me?"

Oh. So I get to have this talk with him. Fuck. "Dee, your friends are all White — "

"Jacob's Korean."

" — or Asian."

"I'm half-Asian."

"Yeah, and half-Black, which to the average White cop means all-Black."

"I know all this shit, Nee — be respectful, don't run, show your hands, blah-blah-blah. It completely sucks that I have to know it and my friends don't. Like I'm some kind of monster."

"You're not the monster in this story. But what if some night somebody thinks the phone or spray can or pop bottle is a gun?"

"I would never — !"

"I know, Dee. But the real monsters don't. And the thing with monsters is, you can't tell who's a monster until they're trying to kill you. Why do you think Dad wears a suit and that nerdy bowtie? Why did he wear glasses that he didn't need until last year?"

"What do you mean? Dad's worn glasses my whole life!"

"Mine, too. But he didn't need them. He told me he started wearing them in college, to look more serious.

And more harmless."

"*More* harmless?" Dee protests. "He's a viola player!"

"Yeah, think about that. You're already almost as tall as Dad, and you're only twelve."

"That is fucked up."

"Reality, dude. Fuckin' reality."

He shakes his head and turns away. "Reality blows."

Can't argue with that. I look around and realize I don't know where we are. "Hey, Dee, where does this bus go?"

"I don't know. Which one is it?"

Seriously? OK, I guess I'm the sort-of grown-up here. I look up at the display: 43 to Downtown. Shouldn't be too hard to get home from there. "Let's get off downtown and see what's running the other way."

"OK. Is it too late to do something fun?"

I check the time: almost eleven. "For people your age? Probably."

We get off at a well-lit stop. There are some people around, mostly smoking near a bar up the street. Buses are few and far between this time of night. Dee pulls up his hood and shoves his hands into his pockets.

"Could you leave the hood down? People are weird about hoodies these days."

"I'm cold."

"Well, if you had any sense, you'd have put on a coat, dumbshit." I don't have the heart to tell him to keep his hands out of his pockets, too. I mean, it *is* cold — that's what pockets and hoods are for, right?

A bus pulls up. It doesn't go near home, but I urge

him on. "Let's warm up."

We ride this bus out of the downtown core, toward the Center. Yeah, I know. Makes no sense to me, either. You get used to it.

"I'm hungry. Can we get Mickie D's?" Dee points to the Golden Arches looming a block away and pulls the cord before I can answer.

Is he serious? But growing boy and all that ... "What's the magic word?"

"I dunno — abracadabra? Wingardium leviosa?"

See what I'm dealing with? Such a nerd. I stare at him till he loses his smirk.

"Um, please?"

"Oh, all right."

We get off the bus and jog across the parking lot to the restaurant. The place is busy but not packed. Most important, it's warm. I almost turn right back around when I see two cops having coffee on the other side of the restaurant. But one of them's brown and a woman, and cops need coffee in the middle of the night. And we have a right to come in and buy food. So far, they don't seem to care about us, but I yank Dee's hood down anyway.

"Try to look Japanese."

Dee's already talking about super-combo meals and milkshakes, but I pull him back before he orders. "You got any money?"

"Some." He digs around in his pocket and comes up with about fifty cents in change.

I open up my wallet and between us we have enough for a four-piece McNugget and a hot chocolate.

"They look lonely." Dee dunks a nugget in barbecue

sauce and grins. "Check it out — we are an entire order of fries short of a Happy Meal."

I keep a straight face, but he's so not wrong. "It's not a meal, it's a snack. Now shut up and eat." I take a slurp of hot chocolate and half a nugget for myself, since I paid for most of it, and let the growing boy have the rest. I pull out my phone to check bus schedules. "Shit, I'm almost out of charge." I turn it off to save power. Across the way, the Latina cop gets up and crosses over to our side to throw away the empty cups. I casually place my hands on the table, and to his eternal credit, Dumbshit Dee gets the message and does the same.

"It's getting pretty late," the cop says. "You kids all right?"

I give her a big smile. "Yep. Just waiting for our ride. Warmer in here than at the skate park." I pat the board to back up my story.

"I'll bet it is. Well, you kids have a good night." She joins her partner at the door and they head back out to their squad car.

OK, I didn't need that, but she was right about the hour. We should get our asses home. When the food's gone, we use the restrooms and head back out. It feels colder after the warm restaurant.

"I think the bus we need runs on the other side of the Center. Want to cut across or go around?"

"It's shorter to cut across."

True, but the streets go every which way. Some are a grid and some cut through diagonally, and I always get turned around. I don't let on that I'm lost either way. We cross the street and head into the sprawling campus of lawns, museums, theaters, and a food court, most of which are closed at this hour. The Needle looms overhead, eerie in the gathering fog. We take turns towing each other on the skateboard, and even try to ride it together, but it's not quite long enough. We reach the other side, which doesn't help. Nothing looks familiar. I turn on my phone again to check a map and it announces an urgent voice mail. Oh, shit. I listen as Mom wonders where we are, berates me for turning my phone off, insists I call home ... and then the phone dies before she can finish. And I still don't know where we are.

"Lend me your phone, Dee."

"I didn't bring it."

I'm too tired to even get mad at him. He's shivering in his thin hoodie, and I'm starting to get cold now, too, walking around in what are, essentially, my pajamas. I feel very exposed without the armor of my punk-girl makeup. We start walking again, around the perimeter. We take turns carrying the board, a heavy load for something so small. If we don't find a useful bus stop soon, I don't know how we're getting home. My phone's dead; Dee doesn't have his. Are there still payphones? Doesn't matter; we spent all our money on fucking McNuggets.

A big white SUV pulls up to the curb. The driver gets out and the car does the little beep-beep thing when she locks it with her fob. She's a mom-type, wearing a jacket and shoes suited to the weather.

Dee takes a couple of steps toward her. "Excuse me, ma'am?"

Politest I've ever heard the little snot, but I wish he

woulda warned me. "Um, Dee?" I grab for his sleeve but miss.

SUV-mom stiffens. "I don't carry cash."

"No, I just wondered if we could borrow your phone." Dee's using this slow, calm voice, like he's talking to someone about to jump from a bridge.

"Don't come any closer!" She holds a tiny cylinder in her hand, a fan of keys and saver-club cards dangling below it.

"Dee, look out!"

She squeezes and hits him ... with the bright but not disabling beam of an LED flashlight. With a tremulous whimper, she turns and stumbles back to her oversized vehicle. It beep-beeps again, she climbs into the driver's seat, and speeds away.

Dee watches, shaking his head. "That was weird."

"I hope she doesn't call the fucking cops, or we are screwed. What were you thinking?"

"That she might take pity on poor little us?" He sighs. "Who can save us now?"

Who in-fucking-deed?

"Hey! Whitney! I thought you had to stay home!" I look around. Barbara is leaning out the window of an orange PT Cruiser. And now I recognize where we are, right outside The VERA Project.

"Oh, hey! How was the show?"

"Amazing! You guys need a ride?"

I exchange a look with Dee. "Do we ever. We've had the stupidest adventure. Oh, this is my brother, Hideo."

"Get in, kids," the driver says. "We need to get home before we all turn into pumpkins."

"Dad, how many times do I have to tell you, it's only

the carriage that turns into a pumpkin?"

"So we turn into mice? How is that better?"

"Just you, Dad. We'll be fine."

"But you'll all be walking home barefoot, right? I know there's some shoe-loss in there somewhere."

These people are nuts, but not in a bad way. I let Dee and the skateboard ride shotgun. Barbara scoots over and I climb into the backseat with her and Carol Anne. "Carol Anne, what are you wearing?"

"She's not Carol Anne, she's Miss Space Girl 1962."

"I hope you plan to wear that on stage."

"If we ever play a gig, I might."

"Don't say 'if,' say 'when.' Anybody got a phone I can borrow?"

Barbara hands hers over, and I call home. Dad answers, which is a relief; he's generally calmer than Mom. "Hi, Dad. My phone died and we had some bus trouble, but we're on our way home now. We ran into a friend who offered a ride." Barbara suddenly grins like crazy. What's that about? I finish the call and hand back the phone. "Thanks, Barbara; you're my hero."

5

SISTERS

STORM

Don't tell anyone I'm spending Saturday night at home, wasting time online. In sweat pants. Not yoga pants. Straight-up give-up-on-life pants. How lame is that? But it's been a rough winter. So I'm chatting online with Whitney P, which is more than all right. You wouldn't know it to look at us now, but we've been BFFs since kindergarten. I don't have to explain things to her. If I'm home on a Saturday night, fine. So is she, on guard duty, sounds like. She makes it sound terrible, but I'd take a little brother over a big sister any day.

"Girl, I'm tired of the pity party. We should do something fun."

"What, this isn't fun?" Whitney laughs and her microphone goes staticky. "You're right. But not shopping. I'm sick of the mall."

"Never thought I'd say it, but me, too. I'm thinking something ... different. Something Heather would hate."

And the next thing I know, I'm considering joining an all-girl punk band, even though I don't play an instrument. Completely out of left field, but in a good way. Heather would absolutely hate it. And Whitney thinks it would be good for me.

"Good for me, how? Like kale?"

"What the fuck does kale have to do with it? I just think it'd do you good to have some fun with a different group of people. Like a cultural exchange."

"I'll think about it. Maybe I could — "

"Oh, shit, he's making a break for it. Seeya!"

And she's gone. So I text Jackson.

what do you know about this band of whitney's?

not whitney's, barbara's. why do you ask?

w wants me to be in it. should I?

exactly what you need. do it

Well, there you go. If Jackson says do it, I'll do it. But, Barbara. Barbara? That mousy, badly-dressed girl in the drama closet? She looked like a complete loser. I'm supposed to hang out with losers?

But Jackson says ...

Thursday after school, Whitney texts me: meet us in the band room

So I head down there. I don't know what to expect

— is this an actual practice, a planning meeting, a try-out, or what? Whitney never said, so maybe she doesn't know either. Or maybe it doesn't matter. I'll play it cool, but I'm excited to try something new.

In the hall outside the band room, that weirdo Oakley almost plows into me — head down, hands in pockets. Messy brown hair flops over his eyes, like he hasn't had a haircut in six months. I wouldn't recommend the beard he's working on either, but he hasn't asked me.

"Excuse you!" My sarcasm doesn't stop him as he heads outside. "Creep."

A marching rhythm on snare drum leaks from the band room, so I guess they've already started. I push the door open and slip in quietly. Whitney's at her drum set, with Carol Anne and Barbara standing facing her. This place seems absurdly huge for a three- or four-piece band, but too big is better than too small. Broad tiers stair-step from the entrance at ground level, next to the music teachers' office. The drum set is at ground level, too — near the piano, for jazz band — but the other percussion stuff — tympani and xylophones and whatever — are on the top tier.

Carol Anne starts playing something I don't know, and Whitney adds the marching riff I heard from the hall. Barbara nods and smiles, then starts singing.

... where I could see
and not get squashed ...

She looks around and loses all her color. I mean, I half expect her red hat to turn white. She stops singing.

"Oh, no. No, no, no, no, no. This is not happening. Not her."

Her appears to be me.

"What's wrong, Barbara?" Carol Anne looks between us, clearly as baffled as I am.

"Storm. I can't … I never … she'll …" Barbara gives up trying to make sense and presses her forehead against the wall. "Please … just go away."

Seriously, this is not what I'm used to. I walk into a room and people go out of their way to make me happy. If I ask people to move, they move. If I ask people to leave, they leave. Not the other way around.

I turn to Whitney. "What's going on?"

She lays down her sticks. "Shit, I forgot they didn't know I'd asked you. Sorry, Barbara, I thought I'd said something, but Saturday was so fucked up. I figured it'd be OK, since we've barely started."

Barbara faces us again. "Anyone but her would be OK."

I'm struggling to stay calm. I mean, I don't even know this girl. "Look, I'm sorry, but Jackson said I should — "

"Wait — Jackson said?"

"Yeah, as soon as Whitney suggested I join you, I ran it by Jackson. He said, and I quote, 'Do it. Exactly what you need.' That's why I'm here. It wasn't my idea to hang out with you losers."

"Losers?!" Now Barbara's cheeks are as red as her cap. She gets right up in my face, or as close as she can, being shorter and in flats. Maybe it's my imagination, but there's heat coming off her like she might go up in flames. "I'll have you know Carol Anne is an incredibly talented musician with more style than you'll ever have. And Whitney is a genuine punk. We're not asking you

57

to join us. You should be begging us to let you in."

Wow. Lots of spirit for a loser. "OK, calm down. I get it. I have nothing but respect for Whitney and Carol Anne. But what's up with you, Barbara? What'd I ever do to you? I don't even know you."

"Nobody knows me, and it's all your fault."

"No offense, but you don't look like the kind of person I'd even bother with."

"No shit! You were so mean to me I turned invisible to make you stop."

I try to remember her, I really do, but ... nothing. "When did this supposedly happen?"

"Third grade. We were eight. You called me names and stepped on my ants."

OK. I still don't remember Barbara — or her ants — but the timing adds up. "I was mean to a lot of people. I think I've gotten better since then. And so have you, because I see you plain as anything. You're not invisible."

"Not anymore, since Jackson gave me a magic hat."

Jackson again. So it's not only me, and I can't help a stab of jealousy. But he never said I was his sole ... client. "Let's ask Jackson, then — should I be here or should I not?" I pull out my phone and start to scroll through my contacts.

Barbara whips out her own phone. "I'll do it myself."

Right. He gave her his card, that day in the drama closet. Something about shopping, though I can't imagine he helped her with this outfit. Maybe the hat.

We all stand around awkwardly while Barbara texts Jackson. Finally she looks up from her phone. "He says

I should give you a chance."

"Do you trust him?"

She nods.

"So do I. Friends?" I hold out my hand.

She stares at it. "Not friends. But, truce." She takes my hand and shakes. Her nails are in appalling shape, but she has a surprisingly strong grip.

Whitney puts an arm around each of us. "Fuck practice. We need ice cream."

Barbara resists Whitney's suggestion at first. "We shouldn't quit yet! We haven't even tried — "

"We're not quitting," Carol Anne assures her. "Think of it as a get-acquainted meeting." She turns to me and Whitney. "I take it you two know each other pretty well, but the four of us don't really run in the same circles. It can't hurt to do something low-key."

Carol Anne's diplomacy eases the tension. We leave school and head down the street. Barbara walks faster than anybody and is soon half a block ahead.

"You guys hang back," Whitney says, and trots off to catch up. She says something to Barbara that I can't hear, but I assume it's about me because what else do they have to talk about? Also, Barbara looks back at me for a sec.

"So what's her deal?" I ask Carol Anne. I don't know her that well, either — fat girl, and all that. No, that's Heather talking; she's not really that big. I prefer her vintage feminine style to Barbara's sloppy grunge-boy look. Also, she might be sane.

"I'm not sure. I never saw her before last week, so maybe the invisibility thing is true."

"You don't think she's kind of, maybe, a little bit

crazy?"

"She might be. She's got guts, though. Think about it — she's apparently spent the last several years doing nothing but going to school, listening to music, and writing songs. Oh, and going to shows *by herself*. No extracurriculars, no group of friends. Then, out of nowhere, she wants to start a band? And the way she stood up to you just now? Nobody does that."

"Oh, like I'm so scary ..."

"Storm, you have no idea. But Barbara ... one minute, she's got no confidence, the next she's kicking a guy three times her size. And she writes a damn good song. I want to see how all this turns out."

I want to hear more about that kick, but now we've caught up to Barbara and Whitney, so it'll have to wait. They're in front of a place that sells frozen custard. Is that different from ice cream? My parents' foodie friends would know. Barbara's talking with a scruffy old guy at the curb. We catch up in time to hear him say, " ... but I was in the hospital with pneumonia for two weeks." He has a gravelly voice, like he's been smoking since he was nine.

"Well, I'm glad you're back. I'll take a paper." Barbara counts out two dollar bills and hands them to the guy in exchange for a small newspaper.

I wait until we're inside to ask. "What was that about? You know that bum?"

"Pete's not a bum, he's a vendor. I buy a *Real Change* from him most weeks, but I hadn't seen him lately. Drag to get pneumonia, but I'm happy he has a place to live now."

"I don't give money to panhandlers. Dad says they

just spend it on drugs or booze."

"He's a *vendor,*" she repeats. "And it's a pretty good paper."

"You're kind of a do-gooder, aren't you?"

"No; I just know how it feels to be invisible." She studies the menu, then peers into her wallet. "I guess I'll ... have some water."

I pull out my credit card. "No, this is my treat. All of you, order whatever you want." The appetite I haven't had for months has suddenly come back in a big way. I was planning to ask for frozen yogurt or get a tiny serving, but screw it. I order a big bowl of chocolate, with caramel sauce and nuts. I can't eat all that and have Barbara just drinking water. I about pass out from the first bite, it's so good.

Whitney stares, and then cracks up laughing. "I haven't seen you eat like that since forever."

"Told you, things are looking up."

Barbara pats herself on the cheek. "That looks better. You know, than it did that one day."

Oh, that's right. She saw the bruise when it was too fresh to completely cover up. "It wasn't serious, but Jackson dragged me down to the nurse's office."

"Yeah, he seemed worried."

"He's helped me with worse."

I don't tell her Jackson saved my life.

That sounds melodramatic, but I'm pretty sure it's true. Even before that, he never steered me wrong. I'll never forget the first time I met him. First day of freshman year I walk into school with my hair and makeup perfect, my outfit exactly right — new but worn enough, snug but not trashy, all the right brands — and my attitude firmly in place. *I belong here. I run this show.* While I'm checking out the scene and getting a sense of the pecking order, this absolutely gorgeous guy appears out of nowhere. (He was shorter then and not quite as nicely filled out, but still.) He leans against the wall and says, "Hey, beautiful, let's form a gay-straight alliance." To this day, that's still the weirdest pick up line I've ever heard ... but, hey, it worked.

I go, "What's your deal?"

And he goes, "I can tell by looking you're a queen. Well, I'm your fairy godfather."

Seriously. He said "fairy." So I go, "What, you'll grant my wishes?"

"No, that's genies. I'll give you what you need."

"Oh, really. What do you think I need?"

"Unfiltered opinions, free boyfriend-vetting, and impeccable advice."

"Sounds good. What do you want in return?"

"Don't be mean. Treat your followers with kindness. Don't hurt the little people."

Now, Heather had been training me to be a queen for years, so I admit I hadn't always been the nicest girl up to then. I'd seen my own share of meanness, though. It couldn't hurt to have a protector, or whatever he was offering to be.

As it turned out, he did an excellent job of steering me away from potentially abusive boyfriends. But even Jackson couldn't protect me from Heather.

I won't pretend I had a miserable, deprived childhood. I didn't. Dad rakes in enough dough as a real-estate attorney to afford all the comforts. I mean, the four of us live in a five-bedroom, four-bath house in a nice neighborhood. Designer clothes, tropical vacations, nice cars, all that. I even attended a fancy private middle school. (I missed seeing Whitney every day, though, and demanded to go to whatever high school she went to. Also, I hated the uniforms.)

Dad travels a lot on business, flying around to Housing and Urban Development closings, and Mom has her boards and charity luncheons and all, so Heather and I had a nanny all the time we were little. Rosa would pick us up from school, fix us food, supervise homework, take us to lessons, even put us to bed if our parents were out late. When Heather started high school, Mom decided Heather could look after me, and let Rosa go. And at first it was so cool — I got to be with the big kids. I used to do my homework in the gym during Cheer practice. When I was eight, nine years old, Heather and her friends dressed me like a doll. When I was eleven, she taught me how to do my hair and makeup, how to walk in heels, how to flirt to get whatever I wanted. We looked at bridal magazines and planned each other's weddings. It was fun, pretending I was a model or a movie star. Pretending I was Heather.

Other parts weren't so cool. Sometimes she swatted me when I sassed her or wouldn't do her bidding. As time went on, swats turned to pinches. Shoves. Punches. I did my best to go along with the program — and stay away from stairs when she was around — but it seemed like I always had at least one hidden bruise.

When we were little, Whitney and I took classes in tap dance and tumbling, and I dreamed of being a dancer or acrobat or trapeze artist. Heather straightened me out — our people did not perform. It was acceptable to compete, though, as long as I was better than the others. After Whitney and I graduated from little-kid tumbling, she persuaded us to take up gymnastics, which we did for years. She made it seem like my idea, but I realize now as long as I was in lessons, Heather was free to live her own life. Looking after me must have put a huge crimp in her style. Sorry, Sis — it wasn't my idea, either.

Gymnastics, though ... I loved all the moves; I hated the competitions. I used to throw up before meets, but once I was out on the floor, it was just me and my skills, my own secret circus. As a side benefit, I learned how to fall without hurting myself; useful when Heather got shovey. I stuck it out until my height and boobs gave me an excuse to quit gymnastics and go out for Cheer (like Heather), where long legs and a good figure are assets, and I could still cartwheel and flip. It also got me in with all the right people, according to Heather. (Not Whitney's people, but we had our own secret sign language for when we'd pass in the halls.)

Heather let on she was proud of me, and I thought we'd finally be OK. Then she told me she'd kill me if I got fat.

Part of me must have believed her; I couldn't eat in front of her, and then it got to where I could hardly eat at all. Every morning, I'd get up, put on my warpaint and designer armor, and stride through the school day behind a mask of perfection. *Don't show weakness, be strong, be the best. Just get through high school.* I dressed in (fashionable) layers to hide how thin I'd gotten. Other girls would tell me how great I looked and what was my secret and I wanted to hide in the restroom and cry. *No. Don't show weakness.*

And then, a crack in the armor: last fall, I fainted in practice and ended up spending a week in bed. I encouraged the rumor that I had mono, which was easier to explain than the truth. Added benefit: Heather kind of freaks about germs, so she made herself scarce until I was strong enough to go back to school. Meanwhile, Jackson helped me find foods I could keep down that were portable so I could eat whenever I had any appetite. I've been subsisting for months on mostly granola bars, Greek yogurt, string cheese, and baby carrots. Don't knock it — it kept me from starving, and I stopped losing weight. See? Jackson saved my life. I kind of conveniently forgot to tell Heather I dropped Cheer. When she found out last week, she cussed me out and socked me in the face. She'd been knocking me around for years, but she never went for the face before. It wasn't about the fainting or the weight loss. I was a quitter; I'd never be as perfect as she is.

Through all this, Dad was traveling so much, we hardly saw him for more than a few hours here and there. Mom was there ... and not there. See, she likes a glass of wine or seven every now and then. OK, every night. So she misses a lot. Even sober, though, Mom stayed out of our disputes. "You need to learn to settle it yourselves." Which usually meant a punch in the gut.

I did what I could to hide the bruise on my face, but I'm glad now that I couldn't cover it up completely. I went to find Jackson for advice. Barbara was there, which made it weird, but once she'd left, Jackson gave me what I needed: someone to walk with me to the nurse's office. Jackson has a gift that way. That walk started a whole cascade that might as well have been magic. The nurse put ice on my face and gave me a brochure about intimate-partner violence (!). She thought I needed an X-ray, so she called my dad at his office. Dad took me to Urgent Care (contusion from blunt trauma, no broken bones) where the doctor urged us to get therapy for my eating disorder. (Is it an eating disorder if you want to eat but can't? Because someone has threatened to kill you? I'm kind of looking forward to talking to someone who might know.) Dad was ready to mess up the boy who would hurt his princess, but when he learned who actually did it, he looked like he was the one who'd been punched. By then, it was too late to go back to school, so we went home and told Mom what was going on. She broke down crying, like it was her fault, which I guess it was, but only partly. She promised to quit drinking, so that's a win if she can stick it out. And that night, Dad kicked Heather out of the house. That's a good thing, but I don't know if I'll ever get used to it. I miss her. Sick, right? But we planned each other's weddings ...

Anyway, see why I take Jackson's advice?

Carol Anne's voice brings me back to the band meeting in the ice cream store. Sorry, *frozen custard*. "We were talking in the band room before you came in. Are you two cool with it if Barbara and I record some quickie phone demos so you can learn the songs? Because we're thinking we might have to put off actual band practice until after *Anything Goes* — we're both in the chorus, and practice starts next week."

Whitney raises her hand. "I'm in the pit band."

"I'm, um, playing the lead." They're all staring at

me, ice cream forgotten. "What?"

Carol Anne laughs. "Well, I guess now we know you can sing, if you're playing Reno."

"She'll look great in the snazzy costumes, too," Whitney puts in. "I hope the designer knows you're eating like a person again."

"I told Ms. J I planned to gain some weight before the show, and she said, 'Good.'"

"You can't have mine, but we could order another round." Whitney guards her dish, then turns to Carol Anne. "I was thinking of piercing my tongue next, but looking at your nose stud, I might do that instead. Don't take this wrong; I'm not into girls, but I could totally kiss a girl with a nose stud." Whitney shakes her head and laughs, but Barbara goes beet red. "Oh, no, you're not ... are you?"

Carol Anne laughs. "Barbara's crush is very much not a girl. That's all I'm saying."

Barbara nonchalantly spoons up some ice cream and looks at it as she speaks. "So, Carol Anne, are you going to Marina's sweet-sixteen party tomorrow?" She eats the spoonful as if she doesn't actually care about the answer.

"Um, yeah, I think so." For some reason, now Carol Anne seems flustered.

Barbara's cool attitude vanishes. "Oh, man, I'm sorry! That sounded way cleverer in my head. I'm a bad friend."

"No, you're new at it. *Nice* might work better for you than *clever*, though."

I still don't know what they're going on about. This must be some party. "Who's Marina?"

"Not in your tier," Whitney says. "Is sweet-sixteen even a thing anymore? I had a normal birthday. Well, normal for me — family party and one more piercing." She fiddles with her lip ring. If I remember right, twelve was her lobes (I did mine then, too); thirteen, upper ear; fourteen, lobes again; fifteen, eyebrow. Betcha anything she gets a tattoo for her eighteenth. Then again, maybe not. She has no problem with needles, but blood kind of freaks her out. It'd have to be on her back or something. But maybe I'll get one, instead ... if I'm really free of Heather.

Carol Anne nods. "Did all your aunts and uncles want to know when you were getting your license?"

Whitney laughs. "Yeah, what's that about? I've seen how people drive! Storm, yours was more of a big deal, wasn't it?"

"Well, we went to Hawaii, if that's what you mean. And I got a car. Speaking of which, if anybody needs a ride — "

"Shotgun!" Whitney, of course.

Carol Anne laughs. "No, thanks, I live close."

"Yeah, so do I." For some reason, Carol Anne frowns at Barbara, who shakes her head. "For my sixteenth birthday, my folks took me to lunch. Then I, um, donated blood. All three of us did."

Whitney very deliberately sets her spoon in her ice cream dish. "You did this voluntarily? On your birthday?" Probably nobody but me hears the quaver in her voice.

"Yeah, I did my service hours there, and I wanted to donate as soon as I was finally old enough. How else is someone like me supposed to save a life, right?"

I have no reply for that. Barbara is one weird girl. I study her carefully, but there's still not much to see. She gives blood and she buys the homeless paper. I don't care what she says. She's totally a do-gooder.

6

ANYTHING GOES

BARBARA

I was high. That's the best way I can explain it. (I mean, I'm guessing. Someday, maybe I'll try pot and find out if I'm right.) In those first days after Jackson gave me the hat, I felt like I could do anything: talk to people, start a band, fly. A guy stepped on my foot at a show and I kicked him! And got away with it. How powerful is that?

It lasted a week, and then Storm showed up at our first practice. I couldn't breathe and I thought I might faint. But Whitney — and Jackson — thought she needed to be there for some reason. I never had friends before and I didn't want to lose them over something that sounded so stupid. I mean, can you imagine? *"Why can't she be in your band?" "Because I'm afraid of her." "Why?" "I don't know!"* Easier to let her in.

While I was still not in my right mind, I also let Jackson talk me into signing up for the chorus of *Anything Goes*, our spring musical. Nuts, right? I mean, I am so not a theater person. Meanwhile, I'd persuaded Carol Anne to do it with me, so I couldn't very well back out. But because of play practice, the band had to go on hold before we even started. I figured that would be the end of it. Some dreams are too nutty to come true.

Ten minutes into our first chorus rehearsal, I no longer think it's a terrible idea. I mean, duh — it's singing in a group from sheet music. This is what I know. We work in sections at first. The music is great, the lyrics are funny. Some of the other sopranos are having a surprising amount of trouble with the part, but I guess not everyone reads music so I shouldn't judge. The three main culprits are a group of interchangeable blondes from Storm's usual posse, so it's also possible they want to be the center of attention. Sorry; there I go again. People like that bring out my judgey side.

Once we kind of know it, we join the rest of the chorus to run through the song with all parts. It's rough, but already it sounds pretty good. I'm doing my best to watch the director, Mr. D, as well as my music. He moves away from his stand a lot to listen to each part. He occasionally frowns at the tenors or basses, where most of the cutups seem to reside. We get through the song, and I figure he'll have us mark some dynamics or rehearse a part.

He looks straight at me. "You, Miss ... "

"Me? Um. Bernsen. Barbara Bernsen."

"What are you doing here, Miss Bernsen?"

And it was going so well. I'm afraid I'll faint or throw up, but I manage to answer. "I signed up to be in the chorus. You can check the list, I'm sure it — "

He shakes his head impatiently. "No, I mean why are you in the chorus and not the cast? You have a lovely voice, perfect for Hope Harcourt."

Well, I still might faint. "Really?" I squeak, no lovely voice anywhere in evidence. "I mean, I didn't try out. I can't act or dance." I don't add "or be seen," which was still true at the time of try-outs. What director would want an invisible ingénue? (Maybe Invisible Ingénue would be a good name for the band. Or, you know, not.)

"Next year, try out. I hope to add you to my concert choir, too."

"Thank you. I'll think about it."

My face must be so red, because it's burning up. Everybody's staring, exactly what I've been avoiding for years. Over in the alto section, Carol Anne grins and gives me a thumbs-up. That helps. And after I calm down, the recognition still feels good.

Out in the hall after practice, Storm's three friends gather around me. Chloe, Zoe, and Dakota. They're made up to look like they have anime eyes, so I feel like I've stumbled into a cartoon. Although all blondes, they're not so identical up close. Chloe has Asian features and wears her hair in a tight ballerina bun. Zoe's a light-skinned black girl with golden ringlets. Dakota's a white chick, her hair in a long, smooth fall.

"Ooh, it's Miss Lovely Voice." Chloe's tone is mocking but her smile seems friendly. "How do you sing so fancy?"

"I ... sang what was on the page."

Zoe's laugh is like breaking glass. "I can't believe she thinks she's going on stage with that hair."

This thought has actually crossed my mind, too. "Yeah, I might cut it." Maybe now that I'm getting to know the cool people, I can come up with a better look. "What do you think — "

"I didn't say you could talk." Dakota flicks my cap with her fingernail. "You're so special, with your little hat."

"You heard Mr. D: you don't belong in the chorus."

Too late, I see what's going on. It's third grade all over again, only so much worse now that I've had my moment of visibility. But what could these mean girls possibly get out of humiliating a nobody like me?

And also, what happened to my resolution to not give a shit? I don't know whether it's the unfairness or the stupidity, but something snaps. I stamp my foot; the sound echoes more than you'd expect from a sneaker, but these hallways have strange acoustics. "D-don't diss the hat." Yeah, that sounds real tough. I am a total loser who doesn't belong in the chorus of a high-school musical, let alone the cast. What was I thinking?

They screech and move in closer. Chloe throws an arm around my shoulders. "Look how cute she is — she wants to fight us!"

I force a smile and let out a weak giggle. "Oh, I've never hit anyone in my life." Yeah, like that wasn't obvious. If I had my Docs on, I might kick them in the shins, but I'd rather they leave me alone so I can go tell Mr. D I'm quitting the show.

Or, you know what? I have this sudden insane certainty that I could take all three of them in a hair-pulling contest. Yeah, bring it on. My hands squeeze into fists, and I swear I can already feel the strands against my palms.

Dakota grabs the back of her head and spins to look behind her. "OK, who did that?" But there's no one there. Funny timing; I probably shouldn't laugh, though.

Chloe frowns and loosens her bun, like a pre-fight ritual. Over Dakota's shoulder, I catch a glimpse of Jackson and Storm as they leave the room where the cast had their rehearsal. Maybe Jackson will help me out here. No, he turns the other way before I catch his attention, deep in conversation with Storm. But she sees us and turns around. No doubt she wants to get her digs in, too.

"Hey, B, good practice?" Storm smiles, a nice smile. These other girls look like posers next to her. And I'm B now? Never had a nickname before. Well, other than the gross one she gave me in third grade.

"Yeah, um, pretty good."

"Will you excuse us, ladies? I need a word with Barbara."

"Yeah, sure, Storm. See you tomorrow." Dakota backs off and the other two join her.

Zoe runs her hand through her curls. "Girl, my

scalp is burning," I hear her mutter. "Stupid chemicals."

Chloe shakes her hair out. "I hear that. It's like somebody's yanking on it."

Huh. What's that about?

Storm doesn't even wait for them to get out of earshot. "I listened to your demo. You rock, girl! This is going to be so much fun." She looks past me for a moment. "OK, they're gone. How bad were they?"

"I, um, oh, not that bad. They didn't appreciate that Mr. D complimented my voice. Don't know why they care."

She sighs. "They have so much to learn, but I don't think they'll bother you again." She turns and walks away, waving over her shoulder. Farther down the hall, Jackson smiles and applauds quietly. When she catches up to him, they high-five and continue down the hall together.

OK, what just happened? Is Storm on my side now? Whether or not she meant it, people heard her tell me that I rock. She called me B. I don't know what to make of this girl, but now I have to be in the show. It's a moral imperative.

Several practices in, when we have the songs learned, things get a lot more challenging. First, all chorus members are supposed to come up with a character and backstory: age, social class, why we're on this ocean liner. I'm at a loss because I don't think I can get away with "the invisible girl."

Carol Anne comes to my rescue with a brilliant idea. "I want to be a snooty old rich lady. You can be my wide-eyed, innocent niece."

"Sure, I'll just be myself."

"In better clothes."

Second challenge: we start having choreography rehearsals. Yeah, we're not only expected to sing, we have to dance. Have I mentioned I can't dance? I can sway, fine. Head-bang, OK. Jump up and down and wave my arms, sure. Dance in any organized way, not so much.

Fortunately, I'm not the only one. The people with decent moves (like Chloe, Zoe, and Dakota) get to do the actual dancing, while the rest of us get simpler steps. Before I know it, we're rehearsing on stage with the cast, and that's when I get the surprise of my life. You know who can dance? Storm. She sings fine, acts OK, but I think she got the lead because she can tap dance, like for real.

The leads and principal characters have costume fittings for multiple costumes. (Storm is clearly delighted with her spangly showgirl outfits. They look amazing on her in a way they never would on me, though I can't help thinking of that sparkly purple dress hiding in my closet.) Things are different in the chorus. One afternoon, the designer drags several racks of costumes into the hall and we're instructed to find something that fits and suits the character we've created.

Carol Anne dives right in and finds an elegant, matronly dress and one of those furs with the head and tail still on. Horrible, but it matches her hair and definitely suits her snooty-old-lady character. Meanwhile, I'm lost and overwhelmed until somebody grabs my green cap off my head and replaces it with that straw cloche Jackson had me try on way back when. I spin around and there he is.

"You looked like you could use some help."

"Boy, could I! Where do I start?"

"The racks are arranged Small Medium Large, so I'd say in the middle. What do you need?"

"A travel outfit and something dressy."

"Are you young or old?"

"I'm Carol Anne's niece, so young, I guess."

"Easy." He reaches into the middle of one of the racks, for all I know with his eyes closed, and extracts a classy tailored suit in dark green tweed. "What about this for the travel outfit? It goes with the hat."

I take the hanger while he goes back in. He comes back in no time at all with something fluttery and floral.

"There you go, a perfect party frock."

"Frock," I echo, dazed. It's not a word I've ever had a chance to use before, so I say it again. "Frock. I like that better than 'dress'."

"I thought you might."

"Thanks for the help. I wasn't sure you'd have time." Jackson has a large role, though not the lead. He has plenty of lines, songs, and dance steps of his own to worry about without my wardrobe problems.

"No problem. I volunteered to help anyone who needs it."

"Good — we're supposed to wear our own shoes, but I don't have anything that'll work. Want to go shoe shopping with me sometime?"

Jackson laughs at that. "I thought you'd never ask."

During full rehearsals, the chorus has a lot of

downtime between numbers. We're supposed to be quiet, so a lot of people do homework. This is all new to me; I wonder if all extracurriculars are like this — an extended study hall with the distraction of an activity. It's hard for me to focus on reading assignments, but math problems aren't too bad. I can finish two or three between chorus numbers without completely losing my train of thought.

Sometimes, I let my attention wander to a different show. Whenever the stage crew is around, Carol Anne kind of drifts over and hangs out with Marina. There's nothing obvious going on, but they chat enough to get shushed, and then they have to move closer together. Which neither seems to mind, but then they sort of jerk apart, so I don't know. I have no skill of my own at flirting, so I can't tell if they're doing it right. I'm happy to watch the show whenever Jackson's on stage. I was surprised he didn't get the lead, but he's good in a comic character role. I hope they don't cover up his looks too much when we get to makeup.

7

HALF A BUS CLOSER TO HOME

I wonder what it's like to live right next to a bus stop. It'd be ironic if those people never rode the bus. I'm meeting Jackson on a Saturday afternoon to ride over to Value Village. There's a stop not too far from my house for a route that runs close to his house. It's no use for where we're going, though. For this expedition, we're catching a bus where the nearest stop is almost half a mile south of my house, a little more than that north of his. That must be why some people drive. Good thing it's not raining. Not that we'd let that stop us, or we'd never go anywhere.

He's already at the stop, and greets me with a big

smile. "Ready for another treasure hunt?"

"You bet!" I've learned it's more fun if we don't call it shopping. I can get into the adventure of searching out lost gems more than I can being a mere consumer.

I eat lunch with Jackson or Carol Anne almost every day at school, which still feels new and different, and every couple of weekends we go on these thrift shop excursions or to the movies. Much as I like Carol Anne and Whitney, I think of Jackson as my best friend. I don't know what I am to him, but as long as he wants to hang out, I am there.

The hat racks are a bust this time, but I score a Velvet Underground T-shirt — black with a hot pink banana. Jackson lucks into a couple of vintage tropical-print shirts, one red, the other, green and orange. Not cheesy polyester, either — one-hundred percent silk.

"Are you sure you need both of those?"

"Summer's on its way, and wheedling doesn't become you, Barbara." He winks at me and I literally (by which I mean figuratively) die. "If you're nice, I might let you borrow one sometime."

"Cool."

"So, shoes for the show?"

"What, here?"

"Why not? We found those Docs here. Come on, it won't hurt to look."

Not to look, but maybe to wear. I keep that thought to myself, but really, any shoes in good condition must be hellish, because why would someone donate comfortable shoes?

There are a lot of shoes in my size though, and I think I've lucked out when I find a pair of silver ballet flats. They're soft leather with rubber soles, which seems perfect. Unfortunately, they're too wide in the heel and keep slipping off every time I take a step. Back they go. A brown pair fits in the heel but they have weird toes that pinch. I put them back on the shelf, and continue the search.

"Hey, Cinderella, try these!" Jackson holds out a pair of pale pink pumps with round toes and a small heel.

"Really? Pink?"

"Why not? Your Velvets shirt has pink on it."

"Totally different."

"Well, your party dress is a pink and green print, and they'll give the green suit a nice girlish touch."

That's right — they're for the character, not for me. I try them on and not only do they fit, I can walk in them without falling. I try one of my simple dance steps, and I'm still upright. And they're on sale, only $3.99. "OK, these should work. Who knows, I might even wear them someday in real life."

"Be sure to send invitations, because I want to be there."

As if that weren't exciting enough, we decide to go back to Jackson's house for a movie and some food. I can't believe I'm finally doing normal friend things with someone, and it happens to be a real Someone! How did this happen?

On the bus, I take out my new shoes to admire them again. "I wish I'd had these for Easter."

"Do you even dress up for church?"

"Not usually, but for Easter, yeah." I put the shoes back in the bag so I can look at Jackson, which is no sacrifice at all. "You know, I still haven't seen you there."

"I told you, you're not supposed to see me."

"And I told you the sound's better in the middle. I mean, if you're there for the music — "

"Fine, just don't make me stand up and be welcomed."

"I wouldn't. I might introduce you to the choir director."

"I'll wear a lot of things, but I draw the line at choir robes."

"OK, OK! So you know, we don't wear robes in the summer."

"I'll think about it."

I'm not sure if that counts as evangelism, but it's probably the closest I'll ever get. I'm terrible at talking to people about pretty much anything, so with something as sensitive as religion it's ten times worse. I mean, do I really believe in God myself? I do believe, if there is one, we're the only hands and feet he (or she) has. And if there isn't one, all we have is each other, so I guess I'd still go to church. How do I say that out loud to anyone without tripping over my words? But Jackson's already interested, at least in the music. So I can share that much good news, anyway.

What I said about this bus route is still true on the way back: the closest stop is half a mile from Jackson's house. Oh well, I don't mind walking. When I head up the aisle to the front door, though, he holds me back.

"Back door's better."

"Why's that?"

"It's half a bus closer to home."

I spend most of the walk to his house making up a song off that one line. I've been trying to write a song about how he gave me a hat and made me visible, but this is better.

His mom's in the kitchen when we get there. "Any luck?" She pulls a pan of brownies from the oven.

Jackson displays his silk shirts. "Pretty good. OK if we order pizza?"

"If you get enough for us, too. Brownies will be cool in time for dessert."

"They smell amazing!" Seriously, is there a better scent in the world?

"Thank you, Barbara." She leans in close and stage-whispers, "It's always good to see you, but do you think he'll ever bring a nice boy home?"

I love this because Jackson blushes, and I so rarely see him act like a regular awkward teenager. Nice to know he's actually human. He turns his back and pulls out his phone. While Jackson's ordering pizza and hot wings, his dad comes in.

"Barbara! Knock knock!"

"Um, who's there?"

"Interrupting cow."

"Interrupting cow, wh — "

"Moo!"

"Ha! An oldie but a goodie."

"Knock knock!"

I roll my eyes. "Who's there?"

"Little old lady."

I know where this is going, but I play along, anyway. "Little old lady who?"

"I didn't know you could yodel!"

He goes out laughing. Dads are so easily amused.

Jackson finishes the call and shakes his head at his dad's retreating back. "Sorry about that, Barbara. Just what you wanted, jokes that haven't been funny since second grade."

"Hey, you've heard the level of humor at my house. I feel right at home."

I follow Jackson into the family room to pick a movie while we wait for our food. It's not a big room, but it has the most comfortable couch in the world and a way bigger flat screen than at my house. We have a lot of the same movies, but his are Blu-Ray; we're still chugging along with DVD. Don't get me started on streaming. Parents have to be brought along gently.

Jackson pulls out a few boxes but puts most of them back. "Just, if he comes at you with Interrupting Starfish or Procrastinating Cow, do not give in. Walk away."

"I don't remember those."

"You don't want to. How about *Avengers* again?"

"Sounds perfect." But I'm still thinking about the very ordinary goings-on in the kitchen. "Jackson, were your parents this relaxed when you first came out?"

He snorts an adorable little laugh. "Pretty much. I think they knew before I did, so it wasn't a huge surprise. I got lucky."

"I feel bad for kids who can't be themselves at home."

"Yeah, like poor Storm. I'm glad she finally spoke up about Heather."

I wasn't thinking of Storm so much as Carol Anne, but it's not my place to clarify. I guess they both fit the category, in different ways.

The food arrives and that whole conversation gets shuffled off to the side. We settle in to watch *The Avengers* for the third time. Weird how superheroes cause as much damage as the villains they're fighting. Kind of amazing there's any city left in that universe. But it's one of my favorite movies, anyway.

This is exactly the kind of ordinary fun I used to imagine when I tried to picture having friends, so of course I try to spoil it. "Jackson, you must know twenty or thirty cooler people to spend a Saturday with. Why me?"

"What do you mean? You're my friend."

"But why am I your friend?"

He turns and looks at me intently. It kind of makes me giddy. "Because you don't think you're interesting."

OK. What's that mean? I'm not interesting. "But what about you? You're always giving everybody what they need. What do you need?"

He gives me a smile like a day in July. "This."

"This? Delivery pizza and a Marvel Blu-ray?"

"This, kicking back with my lowest maintenance friend who shares my taste in movies. Storm's great, but she doesn't get this stuff."

"I find it hard to believe we're your only friends."

He pauses the movie. "Let me show you something."

Jackson gets up and I follow him upstairs to his bedroom, which is a secret thrill for me because I'm lame like that. The decor has a distinctly masculine vibe — blue and tan striped bedspread, swimming trophies on the windowsill, no purple or rainbows to be seen. Not that there's anything wrong with that. Maybe more to the point, the bed is made, the desk is tidy, and I could believe the rug has been vacuumed in the past month. This can't be said of my room.

"Wow, do you actually clean your own room?"

"I wouldn't want anyone else to! It's my space, my stuff."

"I wish I could. I'm good at organizing information, but stuff ... not so much. What did you want to show me?"

"This." A corkboard over the desk displays several colorful sketches. "I've got binders full of this stuff, but these are my favorites right now."

"What am I looking at? Is this a robot?"

"Power armor. And these are superhero outfits that actually make sense."

"So ... you're a closet nerd?"

"Exactly! I'd love to design for the movies someday — sci-fi, fantasy, comic book stuff. But I don't only draw them."

I don't know why I'm surprised, considering his understanding of clothing and theatrical costumes, combined with his taste in movies. "How many have you actually made?"

He slides open his closet door to reveal an array of colorful Spandex. "All but the armor."

"I, uh, wow. When I said 'closet' I didn't know I was being literal. Do you actually wear these things?"

"To Comicon, every year since sixth grade! Nobody knows but my parents, and now, you."

"Seriously, nobody recognizes you? I can't imagine you're the only one from school who goes to Comicon."

He waits while I figure it out. "Oh, yeah — the suits all have masks. Jackson! You have a secret identity!"

"I don't show this side of myself at school, but I figured you'd get it. You're cool that way."

See how awesome he is? My weekend is officially made.

After the movie, I gather my stuff and catch the bus home. My stop isn't too far from my house, but I think of Jackson and get off by the door that's closer to home. I will definitely finish writing that song.

8

IT'S DE-LOVELY

Dress rehearsal brings the part of the production I've been dreading. I'm OK wearing a dress a few times. I've been practicing walking and dancing in my pink shoes, so I shouldn't look too dorky onstage. But now I have to face my old nemesis: makeup.

The leads have parent volunteers to help them, but chorus members are on our own. We have general instructions based on our characters' ages, but the girls' instructions seem to assume some experience with makeup. I'm OK with step one: apply cold cream to face. After that, not so much.

I watch Carol Anne put on foundation and draw

crow's feet and frown lines on her face. It looks cartoonish, but with the silver streak sprayed in her hair, she could almost pass for an old woman. She adds a red dot to the inside corner of each eye.

"What's that for? No one will even see it!"

"It's supposed to make my eyes less prominent. You're a young character; you'll have a white dot to make them look bigger."

"No, I'll put my eye out."

"I'll help you tonight, but tomorrow, you can do it yourself."

She applies foundation and eyeliner and rouge and mascara. I see a clown face in the mirror, but she assures me it has to be exaggerated in order to look normal under the stage lights. If she's wrong, at least we'll all look ridiculous together. Worse than that is the feel of it on my face. I already can't wait to wipe it off, and the show hasn't even started.

I'm nervous before our first number; then we're into it and I forget to worry. There's an audience out there in the dark, but I can't see them. The sounds of laughter and applause actually help.

Because it's technically a rehearsal, we're allowed to sneak around to the back of the auditorium to watch some of the scenes without a chorus part. From this distance, the makeup doesn't look silly at all. Probably two-thirds of the seats are full, mostly with students and teachers. There's a group of stoners smarting off in the back row. I'm not sure why they bothered to come — the only one of them paying any attention to the show is that guy I gave the earplug to that time. Oakley? I think that's his name.

Storm stands behind the back row, watching with her arms crossed. Wait ... why is she out here, and in street clothes? Isn't she supposed to be on stage? Yes, there she is, singing and dancing and looking like a star, an infectious smile on her face. They must learn that in dance class. I sneak a second look at the person at the back of the auditorium. There is a resemblance but in better light, I wouldn't have been fooled. She's several years beyond high school, and watching the show with an expression like she just ate soap. The light dawns: this must be the legendary Heather. I do not approach.

For actual opening night, I do most of my own makeup, but beg Carol Anne to do my eyes again.

She gives a big dramatic sigh, then smiles. "Just this once. Your hair's cute, by the way. Suits the period."

"This show was a good excuse to try something different. I'm lucky a bob looks good with my other hats."

"Nervous tonight?"

"Not as much as last night. Is that weird?"

"Well, the dress rehearsal was reassuring. My parents and a bunch of my cousins are out there tonight, though, so I've got some butterflies going."

"Mine, too. And my grandma. I'm so excited for them to see it."

The time drags before the show starts. We can't go out front tonight; we have to stay in the wings or backstage. The overture takes forever. It's still hard to believe that's punk girl Whitney playing the elegant, jazzy part, but I watched her in rehearsal. No way anybody that good would actually want to be in a band with me.

Then the curtains open and the show begins. I don't *feel* nervous — I don't have lines, and I know all the songs by heart — but I must be, because something funny happens with time. Before I know what's happening, we're in the middle of the first number, and then suddenly, it's intermission. Part of me wants it to slow down so I can savor the experience of being onstage, in costume, under lights, singing (and sort of dancing) with a big group. The show is so funny and we've worked so hard, it seems a shame to let it flash by like this. On the other hand, it's really hot under those lights, so maybe it's just as well time is zipping past. I'm sure I'm missing a lot of what happens when the chorus isn't on, but I know the jokes are hitting because I recognize my mom's laugh. Soon enough, it's time for curtain calls. Storm and the girl playing Hope get all these flowers while they take their bows. The chorus doesn't get bouquets, but we receive a rousing ovation for our work.

I spoke too soon. Lots of girls in the chorus get big bouquets afterward from their family and friends. I'm feeling left out.

"There's the star of the show!"

I'd know that beautiful low voice anywhere, and turn to meet Grandma's hug. She gives me three roses that match my shoes. Nobody ever brought me flowers before, so this little bouquet means everything.

"Thank you! Did you really like it?"

"Loved it! And you were de-lovely up there."

"Oh, I was way at the back! Nobody could see me."

"Not true." Mom comes up beside her and I realize all three of us have the same haircut. The only difference is color — mine is brown, Mom's is brown with gray streaks, and Grandma's is all silver.

Dad joins us, too. "They're right. You looked like a born performer."

"Good thing we have three more shows, then."

Not too far away, I recognize Whitney's little brother with their parents. Well, not so little, but you know what I mean. He doesn't look thrilled to be here, but I'm sure Whitney will be glad he's not out getting into trouble. Carol Anne is mobbed by what must be her cousins. And there's that one scruffy-looking stoner who was paying attention at the dress rehearsal. Weird that he'd buy a ticket to see the show again; must be a music lover or something.

"Hey, you!" Jackson spins me around and gives me a hug. Both make me dizzy. "How does it feel to make your theatrical debut?"

"My feet hurt, I'm starving, and I can't wait to get this goop off my face."

"So you loved it."

"It was fun," I admit. "You got all the laughs, though. How come you didn't get flowers?"

He shrugs. "Tradition."

"Well, that's not right. Here." I separate one of my roses from the others and give it to Jackson. He lights up with a smile that makes me wish I could give him a huge bouquet.

Grandma clears her throat. "Are you going to introduce me?"

"Grandma, this is my friend Jackson Durand.

Jackson, my grandmother, Nora Adams."

He takes her hand and kisses the fingers. "Pleased to meet you, ma'am."

"Well, not every day I meet such a polite teenager. So, are you two ... "

"Grandma! No, Jackson is my fashion advisor and I'm his project."

"I wondered who picked those shoes, because I couldn't imagine it was you."

She knows me too well.

9

SINGIN' THE BLUES

Woke up this morning
Didn't want to go to school

So, yeah. I'm singing the blues. The show's over and I don't have anything to look forward to except finishing another school year. Bleh.

Sure, I know I was originally against the whole idea of being in the musical, but it turned out to be the most enjoyable part of high school so far. It wasn't a garage band, but I was part of something. I even went to the cast party, on the assumption that it was a celebration of what we'd all accomplished and would therefore be a good time even for someone like me, who hadn't been to a party since about first grade.

My mistake. The organized part of the party was fine. The director gave shout-outs to the leads and principals, of course, but also to the hardworking chorus (thank you!) and the pit band (who all bailed on the party to go do their own thing). We were then instructed to have a good time, but I forgot that I didn't make a whole lot of new friends during the show. I could tell Carol Anne wanted to hang out with Marina; she didn't need me getting in the way. Jackson tried to make sure I was all right, so I lied and said I was so he could have fun with his real friends. Storm acknowledged my presence, which in the past would have terrified me but now I can deal. But that left me by myself. At a social event. Oh, help.

I took up a position by the snack table and spent most of the night directing people to the bathroom or letting them know whether I'd seen whoever they were looking for. It occurred to me that the best way for me to be at a party is to have a job. Not hosting, because that would require plans and invitations and actually knowing people, but having a responsibility so I'm not standing there getting depressed. Not to say I didn't end up feeling low. I called home while the party was still in full swing and begged a ride home. I am such a loser.

I drag into school on Monday, and everything seems empty. Now I'll have time to catch up on schoolwork, but who cares? At least it's a nice day in May. I take my lunch outside so I can feel sorry for myself in the sunshine. I wasn't looking for anyone, but there's Carol Anne, already on the steps with her guitar.

I plop down next to her.

"Hey, I was wondering where you'd gotten to. You left the party early."

"Yeah. I was ... tired."

Whitney surprises me by sitting on my other side. "So, we still doing this band thing? Because I've been listening to your demos and I can't wait to start."

"Really?" I can't hide my shock and I don't try. Somebody else likes my nutty idea?

"You bet!" Carol Anne says, and starts strumming "Huge Guy in the Mosh Pit."

My gloom lifts, just like that. "Yeah, I want to if you do. Does Thursday still work?"

"I don't see why not. I'm not sure Dad knows we ever stopped. Should I tell Storm, or do you want to?"

"You think she's still interested?" Storm was nice to me all through the show. Not in a let's-have-lunch or come-over-to-my-house way, but, you know, like I existed and wasn't loathsome. So why am I still nervous about her? Habit, I guess.

Whitney grins. "I'll find out for sure, but I'm pretty sure she's interested."

And we're off! The four of us get together that Thursday after school to see what we can come up with. So of course the first question has nothing to do with music.

"A kickass band needs a kickass name," Whitney says. "So what do we call it?"

I'd be lying if I said I hadn't given it more than a little thought. "I like Cupcake Time."

"Hell, no," Whitney says. "Cupcakes are over. Besides, nothing about 'Cupcake Time' says riot grrrl.

What about Plague of — "

"Cole Porter preserve us! No plagues. No turtles," Carol Anne says. "That ship has sailed."

Storm holds up one finger. "I like Storm."

Of course she does. "No," the rest of us say in unison.

"And I don't want us to be Barbara and the Bumblebees or anything like that, either," I put in. "Let's come back to it later, after we've learned some songs."

"Do we have to wear matching outfits?" Storm asks. "Because I'm not dressing like Barbara."

I take deep breaths and remind myself that she no longer has power over me. Besides, what's the problem with how I dress? I'm wearing my new Velvets shirt and my even-newer fuchsia beret that almost matches. "Don't tell me what to wear, and I won't tell you."

Storm rolls her eyes. "Here we go again."

Before the argument can work up any steam, Mr. P interrupts. "Hey, girls! Got everything you need?"

"Yeah, Dad, we're good here." Whitney looks like she wants to crawl into a hole, but her dad seems pretty nice, for a teacher.

"OK, glad to hear it." Mr. P twiddles with his bowtie. "You're technically one of the chamber ensembles, so my responsibility."

"Cool," I say. "Thanks."

"I know you haven't had a lot of rehearsals, so I put TBA on the program."

"Um ... program?" I hate when my voice squeaks like that.

"For the spring chamber concert? Next Tuesday?

Each group presents a work of their choice. Obviously, you won't be playing from the standard repertoire, but— "

"OK, Dad, we get it. Thanks." Whitney keeps her cool until her dad leaves the band room. "Fuck! Since when does 'technically' mean 'actually'?"

"Yeah." I feel dizzy (actually, not technically) and sit on the lowest tier. "What I said back whenever about a garage being a chamber? That was a joke."

Whitney hits a cymbal. "Apparently not. So what are we going to play?"

I started this band to play my songs, but that suddenly feels kind of self-serving. Especially now that I know how good Carol Anne and Whitney are. Why would they want to play my silly songs, especially for the chamber concert? "Maybe we could try something we all know?"

"The new Taylor Swift record is so good!" Storm gushes. "Can we try something from that?"

Carol Anne taps her fingers on her guitar. "I haven't had a chance to listen to it yet. What about something older?"

We end up trying a couple of Beatles songs because everyone knows the Beatles. But who knew those simple-sounding songs were so hard? It's a trainwreck. We have better luck with my old favorite, "Rockaway Beach," but it's still kind of a struggle.

Whitney rocks back on her throne. "OK, now that we're warmed up, let's try that one of Barbara's about the huge guy. One, two, three, intro!"

Whitney and Carol Anne play a marching riff on snare drum and acoustic guitar, and we thrash through

"Huge Guy in the Mosh Pit." It's rough and messy, but already better than any of the covers we tried.

"We're doing that one for the concert — a stripped-down, acoustic version, just like that." Whitney puts down her sticks. "But the first thing we need to fix is Barbara's voice."

"What's wrong with my voice?"

"Nothing ... and that's the problem. How do we scuff it up a little?"

"I'm not shredding my cords."

"No, that's not what I mean. I think we should save that sweet choir-girl voice as a secret weapon. What's your low end like?"

"It's OK, but I don't have any power down there."

"That's what amplification is for. Carol Anne, can you try that song in D?"

Carol Anne fiddles around with some new chords, and then starts playing the same song, but lower. It's less comfortable to sing, that's for sure. It doesn't sound like me.

Halfway through the first verse, I have to stop to clear my throat. "It's hitting right in my *passaggio*!"

"Ooh, me, too," Whitney purrs.

Carol Anne laughs. "Whitney, do you even know what a *passaggio* is?"

"I mean the break between my chest voice and mid-range. It's a lot of work to sing in the cracks, and it doesn't even sound good."

"No, it sounds *great*," Carol Anne assures me. "Very punk. Have some water and try it again."

The second time, I get through the song and I'm starting to hear what she means. It's still hard, but the song has some edge now. We do it again, and Carol Anne and Storm start throwing in some shouts and harmony vocals. This is really happening!

"OK, we've learned a song." Storm applauds. I don't know her well enough to tell if she's being sarcastic. "Now can we talk about stage outfits?"

"We're a punk band; wear whatever you want."

"Whoa, chill! I just asked a question. It's not a personal attack."

It's not? Oh. Right. I try to smooth the frown from my face, relax my fists. "Sorry. I'm still not used to, you know, people."

"We're such a long fucking way from playing any shows," Whitney says. "For the chamber concert, we'll have to wear black. For anything else, let's agree that we don't have to match, and we'll plan the details when the time comes."

Storm has her finger in the air again. "Can I say one more thing, though? This isn't a personal criticism, because I know Barbara's sensitive, but can you do anything besides stand still and sing?"

I want to sink through the floor. The thing is, she's right. If we ever do a show, I'll sound great but look pretty stupid. "You know I can't dance."

"You don't need to dance. You just need a couple of basic moves, like in the musical, so you don't look like you have a stick up your butt."

As if I didn't feel mortified enough. "If that's how I look, maybe I should quit now."

"Too late to quit — you've got us all involved." Storm's smile is the nice one again, like that day after play practice. "You didn't have to let me be in your band, but you said OK." She leans in closer. "In return, I will teach *you* how to move like a rock star."

10

THIS IS AN EMERGENCY

When I come out of school, I don't feel exactly like a rock star, but I feel pretty good. Although I've been singing and attempting to move for the last two hours, I'm not tired. Well, my voice is tired, but I've got back some of that do-anything energy I had when I first became visible. Chamber concert? Bring it on.

We weren't sure how long we'd practice; I text Mom so she won't worry.

walking home now

Nar? (momtext for "Need a ride?")

too nice out for that! seeya

It's not much more than a mile to my house; a good

walk, and it's not even five o'clock yet. It won't be dark for hours. Mom and Dad worry when I walk after dark, so all winter I rode the bus home when I stayed late, even though I see more creepy people on the bus than on the street. Whatever. It keeps the parents happy.

So I'm walking up 15th with Dead Bars singing "Tear Shaped Bruise" in my right ear while I keep my left ear tuned to the road. In an hour, traffic will be heavy, but for now, there's not much to speak of. I pass under a big lilac bush where the street curves around the reservoir. A month ago, it was in full bloom. I love the smell of lilacs almost as much as brownies. Now it's a mass of green leaves and crispy brown flower skeletons. I wonder if the others would like Flower Skeleton as a band name. Probably not.

Some major engine noise drowns out the punks in my earbud. A giant, shiny pickup truck roars by, blasting heavy metal. A guy's voice yells something like, "You're too fuckin' ugly!"

I jump back from the curb, my heart drumming, more from the surprise than the words. In one of those futile gestures, I make a finger gun and fire a bolt of rage at the back of the truck.

Or not so futile. The right rear tire blows out. The truck swerves, overcorrects, crosses the other lane and the opposite sidewalk. It misses a power pole by an eyelash and smashes into the chain-link fence around the reservoir with a solid crunch — dead-center on a steel post. The engine revs and dies. Steam puffs from the radiator. The heavy metal soundtrack continues unabated.

"Oh shit oh shit oh shit!" I'm tempted to keep

walking, but I dig out my phone and call 911, because what if somebody's hurt? Oh, God. *What if somebody's hurt?* While it's ringing, I look both ways and dart across the street. This isn't my fault. Just a coincidence.

"911 emergency. What is the nature of your emergency?"

"I just ... " ... *blew out a tire with my mind.* "There's been ... "

"Are you injured? Do you need an ambulance?"

I reach the truck and try to catch my breath. "It's not me! I mean, I witnessed an accident on 15th Northeast, at about 73rd. One vehicle and a fence. I'm looking to see if anyone's hurt."

The deflated airbag spills from the steering column into the driver's lap. He lolls against the shoulder harness, yelping, "Reset! Reset!"

I recognize him from school — Otis Somebody or Somebody Otis. Same thing with his scruffy-looking passenger, Oakley, but I never knew if that was a first name or a last name, either. He's giggling hysterically. Good, I didn't kill them. (Because not my fault, right? Right? Then why did I feel something when I fired my finger gun, and why did it feel so good?)

I open the driver's door and climb up on the step to turn off the music. I don't usually mind metal, but it seems ... inappropriate.

"These guys both look pretty shaken up." I'm pretty shaken up myself, but I'm not telling her that. "They're not making any sense, but they're breathing, and I don't see any blood or bones."

"Don't try to move them unless the vehicle is on fire. Police and paramedics are en route. Please stay there so you can tell them what you saw."

"All right." As I put my phone back in my pocket, Oakley fumbles with the door handle. I walk around the truck to open the door for him. "Look, maybe you should stay in your seat till the paramedics get here."

Still giggling, he slides out of the truck, almost falls, regains his balance. "The look ... on your face ... when I yelled ... oh, God! And that ugly hat!"

My anger flares and any sense of guilt flees. Of its own accord, my fist clenches and pops him right in the nose. That feels good, too, even if it hurts my hand.

He sits down hard. "Bitch! What'd you do that for?" Tears fill his dark eyes.

"Asshole!" Strong language for me; I don't usually swear, no doubt a result of having no friends in those formative middle-school years. "Why'd you yell at me?"

"I dunno, 'cause it's funny?" Blood trickles from his nose. "Otis thought it was funny."

"Well, it's not. And it's not an ugly hat. It's a raspberry beret, the kind you find — oh, here!" No point in wasting a good song reference on a guy who's bleeding on himself. I dig a pack of tissues from my pocket and give him one. Because, yes, I'm the type of person who's always prepared for anything. Anything except superpowers. Which I absolutely don't have because that's impossible.

What's actually funny is that when the cops come and Oakley tries to tell them I hit him, they figure he's in shock and don't even write it down. In return, I tell them about the tire blowing but leave out the drive-by aspect. I hang around long enough to hear that the truck had been reported stolen — seems Otis "borrowed" it from his brother without permission. And hadn't had his license long enough to drive around with teenage passengers. Heh.

So I'm both shaken and smug when I finally head for home. I probably should wait for a bus, but it's still light out and I'd rather walk. I think about the coincidence with the tire all the way home, but I can't make sense of it. At least the walk works off some of the adrenaline.

My phone vibrates in my pocket.

Where r u?

Oops, I guess I should've let Mom know I'd be later than I thought. It's hard to think when weird stuff starts happening. I'm almost home, anyway, so rather than take the time to reply, I keep walking. Then I see something funny enough to take my mind off everything. The sign lights up at the mini-storage place ahead of me. Vertical blocks spell out HEATED STORAGE. No big deal; I've seen it hundreds of times. Except now, the third block is burned out, so it reads:

H S
E T

T R
E A
D G
   E

Band name, maybe? "Thanks, guys, we are He Ted."
Like, "Me Tarzan. You Jane. He Ted." See, it's ironic
because we're all girls and none of us is named Ted.
Yeah. God, it's hopeless.

I can hear Mom in the kitchen when I get home a
few minutes later. "Sorry I'm late," I call, hoping she
won't ask why.

The whole house smells like fresh-baked bread. Oh,
yeah — pizza night! She's been making it every
Thursday for as long as I can remember because it used
to be the only food I actually liked. I learned only
recently that she used to make it more nutritious by
slipping whole-grain flour into the crust and pureed
vegetables into the sauce. She doesn't have to do that
anymore because now I eat like a normal person, but I
still love pizza best. I hang up my stuff and go in to
help.

"What made you so late? I was starting to worry." She ladles sauce over the partly-baked crust.

"There was an accident on 15th." I go to the sink and wash my hands. "I, um, called it in and they told me to wait so I could give a statement." Should I tell her I think I caused it? No way.

"How awful! Was anyone hurt?"

"Not seriously, I don't think, but the truck was pretty messed up."

"Just one vehicle?"

"Yeah, they ran into the fence around the reservoir."

"Oh, dear; that's a tricky curve. Drunk driver?"

"Inexperienced, I think — some kids from school. No one I know," I hasten to add, because she's met Jackson and Carol Anne and completely adores both of them. "A tire blew out."

"That would do it. They were lucky you were right there. I'm proud of you for being so responsible and mature." She gives me a shoulder hug that leaves a floury handprint on my black shirt. "You're my little hero."

I give her a weak smile and focus on arranging cheese and pepperoni slices. I don't feel like a hero. I just hope I'm not a villain.

11

HUGE GUY IN THE CHAMBER CONCERT

It's a classic nightmare scenario: onstage, unprepared, not dressed right. Only it's not a dream. It's the Spring Chamber Concert.

After our one rehearsal, we're performing in the most unlikely venue imaginable. Even worse, for some reason we're closing the program. What was Mr. P thinking?

The other ensembles — two string quartets, one piano trio, a wind quintet, a couple of string trios, and a few duos — have all been working together since the beginning of the semester on classical chamber repertoire. They've chosen their best pieces and polished them in rehearsal until they shine. They all look refined, too, in their black dresses and dark suits, playing with confidence and intensity in front of their friends and families.

And us? Well, Storm has a black evening gown, so she looks like she belongs. Carol Anne is presentable, too, in a black sheath and pearls. Whitney and I are wearing black, at least ... jeans and plain T-shirts, but black.

I wish we could have gone first so I could enjoy the rest of the concert. A lot of the music is familiar. I couldn't tell you the titles without looking at the program, but it's like meeting old friends. It's not that hard to imagine an alternative reality where, if I hadn't been invisible, a lot of these music-geek kids would be my friends. The music is exactly the kind of thing my mom listens to while she works on her freelance editing jobs. She says the structure of chamber music helps her focus without distracting her with words. Anything with lyrics — choral music, opera, folk and pop songs — she saves for her downtime. Come to think of it, I listen to instrumental tracks when I'm doing homework. I'm exactly like my mom! Except she's not about to die on stage. (And she's not here. They think I'm at Carol Anne's house, working on a school project.)

We leave our seats in the front row and wait in the wings during the piano trio's performance. They finish to enthusiastic applause, leave the stage, then go back on for a second bow when the applause continues. Maybe they'll do an encore and we can delay the inevitable ...

Mr. P steps onto the stage. "Thank you for that fine

performance! Next up, we have four young ladies who joined the program partway into the semester. I'll let them announce their piece. Please welcome Barbara, Carol Anne, Storm, and Whitney!" He moves the microphone to the center and leaves the stage.

We walk out from the wings to polite clapping, Whitney carrying her snare drum and sticks, Carol Anne with her Martin, Storm with a tambourine, and me with nothing but nerves. This is the same stage where we performed *Anything Goes* not that long ago. It's so big and empty without the sets and props and other performers. I'm glad I'm not out here alone. We form a semi-circle around the microphone, so we at least look sort of chamber-y. With the lights in my eyes, I can't see much out in the audience. There's an understandable amount of muttering.

I step up to the microphone for the first time in my life. "Hi, um ... " The PA squeals with feedback. Mr. P motions for me to back up a step. "Sorry! We're, um ... " *Woefully under-rehearsed? Completely out of our minds?* "We're not one of the standard chamber groups." That gets a friendly laugh. "So we're not presenting a piece from the standard repertoire. This is a new, original work by a, um, local songwriter."

"It's by Barbara!" Carol Anne shouts.

My face ablaze, I continue the introduction. "Right, I wrote this song. It's called 'Huge Guy in the Mosh Pit.' We'll play it now, I guess."

Whitney counts it off. There's something bracing about the snare drum after an evening of strings and woodwinds. Carol Anne's guitar sounds great in this room's acoustics, too. If I were singing in the strong part of my range, I probably wouldn't need the mic, but I'm glad to have a boost. We do the song like we worked it out in rehearsal, including the rave-ups and shouting. Except I don't try to move.

When we finish, we're greeted with mostly puzzled silence. I imagine crickets. A few people clap. Then somebody way in the back whistles. "Yeah! Rock and roll!" The rest of the audience laughs and claps a little more. We take a quick bow and beat it offstage.

"We are never doing that again," I declare.

"Oh, come on, what kind of band will we be if we don't play any shows?" Whitney removes her snare drum from the stand and zips it into its case.

"No, I want to play shows." I realize only as I'm speaking that I mean it. The playing part was awesome. "We've got something. But we're never going out unrehearsed like that. I thought my heart would explode."

"Maybe we shouldn't play the chamber concert," Storm says. "That was just weird. Although I must say, it's nice to see people dress up for a change." She smiles at a sandy-haired cellist as he hefts his instrument case.

He turns red, but smiles back. "You guys were fun. We should always end the concert like that."

"Yeah? You liked it?" I still can't believe I lived through the performance.

"We're not all stodgy. Some, but not all. I'm Sean, by the way."

"Hi, Sean, I'm Storm." Like he doesn't know that. "You probably know Whitney already. This is Carol Anne, and the one who looks like she's in shock is Barbara." Well, thanks for that, Storm.

"Hey, everybody. I'm pretty sure that was my little brother whistling; you must have been his favorite part of the whole concert."

"Then it's decided," Whitney says. "When we play for the concert in December, we'll have something polished and ready. We will knock their formal black socks off."

12

BRUISES AND BROKEN STRINGS

CAROL ANNE

I can't believe I broke a string. I change them every couple of months, so they don't usually get a chance to break. In fact, I changed them last night. That wouldn't usually be a problem, but then, I don't usually play this hard. "Huge Guy in the Mosh Pit" begs for an aggressive strum, but I guess that was more than unstretched strings could take. Sure felt good, though.

"I guess we're taking a break." Barbara's voice sounds ragged. She takes a long drink from a water bottle.

"Thank fuck," Whitney mutters as she stands up. She props her foot on the piano bench and stretches her leg, massaging the calf.

"I'll just change the one string, so this shouldn't take long." I open my case and pull out a spare set.

Storm sets down the tambourine and rubs her palm. "Take as long as you need. This hand will never be the same."

Barbara leans against the wall, the picture of dejection. "I'm sorry, you guys. We could quit now, before it gets any worse."

WHITNEY

My leg is asleep all the way up to my ass and I can't feel my fucking foot. I need a drum throne with a better seat — this one bites into my leg. So you better believe I am past ready to stand up by the time Carol Anne breaks a string. It's a fucking miracle.

We've been playing "Huge Guy" over and over. One, it's the only song we all know, but, also, two, it's fun, and only gets more solid every time through. But I feel like I'm risking nerve damage here.

"I guess we're taking a break."

Shit, what happened to our choir girl? She's starting to sound like a smoker. I guess we all need a break. "Thank fuck." I stand up — carefully — and shuffle over to the piano bench to stretch my tingling leg. My arms feel better than my legs, but they're starting to ache from the pounding.

Looks like Storm's a little sore, too. Or a lot, based on that wince. Well, she's been laying into that tambourine like it did her wrong, so no surprise there.

Barbara takes a long drink of water. It helps her voice but not her mood. "We should quit now, before it gets worse."

STORM

That's gonna leave a mark. A few bruises is nothing new, but I don't usually give them to myself.

I started out hitting the tambourine with my hand, but I decided I'd better stop before I broke a bone or something. I've seen backup singers beat the tambourine on their hip or thigh, so I tried that. Yeah, I'm not breaking that bone. I bet I'll have a massive bruise in the morning, though.

I'm not the only one ready for a break, but it's the guitar that takes it literally. Carol Anne opens her guitar case and pulls out a pack of strings. While she's changing the broken string, Whitney stretches her leg and rubs her foot.

I massage my sore hand and walk around. Shake it off, as my girl Taylor advises. OK, I'm pretty beaten up, but I'd rather get bruises doing something fun by choice than the old way. Even better would be to figure out how to do this without hurting myself.

Barbara drinks some water and rasps, "We could quit now, before it gets any worse."

I turn toward her, alarmed. "Oh, hell, no. We can't quit now. It's just getting good."

"It ... it is?"

"Fuck, yeah!" Whitney chimes in. "We've got that song, though. Maybe we should work on something else for a while."

BARBARA

What have I done? Carol Anne broke a string, Whitney can barely walk, and the way Storm's wincing, she must have pounded her leg to mush. My voice is feeling pretty rough, too. Wasn't this supposed to be fun? Maybe we should quit now, save ourselves a lot of trouble. We could stop thinking about names and stage outfits.

Oops. I must have said some of that out loud, because Whitney and Storm refuse to consider it.

"Maybe we should work on something else for a while."

As Whitney says this, Carol Anne finishes installing the string and tuning it up. She plays a familiar three-chord intro, Whitney dives back behind the drums, and we all try to sing "Louie Louie." I don't know all the words because who does? Also, I'm laughing too hard. Nothing like an indestructible garage-rock classic to fix my mood. It kind of falls apart, but then they segue into "Barbara Ann," which makes me blush.

"OK, I guess we're doing this," I say as they wind down. "Maybe we should be a cover band, after all."

"Sure, we could try that," Carol Anne says. "But what about working on that other one we demoed? The bus one. It seemed lower impact than 'Huge Guy.'"

"Oh, yeah, I like that one." Storm picks up the tambourine and taps it lightly against her leg. "And I'm sure it calls for a more restrained tambourine part."

Carol Anne listens to some of the demo on her

phone, then starts playing. She stops after a few bars and starts over in a lower key. Is this going to happen with everything I write? Yeah, probably. Whitney picks up a pair of bongos and adds a light beat under the guitar. Carol Anne turns to her with a smile and a nod of approval. I can't argue with them; it sounds pretty good. I pull up the lyrics on my phone and when the verse comes around again, I start to sing.

Went to the thrift store with my best friend ...

It's low for me, but less of a struggle than "Huge Guy" was at first. I didn't envision such a relaxed tempo, but it feels good for now. Maybe we can work up a quicker version, too, once we know the song. I'm glad now that I sang it for Carol Anne soon after I wrote it. I almost didn't; it seemed so personal. But most of my older stuff doesn't have much to do with my life now. This band deserves new material, so I guess I need to write faster.

The next time through, Carol Anne tries out a harmony part that sounds so good I stop everything so we can all hear it again and record it before we forget.

"Storm, can you do something like this on top?" I demonstrate what I'm thinking, she tries it, and then we put it all together. "Yeah! That's sweet."

"Well, of course it is," Storm says. "You wrote it about Jackson. It's a loooove song."

"No, it isn't." Right. My red face says different but I won't back down now. "I mean, yes, he's in it, but it's about having a safe place to go home to." Even as the words are leaving my mouth, I remember, in spite of appearances, Storm hasn't always had that kind of place. "It's about family. That kind of love."

"Uh-huh." Storm gives me an infuriatingly knowing smile. Makes it hard to feel sorry for her.

Carol Anne steps in and saves the day. "So, we're running out of school year. Can we keep going over the summer?"

"Drums will be at my house, but that shouldn't be a problem," Whitney says. "We'll be away at Yellowstone for a couple of weeks, though, and I got a job at the mall — food court this time, three days a week."

"Yeah, I got a part-time job, too," Carol Anne says. "You know that cool little vintage shop on the Ave? And we're having a big family reunion. But we should be able to work around that, right?"

"I'm not doing anything but Cheer Camp and three weeks in Europe, dahlings." Storm pretends to smoke from a long cigarette holder.

"OK, we'll play it by ear and squeeze in whatever practices your busy schedules can take." I'm feeling like a slacker, with no particular plans at all. Maybe I could still get a job, to complicate things further. "I'll ... see if I can come up with new material. Because we need more than two songs."

13

PUNK ROCK GIRL, COUNTRY RADIO

Between band practice and schoolwork, the last weeks of the semester pass in a blur. This is the first year I've had anything to distract me; now I get why kids fall behind on assignments. But I caught up (thanks to a spreadsheet) and passed my finals; school is the one thing I've always been good at, besides singing. With another school year in the record books, I come home on the last day and empty my backpack onto my desk, but I'm completely unmotivated to actually sift through the stack of papers for what to keep and what to recycle. No rush; I've got the whole summer.

For as long as I've been in school, Mom and Dad

have always taken me out for dinner to celebrate the last day. That meant a lot of pizzas and burgers in the old days, but this year, they want to take me someplace nice. Who am I to argue?

But, wow. White tablecloths, cloth napkins, oil candles. Maybe I should have changed out of my jeans and T-shirt. Not that I have much that's dressier. I don't think that sparkly purple number would fit in here, either. Unexpectedly, I'm saved by the weather. No June Gloom today, so the hostess offers the option of a table on the patio. When Dad looks to me, I nod vigorously. Outside equals casual; maybe I won't feel so underdressed.

There's no water view, which Dad says would cost even more, but herbs growing in pots and raised beds make it feel and smell like a garden. Bees buzz nearby, but they have flowers; why would they care about us?

"What lovely anise hyssop," Mom exclaims of the plant with the bees. Grandma's a botanist, so there's hardly a plant Mom can't name. "And nasturtiums! Now it's really summer."

We order drinks, and I study the menu. At the family restaurants I'm used to, steak or shrimp is usually the most expensive item, and I know to ask permission before ordering either. Here, though, even the burger is up there.

"I've never had lobster," I muse. "What does 'market price' mean?"

Dad snorts. "It means, 'If you have to ask, you can't afford it.'"

"That's sort of what I thought." I flutter my eyelashes and attempt to look sweet. "May I order lobster?"

"I'll buy you lobster when you graduate — "

"Well, that's not much longer — "

" — from college."

"Two-year or four?"

He holds up four fingers.

"I guess I'll have the wild Alaska salmon, then." He pretends to choke but doesn't say no, so I guess it's all right. Then he orders the same thing. Yeah, it's all right.

When my lemonade and their wine arrive, Mom raises her glass. "Here's to one more school year behind us." We clink our glasses and drink. The lemonade here is excellent, but I almost choke when Mom adds, "So how does it feel to be a senior?"

"What?" I sputter. "I'm a ... oh. That's gonna be hard to get used to."

"Tell me about it!" Dad shakes his head. "Guess I better start that college fund."

"Nice try." He's been pulling this joke for years, but I know my parents and grandparents have all contributed to a fund for me. It's not huge but it'll help. Wish I knew what I wanted to use it for.

Mom holds her glass up to admire the ruby color of the wine. "So, Barbara, are you relieved to be finished with another year?"

"I'm relieved to be done with classes, but I'll miss seeing my friends every day." Just saying 'my friends' still gives me a thrill, and now a lump in the throat.

"But you'll still see them. Aren't you keeping the band going over the summer?"

"When everybody's free, but that's less often than

you'd think. With vacations and summer jobs, scheduling practices will be a nightmare."

Mom's chuckle holds more sarcasm than sympathy. "You have no idea; none of you are even working full-time."

"You're really making me want to grow up, you know that?"

Regardless, it'll be a chore getting everybody together. Even I found a weird little sort-of job, a few hours a week as a "shelf monkey," re-alphabetizing movies at the neighborhood video store. I know, right? So nineties. But perfect for someone who can fade into the background, and it's a very funky little shop. I'll get paid in video rentals, which ought to help the family entertainment budget. And if a real job opens up, they'll already know I'm reliable.

"You can get together with your friends even if it's not the whole band, right?" Mom presses. "There are other activities — swimming, canoeing, hiking ... "

Swimming. There's a thought.

" ... and it's been years since you had a birthday party."

"When did I ever have a birthday party?"

"Didn't we do something when you were four or five?"

"Maybe." I have the haziest of memories — a butterfly cake, melting ice cream, kids screaming. But four is pretty small. What little I remember is probably from a snapshot of the actual event. "No, that's a good idea. Birthday party with my best friends."

"And of course tomorrow, we're heading out to visit Barb and Tom."

I don't mean to groan, but it slips out before I can stop it. "Do I have to go?"

"It's only one weekend. And they've put in a pool."

Every year, as soon as school's out, we go visit Mom's old roommate — the one I'm named for — and her family on their farm. They grow cherries and grapes and make wine. It's kind of fun to get food and drink from the source, but this is the last weekend before everybody starts working. The pool is tempting, but not that much.

"Why don't you see if one of your friends can come along?" Mom adds, probably based on the look on my face.

That's more like it. I pull out my phone and text Jackson. It's still a thrill to get his reply. Until I read it:

can't, starting work tomorrow. have fun!

Thanks a lot. I try Carol Anne next and don't even get an answer. I don't know Whitney well enough to invite her out of town, and I'm not even considering Storm. I'm about to get whiny about it when a woman's voice from the next table stops me cold.

"The drink I didn't have last time is the drink I should've had."

I lunge to grab the pen from Dad's pocket. I probably shouldn't write on the cloth napkin, though. I remove the coaster from under my lemonade and scribble the line before I forget.

"Barbara, what are you — "

"Sh! Song!" I study the line, cross out *time* and replace it with *night*. That'll do for now. I stuff the coaster into my pocket and hand the pen to Dad. I don't know what I'll do with this windfall, or what it even means, but I'm happy to have it written down. "So what time do we leave?"

If I had any say, we'd be leaving after noon, but Mom and Dad want to hit the road early, before it gets hot and crowded. At least they have the decency to wait until the sun's up, but it's still pretty early. I've lost the positive attitude I had last night. We pack whatever we need for overnight and pile into the car with a plan to stop for breakfast on the way. That's fine by me; I'm still full from last night's dinner, which was amazing. I ate it all, including the nasturtium petals in my salad. They tasted peppery — not at all like I imagined flowers would taste. We all shared a warm rhubarb crisp for dessert, but Mom and Dad let me have most of it.

Mom's driving the first leg, which means Dad's in charge of music. He slides the new Sonics album into the CD player, so I leave the earbuds out for now. There's not a slow or quiet song on the whole album, so you'd think it would keep me awake, but I doze off a few songs in. I'm so not a morning person.

I vaguely hear the end of the album. When Dad ejects the disc, the radio comes on, tuned to NPR, but we're far enough from the transmitter that the reception is staticky.

"Are we there yet?" I mutter.

"Another twenty minutes to breakfast."

He turns off the radio and I continue to doze until we're pulling into a café in the mountains. We're no more than an hour from home, but it feels like we've traveled somewhere. I've got more appetite now, and I remember the waffles here. Maybe this trip will be all right.

Back on the road, I watch the scenery fly by at seventy miles per hour. Now Mom's in charge of music, so we're listening to something classical. It's not choral, so I haven't been paying attention, but it goes well with trees. It doesn't seem very long before we're out of dense mountain forest and into dryer country — pine woods and sagebrush and grassland. Not much to look at. What did I used to do when I was bored, before I had friends? That's right. I put in my earbuds and disappear into a book. This would work better if I weren't near the end of the story and if I'd loaded more music on my phone. I run out of book about the time things start to repeat. I'm left to listen to Mom's music and stare at the dull scenery.

I decide to give Carol Anne another chance and send a no-drama text.

hey

Ten minutes pass. I need to be more emphatic.

hey!

Nothing. Seriously? Time to go extreme.

HEY!

Still no answer? Fuck it. I give the screen a furious swipe. "Oh, shit!" I blurt as a crack follows my finger across the gorilla glass.

"Barbara! Language!"

"Sorry, Mom." Good thing she can't hear my thoughts. "My phone — the screen's cracked!"

"Well, how did that happen?"

"I, um, don't know." She wouldn't believe me if I told her. I can't explain it myself. "I ... must have dropped it or something." Right. I dropped the phone I begged for last Christmas, the phone I'm absurdly careful with to prove I can be trusted? Like she'll believe that, either.

"Does it still work?"

"Yes."

"Then the crack is a good reminder to be more careful."

She's right. Doesn't mean I don't want to pitch the stupid device out the window. How could my finger crack that tough glass, though? I stare at the offending digit and see a blown-out tire, a truck running off the road. No, that's ridiculous. It's just another coincidence.

The CD ends and Mom pops it out. The radio comes on again, but this doesn't sound like NPR.

God is great, beer is good, a man's twangy voice sings. Mom reaches to turn it off.

"Wait!" I've never paid much attention to country music before, but a line like that deserves notice. I listen to a few songs, and they're not that far from the rock and roll I like. There's more steel guitar and a different vocal style, and the subject matter differs some, too. More patriotism and pickup trucks than you find in the average punk rock song. A lot of drinking and cheating, too. There's usually a story. "OK, that's enough."

We're back to more Beethoven or whatever. I pull the coaster from last night out of my pocket and study that strange line. Maybe it belongs in a country song. Can I write a country song? For that matter, can I write about drinking? I've never even had a beer. (See above, formative middle-school years.)

After what seems like all day but is only four hours, we leave the interstate for a state highway, then a county road, and finally a long gravel drive, cherry orchard on one side, acres of grapevines on the other. We finally stop in front of a big house — not an old farmhouse, a new one, but designed to look historic. Last year, it was habitable, but still unfinished. Now, it looks done, like it's always been there. The new Barrelrace Cellars tasting room and gift shop sit at a right angle to the house. The image on the sign shows a rider in a cowboy hat, flat to the back of a galloping horse as they round a barrel in a rodeo arena.

I climb out of the backseat, relieved to stretch my legs. The hot air is a shock after the air-conditioned car. It's so dry I can already feel my lips chapping. It smells like dust and sweet hay, with a faint stink of manure. Oh, right. This is farm country. Great.

"Welcome!" Mom's friend Barb greets us from the shady porch. She reminds me of a Lego person — small and blocky and cute. She looks comfortable in a sleeveless blouse and knee-length shorts. She has reading glasses perched in her short blond curls. "What do you say to a swim before lunch?"

"That sounds great!" I'd forgotten about the pool. That could make the visit bearable.

"Hey, there's my little namesake!" Barb steps down to give me a hug. The "little" is funny — she's now three or four inches shorter than I am.

"How hot is it, anyway?"

She checks the thermometer on the porch. "This says ninety-eight. We might hit a hundred today, but yesterday was a hundred and three."

"But it's a dry heat," Dad says solemnly.

I roll my eyes and he pretends not to notice. We grab our bags and follow Barb into the house, which is blessed with central air.

"See what you think of how I've decorated your rooms. With the whole wine thing taking off, we're thinking of doing a B&B," she announces. "If people are staying here, they'll start their tasting here, too."

Mom chuckles. "And buy a few bottles to stash in their room. I wondered what you were going to do with all this space."

Mom and Dad's room has a big bed buried in ruffled throw pillows. I don't get it, but I wouldn't mind the bookshelf full of classic novels. My room across the hall has an antique daybed and a smaller collection of both pillows and books. I close the door and unpack my swimsuit. I haven't even looked at it since I got home from camp last time, almost a year ago. It's a plain black racing suit. (Not that I'm fast. I'm good enough to pass the swim test at camp: length of the pool, no drowning. Very little speed required.) The most this suit has going for it is that it stays put no matter what I do. But the bottom is all pilled, and when I get it on, it's tight across the chest — a good sign that it's time to think about a new one.

Mom's already out by the small pool when I get there. She passes me a tube of waterproof sunscreen. The patio and pool are about two-thirds in the sun in the middle of the day, so I'm glad she remembered it. We both tend to burn. I grease up and step into the water. It's cold, but that's what I want. I tiptoe down the steps until the water's up to my waist, then plunge in over my head. Ahh!

I surface in the deep end and float on my back. Mom and Barb sit on the steps in the shallow end, laughing and catching up. I pick up bits of the conversation whenever my ears are out of the water.

"Barbara's smart to go with a one-piece. I'll never forget what happened with your string bikini and the high dive. Who were you trying to impress? Not Steve."

I go under. My mom, in a skimpy bikini? Hard to picture her showing that much skin, especially for the benefit of someone not my dad. When I pop up again, Mom's laughing so hard, she has to wipe her eyes.

" ... but at least I managed to find my top!"

OK, I think I'll look for another one-piece. Barb splashes at Mom and misses, getting me right in the face. "Hey!"

"She didn't mean it, Barbara." Mom turns to her friend. "Barbara hates to be splashed. I think it's the only thing she dislikes about swimming."

Dad decided he preferred a nap to a swim, so it's just us girls in the water. When we've had enough swim time, Barb fires up the grill and makes burgers for lunch. The aroma draws Dad out of the house to join us. There's a salad, too ... with nasturtium petals, like at the fancy restaurant, so that must be a thing.

I go inside to rinse off and put on shorts and a T-shirt. As I return, Barb's husband Tom tractors up to the back gate with a box of sweet cherries, just picked. Tom's a tall guy, neck and arms burned brown, bald head protected by a seed cap. He doesn't talk much, but when something's funny he has a deep, rolling laugh that's contagious.

Barb scoops up a bowlful of cherries and adds them to the patio table. She smiles when she sees me eyeing them. "Barbara, stay out of the cherries or no one else will have a chance at them!"

Sure, hog the cherries one time, and they never let you forget. When she goes in the house for buns and condiments, I grab a cherry and pop it into my mouth. It's sun warm and bursting with juice. Tom catches me spitting out the pit. He winks and zips his lips.

When everything's ready, we sit in the shade of the big umbrella. As always after swimming, I'm famished. "This is the best burger I've ever eaten." The juice runs over my hands and the bun is disintegrating. It might have been better to stay in my swimsuit.

Mom nods in agreement and licks grease off her hand. "I'll bet the beef's local."

"Yep — from a steer our new neighbor raised for 4H," Tom says. "Can't get much more local than that."

14

A GOOD HAT

After lunch, the adults go over to the tasting room. I could go, too, and hang out in the gift shop or something, but really — what could be more dull than a bunch of grown-ups standing around talking about wine? And while I'm on the subject, how could anybody taste all those weird things they say they taste? I opt to stay in my room and nap.

Only I'm not sleepy. I text Carol Anne again — *hey?* — but get no reply. I even go to the extreme length of calling her, but it goes straight to voice mail. Apparently she has better things to do than wait around to hear from me. I try Jackson; same result.

He's either working right now or he's found someone much cooler to hang out with. Sure, I go out of town for one day, and everybody forgets about me. I look at the cracked screen and set my phone down extra carefully. I pick a book off the shelf, but it doesn't grab me.

I feel so out of place here — a punk-rock girl listening to country radio. I stop everything and dig my notebook out of my pack, because that's a pretty good line. I scribble it down and start a list of what might go into a country song: whiskey, betrayal, feeling sad, a punk girl who's almost seventeen and doesn't drink ...

I don't know if that's going anywhere, and anyway, what am I doing indoors when there's a swimming pool?

I squeeze back into my damp suit, slather on more sunscreen, and head back outside. The heat smacks me like sheet metal, so I waste no time jumping into the cool water. I don't think I've ever had a swimming pool to myself before. That means nobody can splash me! Pretty soon, I forget I'm supposed to feel lonely. I'm doing a lazy backstroke when a lanky kid in a cowboy hat rides up to the back fence on an actual horse. This is so not the city.

"Hey! Barb invited me over to swim." It's a high-ish, husky voice, like maybe it changed only last week. "That OK?" The rider swings down off the horse in one smooth motion and loops the reins over the fence rail.

"Oh, um, hey. Yeah, fine." Not fine at all, in fact. Hard enough to talk to a boy I don't know (which would be pretty much every boy except Jackson) when I'm wearing clothes. In a swimsuit? I'd almost rather drown.

"I'm Bailey." Standing on one foot, Bailey yanks off a boot to reveal a long, narrow foot.

"Hi, I'm Barbara."

"You related to Barb?" Reverse procedure to remove the other boot.

"My mom roomed with her in college."

"Cool. You sure are pale."

My, a tactful one. "I don't tan, and we don't get much sun."

"Oh, city folk!" The cowboy hat comes off, freeing a long brown ponytail. Under the Western shirt and high-waisted jeans is a tiny American flag bikini on a lean and deeply tanned but definitely female body. Bailey's a girl, and I barely manage to not say it out loud. She cannonballs into the deep end and surfaces with a loud, "Whoo!" By some miracle, the bikini stays on. Doesn't mean I'll risk one.

After I clear the splash from my eyes, I take a guess. "Do you raise steers for 4H?"

"Yeah, since I was twelve. Before that, it was rabbits and sheep."

"How do you stand the smell?"

"What smell?"

I can still detect the manure reek, even over the pool's chlorine scent. She can't smell it?

She smacks me lightly on the arm. "Kidding! You live in the country more than a day, a little shit smell doesn't bother you. It smells like money."

"Money?"

"That's what my dad says — he raises hay and cattle. And I'm saving my prize and sale money for college. I want to be a veterinarian."

"Wow, ambitious." Compared to me, anyway, with my non-existent plans.

She nods. "At least eight years of school, but I like a challenge."

"You don't think it'll be kind of gross?"

"Aw, I been touching gross stuff as long as I can remember. I already help Dad doctor our stock; I might as well get paid for it."

"And you don't mind people buying your animals to eat?"

"What else you gonna do with a steer? Barb and Tom bought half the last one."

"Yeah, I, um, think we ate him for lunch. Sorry."

Bailey throws her head back and howls. "Good riddance, I say. I named him Sugar, but I ended up calling him SOB. Ornery, but delicious."

"What do you call your horse?"

"Swift — you know, like Taylor? I love her."

"Heard of her." Not my thing, but Storm's a huge fan. "Is Swift swift?" I grin.

"She's turning into a good barrel racer. That's us on the sign for the winery; label, too. Ever been to a rodeo?"

"Once at the state fair, I think, a long time ago. I've never been on a horse, though."

Bailey studies me. "You must be on the swim team."

"Not even close," I snort.

"Why the racing suit, then?"

"I never have to think about it." I definitely have to go shopping for a new suit. "My friend Jackson's on the swim team, so I've been to a couple of meets."

"If we had one, I guess I'd be on it."

"Yeah? You go out for sports?"

"Pretty much everybody does in a school our size, but I would, anyway. Fall's volleyball, winter's basketball, spring's track and field, summer's rodeo."

"Sounds like a lot, on top of raising a steer."

"And chores, and babysitting, and homework. And band, of course."

"Do you play bass?" What are the odds, right? But I can't help myself.

"No, tenor." Bailey floats on her back and spouts water into the air.

"Wait, what?"

"Tenor sax. And clarinet in concert band, but jazz band is way more fun."

Sounds like everybody really does do everything. "How big is your school?"

"Almost 150!" Bailey says it like that's a lot. "What about yours?"

"I think about ten times that."

"No way! How do you even keep track of everybody's names?"

"I don't. I only know a few people." I've always wondered how Jackson does it, because he does know everybody. It's his superpower. "The good athletes are kind of celebrities, though. Even I know who they are." Well, some of them, like the basketball-star Hornbaker twins, Jordan and her brother Justin. When either of them comes down the hall, you know it. Bailey would probably love them.

"Well, you must have something you do for fun."

"I was in the spring musical, but I'd never done anything like that before. Mostly I hang out, or go thrift-shopping with my gay best friend."

"Wow, that's so — urban. Does every girl have one?"

I'm not sure, but I think she's probably joking. "No, but they should. I got mine completely by accident, but I'm never shopping with anyone else if I can help it. We don't shop that much, though. Sometimes I go to shows."

"Like, movies?"

"No, music. Punk rock, garage — like that."

"Ooh, so edgy. Is everybody all tattooed and pierced and whatever?"

"Some are. Not me, but my drummer has a bunch of piercings."

"Your drummer? You're in a band? Do you have a record? Are you on iTunes?"

I laugh so hard I almost drown. When I've got my breath back, I try to clue her in. "We've had four practices and learned two songs. We haven't played out yet and we don't even have a name. On the plus side, we haven't killed each other, so maybe someday there will be a record." It's the first time I've voiced this hope out loud. That makes it real.

"That sounds amazing!"

I sigh. They haven't forgotten me, have they? "It's what I've always wanted to do. I kind of, you know, write songs, but I never had anyone to do them with before."

"You write songs! Like Taylor Swift!"

"Well, not much like Tay — "

"Sing me something! What's your best song?"

Like it wasn't weird enough singing for Carol Anne in her bedroom, now I have to sing for a complete stranger in a swimming pool? Maybe not "Huge Guy in the Mosh Pit." I can probably pull off "Half a Bus Closer to Home."

Bailey listens attentively and claps at the end. "That is so sweet. And your voice reminds me of somebody."

I don't see how it could, but a faint memory of my own has been working its way to the surface. "I think I've only met one other Bailey in my life."

"There aren't a whole lot of us. Where and when?"

"Church camp, when I was ten."

Without warning, Bailey rockets out of the water and comes down with a splash that drenches me and half the pool deck. Why does she keep doing that? "That camp at the beach? What year?"

It sounds like the most urgent question ever. I tell her the year and she shrieks.

"Yes! The year it rained every day! That Bailey was me! And now I remember you — we were in the same cabin!"

"You remember me? Really?" I mean, I was less invisible at camp than at school, but still ...

"I didn't recognize your face, but I remember your voice. I always wanted to sit near you at campfire and singing time."

"You did?"

"Yeah, you sang right out, and you actually hit the notes. Remember our theme song?"

Without waiting for an answer, she launches into a chorus of "Our God Reigns." Which I do remember because I never forget a song, so I join in.

"Yeah, I'd know that voice anywhere! I totally expected you to sing on talent night. Why didn't you?"

"I was, you know, dealing with some self-esteem issues. Still working on that, actually. But I was in our cabin's skit."

"Everybody was in the skit, but there weren't any songs. Did you have lines?"

"No, I was the tree."

"The tree. What a waste!"

That does more for my self-esteem than singing at camp would have, but I don't know how to tell her that. "Sorry I didn't recognize you."

"No reason you should! That was the only summer I went to that camp. And I was a total tomboy then."

I don't know how to tell her I thought she was a boy earlier. "So what are you now?"

She brays out a long laugh. "Still a tomboy! But I clean up nice. See this tan? Spray-on, for prom. Even I wouldn't wear an off-shoulder dress with a tank top tan!"

I see another exuberant splash coming before her hands hit the water. I fling my arms up in front of me and yell, "Don't splash me, goddammit!"

The splash never reaches me. It's like it hits a window and falls straight back into the pool. What the heck? The impossible things are starting to pile up, and this time there's a witness.

"Whoa! Barbara!"

"I'm sorry. I didn't mean to swear. I don't like to be splashed, is all." Misdirection never hurts, right?

"No, I get that. But what did you do? It was like a force field or something. Ooh! Like whatshername in *The Incredibles*! Can you turn invisible, too?"

I don't know how to answer that. I mean, I joke with Jackson that I'm still invisible without a hat, but I'm not sure that's true anymore. "I can kind of ... escape notice, if that counts. But a force field? That'd be like a superpower or something."

"Then let's say you have a superpower! Do it again!"

The splash hits me before I know what's happening. I'm so startled, I snort water up my nose. My sinuses are on fire, and I feel anything but super. "Stop doing that!"

I give the water a shove. A huge wave washes over Bailey, knocking her off her feet. She comes up coughing and wiping her eyes. I'm afraid she'll take a swing at me. Here I thought I was making a friend with no help from Jackson, and I have to go and ruin it.

But wait. She's laughing. "Barbara! I think you have anger powers! When you're ticked, you can do amazing things! Did this just start today?"

"Well, there were one or two times where I wasn't sure." I glance at the finger that caused all the trouble up to now.

"This is so exciting! Isn't it? What's it feel like?"

"Scary! But also ... satisfying. Like, instead of being pointless, I can put my anger into something real. It's just like ... wow." But I wrecked that guy's truck. I cracked my phone screen. I almost drowned Bailey. Who knows what I might have done to those mean girls if Storm hadn't come along. "What good is it, though? I gesture, and ... things happen. But I don't know what until after."

"Then don't do this one." Bailey draws her finger across her throat.

She thinks it's funny, but that gives me a chill. "I'll be careful."

"I'm not saying you should fight crime or anything, but I'll bet you could have some fun with it. Let's think about this."

"OK, but maybe not in the pool, because I'm turning into Prune Girl."

Most of the pool area is in shade now, anyway. We dry off and plop down on loungers. It's still warm out, but not unbearable. Bailey tilts her straw hat over her eyes in a passable impression of a cowpoke snoozing out on the range.

"That's a good hat."

She takes it off to look at me. "Aw, this is just my work hat. My rodeo hat is the good one." She reaches over the side of the chair and extracts a phone from her jeans pocket. "Here, you can see it in my profile picture. It's from when I was a junior rodeo princess."

The photo shows a grinning Bailey in a fawn-colored Stetson with a sparkly tiara attached to the front. "Wow. I collect hats, and I agree; that is one good hat. I think I need one."

"Who doesn't? They're not cheap, though."

"Maybe I'll start with a work hat."

Bailey laughs and sticks her hat on my head, then takes a picture. "Yep, you're right. You do need one. Wish I could give it to you, but I need it, too."

"That's OK, they tend to find me."

"Is that a superpower, too?"

"Maybe. It's a lot more useful than the other one."

"So maybe you need more practice. Hey, are you on Facebook or anything?"

"Not much. I have a profile I almost never use."

"It's a total time suck," Bailey says. "I log in to check messages and end up on there for hours."

"Well, I probably wouldn't have that problem. I've only accepted friend requests from people I know, which means three friends and my mom. We talked about a band page, but I can't set it up until we have a name."

"I'm going to friend you so I'll know when you share songs and get famous and everything. Or get your own comic book, whichever. Promise you'll accept?"

"OK, I promise. As long as you'll let me know when you get into veterinary school."

"Deal."

Our hands meet in a resounding high five. Somehow, I've made a friend, with no help from anybody.

"Barbara, did you have a good afternoon?" Barb asks.

We're out on the patio again, eating the chicken and ribs Tom grilled for dinner. The adults have opened a bottle of Barrelrace wine, and I have a tall glass of limeade. Why did I not know limeade is a thing? It's the best.

"Yeah, Bailey came over, and we swam." I'm going for cool and casual, like I always hang out with people

I've just met. I'll leave out the detail about superpowers.

"I thought she might. How did you and Bailey get along?"

"We had fun. Turns out we were at camp together a long time ago."

"Small world!" Barb holds up the wine bottle. "Did she tell you we put her on our label?"

"Yes, and about her steer, and her horse, and her ex-boyfriend who's going into the Navy, and all the sports she plays." I shake my head and grin. "I like her, but she's kind of exhausting."

Barb chuckles. "She's an energetic girl."

"She wants to take me to her church tomorrow." I look to Mom and Dad. "Is that OK?"

Mom smiles in a way I can't decode. "Sure, our only plan is to visit farm stands; we won't head home until after lunch. Do you know what church?"

"No, all she said was to wear long pants."

"That's an odd dress code."

"Yeah, maybe. I'm fine with it." Because I just made a new friend and I don't want to come off as too fussy. I can manage long pants. At least they don't require long skirts.

Farm breakfast is early, but I'm used to getting up on Sunday morning. And also, I hardly slept. This is the red half of the state; what if Bailey's church is some far-right extremist outfit? What if they all bring guns? What if I don't know any of the songs? What if ... ?

OK, enough. I did get some sleep, and breakfast included fresh cinnamon rolls, so I can't feel too bad. I have my jeans, sunscreen, and green cap on by the time Bailey arrives. It's already warm out, at nine in the morning.

"Barbara and Bailey — sounds like a circus," Dad comments. I give him a look, which he ignores.

I follow Bailey out past the pool to the gate, where Swift is waiting. Bailey unties the reins and swings up into the saddle.

"OK, climb up on the fence and get on behind me."

"I ... what? Oh, no, that's OK. I just don't know how to — "

"Oh, here!" She reaches down and whips the cap off my head, replacing it with her straw hat. She plops my cap on her own head. It doesn't look half bad.

Tom comes out and gives me a boost so I can scramble up behind Bailey. I wrap my arms around her. This is not how I ever expected to go to church.

"That's right! Hold on tight and grip with your knees. Giddyap!"

Oh. Lord. Let me tell you something about horses. Horses are big. Really big. I'm, like, a mile off the ground. And the smell — sharp and sour and like nothing I've ever smelled before or want to again. Also, have I mentioned big?

And when they move, they move all over. Side to side, up and down, and of course forward in a huge hurry. If I weren't clinging like a limpet to Bailey, I would have fallen off at the first step. She's yelling. I'm screaming. I press my forehead against her back (crushing the hat brim — sorry, Bailey), squeeze my eyes shut and try to master this balancing act. Eyes shut makes it worse. I open them and get a look at how fast the ground is going by. Not helping! I look out over Bailey's shoulder.

Wow. Snow-capped mountains peek over the surrounding dry hills. Gently rocking, but still a pretty nice panorama. I can barely smell anything over the horse stink, but sometimes I get a whiff of moisture or something growing. Not manure, so I feel lucky.

Bailey turns and shouts, "Well, how do you like my church?"

"Where?"

She waves her arm in an expansive gesture. "Here!"

"It, it, it ... has a nice view?"

She laughs and slows to a walk. "Sorry. That wasn't fun?"

"Some parts were not as terrifying as other parts. I guess horseback riding isn't for me."

"But you never would have known, right?"

"Yeah. Thanks, I guess." I look to the hills and mountains. "This is beautiful, though. Maybe we should sing a hymn or something."

"There's always our theme song."

"It's not raining."

"Yeah, but the verse has mountains, remember?"

I didn't remember it was the same song, but when she starts to sing, it comes back and I join in.

How lovely on the mountains are the feet of him
Who brings good news, good news,
Announcing peace, proclaiming news of happiness:
Our God reigns ...

"How come you never came back to camp after that one year?"

"I started going to horse camp instead. Do you still go?"

"I went last summer. This year I've got too much going on." I hope that's still true. "So ... could we try galloping again?"

"Are you sure?"

"Yeah, I'm feeling braver. And when will I have the chance again?"

"Well, all right! Hang on!"

I'm ready this time. I grip with my knees for all I'm worth and cling to Bailey with one arm while I hold onto the straw hat with the other. The ride is kind of rough as Swift gets up to speed, then smooths out. We're rocking and rolling and racing across the pasture, and the thrill in my belly has almost nothing to do with fear. I throw back my head and whoop.

"That's more like it!" Bailey yells. "Get ready for the postlude!"

We're heading right at an object in the distance, I can't tell what. When we don't change course the fear returns, but I figure Bailey knows what she's doing, or Swift does. Right? We're closer. It looks like ... a steel barrel? Yeah, one of three.

"Oh, shit!" I yell as Swift takes the turn around the barrel, low and tight. I lose my grip on Bailey and start to slide off sideways. This is gonna hurt.

I windmill my arms; against all reason and laws of physics, I move up instead of down. What the fuck? (And when did that word enter my vocabulary?) One more flap and I'm vertical again, suspended weightless for a breath. Then I'm back in the saddle behind Bailey.

About the time my stomach catches up, I wrap both arms around her. The hat can take care of itself.

"You all right back there?"

"It's like flying!" No *like* about it, but I'm not ready for that discussion.

I'm more ready for the next barrel, which is another point on a triangle. It's amazing how close Swift gets without hitting it, or falling over. We round the third barrel.

"Bring 'er home!" Bailey hollers. We gallop full out back toward the first two barrels. As we pass between them, Bailey pulls on the reins. "Whoa, girl! Whoa!" Swift slows to a walk for a more sedate ride back to Barb and Tom's.

"Thanks for coming with me," Bailey says.

"That was pretty cool. I never had church on horseback before."

"I do most Sundays, but I never gave a ride to a superhero before!"

"You probably still haven't." But ... did I fly? No way. That's ridiculous. But superhero or not, I'm friends with a cowgirl. Maybe that'll help me write my country song.

15

SUPERSUIT

First thing Monday, which is not really all that early, I sit on my bed and make the call. I rarely use my phone for calls, but Carol Anne didn't answer my weekend texts or voice mail and this is an emergency. I bounce until she picks up.

"What's the word?"

"Everybody knows that the bird is the word," I recite.

"Perfect timing, Barbara! I was about to answer your texts."

"From Saturday?" Yeah, right.

"I know, sorry about that. My phone slid down

behind my bed and the battery died; I found it and plugged it in about half a minute ago. So, what's up?"

OK, I'm glad I didn't actually lay into her, because that's exactly the kind of thing that would happen to me. "I need to go shopping for a new swimsuit."

She's silent longer than I find comfortable. "Who are you and what have you done with Barbara?"

"Ha ha. But seriously, I put on my old suit this weekend, and one, it's worn out and two, it doesn't fit anymore. Also, three, it's black."

"You wear black."

"Not nothing but, though, unless it's a chamber-music concert. Are you going shopping with me or not?"

"Sure. Just tell me you're not buying a swimsuit at a thrift store."

"No, that's why I need your help. I can't bear the mall on my own."

"Why me and not Jackson?"

"I'm not shopping for a swimsuit with a boy! Not even Jackson."

"All right, let's do this thing."

"And then we can go swimming." Which is the whole point.

Department store, teen section, sales rack. I start pulling out suits and checking size tags ... not that they mean much.

"So, did you have fun on your weekend in the sticks?"

"More than I expected to."

"Bring back any souvenirs?"

"A case of wine, about twenty pounds of cherries,

and a little sunburn on my neck where I missed a spot."
I didn't even know about the sunburn till I got in the
shower this morning. Yowch. "And I made a new
friend."

"Online or real life?"

"Both, but real life first. Bailey's an actual cowgirl.
She even took me for a ride on her horse."

"Huh. So that's how it is, first straight girl to come
along ... "

I stop what I'm doing and stare at her. Is Carol
Anne ... jealous? And why do I feel terrible and good at
the same time? But mostly terrible. Maybe I broke
some rule of friendship, because how would I know?
"I'm ... I mean, did I ... ?"

"Barbara, I'm kidding! It's good that you're making
more friends. Sorry, I forgot how sensitive you are."

"Oh. OK." What was I doing? Oh, yeah, shopping
for a swimsuit.

"Since you don't seem to have this cute cowgirl with
you, did you bring me anything?"

"Well, I'm writing a country song." This rack may
have been organized at one time, but now it's chaos.
Here's a teensy size nothing suit next to something that
would fit two of me. "And how do you know Bailey's
cute?"

"Just a guess. I sense cowgirl influence in the
songwriting department."

"She doesn't know about it yet, but I'll run it by her
for authenticity. And she probably is cute, if you like
athletic extroverts in tiny flag bikinis."

That shuts Carol Anne up for a few seconds. She
coughs. "This Bailey — she doesn't play bass, does

she?"

I laugh. OK, we're still friends. "Tenor sax. I asked. And she lives, like, 200 miles away."

"Good. Ooh, what about this one?" Carol Anne teases me with a skimpy bikini. It would look great on Bailey.

"No. I don't have a bikini body."

She holds up another one that looks like a handful of colorful strings. "You know the best way to get a bikini body? Put a bikini on your body."

"Yeah, um, no. Forget it."

"I thought you were all about being more visible."

"Visible, not naked."

"Fine, be a prude."

"Hey, if you want a bikini, get one; I'm looking for something I can actually swim in." I collect an assortment of suits that might be my size, none of them a two-piece, none of them black. That's as visible as I care to be at the pool.

"I already have my suit, and it is — " Carol Anne breaks off, pointing at the suits in my hand. "Sweet mother of — did that blue one have a skirt? You are not getting an old-lady suit with a skirt!"

I go into the fitting room and close the door without making any promises either way. After the first suit, I try not to look in the mirror until each one is on; nobody looks good struggling into Spandex. Of the six suits, three don't fit at all. Two would probably be fine for lounging around, but not for swimming. That blue one, though ... It fits and it stays put when I move my arms through some strokes, stretch and bend. I like how it looks, too. It has a high-ish neck, kind of like my old racing suit, and a low back with crisscross straps. The flippy little skirt is more about style than coverage — flirty, not matronly, with a spunky white belt at the hips.

I come out of the fitting room to model it for Carol Anne. "Admit it, this one is totally cute."

Carol Anne nods. "You sure don't look like an old lady. Actually, with the skirt and the belt, I'm getting kind of a vintage Supergirl vibe. All you need is red boots and a cape."

I go all lightheaded and have to sit on the little bench in the fitting room. She doesn't know, does she? I never told anyone about that weird episode with the finger gun and the tire, and Bailey's the only one to witness anything else.

"Maybe that's why I liked it." I close the door to peel out of the suit and start getting my clothes back on. "I had a suit kind of like this when I was six. That one had a white skirt, but the rest was blue and it had the same kind of belt. I ran around that whole summer in my swimsuit with red rainboots and a towel-cape, saving the world."

"Hard to be a superhero in a bikini, I guess," Carol Anne concedes.

"I wanted to wear it for my Halloween costume." I leave the rejects in the fitting room and emerge with my choice.

"Oh, man. Did your mom have to tell you the bad news about October?"

I shake my head and grin. "Nope. She got me thermal underwear and dyed it to match. And sewed me a real cape."

"Your mom's the best, but pictures or it didn't happen. Come on, let's go to the food court and bother Whitney."

"OK, but then we're going to the pool." Because I *really* want to swim.

A couple of hours later, we're in the locker room at the community center. Carol Anne is rocking a retro-style two-piece, green-and-white polka dot, modest by today's standards but worthy of an old-school pinup.

I hold out my hand. "Gimme your phone, I'll take a picture you can send to Marina."

She hands over the phone. "Go ahead and take a shot. I don't think I'll be sending it anywhere."

"I thought you guys were hitting it off."

"Yeah, maybe. I ... kind of chickened out."

She poses and then insists on taking some shots of me. I tie my towel around my neck and try to look heroic, but I keep cracking up. Then we lock the phone up and head out to the pool. The building echoes with shouts and laughter. Kids' swim lessons have just finished. We drape our towels around our shoulders and wait by the bleachers while the lifeguards rearrange the lane dividers for open swim.

Carol Anne looks where I'm looking and wags a finger at me. "Now I get the sudden interest in swimming. Naughty Barbara!"

"What? It's healthy exercise." But I'm not even trying to hide my interest. See, somebody else has a summer job. Jackson's lifeguarding and teaching swim lessons.

"You're not going to fake drowning, are you?"

"No! That'd be mean. Besides, I'm a terrible actor. I

just plan to enjoy the view."

"Put your eyes back in your head, OK? How do you like it when somebody looks at you that way?"

"Is that a hypothetical question? It hasn't happened, so I don't know."

"Oh, stop with the invisible BS." Carol Anne glances around at the others waiting to swim. "Two guys at four o'clock, totally checking you out."

I take a peek over my shoulder. "How do you know they're not checking you out? Anyway, those guys are, like, eleven. They probably discovered girls last week."

"And when did you discover boys?"

"I don't know. February?"

"And that's your excuse for acting like a creepy stalker?"

"Mm, maybe." I'm kind of distracted by Jackson climbing out of the pool. I try not to stare. "It's weird, but before the hat incident, I didn't think much about how people looked. I mean, if I heard another girl say some guy was hot, I could see it, but I wouldn't notice on my own."

"So you're saying that because you're visible now, so is everyone else?" Carol Anne shakes her head, but at least she's cracking a smile.

"Well, yeah. I guess it didn't hurt that the first person I saw from under the magic hat was the cutest guy in school." I grin. "Maybe that triggered a developmental thingamajig."

"Fine, but still — would you want someone who's supposed to be your friend staring at you like that?"

I snort. "What friend, you?" Which I immediately regret. I shouldn't talk with my mouth.

154

"OK, this isn't too awkward."

"I'm sorry, Carol Anne. That was such a dumb thing to say."

"It's all right, Barbara. I don't think of you that way, but I will say you are objectively very cute in your Supergirl suit. Does that mean you want to be ogled by anyone but those little twerps?"

"I guess I get your point." Jackson pulls a T-shirt over his perfect pecs and abs and climbs up to the lifeguard chair. He spots us and waves. My sex object transforms back to my best friend. Now I do feel bad for staring. I'm stopping that right now.

But discreet glances are OK, right? Because best friend or not, this guy is seriously a work of art.

16

PRACTICE, PRACTICE, PRACTICE

It took until the middle of July, but we're finally having our first band practice of the summer. Now that Whitney's back from her Yellowstone trip and Storm's done with Cheer Camp, maybe we can come up with some kind of a schedule. If nothing else, it should go better than my attempts at superpower practice. Turns out it's not that easy to make myself angry on purpose. Well, I guess I could go online and read people being wrong on the internet, but I don't want to destroy my computer.

Whitney's drums are back at her house for the summer, so that's where we'll practice. The bus I need stops more than a mile from home, but because of schedules, it's actually faster to walk there than catch a bus close to home and transfer. They obviously don't plan these things with me in mind. Good thing I like walking, especially on a summer afternoon. After July 4, our summers are perfect.

Half a block from the stop, I see the bus I want pull up to the intersection and start to make the turn. Oh shit, it's early or I'm late! I break into a run. I hate running for the bus because it usually doesn't make any difference, but I feel like I have to try. I'm really moving, too, and the bus is pulling up to the stop now, so I might make it if the lights are with me. Yeah, the cross traffic stops the moment I reach the curb. I'm gonna make it!

I put on a burst of speed and have one foot in the crosswalk when a car turns in front of me. The damn driver's not even looking! I scream and flail wildly, but it's too late for either of us to stop. I shut my eyes, then open them again when there's no bone-crushing thud. I'm still running ... up over the roof of the car. Not on it; over it, all the way to the other side of the street. I come down on my feet, still running for the bus. I'm not sure my shoes are even touching the concrete.

I almost plow into a guy who just got off the bus. He jumps out of the way, and covers his nose with one hand.

"Don't hit me!"

Now I recognize him — it's that Oakley dude, the one I punched. He's got a shopping bag, so I guess he's on his way to the discount produce market next to the bus stop. "Of course not! You're fine."

He stares at me. "I thought that car was gonna hit you, but you ... you ..."

"Parkour!" I improvise, and board the bus before he can argue. I tap my pass on the reader and stumble, out of breath, to the first open seat.

Did that just happen?

My phone alerts me to a new text. It's Bailey!

hey, you! listened to your demo. not really a country music fan but the title cracked me up. and you totally have the voice for it if you ever wanted to do a reverse-crossover type thing. seeya!

Why did I assume she'd be a country fan? Because she rides a horse? I mean, Taylor Swift hasn't been country for years. I'm glad Bailey likes my singing, though. I tap out a quick reply.

thanks! I think I just flew

lol! sure you did ... did you?

maybe, maybe not

Did I? I'm not out of breath now, but my heart is still racing. Because that was amazing! Also, I didn't get run over, and I actually caught the bus. About time these powers started being useful.

It's only a couple of blocks from the bus stop to Whitney's house, but I use it for flying practice. It's not that easy without someone trying to run me over. I run a few steps and push off, but I'm only jumping, not flying.

"Gah!" My toe hits some uplifted concrete and ... I don't go down. I travel a good fifteen feet further, parallel to the ground, and manage to get my feet under me before I hit. I wish I could take video so I know what it looks like. Maybe I'm just falling with style.

Whitney's living room is already pretty crowded when I walk in. Her mom's grand piano — a small one, but still, a grand piano — dominates one corner. The drums take up another. The clear acrylic shells make them seem less substantial than they are, but they still hog a certain amount of space. If that weren't enough, Carol Anne brought an amplifier and an electric guitar, in addition to her Martin acoustic.

"Yay, Barbara's here!" Carol Anne calls. She is literally wearing pink pedal pushers, like the song. I guess that's what happens when you work in a vintage clothing store. "I thought it was time we went electric."

"As long as it's OK with Whitney's folks."

Whitney squeezes in behind the drums. "They're both out — they took Dee and his friends to some skateboarding movie, so we've got the place to ourselves until four thirty."

"I'll keep it turned down, since we don't have a PA for the vocals. I just want to hear how it sounds."

There's a flush, and Storm emerges from the hallway. She's wearing those lace shorts that are all the rage, with a floaty sleeveless top and sandals with jewels on them. Of course she looks fabulous, but this is how she dresses down? "Hey, it must be summer! Barbara ditched the flannel."

"But I still have my hat." I make myself smile at her to show I can take a joke and don't care about her opinion of my clothes, even though I do. I wish I could be effortlessly stylish any day of the week. It's hard enough to be stylish once in a while, with a whole lot of effort. But can she fly? I'll take that over lace shorts any day. "How was Cheer Camp?"

"It was great to get back into it, but one more day and I would've OD'ed on spirit. It's a relief to hang out with some normal people."

"I thought we were the weirdos, but OK. Are we ready to rock and roll?"

Whitney answers that with a loud, "One, two three, intro!"

The electrified "Huge Guy" sounds so great I forget to come in and we have to start over. It's totally garage-y, even though we're practicing in a living room. Even turned down, the guitar mostly drowns out my voice, but I kind of don't care.

That song's a good warm-up, so we run it three times, then remind ourselves what we arranged with "Half a Bus Closer to Home." There aren't any bongos handy, so Whitney does something light on the toms. Nobody can remember what we came up with for harmonies, so we make up some new lines that seem to work. Then we run through "Huge Guy" again for the heck of it.

"OK, that was fun," Carol Anne says. "Now what?"

"Maybe it's time to try a cover. Did everybody get the link I sent?"

"'Pretty Gown'? Yeah, but who is that? Should I know?"

"They were on that show we went to in February, the one with Marina's cousin."

"Oh, the old folks! They didn't have a keyboard, did they?"

"Not at that show. I figured we could rearrange that song for guitar."

Storm leans on the piano. "I can't believe Barbara

wants to do a song about a dress."

"Hey, I own a dress! But that's not really what the song's — "

"OK, whatever, forget I said anything."

"I didn't know you wanted to start working on it this soon," Carol Anne says. "If we wait till next time, I can work up the chords. But what about your new one?"

She and I arranged a quick and dirty version of "The Drink I Didn't Have Last Night" a few days ago, but I didn't want to share it until I'd gotten Bailey's opinion, which turned out to be less than expert. Live and learn.

"Yeah, OK. This is kind of a country-ish thing, so we'll want to work up harmony vocals eventually. Whitney and Storm, just listen this time and see what you think."

Carol Anne manages a pretty convincing slide guitar sound on the intro, then drops into a strum pattern when I come in on the verse.

Punk-rock girl, listenin' to the country radio.
Whiskey and betrayal, everybody feelin' low ...

"Cute," Whitney says when we finish. "Is that the whole thing?"

"Well, that's all I've written yet. I don't want to overdo it. Do you think it needs another verse?"

"No, with the punk-rock reference, short is good. What do you think, Storm?"

Storm crosses her arms. "That is such a hayseed song."

"It's an *ironic* hayseed song," I explain as calmly as I can manage.

"Whatever. I can tell I'll need some overalls for this one. And a big straw hat."

Before I can ask what's wrong with a big straw hat, Carol Anne breaks in.

"What were you thinking for harmonies, Barbara? Do you want them on the whole thing, or just the chorus?"

"I thought some *oohs* on the verse, with words on the chorus." I demonstrate a possible high part, then a low part. "Will that work?"

"I don't know." What is it with Storm today? "That's pretty high. We should change the key, like we usually do."

"No, we are not changing the fucking key!" I crack an imaginary bullwhip for emphasis. Maybe not such a good idea but too late now. Nothing happens to Storm, but Whitney's throne topples. She pitches backward onto the floor in a cloud of profanity.

She tries to get up. "Oh, fuck, that hurts!" She sits up carefully, cradling her left arm.

"Oh, shit! Whitney, I'm sorry!"

"What are you sorry about? I've been wanting to replace this shitty old throne forever. If I'd known it was about to break, I would've done it a long time ago."

"It actually broke?"

"Yeah, looks like one of the supports sheared off." She winces. "Hey, Storm, could you get an ice pack from the freezer? I think I sprained my wrist."

"Yeah, sure." Storm hurries to the kitchen and comes back with a blue ice pack and a dish towel. "I've got my car — want me to drive you to the ER?"

Whitney presses the pack to her wrist, grimacing

when it bends at all. "No, Mom and Dad will be back in half an hour. I'll live, but maybe get me some ibuprofen?"

"It ... it's not broken, is it?" I can't believe I broke my drummer. Too shaky to stand, I take a seat on the piano bench.

"God, I hope not. I sprained the other one once, in gymnastics. It hurt exactly like this. They'll take X-rays and have me wear a brace for six weeks, bet you anything. If it's like last time, I'll even be able to play a little."

She's taking it amazingly well, but I don't care what she says. This was my fault. Superpowers don't seem so fun anymore. Even flying isn't worth it. This has to stop.

Storm comes back with the pills and a glass of water. "There you go. Need help up?"

"If you would be so fucking kind."

As Storm is helping Whitney up, she glances over at me. "Barbara, are you OK? You look kind of washed out."

"I feel kind of washed out."

"Took it out of you to drop an F-bomb, huh?" Whitney grins, then winces again. Storm helps her to the couch, where she reclines with her arm on a cushion.

"If I'd known you felt so strongly about the key, I wouldn't have said anything," Storm offers. "I'm kind of bossy sometimes. Just call me on it, OK?"

"I, um, think that's what the F-bomb was for." I manage a weak smile. "Sorry I lost it, though. That was over the top."

"Well, if you can't fight with your band, who can you fight with?"

"I'd rather not fight, period."

"Yeah, good luck with that," Whitney mutters. "Why don't you guys keep working on that song? It might take my mind off how much this hurts."

Now I feel worse. I try to sing to be a good sport, but it's not the same. We'll have to come back to this one later. We end up sitting around on the floor by the couch to keep Whitney company until her mom and dad get back.

"So what's going on the rest of the summer?" Whitney asks. "Big plans? Little plans?"

She obviously needs something to keep her mind off the pain, so I try to help. "I'm gonna try to have a birthday party on the thirtieth, if anyone can come."

"Oh, hell, yeah! Mine's in August, so I'll be sure to do something, too."

Carol Anne smiles. "Yeah, I'll be there. What time?"

"I guess I haven't thought about the details. I'll let you know, OK?"

Storm wipes away a fake tear. "I'll have to miss it — we'll be in Paris by then."

"That is a damned shame," Whitney says with a smirk. "Poor you."

"Well, I'm not sorry about Paris, but you know — Barbara's birthday." She pauses, a frown crinkling her brow. "I don't think I even had a party this year. My birthday was right in the middle of the musical."

"There was a lot going on then." I'm secretly glad she can't come to my party. The possibility was kind of freaking me out.

"We'll take care of you next year, but this isn't about you, Storm." Carol Anne can say stuff like that and no one gets offended. "Barbara, are you doing the same thing as last year? I'd be up for a group blood donation."

"You would? Yeah, I guess we could do that. Is that OK with you, Whitney?"

"Um. Yeah. I mean, fuck yeah!"

Storm stares at Whitney. "Seriously?"

"Why not? I can be a do-gooder, too, you know."

"Not that. The other thing."

"No, I'm down with this. Totally hardcore."

No idea what they're talking about, and before I can ask, we're interrupted by Whitney's parents and brother. We pack up while she's explaining her injury to them, which doesn't include blaming me.

Storm twirls her car keys. "Carol Anne, Barbara, I can give you guys a ride home."

"I'm OK on the bus," I say.

"Oh, come on, Barbara, if she's taking me, she's practically at your house anyway. Grab a guitar and let's go."

Guitars in the trunk, Carol Anne and the amp in the backseat, leaves me riding shotgun in Storm's little yellow Mustang. She's got the top down and she's blasting Taylor Swift, which I have to admit works pretty well on a perfect summer day.

"I hope Whitney's all right." No matter what anybody says, I still think it was my fault.

"She's a tough chick," Storm declares. "She'll be fine."

After that, we shut up and listen to T.S. The

songwriting under all that pop sheen is excellent. I could probably learn a few things.

At Carol Anne's house, Storm and I help her unload her gear, and then it's just the two of us.

I hesitate when Storm gets back into the car. "Thanks for the ride. I could walk from here."

She gives me a skeptical look over her sunglasses. "I'm trying to do a nice thing here. C'mon, get in the car already."

"Yeah, OK, thanks." I settle in and buckle up. The music starts up again, and I focus on that as a way of calming my nerves. "Bailey loves this record."

"Your cowgirl friend? Yeah, it's great."

"I like how she almost rhymes 'sunset' with 'nice dress' on this one. Maybe, um, we could learn it."

"Really?" Storm gives me a quick glance. With the sunglasses, her expression is hard to read.

"Well, it wouldn't sound like this, but yeah. Why not?"

"You don't think two dress songs is too much?" A hint of smile gives me enough courage to be honest with her.

"You know, it's not dresses I have a problem with. Or clothes in general."

"So you just hate shopping?"

"Well, yes, at the mall, anyway. Thrift stores are better, especially with Jackson along. It's just, I know what colors I like, and I know what's comfortable. So that's what I wear, because I have no clue what's cool."

"I thought that's what Jackson was along for."

"He helps, but he doesn't push me too hard."

"Rule of thumb: if cool people wear it, it's cool." She

flicks the lacy edge of her shorts by way of example. "Next spring, the thrift stores will be full of these."

"And they won't be cool anymore! It's too exhausting to try to keep up."

"Now you're getting it. Be careful what you wish for."

"And then there's shoes." I'm on a roll now. "I could put on a nice outfit, but I'd ruin it with comfortable shoes."

"These sandals aren't bad."

"They look amazing, but could you walk a mile in them?"

"Oh. Probably not, but it doesn't come up." Storm pats the steering wheel and grins.

"See, I walked farther than that to catch the bus today. In fact, I had to run for it." I leave out that I flew for it. Didn't I? I'm stopping that, so it doesn't matter.

"Well then, you have the right shoes for the job. Save the nice ones for when you don't have to walk a mile. Don't be a slave to fashion if you don't have to be." She sighs. "You don't know how good you have it, not having to keep up appearances."

Wait. So, *I'm* the lucky one? I guess that's a side benefit of being invisible all those years. "You make it sound like you don't have a choice."

"Maybe I don't. But ask me again after we graduate. By then I might be ready for a change."

17

ANOTHER YEAR OLDER

Being born in late July means I never got to take treats to school on my birthday (not that anyone noticed, me being invisible and all), but I also never had to *go* to school on my birthday. Also, it never rains. Now that I have friends to celebrate with, I kind of regret all the picnics and backyard campouts we could have had. But that's the past. For my seventeenth birthday, I'm finally having a party.

Thanks to Carol Anne's suggestion, the celebration begins at the blood center. Jackson had to work, but Carol Anne and Whitney both show up. Did I think they wouldn't? Of course I did. I'm still new to this friend thing. But they're here, with a parent each to give permission. Once that's done, we finish checking in and wait to be screened.

Mom opted out in order to frost cupcakes, and nobody else's parents want to hang around either, so it's Dad and us girls. "First time?" he asks the other two.

Carol Anne smiles. "No, I gave at a blood drive at school. Piece of cake."

Whitney picks at the Velcro on her wrist brace. "First time for me." I've never heard her speak so quietly.

"Have you seen the size of the needle?" Dad holds his hands up about a foot apart, and continues with wild stories about vampires.

"Um, Dad?"

"Barbara?"

"Knock it off, OK?" I nod toward Whitney. Not only has she been unusually quiet since she got here, now she's starting to curl up in her seat.

To his credit, Dad switches instantly from comedian to concerned adult. "Oh. Sorry, Whitney. You have a problem with needles?"

"Not needles, no." Her voice is even tinier than before. "More like, blood?"

"You know I made all that stuff up, right? Trying to lighten the mood?" He sighs. "And Dad blows it. Sorry, girls."

Whitney sits up straight and leans toward him. "You didn't know."

"So how did you manage all the hardware?"

"That's on my face — if there's any blood, I can't see

it."

A phlebotomist (my favorite big word, which I learned in this very building a year and a half ago) picks up a file from the front desk and comes into the waiting area. "Whitney?"

"You can still back out," I tell her.

Whitney stands and gives us a sickly smile. "No, I got this. Totally hardcore."

"You'll do great," Carol Anne predicts.

I'm called next.

"Barbara! Long time!"

"Yeah, I had a lot of colds this year." I know a lot of the staff from when I used to volunteer in the canteen. "I brought a group to make up for it."

"Well, all right." She closes the door to the screening room. "State your name and date of birth, please."

I do, she laughs and wishes me happy birthday, and we go on to the rest of the drill: vein check, pulse, temperature, blood pressure, iron. That last one requires a quick finger poke; through the window, I can see Whitney in the next room, her eyes averted, so I'm guessing she's up to that step, too. I'm happy to pass; sometimes my iron is too low, and I'd be bummed if I got deferred in front of my friends.

Since everything checks out, we head out to the donation area. Whitney is still getting set up as I lie back in the chair. She doesn't have a choice of which arm to use since she can't squeeze anything with that brace on her left arm. They're making her as comfortable as possible for her first time, with pillows and even a blanket. We start actually donating at about the same time. She doesn't watch the needle go in, but seems intrigued when the blood starts to rush down the tube.

"It's so warm!"

I always like that part, thinking of my warm, living blood being collected for someone who needs it. But this time, instead of rushing, my blood kind of oozes. I've never seen it so slow, and the phlebotomist shares the opinion.

"I'm calling it now; that arm won't make it. Want to try the left?"

"If you can find the vein, go ahead."

The last time I tried to donate from my left arm, they told me the vein was barely bigger than the needle, so I'm not sure this will work. But I have to try, now that I've dragged my friends along. It feels awfully tame after force fields and flying, but this is the only way for me to be a hero now. We start all over, and at least she does hit the vein. It's still slow, but better than before. Meanwhile, Carol Anne is already halfway through even though she started later. So unfair.

I keep squeezing my rubber ball. For whatever reason, the blood flows faster when the phlebotomist is standing there, so she ends up camped out at my side.

"I'm sorry it's taking so long."

"It's not your fault. You're a good sport to keep trying, and you're almost halfway." She nods toward Whitney and Carol Anne. "Interesting idea for a birthday party."

"It wasn't even my idea, but it was cool they wanted to do it." I can't help a little brag. "We're a band. Maybe I'll write a song about blood donation."

"There you go! Something about saving the life of someone you don't even know." She points out a stack of cardboard cartons, labelled HUMAN BLOOD — RUSH. "I heard there's a band using that for a name, but I don't think they've written a song about it yet."

Carol Anne finishes in record time and goes to the canteen for juice and cookies, a bright pink wrap around her arm. Whitney finishes soon after. She goes for a black wrap.

"How do you feel?"

"Fine, I think." She sits up, then lies back down. "Whoa. On second thought ... "

"It's normal to feel woozy the first time. Take it easy till you feel better." They adjust her seat to raise her legs and put ice packs under her neck. "Try wiggling your feet, too."

And me? Squeeze squeeze squeeze for twenty minutes before my pint is finally drawn. At least I can use the time coming up with lyrics, but I'm glad to be done. I reward myself with a bright green wrap to match my T-shirt.

"About time," Carol Anne teases when I join them in the canteen.

Even Dad finished before me, and he started last of all. "Barbara's the hero of the day, trying so hard."

"I'd say Whitney. Very brave. I'm gonna write a song about it."

Dad squeezes my hand. "Considering you could very well have saved a life, you're all heroes. That calls for a party."

Jackson meets us back at my house, wearing the red silk shirt he bought that time last spring.

"Ooh, did you bring that shirt for me?"

He gives me a twinkly smile. "What did I tell you about wheedling?"

"Seriously? You're gonna be that way on my birthday?"

"Wait and see."

The actual party is a pretty low-key affair — pizza and limeade and cupcakes on the back porch, to be followed by a Pixar nostalgiathon in the TV room — but I wouldn't trade it for anything. I invited all three of my local friends, and they came! Bailey couldn't come, of course, but she sent me a gift: a cowboy hat! It's an inexpensive straw one from a souvenir booth at a rodeo, but it looks good on me and I'm wearing it.

Cheese stretches between Whitney's teeth and a slice of pizza. "This is awesome! I've never had homemade pizza before. You're really lucky, Barbara."

I feel lucky to have three (local) friends. "I wanted to send out, but I'm kind of glad Mom insisted."

"The crust is amazing."

"Yeah, that's because of the kale. It gives it just the right texture." I almost get a cramp keeping a straight face as Whitney sets her slice down.

Carol Anne socks me gently in the shoulder. "I'm pretty sure she's joking."

"Yeah, there's not actually kale in the pizza crust." I smile and everybody has a laugh and looks relieved. "It's in the cupcakes."

"Oh, not funny!" Whitney flings an ice cube at me. "Now we're really not naming the band Cupcake Time."

"I'm kidding, OK? It's not in the crust or the cupcakes." I wait a beat. "It's in the sauce."

Jackson shakes his head. "Now you're just running it into the ground. You are the worst liar ever."

I accept his verdict. I've never been a good liar, which is why I'm actually telling the truth: there is kale in the pizza sauce, and they can't even tell. Mom's idea, of course; she figured we'd all need extra iron.

After delicious kale-free lemon cupcakes, I open presents. Whitney's package is wrapped in the Sunday comics and contains a multi-colored felt beanie with a motorized propeller on top. "Cool! Maybe I can wear this on stage sometime!" I set the cowboy hat on Jackson's head (where it somehow looks right at home) so I can try on the beanie and set the propeller spinning. "We're taking a selfie with everybody." I look ridiculous in the best way possible.

"So now you can fly, right?" Jackson says over the hum of the motor. "Way better power than invisibility."

My heart stutters at the mention of superpowers, but it seems like an innocent comment. I turn off the motor and open Carol Anne's present, a warm cap knitted from chunky, bright green yarn.

"I know it's out of season, but I've been learning to knit. That's the first thing to turn out decent."

"Wow, you made this? That's so great, and hey, winter will come again. Thank you!"

Jackson pulls a cream-colored envelope from his chest pocket. "Storm asked me to give you this."

"That's ... unexpected." The envelope is made of heavy, textured paper, and contains a gift certificate. "For a ... mani-pedi? Should I know what that is?"

"Ooh, that's pampering for your nails — finger and toe," Carol Anne explains. "Think of it as a special treat."

"OK." I was thinking of it as criticism, but maybe I should give Storm the benefit of the doubt. I don't know when I'll use this, but maybe I should. My nails don't look that great, even though I've almost stopped biting them. I lay the certificate aside and open the last present, a good-sized box from Jackson. I lift the lid, and there's the other silk shirt, the green and orange one.

He grins at me. "It's not my color, and I remember you admired it."

"Thanks!" I happen to be wearing my lime-green tee, so when I put on the silk shirt, it's almost like an outfit or something. It even goes with the wrap around my arm.

Jackson clears his throat. "The box isn't empty yet, you know."

I lift the tissue paper that was under the shirt and screech. Out comes a fedora in a rich purple felt. It doesn't go with anything I'm wearing, and I don't care. I put it on and Jackson reaches over to tilt it just so.

Whitney whistles. "Glamorous as fuck." She claps her hand over her mouth and looks around for Mom or Dad, but they're safely out of earshot. "I dare you to wear that to church, Choir Girl."

I'm still not sure I'm ready for a fedora in public, but I'm getting closer. "It's not a summer hat. But since you mention it, we're having pick-up choir this week — anybody can sing. You guys should come."

Whitney grimaces. "Sorry, I don't do organized religion."

"I'll ... think about it." That's what Carol Anne's

voice says, but her face — sad, not disgusted — says different.

"Know what? I'll sing with you, Barbara." Jackson to the rescue, when I was sure I'd ruined the party.

"About time. Then you can tell these two party-poopers how much fun they missed." I give them a grin so they'll know we're still OK and I won't mention it again, ever.

"So what's up next week?" Carol Anne asks. "Are we practicing while we wait for Storm?"

"I don't think I'll be able to. Monday, I'm having oral surgery."

Which is the downside of turning seventeen. At my last check-up, the dentist looked at the X-rays of my wisdom teeth and declared this the perfect time to "go in and scoop them out." I guess it makes sense to do it before school starts, but what a drag to be laid up for part of my break.

"The drugs are excellent," Whitney assures me. "We'll visit and bring you ice cream."

I don't know about drugs, but ice cream? And friends to bring it to me? This could be all right.

18

THE BEGINNING OF WISDOM

A big fish tank divides the oral surgeon's waiting room. I like the way it distorts the people on the other side, but otherwise it's identical to the fish tanks at the doctor's and dentist's offices. They all have the same kinds of fish, like maybe they buy a standard package. But the really interesting fish seem to hide the most.

"You OK?" Dad looks kind of pale, but maybe I'm imagining things. He drew caregiver duty today; Mom has a client meeting that's already been rescheduled twice.

"Sure. It's supposed to be routine, right?" They call it surgery, though. I can't help thinking about the prescriptions we filled after my first appointment. Antibiotics and Vicodin and high-dose ibuprofen. How bad should I expect to feel? And how big are the pills I'll have to swallow? I'm glad I'll be out for the actual procedure. "How about you? Are you OK?"

"Till we get the bill." He forces a smile. "You didn't want to go to college anyway, right?"

"I ... what?"

"No, don't worry about it. Insurance will cover a big chunk. That's why we got the high-limit policy."

"Barbara? We're ready for you."

"I'll see you when you wake up," Dad promises, and turns on his e-reader, loaded in advance with a hefty novel. He must expect this to take a while. "Scoop" is maybe a relative term.

The nurse takes me to a room with a dentist chair and lets me get comfortable. Pretty soon, I'm breathing raspberry-scented nitrous oxide and worries vanish. I have never felt so good in my life! I have to write a song about this. I start coming up with one hilarious line after another, but they don't hold still long enough to get them in order. Then a stunning realization scatters the whole project. Of course! Why didn't I see it before? Removing my wisdom teeth will rid me of my superpowers. It's so obvious. When I wake up, I'll be free.

Laughing gas is awesome.

"How do you feel?"

"Amazing!"

"Good, good. I'm going to inject a local anaesthetic, and then we'll start the sedative drip. You might feel a pinch."

She sticks a big needle into my mouth. Who cares? Maybe some time passes and then, far away, there is something like a pinch in somebody's arm. Again, who cares? Not me.

"Count backward from one-hundred, please."

"One-hundred. Ninety-ni ... "

"Excellent, we're all finished. I'll take you to recovery now."

Wait, they're finished? When did they start? I still feel amazing, even with a bunch of stuff in my mouth. And dead lips and tongue. Is Dead Tongue a good band name? No, I can't even say it. I can barely walk, but I let the nurse guide me through the doorway to a little room with a cot. I lie down and she puts a warm blanket over me. I blink and my dad is there. That's a good trick. Wow.

"Howya doin'?"

I give him a thumbs up. "I am so high!" It comes out muffled and slobbery.

He chuckles. "Don't try to talk now. You're still numb, and your mouth is full of gauze."

Oh, yeah. Duh. "Laughing gas is the best!"

"Yes, it is. Don't talk."

I zone out while the nurse goes over post-op instructions. I hope Dad's getting this because I'm not retaining anything. I've forgotten all those great song lyrics already. But what was the other thing? Yeah. I'm free.

19

DISTRACTED DRIVER

I'm sore and swollen for a few days, but I'm also on good drugs. The pills are not too big to swallow. I get to eat pudding and ice cream and mashed potatoes. And I'm cured of stupid superpowers. I know it's true; the laughing gas said so, and why would it lie?

Before I know it, I'm all better and school starts again. And Mom was right — suddenly, we're seniors! I'm not sure I'll ever get used to that. Seniors were always mysterious creatures who had it together — practically grown-ups. That's not me at all. Everybody's stressed out about college applications, which I can't even bring myself to consider yet. I think I'll go to community college next year, take some time to figure out what I want to do besides sing in a garage band. I'm less worried about graduation requirements. I'm fine for academic credits and service hours. I've passed the required state exams. I'm not looking forward to the twelve-page research paper, and I have no ideas for the culminating project, but there's time. Maybe something with the band ...

I'm tossing ideas around on the way to the bus stop — publish a songbook? Cut a record? It starts to drizzle as I'm waiting to cross the highway. Great — at a long light like this one, there should be some kind of weather sensor to make it turn sooner when a pedestrian is waiting in the rain. When it finally changes, a cute little Fiat has the gall to run the red. Apparently the driver's distracted by the corn-on-the-cob she's eating — seriously, corn-on-the-cob at eight in the morning? Sorry, I don't care how late you are. In a fit of pique, I throw a big handful of nothing ... which leaves a baseball-sized dent in her rear hatch.

Um, what?

Crap. The laughing gas lied. I'm not cured, and now I'm worried. Either I still have superpowers, or I'm being stalked by weird automotive coincidences. I hurry across the road now that I finally have the signal. Yeah, it lasts forever one way and about three seconds the other. Once across, I throw some more nothing at a power pole, with no apparent effect. I throw at a puddle; no splash. Not so super and not very predictable. What was it Bailey said? I have anger powers? I guess I'm not angry enough now. If I can't show anyone, I sure as hell don't plan to tell anyone.

But I think I'll try to write a song about distracted drivers.

Carol Anne's late for band practice — not like her at all.

Whitney leaves off her sticking exercises. "She's at school today, right?"

"Yeah; anyway, I saw her at lunch."

The door to the band room swings open and Carol Anne runs in, guitar case in hand. "WE HAVE A GIG!!!"

OK, that could excuse her tardiness. "We do? How'd that happen?"

Another girl follows her in. She hangs back in the doorway but Carol Anne draws her into the room. "This is my friend Maddie. She's having a party after the Homecoming dance and she wants us to play!"

Maddie smiles and ducks her head, so it's like she's looking up at us through her thick lenses, even though she's taller than Storm. "Hi, I'm Madeleine. Trying to go by Madeleine. But, you know, Maddie's fine, too." Her voice is barely audible. Her brown hair hangs straight and limp to her shoulders, and her jeans and sweatshirt ensemble is no more stylish than mine. If she were shorter, she could probably pull off invisibility, no problem. "So, will you? Play?"

Whitney beckons me over and whispers in my ear. "Does she know we can only play six songs?"

That's a generous estimate. I'd say we can play four songs and slop through two or three more. But given a few more weeks to practice, we should be able to work up a passable set. "I say we get to work and put together a good show for ... Madeleine."

She beams. "Thank you! That means a lot. I'll let Carol Anne know the details."

As soon as she's out the door, Storm has a question. "So now can we talk about stage outfits? Could we maybe go formal? Because I'm not wearing jeans and flannel to Homecoming."

I start to object, but Carol Anne steps in. "Storm has a point. If people are coming straight from the dance, they'll be dressed to the nines. It might be fun if we are, too."

Whitney crosses her arms over her chest with her sticks still in her hand like a weapon. "I'm not wearing a frilly dress."

Storm holds up both hands. "Chill, girlfriend. I never said frilly and I never said dress."

"I don't necessarily mind wearing a dress, but I'd rather not spend my hat money on something I'll probably only wear once." I'm not sure I'm ready to bring out that sparkly purple minidress, either.

"I'll go shopping in my closet," Carol Anne says. "I can think of a couple of Aunt Anne's things I haven't had a chance to wear yet."

"That's nice, but we don't all have a closet full of vintage party clothes." Anyway, I don't.

Carol Anne thinks about this for a moment. A big slow smile signals an idea taking shape. "Maybe you do. Do your moms have old clothes stashed away? Or do you have relatives nearby — aunts, grandmothers, older cousins?"

We can all give a provisional yes to that question, though I don't hold out much hope of finding anything good. I mean, Mom's all right as moms go ... but she's from the seventies.

Friday comes and I'm on my way to school in a cheerier mood than usual. Dad's on vacation, and he has to bring me lunch because he lost our bet. Then, same song, different verse: I hop off the bus by the produce market and run to cross the street before the light changes, only to have some yahoo in an SUV block the crosswalk. Well, fuck you, asshole. I have to walk around you? I look right at the driver and flip him the bird — first time in my life. But, whoa! So much birdshit. Dude has to pull over and get out the spray bottle and paper towels to clean it off his windshield.

OK, now I need to tell somebody about these damned superpowers. I thought I could keep them to myself and they'd go away. But seriously, no seagull is that big.

At noon, I race down to the lunchroom to intercept Jackson before he goes in. "Hey, I need to talk to you but not here. Outside?"

"Lots of people need to talk to me, Barbara." Jackson makes a move toward the lunchroom. "I didn't bring my lunch, so I need to go through the line even if we eat somewhere else."

I hold out a Dick's bag. "Cheeseburger, fries, vanilla shake. Did I get that right?"

His eyes widen a bit. Maybe I've surprised him for once. "Why didn't you say so? Ooh, and still hot! What's the occasion?"

"World Series bet — Dad lost." And he likes Jackson, so it wasn't too hard to persuade him to buy both our lunches.

"Didn't know you followed baseball."

"You don't have to follow it to bet on the Series. This was only for Game 4. Come on, before the fries get cold."

Nobody else is braving the great outdoors, even though it's not a bad day out for October — breezy, but almost warm when the sun comes out. The big oak on the corner is starting to turn color; the green leaves look like Carol Anne blotted her lipstick on the edges. I make a note of that line for later. It's not quite there, but I might dig a song out of it. Or a poem for Creative Writing, because that has a due date.

We sit on the concrete planter that encircles the flagpole, halfway down the steps on the south side of the school, where we have a great view of parked cars, a vacant lot, and a bunch of condemned houses. The rest of the neighborhood is nice, but that area has been an eyesore for years. The city wants to turn part of it into a park, but I don't think it will get redeveloped before we graduate in June.

Jackson digs right into his fries. I take a slurp of my chocolate shake.

"So, what's the big secret? No, let me guess. It's about Homecoming. If Zach asks you, tell him no."

That's not even close, but I bite. "Which one, Brown or Morton?"

"Morton. If Zach B asks anyone, I'll have a heart attack."

"What makes you think Zach M would want to ask me? I'm pretty sure he doesn't know I exist."

"Exactly. His M.O. is to lavish attention on a girl who doesn't typically get much. Then he demands a return on his investment."

"That's gross, but I'm nobody's prey." This is neither tough talk nor low self-esteem. It's a fact. Around here, a medium-size white girl with medium-length, medium-brown hair in denim and flannel flies under most people's radar. Even when she wears a hat.

"I thought I'd finally get to give you boyfriend advice. Anyway, as a general rule, if Zach offers you a drink, don't take it."

The warning sits like a stone in my gut. I've heard about creeps like that. Still, I refuse to spend my life on high alert because a few jerks can't be trusted. "I probably won't go to the dance. How about you?"

OK, yes. I'm stalling. I don't know how to say what I know I need to say.

"I'm on Homecoming Court, so I have to go."

"I voted for you. Sorry."

He grins. Jackson could have a whole YouTube channel for his smile alone. I know I'd watch. "It's OK — might even be fun. Not taking a date, though."

"Seriously? You'd have no trouble." Like, if you asked me, for instance.

"The only person I want to ask isn't out to his parents."

Oh, that's right. "Ah. I can see how that might be awkward, you showing up with the limo and the tux and everything. Who is it?"

Jackson slowly shakes his head. "Need-to-know basis. He's not entirely out at school, either."

"Fair enough. I'm not going because I have band business — we're playing for a seniors-only after-party."

"'Bout damn time. Where?"

"Madeleine somebody? Carol Anne knows her. Well, you probably do, too. Tall, super straight hair, wears glasses?"

"Maddie Gowan? I heard she was throwing a party, but I didn't believe it. She's not exactly the party type."

"Yeah, well, I used to be invisible and now I'm fronting a band, so anything's possible."

This merits the signature Jackson guffaw. "You guys better come up with a name and more than four songs."

"And a bass player, while we're wishing. But it's not four songs, it's six now, plus a couple of covers. The name thing might be more of a problem, but it's not your problem."

"Fine. So what are we talking about here?"

I squirm and study the blue and orange graphics on the white bag, though I've lost my appetite, even for a Dick's Deluxe. "It's ... kind of a coming-out thing." My heart bangs a funky rhythm.

"Barbara, I'm pretty sure you're not gay. You were drooling over Thor as much as I was."

"Loki, actually," I correct him. "But there's all kinds of closets." Breathe in. Breathe out. "Do you remember that time last winter when we were talking about superpowers?"

"Oh, how you're invisible and I automatically know everybody?"

"Yeah, that one. Well ... what if I told you I can ... make things happen?"

Jackson lowers his cheeseburger. "I'd say you're drunk on girl power, and I never should have given you that hat."

"Tough, I'm keeping it."

And then I spill the story about the blown-out tire. It sounds ludicrous even to me, and I was there, so this is a good test of whether Jackson is actually my friend. He lets me finish without interrupting, which earns him all kinds of points.

"He shouldn't have been driving. So maybe I used my powers for good, huh?" I have more appetite now that I've told this story. I start on my fries before they get cold.

"Barbara, that was just coincidence. Maybe you should take up boxing, though. Or get anger management."

"Ha ha."

"So you're hanging out with those stoners now? Otis and Oakley?"

"I know who they are. Very different from hanging out."

Jackson leans back and looks up at the flag whipping around in the breeze. "Kind of wish I'd been there, just to see it. I didn't know you could get that mad — enough to hit someone. I'm not sure I've even heard you swear."

"I usually keep it in. I don't know what happened."

"You know what this sounds like to me? Since you've started to have more agency — with the band and being more visible and everything — it makes sense that you'd object to someone who tries to infringe on your personhood that way."

"Did you really use the words 'agency' and 'personhood' in conversation?"

Jackson grins. "I had a counselor who talked like that. But you see what I mean? It doesn't have to be superpowers."

Jackson saw a counselor? He should be one! But with all of us telling him our troubles, I can see how he might need someone to dump on. "That was just the first time. But Bailey saw me use a force field to block a splash in the pool. And a few weeks ago, an absurdly distracted driver ran a red light when I'd been waiting forever to cross Lake City Way. Guess what she was doing."

"Talking on her phone?"

I shake my head. "Less common than that."

"Putting on makeup? Shaving her dog?"

I don't even want to picture it, but I'm definitely throwing it into a song. "Eating corn-on-the-cob. For breakfast."

Jackson has to think about that one for a moment. "Well, there's something you don't see every day."

"I know! Can you imagine, getting killed by someone eating corn? I threw a handful of nothing that I'm pretty sure left a dent."

"Or it could have been a meteorite or plain old road debris."

"Yeah, I wasn't sure, either. Till this morning. I was trying to get to school and an enormous SUV — one of those Armageddons or whatever — blocked my crosswalk. So I flipped the bird at the driver and down came the biggest splat I have ever seen — right on his windshield."

"Birds do that, Barbara." Jackson picks up his shake.

"That's the other reason I started wearing hats. But this, I swear it was like a double-shot of vanilla soft-serve. No seagull is that big."

Jackson puts his shake down without taking a sip, but maybe that's because he's laughing. He pulls out his phone and enters a number. "Hello, Pope Francis?" (So maybe he really does know everyone.) "I've got somebody here I want to put in for sainthood."

"Oh, fuck you." I can't believe how casually that came out. I'd better sit on my hands. "I'm no saint."

"What do you mean? Apparently you're a miracle worker, like Super Jesus." He gives me an infuriating smirk, which I would not watch on YouTube. Well, OK, I would, but still. "Oh, that's right. You don't believe in miracles."

I have no quick answer for that. To Jackson's credit, he waits. "For some reason, it's easier to think of it as superpowers. Emotion-driven reality manipulation through gesture."

"Somebody makes you mad, and you give them instant karma."

"Yeah, kind of like that."

"Huh. So let's say you can make things happen. You're gonna need an outfit. I'm thinking blue, like your swimsuit, but with more coverage and no skirt. Maybe a cape and some over-the-knee boots — "

"As long as you remember I don't wear heels." He's totally humoring me, I know it. Maybe it's better that way. "And capes are cool, but are they practical?"

"I'll make it quick-release in case it gets caught on anything. Or no, maybe a flowing coat instead. I mean, you won't be flying, right?"

"I might be, but whatever. I have a more urgent need: a dress for Madeleine's party."

"OK, now I have to go to this shindig, if you're wearing an actual dress. So once you have your outfit, will you only use these so-called powers to punish bad drivers, or to do something real?"

"You're going to say, 'With great power comes great responsibility,' aren't you?"

"Now I don't have to. But you can't argue with Uncle Ben."

"So, what, I'm supposed to battle evil?"

"Why not, as long as you don't hurt anyone?"

Yeah, he's humoring me. Is he forgetting I already punched that guy in the nose? "Kind of abstract — how do I know what to look for?"

"A liberal, feminist church-goer like yourself should know it when she sees it. What'll you call yourself? Birdshit Girl?"

"Right. I can't even name my band."

"Good talk, Barbara. I have to get to class, but good luck with the superhero thing. Just be careful where you point that finger gun."

I don't know what I was expecting. At least he listened. We wad up the Dick's bags and toss them in the food waste on our way back inside. The Commons is the usual zoo with everybody trying to get to their lockers at the same time. I should have come in a side entrance, but it's too late now. I weave through the crowd. I'm still a long way from my locker when I hear ... no, not a cry for help, but kind of a pathetic whine.

"Come on, guys, give it back."

The crowd divides and flows around a knot of boys,

five tall and one short. The tall ones are tossing something over the head and outstretched hands of the shorter one. At first I think it's a phone, but as I get closer I can see it's a graphing calculator, which clues me in to who the short kid is. For no good reason, these guys are tormenting Zach B when they should be begging him to help them pass 12th grade.

Seems evil enough to me. I don't shoot anyone. I bat the air and the calculator falls into Zach's hands. He almost drops it but manages to hang on. But now what? The idiot crew is still around him. I take a deep breath and sweep into the thick of it.

"Zachary B, just the man I was looking for!" I link my arm through his and keep walking. "Last night's calculus homework didn't make any sense at all."

This should work. They have no beef with me; they probably don't even know me, and like I said, I don't look memorable.

"Careful, Zach — that chick's crazy!"

Zach looks over his shoulder, but I propel him forward. "Keep walking." We reach a crossing passage, I hang a right, and only then do I let him go.

He looks me over warily. "Barbara, right? Are you even in my calculus class?"

"No, pre-calc. I thought you might want a good reason to end that conversation."

"Yeah, thanks for that. Why'd Travis Oakley call you a crazy chick?"

Ah. Last name, then. Fashionable first names are one thing, but who'd want to be named for sunglasses? "He believes I broke his nose. He'd been in a car crash and he was hysterical."

"Oh. That makes more sense, I guess."

"I didn't break it; I just hit him a little bit. He was pissing me off."

Zach give me a wary look, then nods. "He does that. We used to hang out in fourth grade, and he never knew when to quit. Doesn't explain what he was doing in that crowd of meatheads."

"I think he was watching."

"Yeah, he's always trying to be part of the group. So, if you don't need help with homework, what can I do to thank you? Are you going to Homecoming?"

"No, but my band's playing for an after-party. Do you know any girl bass players?"

"Sorry, no. I'm taking a class in sound engineering at VERA, though. Is that any good?"

"Seriously? Because Madeleine's dad's renting a good PA, but we need someone to run it."

"Cool, I'm your man."

About half an hour later, it occurs to me that maybe Zach was trying to ask me to the dance. I still have a lot to learn about being visible. Anyway, I wouldn't want to be responsible for Jackson's heart attack.

20

GRANDMA'S HOUSE

"Are we there yet?" Jackson does the little-kid-in-the-backseat whine perfectly.

"Next stop." This bus ride takes forever, but finally I can pull the cord. We get off in a neighborhood of big houses with bigger lawns. Scattered tall trees hint that this neighborhood, like mine in town, was carved out of a forest. That's about all they have in common. The morning hums with mowers and leaf blowers because, yeah, October. The leaves fall but the grass keeps growing.

"I thought we were going shopping. What are we doing here?"

"Not shopping; a treasure hunt," I correct him. Leaving the bus stop on the main drag, we have to walk in the street, because out here in darkest suburbia, they haven't discovered sidewalks yet. Actually, that's true a few blocks north of my house, too. Oh, God, my neighborhood used to be a suburb! Mind blown. "This way, through the park."

A paved path leads through a stand of firs into a large open space. We follow it past picnic shelters and a playground, buzzing with little kids on this sunny fall day. I used to be one of them, but all the play equipment is new since then. That makes me feel old. Maybe I really am a senior.

We stop to watch some teenagers throw a Frisbee for their dog. The dog is athletic and adorable; the boys aren't bad, either. But we have a destination and soon continue on our way.

"So Storm goes, 'We should dress formal,' and Whitney's all, 'I'm not wearing a frilly dress.' Carol Anne hopes we can all go vintage, but I dunno ... "

Two women in running tights jog past us. A guy in a Seahawks cap lounges on a bench alongside the path. He follows the joggers with his eyes and says something I can't hear. He turns back, smiling. "Hey, Party Hat, where's the party at?"

I almost say, "At Maddie's," but that would mean he was talking to me, which is silly because I'm ... not invisible. Oh. I turn to Jackson to get his reaction, but he's not there. Where the hell is he? And how long was I talking to myself?

"Hey, girl, I asked you a question."

Carol Anne would ignore this guy. Whitney would

go on the offensive. Being me, I come back with, "Why?"

"'Cause I want to talk to you. Got any goodies in that bag?"

That line's so dumb, I don't even have an answer for it. Oh, and there's Jackson, still back by those Frisbee dudes. Some friend he is. He must have seen me giving him the stink-eye, because now he's catching up.

As Jackson comes alongside, Bench Guy says, "Oh, sorry, is she with you?"

"What?! Why are you apologizing to him?"

Jackson holds up his hands and backs away. "If you made her angry, you're on your own, dude." He winks at me, which pisses me off more. He's still humoring my delusion of superpowers.

"Why would I make her angry? I just wanted to compliment the hat, make a girl's day. No offense meant."

"Good," I say, but I'm still kind of steamed. Why should I care what a total stranger thinks of my hat? I turn and stalk away.

"Aw, don't go away mad. Let's kiss and make up."

Seriously? I stop. I turn. I blow a kiss that pins him to the bench and knocks the cap right off his smug little balding head. "You want to make a woman's day? Go call your mom, because nobody in this park wants to hear from you!" He grips the back of the bench and watches me with a dazed stare.

Jackson grabs my waving finger. "Careful, that thing might be loaded." He steers me away, but calls over his shoulder, "I warned you."

I wrench my hand away and turn back long enough to point two fingers at my eyes, then at the guy. The universal sign of *I'm watching you.*

"Are you sure that's such a good idea?" Jackson asks. "You know, considering the whole reality manipulation thing?"

"I don't care! Who does that fucking asshole think he is?"

"Whoa, Barbara, language." Jackson sounds equal parts shocked and amused. "My guess is he thinks he's nobody. He makes a lot of noise so he knows he exists. You, on the other hand ... " Jackson gazes at me with obvious admiration, which I have to admit I like. "You pretend to be nobody, but you know you're somebody."

"More like, I forget I'm not invisible."

"Pretty neat trick, blowing his hat off. That was you, wasn't it?"

"So you finally believe me?" The anger's mostly gone now, and my legs go wobbly. "I don't have a lot of control."

"Could have fooled me. Better be careful, though. Nobodies like that resent somebodies. And if you're gonna start cussing, watch your language around adults."

"Obviously. Come on, we're almost there." Not a moment too soon. Time to get this day back to normal.

"Where's there?"

"Grandma's house."

"Should have figured, with the shortcut and all. Where's the basket of goodies, Red?" He flicks my cap.

"Don't you start." I let the silence curdle, then give in. "OK, I coincidentally have a loaf of Mom's bread in my bag, but that has nothing to do with anything."

As we're about to cross the street, my vision goes split screen. I can still see what's in front of me, but I can also see what's behind me. Not directly behind, but back in the middle of the park, where that guy gets up, finds his cap, and starts back along the footpath. I sink down to sit on the curb. Apparently normal is too much to ask for.

Jackson crouches next to me. "Hey, what's the matter?"

"You were right. I probably shouldn't have gone eyes-on-you at that guy. Now I can see him."

"What, like a hallucination?"

"If it is, it's the most boring hallucination ever. He's just walking through the park." I smirk. "Keeping his eyes straight ahead, I might add. But it's disorienting, seeing two things at once." After a moment, I go back to seeing only what's in front of me. "OK, that's better. Let's go."

The houses on the other side of the park are older and smaller, and they don't all have huge lawns. We cross the street to a pale green split-level, its yard landscaped with native shrubs and flowers. I ring the bell.

"Why all the secrecy? You could have just told me where we were going."

"I didn't think you'd come to the 'burbs voluntarily. So lame, right?"

"Hey, everybody's got family in the suburbs. There's no shame in it. Well, unless you're related to that guy in the park. You OK now?"

"Yeah, I — "

Grandma opens the door. She looks trim in her blue turtleneck and gray slacks. "Barbara! Come in." She looks past me, out to the driveway. "Your mother didn't bring you?"

"No, she had some church meeting so we came on the bus. She'll pick us up later."

Grandma's face crinkles in a smile as she gives Jackson the once-over. "We?"

"Grandma, you remember Jackson Durand? You met at our show last spring."

"Oh, yes, your *fashion adviser*. Nice to see you again, Jackson." They shake hands like grown-ups. "Well, come on in, and let's see what we can find. You'll stay for lunch, of course."

"Wouldn't miss it."

Grandma leads us up the stairs to the main level. "I don't remember exactly where everything is, but I stored a lot of old clothes in Lisa's room. Guest room, I mean. Feel free to paw through it and see if there's anything you like. I'll be in the kitchen if you have any questions." She shows us into the tidy bedroom. A colorful quilt covers the bed, which seems intended to go with the old-timey photos of ancestors on the walls. Except the quilt blocks are all of test tubes, microscopes, amoebas and stuff.

"Door open, OK?"

"Grandma! Don't you trust me?"

"I taught high school biology too many years to trust any teenager. Humor me."

"Fine, door open, but believe me, there's nothing to worry about." Not for lack of wishing, but I'm not telling her that. Or Jackson, for that matter.

She leaves us, and I roll my eyes at Jackson. "This thing adults have with the door being open — seems like everybody but me must be getting it on all the time." I open the closet and pull the chain to turn on the light. Zippered storage bags hang on the rod.

"Believe me, it isn't just you. In spite of that, your grandma seems cool."

"We like her. Eighty years old, and she still grows a vegetable garden every year and does all the work herself. She has a guy to take care of the trees and clean the gutters — anything with a ladder. Mom wants her to hire a housecleaner, too, but Grandma doesn't see the need."

"Well, one person doesn't make much mess. Science teacher, huh? Is that why the quilt with all the science-y stuff?"

"Yeah, it was a retirement gift. Either her friends really liked her or they had a lot of time on their hands." Just then, I get another flash of the creep from the park. He enters a house similar to the one we're in and heads straight downstairs. The basement is set up as a small apartment, packed with sports memorabilia. I lean on the bed and rest my head on the quilt. "This is getting old fast. That guy ... "

"Another vision-y thing?"

"If that's what you want to call it." An older woman enters the scene, carrying a tray with a sandwich and a can of beer. "Lord, I think he lives in his mother's basement."

"How cliché."

"No kidding." I blink as the scene fades. To focus my mind again, I point out a quilt block in shades of green and red. "That's my favorite block."

"Ew. Frog dissection?"

"I know, right? Amazing realism for cotton prints in two dimensions."

"I can almost smell ninth-grade biology." Jackson unzips the first storage bag. It holds a man's suit. "You know that formaldehyde smell?"

My mood dips. "Um, yeah. I had that class same time you did."

He starts and turns his attention fully to me. "You mean, the same section?"

"Yeah. You and Storm were lab partners."

He nods. "You're right. Who was yours?"

"There was an odd number of students. I didn't have a partner." Hadn't thought about that in years, but recalling it now, I still feel kind of lost.

"I'm sorry, Barbara. I wish I'd gotten to you sooner."

"It was probably less confusing for everybody that I worked by myself. And better than field trips in grade school, when the teacher was always my buddy. But what's the thing with you and Storm? Did you grow up together or something?"

A slow smile blossoms. "Not quite. First time I saw her, first day of high school, she walks in like she owns the place. I wasn't sure how well I'd be accepted, but I figured if I got in good with someone like that, I'd be OK."

"Wait. *You* wanted *her* help?"

"It couldn't hurt. But I had a feeling, a girl who already looked that good at fourteen could be a magnet for all kinds of bad. I offered to help her steer clear of nasty boyfriends in exchange for not being a mean girl. I think we've done all right." He unzips the next bag. Another suit. "Your grandpa's?"

"Probably. He died before I was born so I've never seen these, but Mom didn't have any brothers. So, with Storm: you have an ongoing arrangement or something?"

"Well, at first. I'm not sure she needs me so much anymore, but now we're friends. It's a nice habit to check in with each other."

"What about ... other people?"

"I try to help everybody." He looks up at the ceiling with a sweet smile. I go ahead and melt a little while he's not looking. "When I was a kid, my mom noticed I had a special gift."

"Superpower," I mutter.

He snorts. "Whatever you want to call it. Temperament or something. I could join any group on the playground, just ease in there and start playing without being invited. Mom pointed out to me that not every kid could do that, but I could help those kids at no cost to myself. I'd never noticed before, but she was right — there's always at least one kid on the sidelines, waiting to be invited in. So I'd join a group, then once I was established, I'd sort of turn to the kid on the outside and wave them over."

"And you're still doing that, just not on the playground."

"Give the lady a cigar." He applauds in my direction. "It doesn't usually require much more than an introduction of people who'd get along well, or suggesting a club or something. With you, though ...

that was different. I had to improvise."

"What, with the hat?"

"After the hat. The hat was a happy accident. I could tell you needed something, but I wasn't sure what to suggest. The musical was just a decent guess."

"More than decent." A few bags in, I find several weird mid-century maternity tops. Like tents. I mean, what were they thinking?

"I wasn't sure I'd done anything for you till you asked about Carol Anne. Then I knew you'd be OK."

"Wait. You did? Then why ... ?" I gesture around this closet, but I mean everything we've ever done together.

"It couldn't hurt to keep tabs, right? So you'd have at least one friend? And so would I."

"Oh, please. You know everybody. You have loads of friends."

"I might know everybody. Actual friends — people who don't want anything — are less common."

I have the sense to shut up and think about that. It never occurred to me that I had anything to offer Jackson — gorgeous, popular Jackson. I open the next bag so he won't see my red face. It holds a rust-brown pantsuit and a silky rose-colored dress. I pull the dress out and hold it in front of myself.

"Nice color but too mother-of-the-bride for you," Jackson comments.

"Yeah, you're right. I've seen it in the wedding pictures at home." I return it to the bag and zip it up. The remaining bags aren't any more promising.

"Think she's hiding the good stuff?"

"I'll ask. Let's eat lunch first — this is hungry work."

Lunch is Grandma's homemade chicken soup, which alone is worth the trip, along with Mom's amazing sourdough bread. My guy is back, but I can almost ignore him. He has finished his sandwich and is now munching on store-brand cheese curls as he goes online. He logs on to some pickup artist forum or something, but then glances uneasily over his shoulder, like he's being watched — which he is — and logs back out. Huh. Then he's gone again. I can't say I'm sorry.

"So, did you find anything on your treasure hunt?"

I shake myself back to my own lunch. "Not yet. Do you have anything from when you were about my age?"

Grandma considers, then nods. "You know, I think the oldest things are in the basement. I'm sure I kept at least one of my formals."

Jackson pushes away his empty bowl. "If you're interested in giving away any of the suits, I'd take them off your hands."

"Oh, those are business suits, not formalwear. And they'd never fit you, anyway. Lester wasn't nearly so tall."

"I've already rented my suit for the dance. I'm thinking of our drama department at school. It'd be so great to have suits from different decades, and small is good — we always end up with girls in pants roles. The suits could have a second life; they seem to be in good condition."

"They are. Lester always dressed well when he was working."

"What did he do?"

"Insurance, his whole career. By the end, he had other agents working under him, but he made sure to take care of people. Never tried to sell them something they didn't need." She gazes out the window a moment, then turns back to us. "Yes, I think he'd approve if you took some suits. He liked the theater. Now, do you have room for dessert?"

As if that soup and bread weren't enough, she baked chocolate chip cookies, and they're still warm. Of course we have room for dessert.

"Did you bake these just for us?" I lick melted chocolate off my fingers.

"I'm also hosting my book club tonight, but I knew you'd enjoy them. Be sure to wash your hands so you don't get chocolate on the clothes."

I go into the upstairs bathroom to scrub my hands. The pathetic jerk from the park chooses this moment to reappear, also in the bathroom. He looks into the mirror and speaks. I can't hear him, but I'm pretty sure he says, "Do you mind?" He's probably talking to his mom, but I squeeze my eyes shut and when I open them again, he's gone. Good, I did not need to see that. Now I know another gesture never to use without thinking.

When I come out, we head downstairs. Grandma's basement smells slightly musty — nobody is living in it — but it's not spooky or anything. I used to love to play down here when I was little. It's full of my mom's old books and toys, photo albums and old encyclopedias, a ridiculously tiny TV set, an upright piano and comfy sofas and chairs on a linoleum floor perfect for sliding in socks. But there's also a big storage room. Several more zippered bags hang on a rod, and my hopes rise.

Jackson opens the first bag. Two more men's suits.

"Very *Mad Men*," he mutters. "Still seeing your friend?"

"Yuck, I saw him in his bathroom. The episodes are getting shorter, I think."

"That's probably good. It'd be a useful power for a spy, though. Or a detective."

"I'll remember that if I'm ever one of those things." My bag holds a hideous mint-green bridesmaid dress. "God, now he's back. In a towel, no less, playing Madden. I'm beginning to feel sorry for him."

He pauses the game and pulls an afghan around his shoulders. He looks around and I lip-read again: "I get it, OK? Stop watching me!" Oh, the irony. Then he's gone.

"Good, that one was over fast."

"Maybe they'll stop now."

"Hope so." More men's suits, a wool overcoat, a woman's sweater suit. Nothing remotely like what I'm looking for. "I give up. Maybe I should buy a dress."

"Wait, there's one more." Jackson bends to pick up a bag that's fallen from the rod, which at least lets me admire his denim-clad rear. Thank you, Jesus. If I have to see visions ...

He hangs the bag and unzips it. "Yeah, that's more like it." He removes the contents and holds it out for me to see.

Well, now. Carol Anne would definitely approve. The sleeveless dress has a sweetheart neckline and a full skirt made of layers of white tulle. The fitted bodice is threaded with silver. I take it and hold it in front of me. The skirt falls about mid-calf.

"Wow. This is so not me, but ... "

"Here's a picture of the one I think you'll — "

Grandma comes in, holding an open photo album. "Ah, you found it. That was my dress from the senior prom."

She holds the album so I can see the photo. A pretty dark-haired girl with glasses like Carol Anne's poses in the dress I'm holding. She's wearing a wrist corsage and heels that lift her up to about chin-height on her date, a skinny boy in a white jacket and horn-rimmed glasses, with his hair slicked back. I don't know who he is, but the girl has Grandma's smile.

"It looks like your size, too; come upstairs and try it on."

"It'll fit," Jackson whispers.

"How do you know?"

"I'm your fairy godfather — it's my job to know. Also, you look just like your Grandma in the photo."

"No, I don't! She was so pretty, and I'm — "

" — not invisible anymore, remember? Go try on the dress, and ask her if she had glass slippers to go with it."

"Oh, shut up. I'll wear my own shoes."

21

BELLES OF THE BALL

CAROL ANNE

"So, going to the Homecoming dance?" Barbara grabs the brim of her hat and pulls it back down as the wind tries to steal it.

"Probably not. You?"

We're walking back to my house after band practice. With a week and change before our debut, I hadn't given a lot of thought to the other big event that night until she asked. I mean, OK, a while ago, I thought about asking Marina to go with me, but before I could work up my nerve, I heard she was going with some guy. I don't need to see that.

Barbara laughs. "For all Storm's help, I still can't really dance, so no. I doubt it's my kind of music, anyway. Better to stay fresh for Maddie's party."

"Find your dress yet?"

"Did I ever! This dress is the dress they invented the word 'dress' for."

I shift my guitar case to the other hand. "A dressy dress, is that what you're saying?" I want to do a victory dance, but I keep my cool. I didn't think I'd ever get real-life Barbara into anything but jeans, let alone an actual party dress.

"The dressiest dressy dress that ever was ... dressed. You'll look at it and go, 'That is the least Barbara-ish thing ever.'"

"So, perfect, in other words."

"I don't know, but maybe I'll outdo you for once."

"Not happening. I found something of Aunt Anne's from her San Francisco hippie days."

"Groovy." Barbara holds up her fingers in a peace sign.

"Like, far out."

And then we totally crack up because we are still so immature.

We drop off my guitar at home and then walk around the block to Maddie's house. Or, Madeleine's house. She's my back-fence neighbor, and I've known her for years as Maddie, but she's trying to get people to use her grown-up name. Anyway, we're going over to see the space and make party plans.

Maddie opens the door the moment I've rung the bell. "Hi, Carol Anne! Hi, Barbara. Let me show you the rec room."

Maddie towers over me, but not in an intimidating way like Storm did before we knew her. Maddie used to hunch, which didn't help. I can tell she's making a conscious effort to stand up straight these days. If only I could get *her* into some better clothes ...

We follow her through the house — no mansion but pretty big for this part of town. Stairs lead down through a small laundry room into a big carpeted space. Some chairs and a couch face a flat screen on one wall, and there's a pretty nice bar setup, but otherwise, the place is empty.

"It's huge! I had no idea this was down here!"

"I know, it's almost the whole basement. I think the finished part used to be smaller — a bedroom or den over there, with a big garage, but the last owner finished the whole thing to be a recording studio."

Barbara squawks at that. "No wonder your folks are OK with having a band. Soundproofing must be pretty good. I like the garage aspect, too."

"Dad had big plans — pool table, arcade games — but it never happened. He blew his budget on the fancy bar, and then my brother and I came along. They throw a big party every New Year's Eve, and that's about it. Until they had this idea of a safe place for us seniors to gather after Homecoming."

"I'm glad they did. This is a good spot for it." When I first heard "house party" I thought we'd be playing for ten or fifteen kids in the living room. Now I can picture a decent-sized audience.

"Yeah, I guess. Do you think people will come? I mean, I passed out a lot of flyers, but I don't know that many people. I wonder if anybody will want to come to a dry party."

Oh. That might make a difference. "Does it have to be dry?"

Her face goes hard. "Yes. I wrote a paper on alcohol poisoning after one of my brother's college friends died of it. It's a terrible thing."

"Dry is good," Barbara says. "I don't know anybody who drinks."

"Barbara, how many people do you know? Four?"

"Well, I guess five now." She grins at Maddie.

I shake my head. "OK, dry it is. We'll do what we can to spread the word, but we don't know that many people, either."

"But one of them knows everyone," Barbara says. "I already put in a word with Jackson. Let him work his magic."

"OK, I hope that helps." Maddie — sorry, Madeleine — walks over to the empty end of the room. "I think we'll have you set up down here. That door goes outside, so that's the best place to bring in equipment. Dad reserved the PA — should we hire a guy to run it, too?"

"No, we've got a guy," Barbara announces. Wow, she's been busy. "You know Zach Brown?"

Madeleine brightens. I know it's a cliché, but she's really pretty when she smiles. "Math team Zach Brown? Yeah. I didn't know he was into music."

Barbara shrugs. "Well, he's taking a class in sound engineering and seemed up for the job."

"Then we're ready to rock and roll. All we need is the audience."

WHITNEY

"So let me get this straight. You're not going to Homecoming, but you need to borrow a festive outfit for Homecoming?"

"For an after-party. My band's playing, and we decided to go all retro-glitzy. You got anything like that?"

You'd never guess it to look at her, but my cousin Donna (once or twice removed, I can't remember which, and older than my parents) was a real party girl in her youth — giant 'fro, metallic jumpsuit, platform shoes, the whole bit. She's about my height and used to be my size.

"I might. Let's take a look. Why aren't you going to the dance?"

"Not my scene."

I don't offer details and Donna doesn't ask. Maybe it's obvious. I don't know why everybody makes such a big fucking deal about Homecoming and Prom and shit. OK, I guess it gives established couples a chance to dress up and have a fancy date and take pictures to annoy their future children with. And I also guess there's no better way to give a special someone the impression that you'd like to be an established couple. But what's with the elaborate public invitations? Some of these things are like marriage proposals. What if, after your big production, you get rejected? Or maybe worse, get accepted and then have a shitty time?

And no, this isn't sour grapes, though I haven't had a real boyfriend since ninth grade. Even then we were at different schools. If Tad and I were still together, we'd probably go to each other's formal events, so it's just as well we broke up when we did. If we had to go to two of everything, we'd go broke or kill each other or both.

Donna looks at me sidelong and tuts. "That spiky green mess on your head! Why do that? You have such good hair."

"Maybe exactly because your generation still talks about so-called good hair." I know, I shouldn't take it out on Donna. It's not her fault, but shit. How much longer will Black women do this to ourselves? (Or more to the point, let the goddamn patriarchy do it to us.) "Besides, you had *great* hair in the day." I point out Donna's graduation picture on the wall, back when she had that gorgeous big Afro. Today, her hair is straightened and lacquered into a 'do that looks good, I guess, but obviously isn't natural.

"And could again, but even that was work," she laughs. "All I'm saying is, you don't need to treat your hair but you do anyway."

She's right, in a way: my natural hair is dark and shiny and curly, but not African curly, I guess because of my mom's genes. I could shampoo it, dry it, and be good to go. When I was in gymnastics, I wore it in a bouncy little ponytail that everybody thought was so fucking adorable. But I happen to know Dad's family gave him all manner of shit when he and mom were first getting serious. Then I came along, with my "exotic" features and "good hair" and a lot was forgiven. Still, I've always felt I'm not Black enough for them, or Japanese enough for my mom's family, in spite of

Japanese language school to balance the hip-hop and tap lessons when I was little. And I didn't want to be adorable. Is it any wonder I opted out and went for the punk look?

It's too much to explain. "I've got my reasons."

She shakes her head and laughs. "As long as it's not for a boy."

"No way in hell."

She leads me into her spare bedroom and opens a big armoire. "Are you hoping for a dress?"

"Pants, if you've got 'em. Playing drums in a dress is a pain in the ass."

"I'll bet." She shifts some hangers, holds out a jumpsuit. "Yes? No?"

The gold knit fabric is spectacularly tacky, but when I take it from her for a closer look, its age begins to show. It's stretched out enough that the neckline is more sunken than plunging, and the sleeves are full of snags and runs. Also: jumpsuit — how do you take a piss?

"I'll pass. Got anything in two parts?"

She digs around some more. "Oh, here's an old favorite. What do you think?"

OK, more sequins than I ordinarily tolerate, but black. "I think I can work with it, as long as I stay away from platform shoes."

STORM

Jackson and I have a weekly ritual where he greets me outside first period on Monday with a deep, theatrical bow. "Good morning, milady. What dost thou need from thy humble servant?"

I almost never need anything, so we have a laugh and go to class. This time, I have a pressing need. "I could use a date for Homecoming: good looking, not too stupid ... "

He straightens with a smirk. "It's this weekend, and you don't have a date? Who have you turned down so far?"

"Nobody! I haven't been asked. What's up with that?"

"You've finally done it, Storm. They all think you're out of their league."

"Well, duh, but you'd think somebody would have the balls to try." I've been taking a break from boyfriends this year, but it's inconvenient when a big event comes up. "I had hopes for that cute cellist, Sean."

"Not a bad choice, if you're branching out from your usual type."

"Also, he owns his own tux. But he took the safe route and asked one of his orchestra friends — an oboe player."

"There's nothing safe about an oboe player."

I bat my eyelashes. "We're both on Homecoming Court; maybe you and I should go together. As friends, of course. I know I can count on you to look good."

"Decent idea, except I already told Barbara I wasn't taking a date."

"What, you can't change your mind?"

"It's the principle of the thing." He considers. "Actually, I have a better idea. I know someone who needs a date but he doesn't want to ask anyone."

"What, shy? Afraid of rejection?"

"Opposite problem. Any girl he asks would expect to be his girlfriend afterward. He doesn't want one right now, but he also doesn't want to hurt any feelings. I think if you ask him to go as friends, he'd be down with that."

"This isn't another sad, pathetic loser, is it? Don't I do enough being in Barbara's band?" I'm kidding. The band has been a relief, and more fun than I ever expected.

"Far from it. If anyone's in your league, it's Justin Hornbaker."

"Justin? Oo-la-la!" Basketball captain, tall and good looking ... "Does he pass the Durand test, then?"

"You'll have fun, and he'll be a perfect gentleman."

"OK, I'll ask him. But which one of us are you godfathering with this scheme?"

"Who says it can't benefit both of you? You're plausible dates for each other, with no expectation of anything but arm candy and no drama. It's win-win. Plus, when you go to Maddie's party afterward, that'll draw the rest of the A-list."

"So you're using us."

"Hey, you have to go, anyway. As I see it, the party will be a success, the band will have an audience ... so it's not win-win. It's win-win-win-win. No downside."

Justin's in the gym after school, playing pick-up three-on-three basketball with some other guys. There's no such thing as pick-up cheerleading, so I sit and watch a few points. It's no sacrifice; I love watching athletes move. And Justin Hornbaker is a hottie of the first order—tall, blond, ripped, and his team is Skins. Just my type. If I was in the market.

They play until the custodian asks them to leave. I catch up with Justin at the door.

"Hey, Justin. Who won?"

"Oh, hey, Storm. We didn't keep very good track, but I'll say my team. What's up with you?"

"Oh, you know, the usual: looking forward to cheering for you this winter; singing backup with a garage band. Stuff like that."

He laughs and pulls his T-shirt on. Pity. "Wow, a garage band? Did not see that coming."

"It's fun. So, Justin, I understand we have something in common."

"What's that?"

"We both need a drama-free date for Homecoming. I'm thinking we could go together — as friends, no pressure."

"Wow, really? That would be so cool! My mom keeps nagging me to ask someone, but ... "

"I know, it's so hard to keep up appearances. Speaking of which, I'll be wearing a fabulous green dress, so you need to equal but not surpass me. And it's strapless, so I'll need a wrist corsage."

"Got it. Are we doing a limo? Dinner?"

"No reason to go overboard. Do you have a car?"

"No." He gives me a sheepish grin. "Or, you know, a license."

"Not a problem. I have both. Or we could meet up at the dance."

"That doesn't look like much of a date, does it? I'll get the tickets, but I'm fine with you driving. That way,

Mom can take pictures. She'll love that."

"Perfect. Just so you know, we do have to go to Maddie Gowan's party afterward. My band is playing."

"No shit, live music? I was going to skip the party, but now I want to go."

"Right answer, dude. Give me your address, and I will see you on Saturday."

Justin's mom shows me all the pictures she took of Jordan and her date, who did do the whole limo-and-dinner thing and are therefore long gone. She then takes at least twenty shots of us before she lets us leave for the dance. I don't think she believes we're going as friends, the way she has us wrap our arms around each other. I don't mind, but Justin is visibly embarrassed. His ears are bright red. Finally, we escape to my little yellow Mustang. I wish it was summer so we could put the top down. Maybe for prom ...

"Sweet ride!"

"Thanks. Sixteenth birthday present."

"Whoa. So you're Daddy's little princess?"

Yeah, I guess it looks that way from the outside. "My dad is almost never around, so he buys me stuff to relieve his guilt."

"Ouch. Sorry I asked."

"It's actually better than it was." I don't want to get into the whole Heather drama with someone I don't know that well, so I let the subject drop.

"How, um, did you know I needed a date?"

"Jackson happened to mention it."

"I wondered if he had something to do with it. Because, you know, we were talking about

Homecoming, who we wanted to ask or not or whatever." He falls silent, unexpectedly flustered.

I spare a quick glance from the road. "Yeah, Jackson's a great guy, the way he figures out what everybody needs."

"Exactly! A great guy. We're lucky to know someone like that."

I'm not ashamed to admit I like these formal events ... mostly for the fashion show. People who never make an effort otherwise clean up pretty well. People who always make an effort (like me and Jackson) look like stars. And there's always somebody who completely surprises me. Case in point: Maddie Gowan, the quietest, nerdiest, gawkiest girl you can imagine, is completely rocking a short pink dress that shows off legs that won't quit. It's the quiet ones you have to watch out for.

And Justin didn't let me down. His rental tux is black and staid, but he got a multicolored vest with lots of green in it. He's wearing green Chucks with it, so I'm pretty sure we'll have fun.

The music is too loud to allow for conversation, and the room is too packed for any expressive dancing, but we get into it as best we can. Justin has decent moves on the fast songs, but when we slow dance, he's stiff and robotic. I have to place his hands at my waist. When I try to lean against him, he pushes back.

"Leave room for Jesus." He laughs at his joke so I join him, but resign myself to that little gap.

There's a break in the dancing to crown the Homecoming Court. Jackson and I are king and queen, since we're seniors. We share a slow dance, which is no sacrifice. Jackson dances better than any of the straight guys here.

He leans close to my ear. "So you're a queen at last. How's it going with Justin?"

"Fine. He's smarter than he looks — lots of laughs."

"Disappointed this date is just friends?"

"No, that's all either of us want. But I could change it if I wanted to."

He laughs and his breath makes my ear tingle. "I would love to see you try."

"I promised, no drama."

"Smart girl. By the way, this mermaid dress is stunning on you."

"Yeah, I didn't think vintage was my look, but I might have to change my mind."

After our dance, Jackson and I join Justin at a table.

He stands to hold my chair; I didn't realize Jackson meant that "perfect gentleman" thing literally. "You looked good out there, your majesties."

"You two match better," Jackson says. "I'm heading over to Maddie's, make sure the band's ready to go."

"We'll be right behind you," I say.

"Wouldn't miss it! I've been telling everybody," Justin adds.

Is anyone that enthusiastic? But that should get us a reasonable crowd, so I can't complain. It'll be an interesting night.

22

THE DRINK I DIDN'T HAVE LAST NIGHT

BARBARA

Three-fourths of the band gather in Madeleine's basement to set up. Storm will join us later — she's part of the Homecoming Court, of course. Our hostess isn't here yet, either, because she got asked to the dance at the last minute. I'm happy for her. I've gotten to know her better since we booked this gig; she's a sweet, smart girl who should have way more friends than she does. Maybe this party will help.

We set up our gear at one end of the huge rec room. They've disguised the low ceiling and fluorescent tubes with Mylar streamers and strings of Christmas lights, so it'll be festive.

Madeleine's mom is setting out snacks and drinks on the bar, including a bowl of that punch with the lime sherbet in it, which is sort of adorably lame. Like it's a wedding reception or something. At this hour, energy drinks might be more appropriate. Madeleine's dad, meanwhile, discreetly removes all the booze. Fair enough; it's his house. My dad would do the same, if we had enough space for a party of more than the four people I actually know. Or, you know, five if you count Madeleine.

Two of those people — Carol Anne and Whitney — are setting up drums, amps, monitors and microphones. I pass out set lists. We'll start with "Huge Guy in the Mosh Pit" and end with "Half a Bus Closer to Home," the songs we know best, with our other four songs in the middle. I stuck in "Pretty Gown" to pad it out. It's the only cover I felt confident of, and it seems like a good one to do tonight.

"Madeleine wants two sets, so we'll play through this set once, then take a break and play it again in reverse order."

Whitney looks over the set list. "We'll be fine. Do we have a name yet?"

No. I keep thinking about the He Ted sign, so I have an idea, but I'm not sure it's any good; I'm afraid if I put it out in the air, it won't survive. "Trust me, OK?"

Before I can explain further, Zach B comes downstairs for sound check. I thought he wasn't going to the dance, but he's wearing a navy blue polyester suit. Maybe he's Maddie's date? Seems like we would have heard something, like that Jackson had that heart attack. "If it's OK, I'm going to record the show for my class." He looks up from the board and sees us for the first time. "Wow, Barbara's in girl clothes!"

I can't help myself. I twirl. "It's a special night."

Carol Anne's all Summer of Love in a paisley scarf dress and purple granny glasses, with flowers in her hair, even. Whitney's doing a Disco Queen kind of thing with black satin pants and a sequined bustier, punked out with spiky green hair, motorcycle jacket and boots. I'm wearing Grandma's 1952 prom dress, and I even curled my hair, for what it's worth. And I finally used Storm's gift certificate, so I have silver polish on my nails. Even on my toes, which can't be seen. But I know I have silver toenails, which gives me absurd confidence. The whole mani-pedi thing was a strange experience — not unpleasant, just weird for me to be pampered. But I might do it again sometime, for a special occasion.

About the time I finish sound-checking her mic, Storm arrives to put us all back in our places, appearance-wise. Her green satin dress (strapless, with matching opera gloves) elicits a strangled squeak from our sound man. Rhinestones (or diamonds, for all I know) sparkle around her neck, matching her Homecoming Court tiara. And she's with Justin Hornbaker, captain of the boys' basketball team. He's a match for her in a black tux, multicolored waistcoat, and green high-tops. They're both so tall and blond and beautiful, they should have "Perfect Couple" in flashing neon over their heads.

"What's everybody staring at? I know, I look so fat!"

Storm frets with her dress.

Whitney snorts. "Remember, we don't use that F-word. Besides, I'd say, 'Va-fucking-voom!' Where did you find that?"

"Great-grand-aunt Dorcas used to sing with a big band, back in the day. She had such great clothes!"

"And now you get to wear them to sing with a little band." I smile at Storm.

Storm frowns at me. I do everything in my power not to fade out. "Barbara doesn't have a hat."

"I don't have anything that goes with this dress."

She removes her tiara and settles it on my head. "That's better. The lead singer should be seen."

Did she really do that? I stammer out a response. "Thanks, Storm. That's very nice of you." More than nice. Maybe I'm extra emotional tonight, but I have a lump in my throat and if I try to say more, I might cry.

Dressed-up seniors start to trickle in. Jackson, Rat Pack cool in a white dinner jacket, leans on the bar and toasts us with a plastic cup of punch as if it were something much classier. "Nice shoes, Cinderella."

I lift one dainty combat boot (because I still don't do heels) and waste a second picturing us as a couple in our 1950s prom duds. Yeah, I'm hopeless. At least I don't have to see him with some other girl.

Madeleine arrives, adorable in her new pixie cut and pink chiffon minidress. I've never seen her in a dress before. (OK, she's never seen me in a dress, either, but who knew she had such great legs? Not to mention the cutest ankle boots I've ever seen. When did I get to be such a shoe geek? Thanks, Jackson.) She stops off at the soundboard to exchange some nerdy electrical talk with Zach. I join them, in case there's some problem I should know about.

"Hi, Madeleine. How was the dance?"

"Eh, it was all right. But call me Maddie, OK? Madeleine sounds kind of stiff."

"Oh, OK ... Maddie." This is why I never do anything with my name.

"Are you ready to start?"

Oh, that's right. I nod and swallow. I take my place at the microphone. The room's not close to full, but there's enough chatter that I don't see much point in introducing us. Also, if I have to talk, I'll probably throw up. But sing? That, I can manage.

"OK, girls, let's do this thing."

"One, two, three, intro!"

We rip into "Huge Guy in the Mosh Pit," which drowns out the chatter and gets their stunned attention. I can barely hear my vocals over the guitar. For that matter, I can barely hear the kick drum. I guess we should have checked the monitor balance better. I finish the song on faith alone.

There's a smattering of applause, so it must have been OK. That song's pretty hard to screw up. "Thanks, guys. Zach, could I get more lead vocal and less guitar?" Yeah, that sounded pro. I catch my breath and swallow my nerves. "Thanks for coming out. We are ... St. Rage?"

Some dude in the back yells, "Fuck, yeah!" Carol Annee grins and gives me the thumbs-up.

"OK! We are St. Rage and this next song's called 'The Drink I Didn't Have Last Night is the Drink I Shoulda Had.'"

That gets a laugh. Whatever that woman meant, her line turned into a fun song.

A handful of guitar geeks move up close to watch Carol Anne at work, and another little bunch of guys gather to drool over Storm. We do "Focus," the song I wrote about Jackson giving me that first hat. It took a long time to finish, but turned into a fun soul ballad with lots of sha-la-las. Unfortunately, I forget most of the words in the bridge. "Distracted Driver" goes better, and then we do the one cover, "Pretty Gown."

All I want is a pretty gown
Is that so hard?

That song earns an appreciative laugh — for once, even I'm wearing one. I'm not sure what they think of the blood donation one, "I Want You to Have Something of Mine," but it feels hardcore.

By the end of the set, Maddie's rec room is swampy and packed. For whatever reason, seniors of every stripe — in-crowd, nerd crowd, losers — have turned out. I credit Jackson's magic, or maybe Storm's dress.

"Thanks, guys! We're gonna take a break, but don't go away. We'll be back with another set in about ten minutes."

Otis Whatshisname (or Whatshisname Otis) and a couple other stoners amble past the "stage" and open the outside door. Otis pauses to throw devil horns my way. "You guys are sick, man. Killin' it." Clearly, he doesn't know I helped wreck his brother's truck, and I intend to keep it that way. They go outside and leave the door open; the cooler air is a relief even if it does smell like weed.

The band takes a break to pee. I splash water on my

face to cool it. All the curl is gone from my hair, but I still have silver nails and the tiara looks cute; I might have to get one of my own. When we get back to the party, Whitney and Carol Anne grab some snacks, but I'm still too keyed-up to eat. I chug two bottles of water and watch Storm part a sea of admirers in order to focus on Justin. I edge closer. I never learned how to flirt, and maybe it's too late, but if anyone could teach me, it's Storm. Of course, she has that fabulous dress to help her out.

"Warm in here." Storm slips off her wrist corsage and holds it between her teeth while she peels off her long gloves. Everyone she's ignoring watches in fascination. "I don't have any pockets in this dress. Hold these for me?" She hands the gloves to Justin, who puts them in his coat pocket.

Jackson wanders over, too, and takes up a position off Justin's right elbow. Whether she still needs his help, he's always sort of protective of Storm. "Nice work, Barbara, Storm. Hey, Justin."

Justin grins and widens the circle to include Jackson. "Dude! Is this an awesome party or what? Who needs beer when there's live music?"

Yeah, he's kind of a bro, but by all accounts, a genuinely nice guy. I'm already so wound up, it's easy to catch his enthusiasm. "Best party I've ever been to!"

Jackson cracks up at this. "Barbara, your idea of a wild night is staying up past eleven to eat pizza and watch action movies."

I scowl at him, even though he's right. "That was your birthday party, not mine."

Jackson raises his hands in surrender.

Justin shakes his head. "Man, I love movie parties! Invite me next time, too."

"What do you think of Comicon?" I smirk at Jackson as I say this. I probably won't out him, but he should know I can tease back.

"Um, Barbara — " Jackson looks horrified.

Justin lights up. "Dudes! I went last time! So awesome!"

The color returns to Jackson's face. "Really? You liked it?"

"Oh, yeah! Next time, I want to go in costume, though. Like as Thor! That would rock."

"Then Jackson is the man to make that happen. You guys should talk."

Up front, Carol Anne straps on a guitar and starts to tune. Break's over.

"Come on, Storm. Back to work."

Storm taps each of her cheeks with a manicured nail, somehow better than mine. "Kiss for luck, boys." Jackson and Justin obediently lean in and give her a quick peck. Must be nice. Why can't I have a superpower like that?

"So, Storm, are you and Justin a thing?" I ask once we're out of earshot.

"Not yet." She winks. "Jackson suggested I ask Justin to Homecoming, and I always take Jackson's advice."

Well, so do I, but clearly, she's getting a better product.

She peers at me. "Do you have *silver* nails?"

Gulp. "Um, yeah. I used your birthday present, and I thought, with this dress..."

"Yeah, great call. The color goes with the dress, but gives it some edge. Now I wish I'd gone with metallic polish."

I just smile because I have no words. Not even to tell her about my toes.

For our second set, we start at the end with "Half a Bus Closer to Home" and work back to "Huge Guy in the Mosh Pit." It goes better this time; there's even some actual moshing going on. And that neon "Perfect Couple" sign? It's moved. Way in the back, with no regard for anything we play, Jackson is slow-dancing ... with Justin Hornbaker. I glance over at Storm. Not only does she not look jealous, but she wears this smug little grin, like she was in the know all along. Talk about using your powers for good. And I'm not jealous, either. Seriously, I'm not. Maybe I even helped a tiny bit, with the Comicon remark. Anyway, I never had a chance, and I knew it. Besides — Jackson and Justin? Adorable. Jackson and Barbara? Not so much. Still glad I don't have to see him with another girl. I don't know why that makes a difference but it does. Maybe because it's not about me in any way.

Meanwhile, up front, Travis Oakley plants himself between the guitar geeks and the Storm Skye Fan Club. Unlike everyone else, he's dressed down — torn jeans and black Ancient Warlocks T-shirt. I'm guessing he skipped the dance, too. He's taller than me but slouchy, so when he folds his arms and stares, he's more or less at my eye level. It's kind of creepy, but as long as I'm singing, I can't be bothered.

"Thank you, seniors. We are St. Rage. Good night."

Carol Anne switches off her amp. "Good name,

Barbara. Let's keep it."

There's a pop as Zach turns off the PA. Whitney starts breaking down her kit. My ears are ringing — next time, I'll wear earplugs. But what I can hear sounds like people having a good time. Nobody's passed out, nobody threw up on the soundboard; Maddie's party is a success, and we were part of that. I was part of that. Could be the start of a new era for me.

Storm reclaims her tiara and goes off to flirt with a new target. Oakley is still standing there, with his unruly hair and no-longer-stubble-not-yet-beard. I can't pretend I don't see him.

"Can I help you with something?"

"You hit me in the nose."

"I'm flattered you remember! That was, what — six months ago?"

"It doesn't hurt anymore." He continues to not blink. "You're not actually ugly."

"That means so much, coming from you." My knees are starting to shake — adrenaline and low blood sugar, probably. I hope there's some food left.

"You don't have a bass player." So apparently Oakley is still there. "We should hang out sometime."

"Yeah, another time, OK?" I'm more interested in the snack table, but I can't quite see it through the crowd.

"OK. When?"

"I don't know. Later."

"Later. OK. I will see you later."

The lights are still down, but I glimpse Maddie on a couch at the other end of the room, cuddling with a guy I assume is her date. Well, good for her. It's nice to see a shy girl getting some attention for a change. Except, wait, are they cuddling or wrestling? Then the guy gets up. He's drowning in an absurdly big zoot suit, but I recognize him and forget all about Oakley. It's Zach M.

What did Jackson say? He'll demand a return on his investment. I scan the room for Jackson, but he's still involved with Justin. Maddie's parents have been in and out all evening, but right now, they're out. Carol Anne's sitting with Maddie now, so she's probably all right. Still, I keep an eye on Zach. He reaches into his enormous suit coat and pulls out a plastic water bottle exactly like those lined up on the bar. Weird; wouldn't it be warm? Then he empties it into the punch bowl, drops the bottle on the floor like all the other slobs, and ladles up two cups of punch.

Wait a minute. I'm slow, but eventually I get there. I'll bet that's not the good stuff, either. The punch is probably sweet enough to mask vile rotgut. Some people will drink anything; I get that. But it should be their own choice. Otherwise, it's a little bit evil. And I'm supposed to battle evil where I find it, right?

Once again, I don't shoot anybody. From across the room, I push the proverbial huge guy, who stumbles back and knocks Zach M off balance. Zach lunges and dumps a cup of punch ... all over Maddie. Oops. Sorry, girl — send me the dry cleaning bill.

She squawks and jumps up, her pink dress soaked with green punch and clinging to her body. Right away Zach's apologizing, offering napkins and the other cup. I grab the mic.

"Paging Mr. Gowan. Clean-up in the rec room."

My amplified voice startles the room into silence.

Nobody laughs at my lame joke. Zach M turns and glares at me. Zach B looks up from the soundboard. He has the unplugged cable in his hand. This mic isn't even hot, but we'll keep that between us. I put it back on the stand and hope Maddie's dad heard me.

Zach B leaves the board to get closer to the action. He takes off his cheap suit coat and drapes it over Maddie's shoulders. In heels, she's a good head taller than he is, but she glances down at him and smiles before she turns back to Zach M. "No, thanks, I'm not thirsty. I'm gonna go get changed." As she and Carol Anne leave the room, I hear Maddie mutter, "I told Mom this was a terrible idea."

About a minute later, Maddie's dad comes in to tell us to wrap things up. He turns the lights back on and empties the remaining punch into the sink behind the bar. Guests start to leave in pairs and groups, though Jackson and Justin stay to help break down the PA. I'm too exhausted suddenly to be much help.

Zach M jabs his finger at me. "This party was about to get good, till you had to be a snitch. Who the fuck do you think you are?"

Not a tired girl anymore, for one. I'm a fucking superhero. I meet his gaze and wait a beat. "I am St. Rage."

And I flip him two birds. He can pay his own damn dry cleaning bill.

23

GOOD GUY

OK, so maybe plastering Zach M with birdshit was an irresponsible use of superpowers. Doesn't mean I'm sorry. I'm a little miffed that hardly anybody saw it, but maybe it's for the best. Secret identity and all that. Come to think of it, using the same name for my band and my super-self might be a useful diversion. No one will know which I'm talking about, and if you Google it, you get storage companies.

In the weeks since the party, I've had dreams that everybody in school knows about my weird powers. My friends go out of their way not to make me angry. Everyone else goes out of their way to ... go out of their way. Not nightmares, exactly; just stupid.

In reality, the party didn't win me any new friends beyond Zach and Maddie. I'm as unknown as I ever was. Even with a name and a Facebook page, St. Rage (the band) isn't so much as a cult favorite, let alone a big hit. (Bailey gave us a "like," so there's that.) I didn't used to mind being invisible, but come on — I got up in front of people and sang my guts out. I performed three impossible feats. Shouldn't they know who I am? Maybe I'd have to come to school in a poofy white dress. Yeah, right. That's the one thing *less* practical than boots and a cape.

Three good things came out of Homecoming: we got a decent demo recording; Zach M is transferring to another school (so I guess he knows about me, at least); and Zach B and Maddie G are now officially an item. That's nice; it'd be even nicer if she played bass. But even without a bass player, we have approval to record and release an EP for our senior project.

As soon as the Homecoming thing was over, we started rehearsing our piece for the winter chamber concert, so we were a lot more prepared than in the spring. Well, it would have been hard not to be. Nothing like knowing what's coming next! Rather than play one of my songs, we worked up a polished arrangement of a seasonal piece: the old Darlene Love classic, "Christmas (Baby, Please Come Home)." I've been singing along with that record since the second time Dad played it for me; what a thrill to perform it live. And I think Storm was stoked to trade in the tambourine for some sleigh bells. I wore black jeans again, but I borrowed my mom's fuzzy black sweater with crystals on it. I don't think it's a stretch to say we were the hit of the concert. And I wasn't even nervous until afterwards, when Travis Oakley wouldn't stop applauding.

I can't figure him out. He doesn't do anything. He's just ... there. A lot. I can't picture going from the girl who made no impression on anybody for years to the girl in the hat to the girl with a stalker. But I haven't made an effort to ask him what he wants.

Now it's the last week before Winter Break. The mood is generally squirrelly as people try to complete projects while also planning trips or parties or gifts or whatever. Thanks to the demo, the band got on a Teen Music Night at the Eagles club this weekend, so I'm excited about that. It's a showcase kind of thing with six or eight bands, so we're playing only four songs, but still, a real gig, right?

I walk from the bus stop up to school behind a clump of other students, fully half of them in Santa hats. I'm not one of them; my hat's black and furry, with ear flaps. My mind's on tonight's band practice, the last one before the show on Saturday. I hope the teachers don't expect too much today.

The oak on the corner clings to a surprising number of leaves, considering how cold it's been. They're a sad, lifeless brown. The wind rattles through them as I pass, and I could probably get a song out of that. It's not a morning for dawdling outside, but I hang back at the bottom of the steps to let the Santa clump clear the entrance while I tap out a few lyrics on my phone. By the time I shove my phone in my pocket and look up again, I'm almost the only one left outside. The only other kid out here is Oakley. Figures. But he's not looking at me. He sits on the planter by the flagpole with his backpack open beside him, cradling something in his hand. Wait, is that what I think it is?

This is the last thing I need: Travis fucking Oakley, with a fucking handgun. If that's what I'm up against, it's good to know I'm St. Rage (because Barbara doesn't use that kind of language). Bringing the birdshit might not be effective, but I can be a good guy with a finger gun.

He touches it to his head and I make a tiny strangled sound that isn't the least bit super. Then he lowers it and stands up, facing the school doors. Everything in me screams to run away or take cover, like they teach us in those awful active shooter drills.

No, I have to handle this. At least it looks like everyone else is safely inside, and he hasn't fired a shot yet.

"Hey! Oakley!"

He turns away from the school, which feels like progress except now he might point the gun at me. But he's still not aiming it anywhere. "Oh, hey, Barbara."

"Um, dude? What are you thinking? You can't bring a gun to school."

He glances at it. "I guess I just did."

And I guess I'm guilty, too, even if he doesn't know it. "Look, just put it away. Nobody has to know." Except the police, but I don't want to pull my phone out until I'm sure I won't get shot.

"The whole point is *everybody* has to know."

Oh, shit. It's like that, is it? "You're pissing me off, Oakley. Do you know how much of a cliché this is?

What's your plan — mow down a bunch of people and then shoot yourself, or mow down a bunch of people and force some poor cop to shoot you?"

"I haven't worked it out that far. I'm kind of making it up as I go along."

Well, that's something. He's not one of those guys with a notebook full of grudges, pockets full of ammo, and a map of the school. "So, how many random casualties are we talking about?"

"Maybe only one, but I don't know."

"What, exactly, don't you know?" I'm shaking but not from cold. My face is burning with so much fear and rage, I could probably fly all the way home. But not until this is over.

"I don't know how to shoot this thing, or if it's even loaded; and I don't know how to check."

An unstable kid holding a gun he doesn't know how to use — is that scarier than a kid with a gun he does know how to use? I suppose there's a chance it's not loaded, but how do we find out? I hope not the hard way.

Just then, Ms. J, the drama teacher, hurries along the walkway from the parking lot, headed for the entrance behind Oakley. I want to warn her not to come this way, but I can't act like I see her.

My heart's playing a wild drum solo, and I have to remind myself to breathe. Keep him talking. "OK. Then what are we doing here?"

Ms. J freezes, then quietly backtracks. She's safe, but now we've lost that "nobody knows" chance. She's dialing 911 right this second, I'm sure of it, and the school will go on lockdown. I hope everybody remembers from the drills what to do.

Oakley misses the whole thing. "I overheard a girl in the lunchroom say, 'He's so weird. It wouldn't surprise me if he came to school with a gun.' If that's how it is, I might as well find out how it feels."

"See, this is why I stay out of the lunchroom. How do you know she was talking about you?" When he doesn't answer, I push ahead. "Anyway, you don't have to be that guy. Prove her wrong. Do something different, something ... constructive."

"I want to. It's just. So. Hard." He glances at the gun in his hand. "But this ... feels like power."

"That's not power. This is." I point and fire. My shot strikes sparks as it pings off the flagpole and leaves a dent. Oops. At least I hit what I was aiming for. (Considering I never know what might happen, I guess I should be glad it didn't snap off or explode into shrapnel.) Oakley twitches at the sound, but he doesn't seem all that surprised. He saw me fly that first time; maybe he saw all that stuff at the party, too. I point my finger gun at him. "If you try to go inside, I'll have to stop you. And I don't honestly know how much damage this will do."

"Then let's find out." He spreads his arms wide. "I have nothing to live for. You'd be doing me a favor."

The way he says it is so sad and final, but there's a tremor in his voice, like he's not quite sure. My anger drains away. I'm not St. Rage; I'm just Barbara. Now I wish I had the cape and boots so I could at least look heroic.

I open my hand and let the finger gun go. "I do." My voice sounds shaky and small, but I think he's listening.

"We're playing a show on Saturday. After break, we're making a record. Jackson's going to help Justin come out to his parents so they can go to prom together. Zach B, of all people, has a girlfriend! Everybody in this school has something to live for."

"Except me."

I take one step up. "Even you, Travis. Maybe not today. But if you put the gun down, tomorrow, you will."

"Nobody likes me, I'm flunking algebra, and I don't have a senior project. None of that will be different tomorrow."

"Algebra and a senior project? Those can both be fixed; there's time."

Travis gestures with the gun and it's all I can do not to hit the ground. "You wouldn't understand. You have friends; it's easy for you."

I move up one more step. "Travis, I have ... " I have to stop and think, which the gun doesn't help, " ... six friends; maybe seven. A year ago, I didn't have any."

"I always do it wrong. Nobody tells me I'm doing it wrong until they're all irritated and don't want me around. I'm not a mind reader, you know?"

"I'm trying not to be irritated, but this gun thing? That's wrong." Thank you, Captain Obvious, but it's the best I can do. I've never been so freaked out. "But what about Otis? He's your friend, right?" I move closer. Now we're on the same level.

"Alex Otis? I was his sidekick, doing whatever dumb thing he came up with. Pranks and shit. Until he decided I wasn't funny anymore. He blames me for wrecking his brother's dumb truck."

"You weren't even driving!"

"I tried to grab the wheel — he was swerving all over the place after the tire blew."

"So maybe it would have been worse if you hadn't. Anyway, he should blame me — I blew out the tire." I mime with the finger gun and he flinches, but nothing happens.

"Wait, *you* did that? Whoa. And then you punched me out."

"Yeah. I'm sorry about that."

He touches his nose. "It really hurt. But you were right. I was being an asshole, all to make stupid Otis like me."

Travis is shivering. He doesn't have a coat on, just a fleece pullover.

"You look cold. Here, put this on." I take off my hat and hold it out. The wind slaps my head and blows hair into my mouth. I can't believe that ever happens to Wonder Woman.

Travis's eyes widen. I never noticed before — they're dark blue, almost violet, and kind of soulful. He slowly reaches out and takes the hat. "Are you sure?"

"I have a hood." I unzip my collar to deploy the hidden hood. It's not as warm as the furry hat, but it keeps my hair out of my face.

"This is a dorky hat."

"It'll keep your ears warm. Here, let me hold that."

And simple as that, he hands me the gun to hold while he puts on the hat. What was I thinking? Now *I'm* the kid with a gun at school. No drill could have prepared me for this. I want to do the spider-on-me dance and fling it away, but I've heard they sometimes go off accidentally when dropped. I restrain myself and hold it gingerly by the grip. I grab Travis's hand and walk him down the steps and across the narrow street in front of the school, over by the condemned buildings. I don't know if it'll help, but it's away from school, and there aren't any people there to get hurt if things go wrong. I set the gun down and give it a kick. It's kind of a lame kick and it doesn't go far, but he can't reach it. I hold both his hands to make sure.

He squirms. "Um. I don't really like to be touched."

"I'm not touching you; I'm restraining you."

"Oh. OK. I thought you might try to hug me or something."

"You're safe; I'm not a hugger. Where'd you get the gun?"

"Found it."

"Oh, please."

"No, it's true. My bedroom has a tiny little balcony, over an alley behind our building. When I can't sleep, I go out there and sit in the dark. Last night, a guy ran up the alley and tossed something small into the dumpster. It went *clang,* which seemed weird for something that size, so I went to check it out."

"And you decided to bring it to school?"

"No, I put it in my pack so I could turn it in to the police."

"Why didn't you just call them?"

"I don't think so well at 3:00 A.M. And I don't have my own phone because I keep losing them, so I'd have to use the landline, and that might wake Mom."

"I guess I get it. And you had the right idea — whoever tossed it must be a criminal." I wish there was still a chance to lend Travis my phone so he could call the police himself. But I'd have to let go. "Why'd you change your mind?"

"I didn't remember it was in there until I was almost at school."

"How do you forget a thing like a gun in your backpack?"

"Hey, I was late for my bus. It's ... been a bad morning. But when I saw it again, I remembered what that girl said. It seemed like ... destiny." Travis raises his face, like he sees his destiny in the wintry clouds.

Maybe only one ... I feel sick. "Were you planning to kill me?"

He comes back to earth and stares at me. "No, I meant to kill me, but I was too scared. Why would I want to kill you?"

"I don't know, but you've been stalking me!"

"No, I haven't. You said we'd hang out later, and I wanted you to know where to find me when it was finally later. See? I always do it wrong! I don't want to kill you, Barbara. I, I, I ... want to *be* you."

"You mean you want to be Invisible Girl? Or you want a weird superpower that you can't quite control?"

His eyes go unfocused, and he almost smiles. "A superpower would be cool."

"Trust me, it's not that great."

Travis does a whole-body shudder, like he's trying to shed several skins. "But that's not the thing. This is the thing: you're not all popular and phony and shit; you're real, and you're doing something you like with people who like you."

I almost don't get it, and then I do. "What, the

band? You want to play in a band?" This seems like such a minor wish, though I know how it feels. "Being in a band doesn't make your problems go away."

"But does it make it worth having problems?"

That stops me for a second. "You know, it kind of does. Do you play?"

"Yeah, bass; I thought you knew. I've been dropped from five groups already."

I shake my head. "News to me." I'm no better at seeing people than I am at being seen. There's so much to learn. And bass. Too bad we're an all-girl band.

Sirens in the distance. Helicopter overhead. I hope they know no one's hurt, no shots were fired. Well, except mine. I glance up at the dented flagpole. Geez, am I on the hook for the damage?

Travis looks around uneasily. "What happens now?"

"I think we get arrested."

"We? That's not right; you're the hero."

I shrug. "They don't know that. And here we are together, like Bonnie and Clyde."

He goes pale and starts to shake. "I don't want to die in a hail of bullets."

In a weird way, that sounds like a step in the right direction. "Yeah, let's not do that part. Come on, hands up."

"Don't shoot," he whispers. Unless that's me.

I release him and take a deep breath. "Don't make me regret this." I point two fingers at my eyes and then at Travis: eyes on you. My heart's hammering as hard as it does when I'm angry, so I suspect it will work. Then we both raise our hands over our heads as cop cars block off both ends of the street.

Officers approach with guns drawn, yelling at us to lie down and put our hands on our heads. Travis is shaking so much he can hardly stand, and I'm feeling unsteady myself, so it's kind of a relief to get down on the ground, even if the pavement is cold and gritty. Apparently we're not doing it fast enough; a cop grabs my shoulder and shoves me down, then presses a knee into my back. Ouch. It takes everything I have to keep St. Rage at bay; she's pissed but she would be no help. When asked, I tell them where the gun is. Other than that, I keep my mouth shut.

There's some confusion about which of us is the shooter — Travis wasn't wearing a hat when the first call came in. We both get cuffed and read our rights. It's scary and painful and far from my normal Thursday, but nobody's dead. The police have the gun now; it might help solve a crime. And maybe Travis will get some help. Maybe I will. So it has to be better than it was. Than it might have been.

Travis cooperates, but grows frantic when he sees me in handcuffs. "You shouldn't arrest her! She didn't do anything wrong!"

"Travis! Shut up till we have a lawyer, OK? I'm fine."

The cop steers him toward a waiting squad car. "Yeah, listen to your girlfriend."

"He's not my boyfriend."

"Oh, great. A lovers' quarrel."

I should shut up, too. Let it go. Do I really want to risk the one thing that's going well for me? But I have the power. I have the responsibility. "He's not my boyfriend," I repeat. "He's my bass player."

24

ONE TWO EYES ON YOU

I got *arrested*. I'm in the back of a fucking cop car, cuffed, heading for wherever it is they take teenagers who get arrested. Can I call it "juvie"? That sounds really street, but not anything like me. God, what have I done?

Travis is in another car, but I can see him thanks to my super eyes-on-you vision. He's making a heroic effort to hold it together, which reminds me how things could have been a whole lot worse. Nobody's dead. I went into it thinking I was fighting crime and wound up preventing a suicide. I don't know what I could have done differently, so I have to believe it'll turn out OK somehow.

I'm still scared.

I lose all sense of time. Nothing is familiar, I'm coming down off a huge adrenaline rush, and as if that weren't weird enough, I keep having visions of Travis. We get checked in or booked or whatever you call it — fingerprints and everything — and at some point I get to call home. When Mom picks up I spill an incoherent stream of words, but she must catch the gist of it because she says, "I'm calling Janice, and then I'll be right there."

That makes me feel a lot better. One, I need my mom. Two, her friend Janice is an established defense attorney in town. Mom used to paralegal for her before I was born and she's kind of an honorary aunt to me. She'll know what to do.

I wait what feels like a long time, but it's hard to tell in a windowless room with no clock. Is it still morning? It must be, but it feels like days have passed since I first saw Travis with a gun in his hand.

Somebody must have asked if I was hungry and I must have said yes because they bring me a sandwich, even though there's a perfectly good lunch going to waste in my backpack. Behind the sandwich comes the great news that Mom and Janice are here, and that I'm not being held. I'm a witness, not a suspect.

Nothing like detention to make you appreciate freedom. When those cuffs come off, I want to turn cartwheels, even though I can't turn cartwheels. But while I'm giving my witness statement, I have another vision of Travis: alone in an interview room, rocking in his chair.

I break off from telling them about the moment when Ms. J came into view. "Travis shouldn't be alone."

The officer taking my statement looks up from the form she's filling in. "He's not your worry now."

"He is, too! He wanted to kill himself. What if he — " I see him bang his head against the table once, twice before the vision dissolves, " — I don't know, cracks his skull on the table? Could somebody please just check?"

The next time I see him, he's not alone, which I hope means they're taking me seriously. Then his mom arrives (alone, no lawyer), a small, dark-haired woman, younger than my mom but looking really tired. She hugs Travis and he squirms. Then the vision ends, and I hope whatever I've been saying makes sense.

" ... so I'm one-hundred percent convinced he didn't plan to harm anyone but himself. I think he wanted ... an audience? A witness? Something. Oh, and I touched the gun, too, so it'll have my fingerprints on it. But they should check for a third set, because Travis said he saw a guy throw it into the dumpster. So if there was a shooting or a robbery near Travis's place like around three in the morning..."

"Thank you; we'll keep that in mind. We're almost done here, and then you're free to go."

I get all my stuff back — backpack, phone, superfluous lunch — but not the hat, which must be with Travis's stuff. He can have it; I don't think I could wear it again. On the way out, we meet Travis's mom in the waiting area. She gives me a hug and I let her, seeing how Travis didn't want to.

"Ms. Oakley, does Travis have a lawyer?" I'm really worried he'll say the wrong thing and get himself in even worse trouble.

"You can call me Sharon. I ... haven't had a chance to call anyone yet."

"Aunt Janice?" I put on a pleading look.

Janice gives Sharon an encouraging smile. "It seems Barbara won't need legal help. Let's talk."

Mom and I leave them there and go home. It's too late to go back to school, and I don't want to, anyway, even for band practice. Mom leaves a message for Carol Anne because I can't even do that much.

"Barbara, do you want to talk about it?"

"No. I want to stop talking about it."

I take a long shower, then climb into bed and pull the covers over my wet head, even though it's nowhere close to bedtime. I don't sleep but I'm not sure I'm awake. I see a few more glimpses of Travis, but I can't tell where he is or what's going on. Late in the day, I see him in what looks like a hospital room, curled up on the bed, shaking. He freezes, then turns his head and looks straight at me. As the vision fades he pulls up the covers. I hope he can sleep because I can't.

Or rather, I can but I don't want to. As soon as I drop off, I'm back on the school steps with Travis and that damned gun. Sometimes it's just us, sometimes we're surrounded by a crowd of kids. It always goes wrong: he shoots me, I shoot him, he shoots into the crowd, I topple the flagpole and crush the masses ...

After a few of these, I give up on sleep. I get on the computer and find my newsfeed full of a story I already know too well. No names because we're both minors, but loads of speculation and rumor. I feel like I should at least post that I'm all right, maybe dispel some of the crazier ideas, but I don't know where to start, and I'm afraid if I start I won't be able to stop.

I don't have much sense of Friday, other than staying home and hiding out from the world. I turned my phone off, stayed off the internet, mostly stayed in my room. I managed a couple hours of sleep between nightmares, and now it's Saturday.

Saturday? The show! It's all I've thought about for weeks but now it doesn't seem right that such a thing is still on. It's from Before. Maybe I should text the others, see if they want to cancel. Because how can we possibly —

"Barbara?" Mom breaks into my quiet freak-out. "Sharon Oakley's on the phone. She wants to talk to you."

I'm not sure I want to talk to her, but Mom passes me the handset before I can say anything.

"Um, hello?"

"Oh, Barbara, I hope it's all right. I got your home number from the school directory. Travis wanted to make sure you were OK."

"Tell him not to worry about me." Because I've finally stopped seeing him and I don't want to think about him at all anymore. Not that I can help it. "How ... how's he doing?"

"Well, they got him in right away for his psych evaluation, so that's good, I guess. I just hope he can stay out of juvenile detention. That boy wouldn't last a week in jail."

"Is staying out likely?"

"Janice thinks she can get the charges reduced to minor in possession. She called it a gross something or other. Misdemeanor? I think that was it."

"That doesn't sound so bad."

Sharon sighs. "It could still mean up to a year in jail, but if we can convince the court that Travis wouldn't do well there, he could maybe serve his time at home."

"Let me know if I can help." Why am I offering more help? Stop talking, mouth!

"You've done so much already. But Janice might ask you to write a letter to the court."

"Yeah, sure. Whatever helps."

After a silence long enough that I think we've been disconnected, Sharon comes back. "Did you really tell him he could be your bass player?"

"Oh, I, um..." So I guess I said that out loud. See? I should never talk.

"It's OK if you didn't, but in that case, you should let him know so he doesn't get his hopes up."

"I might have said something. So he wants to try it?"

"More than you know."

By the time I remember I was going to text the rest of the band, it's too late. So I get to do a show on almost no sleep — fun! They better not expect any dancing or stage presence from me tonight. Fortunately, I have an outfit with enough stage presence for all four of us.

25

ICE AND FIRE ... AND BIRDSHIT

CAROL ANNE

Whitney and Storm are waiting for me in front of the Eagles Lodge for load-in. I'm psyched — only our second time out and we get to play a real show! Provided, of course, our lead singer actually shows up. Her mom called Thursday to let me know Barbara wouldn't be at band practice, but she didn't give details, and I haven't heard from Barbara at all. The three of us worked on the set with me and Storm trading lead vocals, but it wasn't the same.

"Any word?" Whitney asks.

I'm about to say no, when a familiar orange PT Cruiser pulls up to the curb. Barbara climbs out of the back seat and says something to her parents before she closes the door, and they drive off in search of parking. Barbara stands there for a moment. She's not wearing a hat, and she looks ragged around the edges.

We gather around her. Whitney grabs her arm. "I heard you were in jail!"

Storm gives a half-smile. "I heard she killed a man."

I can barely whisper. "I heard you were dead."

"Oh, wow. I'm sorry. I didn't feel like talking about it." Barbara puts on the purple fedora she's holding. Jackson gave it to her for her birthday last summer, but I think this is the first time she's worn it in public. She added a gold tinsel garland for a hatband, something that can only work in December. "I wasn't exactly in jail; just detained for a few hours. Then I had to give a witness statement."

Whitney picks up her snare drum case. "So it's true! You got involved with the shooting?"

"Nobody got shot."

We climb a long flight of stairs up to the venue, and I'm glad all the bands are sharing drums and amps. It's one thing to tote a guitar or snare drum up a flight of stairs, quite another to haul a band's worth of gear.

"So you were playing superhero again?" I only heard about what happened at Maddie's, but from credible witnesses, so I believe Barbara did something ... unusual.

"Not so super, but it turned out all right." Barbara doesn't seem interested in giving details. In fact, she seems exhausted and like her mind's somewhere else.

A kid brought a gun to school, and everything is somehow "all right"? Nobody was killed or hurt, so maybe that's true. I try to lighten the mood. "I think the definition of 'all right' would be you somehow pulling a bass player out of this mess."

Barbara looks at me sidelong. "Actually, I kind of did."

"She's not sitting in tonight, is she?"

"Um, no. We'll talk about it after."

The venue is a big empty room with a stage at one end, raised bench seats along the sides, and a small 21+ bar area at the back. A guy with a clipboard meets us in the middle of the room. "Which group are you?"

We all look at Barbara, who takes a moment to come out of her fog. "Oh, right. We're St. Rage."

"All right, I have you playing second, but since nobody else is here yet, I'm going to have you help me do a line check. Then you can stage your gear on this side. When you're done playing, leave the stage over there so the next group can come right on."

We dump our heavy coats with the instrument cases and step onto the stage. This gives us our first look at each other's stage outfits. We decided for this Winter Break teen band showcase, we'd all wear shiny, sparkly things — kind of a Christmas ornament theme. Whitney's in her black disco outfit with the sequins again, and Storm's wine-red beaded sweater dress looks luscious on her. And I finally get to wear my silver dress onstage! Barbara's slow to join us; at first it looks like she's wearing a plain, dark dress, but at least it *is* a dress. Then she steps into the light and explodes in sparkles.

"Holy Tina!" I blurt. It's *that* dress — short, purple, covered in prismatic glitter. About time it came out of the closet. As it were. If it gets to make its debut under stage lights, then OK, I can think of worse things. I'm just glad to see her at all.

"That had awesome drama," Storm says. "You should enter that way, after we're all up here."

Doing the sound check is not so bad — we use the opportunity to warm up and run through part of our set. On the gig schedule, we'll follow a bluegrass outfit called Redneck Pagans. They're not using the drum kit, so Whitney leaves her snare drum set up. (What is it about the snare drum? It rarely matches the rest of the kit, and it's the one thing drummers don't like to share.)

By the time we're done and off the stage, the other bands have arrived or are coming up the stairs.

"Hey, Whitney, are you playing tonight?" It's a guy named Jad or Tad or something — I recognize him from Plague of Turtles. Singer, I think.

"I am. Are you?"

Straight guys really are that dumb, because Jad/Tad doesn't seem to notice that Whitney's breathing ice. "Oh, yeah, figured you knew. We formed a new group, Sack o' Hamsters. This is our drummer, Ike."

It's the entire lineup of Plague of Turtles, minus Whitney, plus this Ike character. They're all grinning, but Whitney looks like she could shatter the whole frozen lot of them. She rolls her shoulders and lets out a deliberate breath. "Cute name. Well, break some legs."

Redneck Pagans is a hoot, and four songs go by way too fast. Then it's our turn. Whitney takes her place behind the drums, Storm picks up her tambourine, and I strap on my Strat. When we're all in place, Barbara steps to the front. The glitter is blinding, but her entrance would be more effective with more strut. As it is, she's still dragging.

We start with "Huge Guy," which could follow anything and change any subject. I glance over at Barbara during the intro. She's bowed over the mic like she's asleep or something, but then her head snaps up and she tears into the vocal. Wow, far from being out of it, the girl is on fire.

I relax some and look out into the crowd. Now I'm glad all the songs are so familiar I could play them in my sleep, because what do I see? Marina, in the front row, eyes on ... me? The song ends and I have to change gears for "The Drink I Didn't Have Last Night." That song's so short it's always over before I want it to be.

I lost my nerve and didn't try to kiss Marina at her birthday party. Then we flirted for weeks during the musical, but never quite came out (ha ha) and said what we might have been thinking, if it was more than just me. I failed to ask her to Homecoming. We hang out sometimes, but I'm pretty sure it's going nowhere. But then here she is at the show, looking up at me.

On the next song, "Distracted Driver," the crowd starts to join in on the call-and-response parts. Very cool. Then we vamp while Barbara introduces the band.

"Thanks for coming out, everybody. We are St. Rage! On guitar, a guitar goddess come to earth, Carol Anne Cochran!" I'm sure my face is red, especially with

Marina grinning up at me. "On backing vocals, the smashing Storm Skye! On drums, the mighty Whitney Pratchett! I'm Barbara Bernsen, and I don't drive!"

We finish the song and transition to the gentler "Half a Bus Closer to Home."

When you have to go there,
they have to let you in.
Half a bus closer to home.

"Thank you! Good night!"

And then our set is done. I come off the stage, put my guitar back in its case, and high-five my bandmates. It's too noisy to review our set, but everybody's excited about how it went. Around us, the crowd's responding loudly to a death-metal outfit called Human Blood Rush. (If we'd known, we could've played our blood-donation song!) I doubt I'll be able to find Marina in the crush. But when I turn around, Marina has found me. She screams something I don't catch and throws her arms around me and kisses me. On the mouth. For a really long time. Because I'm totally kissing her back. I don't usually care for death metal, but Human Blood Rush is my new favorite band.

After the show, Barbara's folks meet us at the back of the hall. Apparently, they stayed for the whole thing. Pretty brave considering all the teenage stink and noise in the room.

"We'll go get the car and pick you up out front," Steve says. (Yeah, he insists I call him Steve.) "We had to park a long way off."

"Carol Anne, can we give you a ride?" Lisa asks. (Ditto). "And ... ?"

"Marina." Marina dimples up — always a thrill to

see. "Yeah, that'd be great if you have room."

"No problem."

They leave to get the car and we text our own parents to let them know they're off the hook. Storm rode with Whitney and her folks (who didn't attend), so we all stand out on the sidewalk and debrief the show while we wait. It was so warm inside, we don't even zip up our coats. Barbara's quiet again. I'm still in my happy place because Marina and I are holding hands and nobody seems to have a problem with it.

"So tell us about this bass player already," Whitney says. "Who is she?"

Barbara's breath fogs the air. "Not she. He."

"Um. OK, I guess. Was he here tonight?"

"Yeah, about that. No. He's, uh, at Children's Hospital for a few days."

"Shit, what happened? Not a bass-playing accident, I hope." Whitney looks around at us with a smirk.

"No. Mandatory psych evaluation. Then maybe ... juvenile detention."

Whitney's jaw goes rigid. "Who. The fuck. Are we talking about?"

"Travis Oakley, all right?"

"Oh, hell, no! That asshole? He could have killed us!"

"He didn't shoot anyone, and I don't think he wanted to. Well, except himself."

"And you know all this how, exactly?"

"I was there. I talked him out of it."

"Wow, Barbara." I can barely speak. Now all the jail talk makes sense. I thought she got swept up in the aftermath, but while we were all on lockdown, she was out there. With him. "You *were* playing superhero again."

"Not playing. I could have killed him."

"Well, why didn't you?" Whitney spits.

"Because Travis just wanted someone to see him. I know how that feels. I gave him the only thing I had to offer."

This turn of events makes me dizzy. "We really don't need a bass player that badly."

"No. I think he needs us."

WHITNEY

My mind is fucking blown. Barbara found us a bass player, and oh, by the way, it's that weirdo Oakley, who by the way almost shot up the school two days ago? I felt betrayed enough that Sack o' Hamsters got to play in the middle of the lineup, when the audience was bigger. Now this.

"We really don't need a bass player that badly."

Thanks for the understatement, Carol Anne. I'm too pissed to say anything, which if you know me, that's pretty damn pissed.

"No. I think he needs us." Barbara locks eyes with Storm for a moment. Storm looks away first, which would be interesting if I felt like thinking about it, but now I'm more interested in yelling.

"What are we, some kind of shelter for strays? No fucking way!"

"This isn't up for a vote," Barbara says. Wow, where'd all this backbone come from?

"So we're done. Great." I don't want to be done. We

killed it tonight. Way better than fucking Sack o'
Hamster Shit.

Barbara closes her eyes and drags her hands over
her face. "I'm so tired; I'm not saying this right. This
band is the best thing that ever happened to me. It's
like ... a force for good. The last thing I want is to ruin
it, but maybe we can, I don't know, share it."

"Sharing implies consent."

"I know. I'm sorry, I should have asked you guys,
but it all happened so fast. I kind of promised we'd at
least give him a shot — " Barbara's mouth goes round,
horrified, " — give him a try. If he's a bad fit, fine."

"I don't think we're worried about a fucking *bad
fit*." Do I have to say *violent lunatic* out loud? I'm
pretty sure we're all thinking it.

"He won't hurt you. I won't let him." Barbara's
voice and eyes go hard. It's freaky, but I'm inclined to
believe her. "Not that I think he'd even try. Anyway, we
don't have to decide tonight. It could be months or
even a year before he can play with us. But whenever he
gets out, he doesn't have much of anything else to look
forward to." She blinks and swallows. "Somebody our
age shouldn't be thinking about killing himself.
Somebody I've talked to."

I must have a hard heart, because her tears don't
move me a bit. "If my brother brought a gun to school,
we wouldn't be having this conversation because he'd
be dead."

Barbara turns and looks at me for a long time — not
angry, not trying to make me back down. Seeing me.
She nods slowly. "Yeah. I thought about that. It's not
right, but our skin might have saved us."

"Our?"

"Well, I was out there with him. For all the cops knew, we were in it together."

My anger kind of dies down as I try to imagine what Barbara's been through these past couple of days. She did it for us. And ... for him? For Travis Oakley, the loser's loser? "I still don't like it. Bad enough you're bringing a guy into an all-girl band. Does it have to be that creep?"

"He loves music. He likes our music. And he'll be getting some help — like, psychiatric help."

Storm shoots me a bitter smile. She's been seeing a therapist for almost a year. It hasn't been easy for her, but yeah — it's been some help. Still not happy about Oakley, but then I look past Storm's shoulder. Tall, blond, aggressively made up — here comes a monster I know too well, in puffy coat and high-heeled boots.

"Shit. It's Heather."

STORM

Our fun night takes a turn for the weird when Barbara and Whitney start arguing about whether to let Oakley be our bass player. Is there any question? I don't know what Barbara's thinking but that guy —

My train of thought derails when Whitney looks at me and does a double-take.

"Shit. It's Heather."

A goosebump-thrill runs down my whole body. I don't even want to look. I take calming breaths the way my therapist taught me, then slowly turn to face my sister. I haven't seen her in months. I'm glad we're not alone.

"What are you doing here?" I clamp my jaws together to keep my teeth from chattering.

"I might ask the same of you." Heather glances over our little group. "Quite the pack of oddballs you've assembled; and what gaudy costumes. Please tell me you're at least the star of this circus."

"I'm the backup singer."

Barbara steps up beside me. "Which everyone knows is the coolest role in the band." She glances up at me, clenching and unclenching her fists. "Say the word and I'll bring the birdshit on this bitch."

I so want to say yes. I was one of the privileged few who saw what happened to that jerk at Maddie's party, so I have a pretty good idea what Barbara can do when she's angry. She's scary, but Heather, even without superpowers, is scarier. "Thanks, but I've got this."

"You're going to fight me? The poor little baby who had to drop Cheer?"

"I'm back on the squad — captain this year. Stronger than ever."

"And also?" Whitney chips in. "She's with us, so you can just fuck the hell off."

"No surprise Skankney's still sniffing around."

"Fuck you, Heather."

I'm no street brawler, but a fight is seriously tempting right now. The three of us — Whitney, Barbara, and I — could probably take her. (I don't know whether we could count on Carol Anne and Whatshername, who is apparently Carol Anne's girlfriend — who knew?) On second thought, I think I'll try to be the grown-up.

"I don't need to fight you, Heather. I could call and report you for violating the protection order." Now my legs are shaking. I lock my knees and cock one hip forward in a tough pose. "What are you doing here?"

"Chill, Sis. I'm not threatening you, and I'm not in your house. I need to tell you something, but you block my calls."

"No shit. Who told you I'd be here?"

"I put it together — things Mom said, a listing in the paper."

That's unnerving. When I felt safer all these months, was that an illusion? "OK. What's your big news?"

"I'm getting married on New Year's Eve."

"Sounds romantic."

"Jared says it'll help out on his taxes."

"Well, I hope you'll be very happy." It's always been her ambition to marry a rich man. Now comes the part where she asks me to make nice for the sake of family. To be a bridesmaid, like we always planned.

"You're not invited."

That punch knocks the wind out of me. Why should it hurt? But it does. "Thank you for making the decision and saving me the trouble."

"You cold little bitch. You don't even care!"

I care so much my throat aches, but I force my voice to work. "Why should I care?"

"Because I practically raised you!"

"Yeah. I guess you did the best you could, considering." Everything I say comes out snarky; that seems to be the only way I can hold it together. I don't dare let up now, though, or it'll be no end of tears, and I can't show her that. Not now.

"What's that supposed to mean?"

Like she doesn't know? "It means you shouldn't have had to. We're children of an alcoholic. You coped your way, I coped mine, but none of it was good."

"Where's all this psychobabble coming from? You're not seeing a shrink, are you?"

"A therapist. Yes."

"So you really are crazy?"

"Hey, thanks to therapy and meds, I can almost eat like a normal person again. I was starving before."

Heather smiles. Even her smile is mean. Was it always like that? "But you had a thigh gap to die for."

"Yeah, literally. You said you'd kill me."

"I wouldn't have! You never could take a joke."

"Real funny. You know, there was a time I wanted to be like you." I can still remember us laughing together while she taught me to do my hair and makeup, how to walk in heels. So long ago. "I don't anymore. I want to be like me. Now get out of here before I report you."

I hold up my phone, ready to make the call. She lifts her hands in surrender, pivots and sashays off like a runway model. Nobody says a word while we watch her walk away.

Halfway down the block, she staggers a few steps — not like she tripped, but like she was pushed. Something white splatters on the back of her fancy new coat. Whitney stifles a laugh.

I glance at Barbara, who suddenly has a look too innocent even for her. She shrugs. "What? You expect me to stand here and do nothing?"

"Worst superhero ever." I give her a hug, which is not like either of us. "Thanks, Barbara. So now are we friends?"

She grins. "Absolutely."

I look around at the others. "This might sound crazy, but I'm less worried about Oakley than about Heather. If Barbara thinks he's OK, maybe we should give him a try."

26

THE NIGHT BEFORE CHRISTMAS

BARBARA

I'm not sure how I got through the show. After two nights with basically no sleep, I could barely stand. I dragged myself onstage in my glittery dress, convinced I would ruin the night for everyone. But when that familiar marching rhythm kicked in, I jolted to life. I hope somebody recorded that performance, because I probably couldn't duplicate it if I tried. All the feelings I couldn't put anywhere else, I poured into those songs. But after our set, I was done. I sat down and vegged off to the side for the rest of the show. Which gave me a front-row seat for a pretty spectacular kiss. I was right about Marina. Score one for me.

It was stupid to bring up the bass player issue, but when else would I do it? Travis was on my mind and I was too tired for filters. I wasn't in any shape to argue, and it could have spoiled a good night. I'm perversely glad Heather came along and interrupted. A year ago, I would have laughed at the very idea of me uniting with anyone in defense of Storm, at the idea that she might need me to. I wanted to call in an air strike so bad. Probably a good thing Storm insisted on handling things herself. But I couldn't resist a parting gesture. I'm not a superhero. I'm a pettyhero. So sue me.

Anyway, just like that, we're all friends again. It's still a huge surprise when Storm hugs me, and even more of a surprise when she says, "If Barbara thinks he's OK, maybe we should give him a try." It's not a done deal, but I figured she'd be the hardest to persuade.

When Mom and Dad pull up to the curb, I crawl into the backseat while Carol Anne stows her guitar in back. Then she and Marina climb in after me. The confrontation with Heather amped me up, but now I'm crashing again. My eyes droop and the last thing I hear is Dad asking where Marina lives and Mom saying we were the best band in the show. She would think that, but it's still nice.

"That's not power. This is."

I aim and fire. Travis falls back, a hole in his chest the size of a basketball.

"But I was aiming at the flagpole!"

"No!" I jerk awake.

"Are you OK?" Carol Anne asks.

"Um, yeah." My heart's going about a thousand miles an hour, but I try to hold my voice steady. "I guess I dozed off for a sec." I rub my eyes. "Where's Marina?"

"We dropped her off twenty minutes ago." Carol Anne climbs out and Dad pops the hatch so she can collect her guitar. "Hey, I'm gonna be around the whole break. Wanna do something after Christmas?"

It sounds like a real question, not fake friendliness. "Yeah, OK. Thanks."

"All right, I'll be in touch. Thanks for the ride."

Back on the road, Mom looks around at me. "Barbara, are you all right?"

"Sure." I stop to think, because that was a real question, too. "I don't know. Not really. I need to sleep for a week."

"You can skip church tomorrow."

"But the choir — "

" — can get along without you for one Sunday. Barbara, you were the body of Christ on Thursday morning. Jesus will understand."

Is that what I was? The tightness in my chest loosens some. I know I need more help than just a good night's sleep, but at least it's a place to start.

For the next couple of days, I pretty much just sleep and eat. Cookies, mostly, but some real meals, too. I emerge from my fog on Christmas Eve, my favorite day of the year.

When I was little, Christmas Day was my favorite, for obvious reasons: lots and lots of toys. Every

Christmas without fail, Mom tells the story about when I was a toddler and they put me to bed on Christmas Eve, decorated the tree after I fell asleep, then got me up and took me to church without giving away the secret. Apparently, I sat up through the whole service, eyes wide open, and even held a lit candle during "Silent Night." (Which sounds like questionable parenting, but on the other hand, there's such a thing as too safe.) I don't remember any of that, but I do remember waking up the next morning to a fully decorated Christmas tree that hadn't been there the night before, surrounded by presents, most of them for me. Christmas came to my house. Obviously, it was magic.

It's different now that I'm older. I get that it takes people to make the magic happen, so now I'm one of them. We don't always wait until Christmas Eve to put up our tree, but we're usually later than our neighbors. This year, they waited for me, and I'm glad they did; I needed to be part of the ritual. I love to decorate it with ornaments I've known all my life. I love the anticipation that comes from preparing for the next day: wrapping gifts, making food, hanging stockings. And yes, there is something magical about going to church in the middle of the night and singing carols by candlelight. It doesn't matter whether or not I believe the story is literally true. Somehow, the power of the Universe came to live as one of us losers. All I want tonight is to sing about it.

We leave the house early and drive around to look at the lights. So many people go all out — it's a real show even though it's not organized at all. That puts me in a festive mood. Then we drive past the church. The stained glass windows gleam like jewels lit from within, and surpass any twinkly LED display.

The choir is doing five anthems this year, and I like all of them, but I'm most excited and most nervous about one of the congregational carols, "Lo, How a Rose." A quartet of soloists will sing the first verse — unaccompanied — and I'm the soprano.

When I walk into the choir room to get my robe on, the rest of my section is happy to see me. I haven't skipped a Sunday in, I don't know, ever, so I don't feel guilty, but it's nice to know I was missed. Elaine, our choir director, is especially relieved.

"Am I glad to see you, Barbara! You're feeling well? In good voice?"

"Yeah, I wasn't sick. I played a show Saturday night, and it went pretty late."

"I hear you write songs. I hope you'll write one for us someday."

"They're not really that kind of songs."

"Well, you never know."

So now I'm imagining a choir of middle-aged and elderly singers belting out "Huge Guy in the Mosh Pit" in four-part harmony.

"What are you grinning about, Young Barbara?" It's "Old" Barbara, the alto of our quartet (who's I don't know how old—older than Mom, younger than Grandma).

"I'm not sure I can explain. Do you know what a mosh pit is?"

She shakes her head and gives me a questioning look. "Is it something to do with NASCAR?"

"No. Never mind, I was laughing at myself. Merry Christmas!"

We head up to the sanctuary to run through everything. Rehearsal goes reasonably well for that late at night, but I'm glad I stashed a water bottle under my seat. My throat goes dry just thinking about my quartet part. Then the organist starts his prelude, a sprightly French noel, and my heart fizzes with excitement. Christmas Eve!

All the lights are still on and down the center aisle, candles gleam in tall holders. From this side, the stained-glass windows are dark arches, but I remember how glorious they look outside. I hope they give joy to someone out there tonight. From the choir seats up front, I get to watch people come in. Most of them have dressed up for the occasion, more even than on Sunday. Well, a lot of these people come only once or twice a year, and this is one of the times. There are a lot of ugly Christmas sweaters, too, but they make me smile.

The service begins and we all stand to sing "O Come, All Ye Faithful." A few late coming faithful are still in the aisle. About halfway back, the usher seats a voluptuous redhead in a green velvet peplum dress, her hair done like an Andrews Sister. She takes her seat and is nearly outdone by the girl behind her, a tall blonde in a beaded sweater dress ... that looks familiar. Sure enough, there's a third girl in the group, all in black with bright green hair. Dear Lord, it's Storm, Carol Anne, and Whitney. I invited them to church that one time, but I didn't press it because I'm the worst evangelist in the world. Jackson comes sometimes —

I've finally persuaded him to sit in the middle, and he even sang with us once during the summer — but he's out of town for the whole break. With everything that happened, I didn't even think to ask my bandmates for Christmas Eve. When they spot me, they wave and my cheeks go red hot. I thought I was nervous before; now I'm actually shaking.

Which is stupid. Why should I be nervous singing in front of these three, of all people? But they've never heard me sing like this, here. Praetorius is about as far from garage rock as you can get. They might not get it. But ... they're here. They came out to church *for me*, this week of all weeks. They really are my friends, in spite of the bass player issue. It's the best Christmas Eve ever.

And I nail my solo.

27

RESOLUTION

So it's the day after Christmas — always a letdown. All the preparation and anticipation are over. The presents are all opened, and they're great, but now they're regular stuff, not magical. After our festive day, Dad has to go in to work. Mom's taking a day off, but she's cleaning. I join in, but it's easier to get into "cleaning up for" than "cleaning up after."

When the doorbell rings, I'm happy to get it, if only for a break.

"Merry Christmas!" Carol Anne hands me a gift bag decorated in metallic music notes and tied with a pretty gold ribbon. My gloom instantly lifts — I love getting one more present when I thought they were all opened. "So are you ready to go do something?"

My rescuer! I could kiss her! No, that would be awkward beyond belief. "Um, sure, almost. Come in while I get your present!"

I run to my room to get her gift, five packages of guitar strings, which I barely wrapped in the last scrap of paper on the roll. Making pretty packages is on a par with doing makeup — beyond my skills. "It's not much, but maybe useful?"

"Oh, yeah, absolutely! Thanks. Now yours."

I reach into the bag and pull out a knitted scarf in about fifteen colors, including black with silver threads. "Ooh, fringe!" I've always loved fringes on stuff, like curtains and bedspreads. Is that weird? Yeah, I'm weird. Don't care. "And the green matches the cap you made me!" I'm glad I wasn't wearing it that day with Travis. That black hat was nice, but didn't have any sentimental value.

"After yours, I made caps for everybody I know. You already had one, so I used the leftover yarn to make a scarf."

"So I guess we're going outside?"

It's not actually that cold out, but I wear my cap and scarf with pride. We catch a bus downtown and do all the downtown holiday things. Waiting until after Christmas is a great idea; the crowds are lighter, though with all the schoolkids on break, still pretty lively. Parts are starting to fall off the gingerbread village, but riding the carousel awakens my inner six-year-old. It's pretty tame compared to riding a real horse with Bailey, but I wave my cap and whoop anyway.

We warm up with hot chocolate at Starbucks across from the carousel. With whipped cream, since they asked. And sprinkles.

"So, I never got to thank you for coming to the Christmas Eve service."

"Barbara, I should be thanking you! It was so beautiful, especially that carol you sang with the quartet. I love that song."

"I was so nervous! I didn't think I'd have any spit left. Then you three walked in. I did not expect that."

"I don't know about Whitney or Storm, but I used to love going to Midnight Mass when I was a kid. I miss it so badly sometimes. It wasn't the same at your church, but it was good. Maybe better."

At the word *mass*, something clicks. "I, um, didn't know you were Catholic."

"Well, raised. I don't know if I am anymore. I feel like I want to be something, but ... "

"Bailey has church on horseback."

"*Everybody's* on a horse? Like, the priest and everybody?"

"She goes by herself. I mean, she goes to evening youth group with a bunch of kids, but the horse thing is just her and Swift."

"Cool. I used to be horse-crazy; think she'd let me join her sometime, if I'm out that way? But only if I can be myself."

"Speaking of, how are things with Marina?"

Carol Anne sighs. "On hold. She's out of town till New Year's, but I hope we get to do something before school starts again."

"I know I'm not much of a substitute, but I'm happy to keep you occupied."

She laughs at that. "I thought I was keeping you occupied. Don't you usually do stuff with Jackson?"

"Not the same thing at all!" Except it kind of is. With Jackson away, I figured I'd be moping around home for two weeks. This is way better. Plus, with Justin in the picture, I have to get used to giving Jackson some space.

"The good news is, my dad wanted to know why I was so happy after Saturday, so I told him. And he was mostly kind of OK with it."

"Mostly kind of?"

"He was beginning to suspect, so relieved to be in the know. But it wasn't what he was expecting from his little princess. We're going to do some sessions of family therapy after the holidays."

"Could be a lot worse. Congratulations!" We tap our paper cocoa cups together in a toast.

"Tomorrow, we ice skate."

Yeah, right. I never learned to skate. But Carol Anne has her heart set on it. Maybe I can sit and watch.

"Sit and watch? No way, you're gonna skate!"

I put it off as long as I could. We went to the IMAX first, ate lunch in the food court, and now we're at the seasonal ice rink in a big exhibition hall. It's only open a few weeks of the year, and the only other rink is way up north, so until now, it's been pretty easy to avoid skating. But that was before I knew Carol Anne.

I give in and rent a pair of ugly brown ice skates. Carol Anne has her own skates, dainty white ones with a silver stripe down the tongue. The brown ones are more punk. That's what I tell myself. I lace them up and stand.

"Whoa, these are worse than heels!" I sit back down.

"Come on, it just takes practice."

Carol Anne holds my arm, and we clump over to the opening in the wall. She steps down and glides out onto the ice before turning to face me. I hold the wall and step down. Right away, the blades try to slide off in different directions, and I can't do the splits. I cling to the wall with both hands and pull my feet back together.

"I can't do this!"

"Sure you can. Hold the wall until you feel steady. Or do you want a chair to hold you up?"

A chair? Oh, yeah, a lot of beginners are using plastic classroom chairs for support, holding the back and sliding the feet over the ice as they skate behind. "I don't think I'm ready for anything that might slide away from me. I'll stick with the wall for now."

Carol Anne makes it look easy, gliding on one foot then the other. I hold the wall and scoot forward with no grace or glide. How can this possibly work?

Carol Anne turns and skates backward. OK, that's showing off. "It's a lot like walking — shift your weight from one foot to the other."

It's nothing like walking. Except ... OK, there was a little glide. I'm still holding the wall, but I'm moving forward and not just scooting like an idiot.

"You're getting it! Mind if I take off for a bit?"

"No, go ahead, I'm sure I'll still be here. You won't

try any fancy jumps or anything, will you?"

She laughs. "I never got that far. I can stay on my feet, go backward. That's the extent of my skills." She turns and skates off confidently, but I feel better that she can't do tricks.

Holiday music blares over the ice, mixing it up with the scrape of blades, laughter, and the occasional shriek as someone goes down. A little kid who can't be older than six races past me at insane speed. A couple of show-offs perform spins and jumps out in the middle, but there are plenty of other beginners in need of support, whether from the wall, a chair, or a partner. I've gone about halfway around when Carol Anne catches up again. "You're doing great! Now let go of the wall."

"No way. If I fall, I'll never get up again. People will point and laugh."

"You might not fall. Anyway, what happened to that crazy-brave girl who doesn't give a shit what people think? Who started a band and thinks she's a superhero and faced a guy with a gun?"

That's a punch in the gut. "Thanks for reminding me, I managed not to think about it for a couple of days."

"Sorry. But why would that girl be afraid of a little thing like falling down?"

"Because falling down hurts?" She's right, though. Now I have to try. I let go of the wall and stand perfectly balanced and stable ... until I try to move. Both feet slide out of control and I go down, smack on my behind. "Ow, see?"

Carol Anne makes a heroic effort not to laugh,

which fails. At least she doesn't point. When she has herself under control, she instructs me to get on my knees and then use the wall to pull myself to my feet. It actually works better than I thought it should.

"Now what?"

"Use the wall to get yourself moving, then let go. You're actually more stable when you have some forward momentum — like on a bicycle."

I never learned to ride a bike, either, but I'm not telling her that. We covered this in physics, and I kind of get it. All right, I'll do it for science. I get myself moving, one foot then the other and let go for a couple of steps. At the first wobble, I grab the wall again, but now I know I can do it. I fall a few more times, pick myself up, try again. Before I know it, I'm skating all the way around the rink without holding the wall. Science rules!

"Whooeee!" I can't keep it in and I don't care who looks. I'm skating! Me! It's nothing like riding Bailey's horse, but the thrill is like that. Or like flying, but I didn't have to get angry.

I go around three times, singing along to the canned music and laughing at nothing, and then for no apparent reason, I start falling again. I pick myself up and immediately crash, like my ankles have turned to rubber. It happens again and again, at least five times.

"Goddammit!" I mutter and pound the ice once with my fist. It leaves a steaming little crater, which I take as a message to calm the fuck down. (And that F-bomb's another one.) I hope the Zamboni can smooth that out.

I manage to hobble to the side and lean on the wall

until Carol Anne comes around again. She skates up next to me and stops.

"What's wrong?"

"I have lost the ability to stand up. I just wobble all over the place."

"Are you getting tired?"

"I wasn't, but now I am."

"Show me."

I don't want to let go of the nice friendly wall, but to prove my point, I push off and go down in a heap. "See?"

"You need to tighten your laces." She waits while I crawl back up the wall. "Mine are feeling loose, too. Come on."

We get off the ice. It's as hard to walk on the floor as it was to skate, but I stagger to a seat. The solution can't possibly be that simple, but once I tighten my laces, I can stand and walk. It's a miracle. I go around once more to prove I can, but then I'm done. I turn in my skates and Carol Anne buys us hot cider.

"So you never went skating as a kid?"

"Maybe once when I was really small, but I never got the hang of it. And then ... poof. Invisible. Didn't dare do anything that might attract attention, like falling repeatedly." Come to think of it, what else did I miss? Skating, bike riding, dance ... "I can't believe I wasted my whole fucking childhood!"

"OK, Barbara, calm down. We don't want any birdshit on the ice."

I look down at my hands, clenched in fists in my lap. I don't know what St. Rage thought she was going to do, but there's no place for it here. "Sorry. I'm all right. Sometimes it hits me, how much I missed, and for what?"

"You don't still blame Storm, do you?"

"A little. Mostly I blame myself. Why'd I have to be so sensitive about stupid stuff?"

"Sensitive is OK; it's how you're made, right?"

"It's a shit way to be made."

"No, it's good. That's why you feel for other people. You have a lot of empathy."

"I do? No, I don't. Do I?" If I do, I learned it from Carol Anne. I don't deserve such a good friend.

She smiles and doesn't answer the question. "Speaking of Storm, I think we should do something for her on New Year's Eve, to take her mind off Heather getting married."

"Like what?"

"I don't know, maybe a party? I know, a band sleepover!"

"I've never been to a sleepover."

"Never? You really were deprived."

"Yeah." I pull out my phone.

"Who are you calling?"

"My mom, to ask if we can do it at my house."

It's almost midnight, and the four of us are sitting around in light-up party tiaras and pjs in the TV room, ready to blow our party horns. Well, I'm the only one in actual pajamas — red flannel with cartoon penguins. Mom and Dad have matching sets. Yeah. Carol Anne has a beautiful white nightgown with ruffles and pink ribbons and pearly buttons; I'm not the only one who gets sleepwear for Christmas. Storm and Whitney both wear T-shirts and sweatpants: black Ramones shirt for Whitney, pink glittery Disney Princesses for Storm, I kid you not.

Everybody else sprawls, but Storm sits there in full-lotus, like it's the most natural thing in the world. She tried to teach us some yoga poses, and I discovered I don't have a limber joint in my body ... except for my rubbery ankles.

They've all washed their faces, so I'm seeing them without makeup for the first time. Which, if I'm being honest here, is kind of a shock. The general impression is that they look a lot younger. Nobody here will be mistaken for anything but a high schooler. Whitney's mixed ancestry is more apparent without the mask of eye makeup and attitude. Carol Anne has joined our decade. And Storm? She has great skin and bone structure, so she's still pretty, but the wholesome teenage variety, not the supermodel kind. She must be a natural blonde because her eyebrows and lashes are almost invisible. She took out her contacts so she's also wearing glasses, which I didn't even know she needed. Being Storm, her glasses are stylish even though she never wears them in public. She looks hip and smart, like the librarian alter ego of a superspy. I could almost forget I was ever afraid of her. Almost.

We've had Thai food and ice cream and chips and pop, we've boogied to my party mix, we've watched a couple of movies. Dad went to bed at ten-thirty, but Mom's still awake in the next room, sticking it out till midnight with us.

"We should make resolutions," Carol Anne says.

Whitney tags her on the shoulder. "You first, then."

Carol Anne blushes. "I did mine early — I came out to my dad last week. But I guess I can try to be out at school, too."

"We'll be there for you," Storm says. "Right, girls?"

"So what's yours, Storm?" Whitney seems in a mood to direct, and I'm happy to let her.

"I resolve to not be so perfect." She laughs. "That sounds terrible. You know what I mean. I'm going to try to be myself, whoever that is. I don't have to live up to Heather's ideals. Maybe I'll finally learn trapeze." She shakes her head sadly. "I can't believe she's getting married without me. Well, I guess the wedding's over by now, isn't it? Good luck, they'll need it." She raises a Diet Coke can in toast.

"Now Barbara."

"You're the boss, Whitney. I guess I resolve to continue not giving a shit what other people think, and to learn to control my temper."

"Glad to hear it. I resolve to clean up my fucking mouth." Whitney grins at her own joke. "I mean, I'm practically an adult now. I don't want to sound like my little brother. It's time to act more mature."

"Good luck with that." I don't know how she'll manage, but I don't know how I will, either.

At the stroke of twelve, Mom joins us. We blow our silly little noisemakers and high-five each other. "Well, girls, I'm going to bed. You can stay up if you want, but please keep the noise down. Happy New — " The doorbell interrupts her good wishes. "Uh-oh, a neighbor must have called the cops on you."

Mom's wink assures us that's unlikely, but maybe no more so than a midnight visitor. Mom goes to answer it; we pull on our robes and tag along out of curiosity.

"Yes? Oh, Marina, right? What can we ... Oh, dear, what's wrong?"

And then Mom has her arms around a sobbing Marina. "I ... didn't ... know ... where ... else ... to go!"

"You poor thing!" Mom closes the door. "You must be freezing. Do you want some cocoa?"

"Yes, please. I've been riding buses all night." Marina moves to Carol Anne's arms. "I tried to call, but your phone's off. I called your house, and they said you were at a party at Barbara's."

I doubt she knows how weird that combination of words sounds to me. I find a clean tissue in my robe pocket and give it to her. "I thought you were out of town, or I would have invited you."

"We just got back. We decided to stay in tonight, and I ... " She starts to sob and hiccup again. "I decided I ... needed to start the year honestly. I told them I had a girlfriend, and they ... took it ... badly. They don't ... want me ... around!"

"Motherf — *of* — Tommy Ramone!" Nice save there, Whitney. Way to not break your resolution in front of Mom.

I'm thinking a lot of those words myself, though. I mean, what kind of parents ... "That's awful. When I was pushing Carol Anne to get together with you, I never even thought about how some parents might not be as accepting as Jackson's."

"You didn't push me, you encouraged me when I needed it." Carol Anne gives Marina a squeeze. "Maybe I shouldn't have rushed Marina to come out to her parents so soon, though."

Marina sniffs loudly. Her eyeliner is smeared and streaked down her face, and all over Carol Anne's pretty nightgown. "No, it was time. But maybe I should have prepared them instead of ambushing them."

Storm snaps her fingers, a loud pop. "Stop it, all of you. Don't defend people who are supposed to be the grown-ups. They need to deal."

Mom hands Marina a mug of steaming cocoa. "Storm's right. Marina, I'd like to call your mother and let her know you're safe."

"She won't care. I'll bet they're already asleep."

"That seems unlikely. Give me her number, and then all of you can go back to your party. Barbara? Get Carol Anne a stain stick from the laundry room."

I do my errand, and we troop back to the TV room. Not much of a party anymore. We give Marina a sleeping bag to wrap up in while she drinks her cocoa. We let her have the last of the pad thai, too. As soon as we hear Mom on the phone, we gather close to the kitchen door to eavesdrop.

"Hi, Meg, this is Lisa Adams. My daughter Barbara goes to school with Marina. We gave her a ride that one night, before Christmas? I just wanted to let you know she's at our house. Yes, she's upset, but seems all right. Uh-huh. He said that? But you didn't think she'd actually leave?"

I peek into the kitchen. Mom is pacing up and down, listening and nodding.

"A phase? Yes, I suppose that's possible — teens are changing so fast. Remember being that age? Whew! I know I gave my folks some sleepless nights."

She did? I might have to ask Grandma about that.

"Well, of course you don't, but why should it ruin her life, phase or not? For goodness sake, they're dating; they haven't eloped. Besides, who marries their high school sweetheart these days? You did? Congratulations. You were. Oh. I didn't know. Well, that's one thing you probably won't have to worry about. Sorry, I know it's no laughing matter; I don't usually stay up this late."

Mom makes another circuit of the kitchen and sees me at the door. She rolls her eyes (I think at Marina's mom, not me) and waves me away. Yeah, right. I step back, but we're all still listening.

"Let me tell you, I don't think any of us end up with the kid we thought we'd get. Barbara's been full of surprises this year."

No shit, Mom. You don't know the half of it.

"But don't you think it's a privilege to have that front row seat to someone else's life? You think they're like you until suddenly they're not. But it's still your child, your baby. Well, she's sixteen, of course she's rebellious! That's her job! But this ... it's just who she is. It's not about you."

I look around at the others. Storm's leaning against the wall, studying the ceiling. Whitney keeps punching her fist into her palm. Carol Anne is hugging Marina and stroking her hair, for all the world like she's the mom.

"Have you even met Carol Anne? Well, you should! She's talented and beautiful and generous. She made these darling knit caps for all her friends and family this year. Did she, a black and silver one? Yes, that would suit Marina's style. Uh-huh. Well, would it be so terrible if someday you have a daughter-in-law instead? Dating a girl won't ruin her life, but leaving home at sixteen might. Mm-hm. She can stay tonight — the girls were having an overnight anyway. Yes, Carol Anne's here, too. Ironic, isn't it? And kind of cliché, but if that's your choice ... I'll tell you what — all the parents are coming over for New Year's brunch here. Why don't you join us? We can talk more after we've all had some sleep. Good, we'll see you around eleven. Happy New Year."

As she hangs up, we crowd into the bathroom so as not to be caught eavesdropping, and so Marina can wash her face.

"Um, what just happened?" Marina's calm now, but wide-eyed.

"I think she invited your parents to brunch. And they said they'd come."

Carol Anne looks up from rubbing stain remover onto her nightgown. "Will that help?"

"Can't hurt. Mom's pretty good with people, especially when they're eating her cooking." I should learn to cook. Then maybe I'd be good with people, too.

Marina's cleaning her face, but meets my gaze in the mirror. "Is she like some kind of family therapist?"

"No, she's an editor."

Whitney grins, the first smile cracked since midnight. "Maybe that's it — she has a way with words."

I shake my head, because that's not it. "She has superpowers." And I will never complain about matching pajamas again.

28

WE ALL NEED SOME HELP

After dinner, I usually take my plate to the kitchen and disappear into my room to read and listen to music. Sunday night before school starts again, I stay at the table after I've finished eating. If Mom and Dad notice anything odd, they don't mention it.

"So, you think Marina will be OK?" I play with my fork and talk to my plate.

"There's a good chance of it," Mom replies. "Her mom seems supportive, and her step-dad is trying to come around. If she needs somewhere to go, she knows she's welcome here."

"Yeah, thanks for being so understanding."

"Well, I hope your friends' parents would do the same for you if you were in trouble."

I'm not so sure about that. Jackson's, yes, but I don't know the others that well. Marina ended up staying with us for a couple days, while her parents hashed things out between themselves. She wanted to go to Carol Anne's, but the adults all agreed that was too fraught (their word, not mine, and not as fun as *frock*). So I suddenly had a short-term sister, which let me tell you, was a shock. Either I'm constituted to be an only child or Marina's a bad match for me. We go to the same school and know some of the same people and like some of the same music, but that's about it. I like my routines and my alone time; she's flighty and needy (but to cut her some slack, maybe because of the whole family drama thing). Anyway, I had many reasons to be happy when her folks came and got her with tears and hugs and apologies and plans to meet with a professional. Which reminded me of my resolution. Time to ask for some help.

"Um, about that. See, I think I might be ... " Can't say *a superhero*. "I mean, I think I have ... " *Superpowers?* Not any better. "Stress! Post-traumatic. Maybe."

They exchange a worried glance, then give me understanding smiles. They're freaked out. Just as well to leave superpowers out of it.

"Still having nightmares?" Dad asks.

"Some." They've gotten a lot better, but I can use this. "I think I should talk to somebody who knows about this stuff. So it doesn't, I don't know, fester and get worse and come out in a bad way later. When I'm on my own."

"You're very brave to ask for help. We'll see your doctor for a referral." Mom's calm now, all business. Things are less scary if there's a schedule to organize. "I'll call in the morning for an appointment."

"Thanks. I ... feel better already." And I do. A professional will know how to fix this.

The waiting room has no windows and no fish tank. And come to think of it, no receptionist. (That must be what they mean by "private practice.") But also — mercifully — no piped-in music. Just the glass entrance door, and three closed doors to three counseling offices. There's the usual table of magazines and brochures, though. That's how you know it's a waiting room. Besides the people who are, you know ... waiting.

After all her talk of how brave I am to ask for help and how there's no shame in it, Mom's more nervous than I am. She came with me for moral support (and transportation), but she's starting to weird me out. There's another kid-and-mom pair waiting — a painfully skinny boy with floppy dark hair and gorgeous long eyelashes. They're quietly cracking jokes, so maybe not as nervous as we are, or better at covering it up. I've overheard enough school talk to assure me we won't run into each other in the halls. Even though there's nothing to be ashamed of.

"Hey, Mom, you don't need to sit around here." I give her a steady smile to show how incredibly fine I am. "Why don't you go get coffee? You can get some work done and meet me back here in an hour."

"Are you sure? I can go in with you if you want."

"No, I want to do this myself." I have to do this myself.

"Well, if you're sure. Here's the check for the co-pay. I'll see you in an hour."

Soon after she leaves, the other kid's mom gets up to find the restroom. We sit in awkward silence until I finally blurt out, "So, what are you in for?" And then immediately regret my phrasing, because what if he's doing some court-ordered thing, like Travis Oakley? But then would his mom leave him alone? My guess is eating disorder. Most people assume it's just girls who get that, but boys can, too. Anyway, that's what I read online.

"The lamest social anxiety ever," he says with a crooked smile. "My friends make me barf."

OK, pretty close. "Um, are they really your friends, then?"

That gets a laugh. "It's not anything they do. I want to hang out with them, but I get, like, overstimulated or something just thinking about it. But I'm on meds now that help, and I'm seeing Dr. Myers to learn how to manage my emotions or whatever." He waves in the general direction of one of the office doors. "So what's up with you?"

"I'm not sure what to call it. I'm most worried about some anger issues."

"Whoa, you don't turn green and hulk out, do you?"

That's not too far off, but I shake my head no. "This is my first visit with Dr. Burke, but I hope she can help." I look around desperately for some better topic. "Have you noticed anything weird about this waiting room?"

"What, no fish tank?"

"Oh good, it's not just me!"

He leans toward me in conspiratorial fashion. "I have a theory about waiting room fish tanks."

"Let's hear it."

"You've probably noticed how they all have the same kinds of fish? Well, what if it's actually *the same fish*?"

"Um, what?"

"What if all the fish tanks are connected through a dimensional portal? So when a fish disappears behind the big rock or into the coral thingy and doesn't come out the other side? It's gone to another fish tank. But it's not a closed system — fish die and get replaced, new varieties get popular and have to be added — "

Dr. Myers' door opens and a man in a dress shirt and slacks crosses the waiting room and exits without making eye contact with either of us. Like we're invisible, or he is. Soon after, a small older lady comes out and smiles at the kid. "No Mom today?" She has an Eastern European accent, which seems exactly right for a therapist. I could probably tell her about superpowers.

"She'll be right back." He stands and turns to me. He bangs his fists together and whispers, "Hulk smash," before he follows the counselor into her office.

After he's gone, it occurs to me that I initiated a conversation with a boy my age, and it wasn't completely terrible. Strange, but not terrible. Still, it's probably a good thing we won't see each other again. I don't want to make him barf.

A slim woman with frizzy blond hair comes out of

one of the other offices. "Barbara? I'm Iris Burke." She has an ordinary West Coast accent. I will have to make do.

Dr. Burke's office has a window but still no fish tank. It's like a living room, with a sofa, armchairs, and a rocker arranged around a coffee table. A stuffed bear flops against the arm of the sofa, and a box of tissues occupies a prominent place in the middle of the coffee table. Oh, boy. I pick up the bear in order to sit in the corner of the sofa. He has nothing to lean against in the middle and flops over, which is too pathetic. I hold him on my lap.

"Barbara, would you like some water or tea?" Dr. Burke goes to a small counter at the end of the room where an electric kettle steams next to a pitcher of ice water. "I have black tea, lemon, mint ... "

"Oh, um, yes. Lemon tea, please." My hands are freezing, so I mostly want something warm to hold. But my throat is dry, too, and we'll be talking. If I can figure out what to say.

She brings me my tea and sits in the rocker. "When you saw your pediatrician for the referral, did she prescribe any medications?"

"No, not yet, anyway. I hope I won't need any; I hate swallowing pills."

Mom already filled out some forms ahead of time, and I fill out another one with my personal details. I hand over Mom's check for the co-pay. Our insurance will cover up to twenty-four visits, which sounds like a lot. I hope I'm not that broken.

"So, Barbara, when you called, you said you were concerned about anxiety following a traumatic event?

Trouble sleeping?"

"That's ... *part* of why I'm here. I couldn't say the other thing because I didn't want my parents to hear."

"Well, everything we talk about here is confidential. That said, I encourage you to talk to your mom or dad, too; that is, unless you don't feel safe."

"No, it's just ... they haven't ever seen the other thing, and I don't want to freak them out any more than they already are. But a professional like you — maybe you hear this kind of thing all the time."

"All right. Is this related to the traumatic event?"

"Kind of? This has been going on for a while, but what happened that day made me think I could use some help."

"Let me see if I have this right. There was a shooting incident at your school? And you were a witness?"

"Nobody got shot." How many times have I said that? "A student brought a gun to school, and I talked him into giving it to me. Then I stayed with him until the police came, and we both got arrested. But I was released later that day without any charges."

"I can see how all that might be traumatic."

"It was intense! Going to jail is no fun." I can't get over how articulate I am sometimes. Should I mention how I watched Travis afterward? Maybe not yet. "I was glad it turned out OK and that I could help, but man!" My throat's already dry. I sip the hot tea, which burns my tongue. I set the mug on the coffee table. "I'm sleeping better now, but sometimes I still have nightmares, or I'll be out and a sound or a smell puts me right back there."

"And then you feel what? Scared? That he's going to hurt you?"

"That's not the thing that worries me. I did feel scared at the time, but before that, I was furious — that he was threatening my friends, my school, my day."

"Mm-hm. Maybe that's why you were able to be so brave."

"Well, yeah." I stop myself from saying "duh." "I was angry enough to kill him. In the nightmares, that's what happens." I squeeze the bear. It's very soft and doesn't seem to mind how hard I squeeze.

Dr. Burke nods thoughtfully. "So far, this all sounds like a natural reaction to a terrible experience. I can help you process the trauma. You seem resilient enough to recover."

"But what about my anger? Can you help me with that?"

"Barbara, anger is a normal human emotion. The fact that you wanted to hurt someone in an intense moment doesn't mean you actually would."

I squeeze my eyes shut. "But here's the thing. When I get angry, I have ... " I can't say it aloud. It's one thing to tell Jackson, but this is an adult. She'll think I'm deluded, and she has degrees and everything. I take a couple of deep breaths and try again. "When I get angry, I *feel* powerful. Like I could do anything, but mostly damage." That's so vague. She'll want details, I know it, but I can't tell her about the birdshit. Or flying.

"Do you mean you break things? Throw things? Lash out?"

"I ... oh. I did hit somebody once, when he insulted me. Humiliated somebody else when he tried to mess with my friend. But, no, what I mean is, I get angry and I react without thinking, and in that moment, it's like — I feel like I could flick my finger and totally wreck things up."

"Like a superpower."

"Ha ha ha, yeah, kind of like that. If superpowers were real." My throat is a desert. I sip some tea, which is now cool enough to drink.

"It's a strong metaphor. Have you always reacted this way, or is this something new?"

"Pretty new. Like, the last year or so? See, I used to be invisible — "

"By invisible, do you mean overlooked? Left out?"

I open my mouth to clarify, shut it, and start again. "That works." Like superpowers isn't deluded enough. "Then I started wearing a hat, and people could see me all of a sudden. I was kind of almost normal. And then that guy insulted me and I — " *can't say blew out his tire by pointing at it.* " — I just lost it. When I told Jackson about it, he said I was objecting to someone infringing on my personhood. And something about agency."

Dr. Burke presses her lips together and blinks a bunch of times. I'm pretty sure she's trying not to laugh. "And Jackson is ... ?"

"My friend. The one who gave me the hat. And he actually talks like that — he had a counselor and it rubbed off."

"Well, Jackson might be right. If someone disrespects you and you stand up to them, that's a powerful feeling. It might seem like you could do anything." Dr. Burke looks at me, calm and steady, which is probably something they learn in counseling school. "Let's go back to that day at school. You say you talked the other student into giving you the gun. How did you do that?"

"OK, first I yelled at him, and then I tried to get him to tell me his plans, but he didn't have any plans. I think he wanted to kill himself, or let someone else do it."

"So that's when he gave you the gun?"

"No, he still had it. He said it felt like power, which pissed me off." Should I tell her about the flagpole? There's a mark, but the pole's all scarred and graffitied. It'd be hard to prove which damage was mine. No, I'm not ready to go there yet.

"And what was the shooter's reaction when you got angry?"

Not *the shooter*. Travis. He didn't shoot anyone. But I say, "I think he believed I didn't need a gun to feel powerful. He ... invited me to kill him."

"And how did that make you feel?" If Dr. Burke is shocked, she doesn't show it. She's a pro.

"It's complicated. Before that, part of me really wanted to take him down. But as soon as he gave the OK, I ... lost my rage. I couldn't bring myself to hurt him."

"Interesting. Why do you think that was?"

"Because he seemed so hopeless. I tried to reason with him — convince him that we all had something to live for, which didn't get anywhere. I didn't know what to do, so I gave him my hat."

"You could have killed him, but you gave him your hat?"

"Yeah, he didn't have a coat and he was shivering. I offered to hold the gun for him while he put the hat on, and then I didn't give it back. I don't think he wanted it anymore."

She's watching me, not writing or anything. She glances up at the clock. "Our time's about up. I'm willing to work on your trauma issues, and I can recommend a good anger management group, if you'd like to try it."

"Oh. A group probably isn't a good idea."

"Do groups make you anxious?"

Can I say I'd like to maintain whatever secret identity I have left? Nope, probably not. "I'm not that great in groups. Especially if they're angry."

"Fine, we can work on those issues here, too. Let's meet again in two weeks. Meanwhile, I have an assignment for you."

"What, like homework?"

"Of course. You can't expect to do all your work in a one-hour session every couple of weeks."

"All right, what do I have to do?" I'm thinking she'll have me read a self-help book or take up meditation or something. Maybe keep a dream diary.

She closes her notepad and leans forward. "Anger is a response to a stimulus. Just like how pain tells us something is wrong in the body, anger is a clue that something is wrong in our world. You could treat the symptom and maybe feel better for a time, but that wouldn't fix the underlying problem."

"But if my anger causes other problems — "

"I'm getting to that. Your assignment is to pay close attention to what gets you riled up — or breaks your heart — and think about constructive ways to make things better. Don't just react in a destructive way, but use that powerful feeling. So if someone is disrespectful, you stand up to them, for yourself or for someone with less power. Or you take it to an authority. If a situation seems unfair, maybe you can try to change it."

"Like I have any say. I'm only seventeen — I can't even vote yet!"

"But you can write letters, join groups. And yes, I know there are a lot of things that are outside your control. I imagine we've both waited in the rain for a bus that was late. Neither of us can control the buses or the weather."

We share a laugh about that. Maybe sometime I'll tell her about flying to catch the bus that was early.

Dr. Burke continues. "So should I stand there and fume? Or should I find a stop with a shelter, and maybe invest in a good raincoat and boots for next time? I'll be very interested to hear your insights into what's making you angry, and how you can use that."

Does she mean use my anger, or my insights? Maybe both. Which means, if I'm careful, I have permission to use my powers. I hope I can still fly.

29

SPREADSHEET AND THE

SNOTTY PUPPET HAND

I've had a few days to work on Dr. Burke's assignment. I started making a list, which turned into a chart, because there's nothing like a spreadsheet to reduce stress. (That's actually on the list.) Here's what I have so far:

	A	B
1	**THINGS THAT MAKE ME MAD**	**WHAT I CAN DO ABOUT IT**
2	Drive-by insults	~~blow out tire~~
3		~~punch in nose~~
4		deep breaths
5		turn up music
6	Bad drivers	~~splatter w/ birdshit~~
7		~~throw something or nothing~~
8		pray for everyone on the road
9		lower expectations: assume they're all bad; celebrate the rare ones who aren't
10		learn to drive?
11	Teachers who all assign	~~blow up the school~~
12	homework like I only have their	~~go on strike~~
13	class, all due at the same time	~~whine~~
14		calmly explain the issue & ask for an extension (ha!)
15		make a spreadsheet & get to work
16	Bus is late	bring reading material
17		learn to fly?
18	Bus is early	learn to fly?
19	Person with issues brings gun to	~~splatter with birdshit~~
20	school and ruins my day	~~shoot with finger gun~~
21		trade hat for gun
22		give reason for living (oh shit)
23	General injustice: income	~~splatter with birdshit (but who?)~~
24	inequality, racism, homophobia,	~~shoot with finger gun (but who?)~~
25	misogyny, climate change etc.	buy street paper
26		write a song
27		stand up for myself and others
28		don't drive
29		vote when I'm old enough
30		???

If I ever get catcalled again, that guy better watch out. But other than that, I feel like I should save the actual superpowers for big-deal injustice, if I can figure out how finger guns and birdshit would be any use. But I probably won't change the band's name to

Spreadsheet.

Friday lunchtime. Carol Anne picks out a variation on "Huge Guy in the Mosh Pit," then silences the strings with her hand. "I almost forgot — Maddie says we can use her basement for recording."

"Cool, that'll be perfect." Whitney pats out a quiet fill on the table. "How soon can we get started?"

"Let's not schedule it till we know we're solid on all four songs." I almost said *perfect,* but that's asking a lot. We've had a couple of good practices since break, but we're not ready to schedule a recording session. "If we wait, maybe we'll have a bass player, too."

"Or not," Whitney says.

"OK, whatever." This is still a sore subject, obviously. We need to resolve it, but I don't know when. I hate to bring it up in practice, and I don't have time to argue about it now. "See you guys later ... like maybe next Tuesday." I get up to find a quiet corner for my free period.

Carol Anne glances up from putting her guitar away. "Where do you think you're going?"

"I need to churn out three lab write-ups and finish reading a novel." I'm trying my darnedest to catch up before the semester ends. Our weird schedule gives us a big break in December, and then we come back for three more weeks. Sure, that makes sense. Things went so sideways over the break, I didn't do much work, so I'm behind in almost everything.

"Well, we have honor assembly first, remember? Come on." Whitney takes one arm and Carol Anne the other.

"That's today?" We have these things every month, and everybody is supposed to go. Principal Ernest gives out awards to high achievers and makes inspirational speeches. It's a thing.

I'm so tempted to skip but allow my friends to drag me along. We find seats in the auditorium about halfway back. Whitney goes in first, then Carol Anne, and I end up on the aisle, so I at least don't have to feel crowded. Justin Hornbaker is sitting in the row behind us, and Jackson joins him after we sit down.

I slouch in my seat and think about the work I have to do. The principal drones on and on, and I start to take it personally. Why is he, of all people, keeping me from doing my schoolwork? I hold my hand up at shoulder level and work the fingers like a hand puppet — blah blah blah.

" ... is Student of the Month!" Mr. E announces with apparently genuine enthusiasm.

" ... is Student of the Month!" my hand says in a tiny mocking voice.

Carol Anne turns to me and whispers, "Since when are you a ventriloquist?"

I look at her and my hand says, "Since when are you a ventriloquist?" in that same snotty voice.

We stare at each other a moment, then face forward so we don't start laughing. That is one weird superpower. What possible use could this have? Maybe another spy thing? A surreptitious glance around identifies a test case, across the aisle and at the far end of the row in front of mine. Two kids are whispering together. I focus on the one whose lips I can see and work my puppet hand.

" ... kill for a hot fudge sundae," it says.

The girl in front of us turns around and shushes me/it. Carol Anne grabs my fingers and holds them closed.

I wrench my hand back and return my attention to the stage. I've lost the thread of what Mr. E is saying.

" ... for tremendous courage in a dangerous situation, we award this Certificate of Valor to Barbara Bernsen."

I sit there, stunned, as my hand snottily says, "Barbara Bernsen." I quickly drop it into my lap.

"Go be visible for once," Jackson whispers and gives me an encouraging shove.

What's he mean, for once? But yeah, I don't usually stand up in front of people by myself. I get to my feet and start walking up the aisle to the stage. I wish now we'd sat in the front row, because this is a long hike, even for me. Also, now I have to pee. I finally reach the stage and climb the steps like it's Mt. Rainier. No, scratch that; by the time I reach the summit, I feel like I've scaled Denali. I could use some oxygen. Mr. E shakes my hand and presents a certificate with my name on it.

"Thank you," I whisper and turn back toward the safety of my seat.

Then someone shouts out, "Speech!"

"That's a good idea," Mr. E says. "Barbara, would you like to say a few words?"

Was my raspy little voice not a clue? But I don't think he's letting me out of it that easily. I step behind the lectern and lean on it for support. "Um. Hi." I clear my throat and start over. "OK, so, I'm nothing special

..." ”

"Yes, you are!"

Thanks, Jackson. "I mean, I'm no more special than anyone else. I'm supposedly so brave, but if I didn't have this to hold onto I'd probably fall down, my knees are shaking so hard."

Sympathetic laughter ripples through the crowd. That helps some, but the size of the audience doesn't. When I've performed on this stage in the musical and the chamber concerts, it was dark out there; I couldn't really see the audience, so I could pretend they weren't there. Now, though ...

But there's Carol Anne, and Whitney right next to her. Jackson's behind them, and I hadn't noticed before, but Storm and her crowd are in the row behind him. I focus on them and swallow what I can of my nerves. "So, um, I guess you want to hear something about courage or heroism or whatever. What I'm trying to say is, anyone could have done what I did. I saw what was in front of me and tried to make it better. Maybe that's what a hero does. But when I think about Travis Oakley — "

"Don't say his name!"

Of its own volition, my hand shoots up. "Don't say his name." It's that annoying little nasal voice, far enough from the mic (I hope) that it won't be heard beyond the stage. I close my fingers and move my arm in a meaningless gesture, then stick my hand in my pocket.

"I can f — " *swallow that f-bomb because Mr. E is standing right there. God, I need to pee.* " — say Travis's name if I want to. I think I earned that right. I get that it was a scary day for everybody. But I saved one life that day: his. I'm not trying to glorify what he did or excuse his awful judgment, but Travis was one of us. And I can't help thinking we failed him. I failed him ... " Because what if I'd talked with him after Homecoming, like he wanted to? What if anyone had ever acted like a friend? I look up and there's still a big crowd staring at me. "Sorry, that's not where I meant to go with this. Obviously, it wasn't our fault. Maybe the opposite is true. What kind of world is it where a troubled kid can find a weapon and that's the first anybody realizes he's a troubled kid? But maybe we're the ones who can make things better. We can all be heroes. Sure, we're just teenagers without a lot of power, but we can still give blood, pick up trash, march for justice ... be decent human beings to each other. Save the world a little at a time. OK, um, I guess I'm done now. Thanks for this."

As the applause begins, I pick up my certificate and leave the stage. Jackson stands, and then the people around him stand, and then everybody else who can. A standing ovation? For me? Weird.

I don't return to my seat. Once I'm off the stage, I keep walking as fast as I can, straight out of the auditorium and into the nearest girls' restroom. I shut myself into a stall and take care of business, and then stay there, because now it's all catching up with me. Being visible is all right, but I don't like being looked at, I hate public speaking, and I don't feel like any kind of hero. I let out one loud sob, and then I hear the door open.

"Barbara?" It's Carol Anne.

"Yeah?" I grab some toilet paper to wipe my eyes. My breathing is shuddery with sobs, but I do my best to control it.

"Are you OK?"

"Needed to pee. And, you know, hide out." I flush and zip and come out of the stall. Carol Anne and Whitney are both waiting for me.

"We get it. Storm's guarding the door." Whitney leans on a sink. "Pretty good speech."

"God, how many times did I say 'um'?"

"I lost count." Carol Anne smiles and wraps an arm around my shoulders. "But what did you mean about failing him? I thought you said you saved his life."

"I saved it that time." It's still hard to stand up. I take a seat on the floor under the towel dispenser. "We've been in school with Travis for years. Did I ever have one friendly interaction with him? Did you?"

Whitney considers. "I must have passed him a joint a time or two. Does that count?"

Carol Anne shakes her head. "The closest I can think of was once he was listening to me and playing weird air guitar. Which now that I think about it was probably air bass, but at the time I was embarrassed for him. But Barbara, he's not your responsibility."

"No, I know that. Except, we're all kind of each other's responsibility. Aren't we? Even annoying weirdos deserve enough attention to notice when something's wrong." I shudder as a new thought crosses my mind. "It's probably not too late for Travis to turn things around, but what about the next kid who wants the world to notice him?"

"Chill out, Barbara. Let's deal with one annoying

weirdo at a time." Whitney crouches down in front of me and looks me right in the eyes. "So you really think Oakley's gonna be OK now?"

"I don't know. I think so. I hope so."

"And that it'll help if we let him play bass with us?"

"I'm more sure of that."

She glances up at Carol Anne, who nods. "OK, I guess we can try it. In return, are you ready to put your money where your mouth is?"

"What do you mean?"

"Marching for justice and all that. Dad wants me to take my brother to the King Day march on Monday. It'll be less awful with a friend."

Well, maybe I can do homework on Saturday and Sunday. "Yeah, OK. Probably a better idea than trying to fix things with a snotty puppet hand."

Whitney grins. "We are Snotty Puppet Hand! 1 2 3 4!"

Carol Anne and I answer in unison: "No." Even Spreadsheet is better than that.

True to my word, I go with Whitney and Hideo to a big Martin Luther King Day event — workshops, rally, march. It's a holiday I've never quite known what to do with before, but if I'm going to talk about justice, I better get on board, and this seems like a decent place to start. I went to a workshop on privilege and being an anti-racist ally, which seems to require the superpower of being able to talk to people. I'm not writing it off totally, but there might be better ways for me to be involved.

The rally had some good music, followed by

speeches that mostly couldn't measure up, except when a twelve-year-old kid gave the "I Have a Dream" speech. It was weird to hear a boy whose voice hadn't even changed talking about his four little children, but he knocked it out of the park. Made me kind of wish King had been a songwriter, because there are some sweet lines in there. Go look it up.

Anyway, now I'm ready to get up and move, so it's a good thing it's time for the march downtown to the Federal Building. I'm not big on crowds, so we stay at the outside edge of the group. Some people are carrying signs and banners. I'm glad I'm not carrying anything; it's finally cold enough for Carol Anne's hat and scarf, and I don't want to take my hands out of my pockets.

But I join in on the chants and songs.

"It's like the Sixties or something!"

"Or something." Whitney doesn't look convinced. "You gonna start writing protest songs now?"

"Well, if something comes to me — "

We bump into the marchers immediately in front of us when they come to a sudden halt, and someone behind us walks on the back of my shoe. I hate that; better add it to the list. I wriggle my heel back into the shoe. Somebody's talking up at the front of the march, but I can't hear over the crowd's grumbling.

Hideo's jumping up and down, trying to see. "Why are we stopped? This is lame, and I'm cold!" Snotty Puppet Hand would probably help if I could see who was talking, but if Hideo can't see, then there's no chance of that. I can understand why Whitney worries about him — he's a nerdy goofball, just a kid, but darker than she is and big enough to be mistaken for older than thirteen.

I still wish I could hear. I cup a hand around my ear and it's like I'm suddenly up there, too. Super-hearing? Well, thank you, whoever stepped on my shoe. I have another power.

Hideo ducks out of the crowd and edges forward a short way. Whitney adjusts so she can keep an eye on him, but none of us can go far.

"It sounds like the police are trying to stop the march, or re-route it or something."

"Fuckin' pigs," Hideo mutters, shaking his head.

"Language, Dee."

"Quiet, you guys." Whitney's prim expression kills me. Do I even know this girl? "The march leaders are arguing with the cops. Everybody's yelling, so I'm not sure — Oh, shit, no way! Here, hold this!" I whip off my cap and shove it into Whitney's hands, then leap into the air above the crowd.

Wait, what did I just do? Am I actually flying? It finally worked! Not only that, nobody's looking at me. I'm flying *and* I'm invisible? Cool. This flying thing would be cooler without the tense situation, though. The confrontation looks worse than it sounded. Not only police; police in *riot gear* block the street ahead of us. The lead marchers are refusing to change course; the crowd's shoving pushes them up against the cops' shields. Pepper spray is coming out, and this peaceful march is about to turn ugly.

Flying. Invisible. Can I do three things at once? One way to find out. I fling my hands out to throw down a force field between the marchers and the police as the first pepper spray is loosed. The spray doesn't appear to have any effect, so I guess the answer to my question is yes. Next question: how do I get down?

Oh ... fall. An awkward landing leaves me sprawled in the gutter at the edge of the crowd, right near the front. I should probably practice landing sometime. My heavy coat cushioned the fall, so nothing's hurt but my pride. Still, I'm in no hurry to jump back up; I feel like I just did the mile run in P.E. Around me, everybody is shouting and nobody is listening.

"Miss, are you all right?"

I face the Robocop visor of the nearest officer. Yikes. "Yeah, I'm OK. I ... I tripped." Attention is not what I want right now. I haven't been this close to a cop since that day with Travis.

He moves closer. "You with the march?"

I can't see enough of his face to be sure, but he sounds amused. "Yes. Any reason I shouldn't be?" I don't feel ready to try that ally stuff I learned this morning, but I guess if I have to —

"None at all." He raises his visor and Robocop transforms into a fatherly Black man, with glasses and a graying mustache.

"So, what's with the riot gear? This is a peaceful march."

"Some white supremacist wannabe called in a bomb threat; we can't let anybody near the Federal Building until the bomb squad checks it out." He sighs. "Somebody in charge thought we should be prepared for anything."

"What do you think?"

He looks around and shakes his head. "Not a good look for us on a day like this. But we need to make sure everybody stays safe."

"I get that, I guess, but I don't think anybody understands why you're stopping us. People in the back are starting to shove."

"Yeah, that's bad. Last thing we want is a stampede." He holds out a hand to help me up. I still feel wobbly, so I'm glad of the help. "Think you can talk to your people while I talk to mine?"

Talk to people? Me? "I'll try. Thanks."

He leaves his visor up, which gives me some confidence. I sidle into a gap in the crowd about where my force field used to be. When I'm near the leaders of the march, I form my hands into a megaphone — hey, the ear thing worked. "Listen up, everybody!"

Apparently I'm not wound up enough, or flying really took it out of me, because my message doesn't get beyond the few people nearest me.

"You have to say 'mic check.'" It's my workshop leader, an energetic young woman with a mass of braids emerging from a beanie. "Try it again."

I heard about this during that whole Occupy thing back whenever. Worth a try. I make my megaphone again and shout, "Mic check!"

"Mic check!" the crowd near me roars back, and the rest settle down as the words travel to the back. Gotta love a throng of activists.

"We can't march to the Federal Building!" I wait while this is relayed. "There's a bomb threat!" This part gets passed along, too. Excited muttering runs through the marchers, but they do seem calmer now that they have a reason for the delay. "Please don't push!" I'm not sure this is still needed, but better to be safe.

I look over my shoulder at the police line. They've all raised their visors and appear more relaxed. The officer who helped me up approaches. "You have permission to go to City Hall Plaza as an alternative location. It's only a couple of blocks from here."

I glance at the march leader. She smiles and nods. "Better than standing here in the cold."

"Do you want to tell them? I mean, I wouldn't want to appropriate — "

She shakes her head, smiling. "Kid, just tell them. You're doing great."

Great? Yeah, right. My heart is thudding and I'm ready to get out of this crowd. But, OK ... I started it. I do the mic check thing again, but this time I don't need it. My voice carries like I've got a police bullhorn, so I guess I've recovered. "We're detouring to City Hall. Get ready to march, but no pushing!"

In a feel-good movie, I'd sing the opening lines of "We Shall Overcome" to give the marchers something to do, but this white girl's done more than enough, and they don't need me for that. I lose myself in the crowd before anyone can ask how I did what I did. I edge toward where I left Whitney and Hideo.

"Barbara! Over here!" Whitney waves my green cap in the air.

I join her and reclaim my cap. Not a moment too soon — my ears are freezing. Hideo's not with her, but he can't be far off. "Thanks. Sounds like we'll be moving soon."

"Yeah, so I heard. What did you do?"

"Me? What makes you think I did anything? Besides fall on my butt in the gutter."

"Uh-huh. And where were you falling from, Miss Innocent Face? Last I saw, you were flying —"

"Shh!"

" — flying into the air," Whitney continues in a whisper, "and then you disappeared."

"That's your version. I say I tripped and fell, a cop who looks like your dad helped me up, and we figured out that nobody was listening to anybody else. He got things organized on his side, and I did what I could on ours. That mic check thing is pretty cool, right? Low tech but effective."

"Mic check. Right." Whitney's got her skeptical look on. She waves Hideo over as he works his way back to us.

"We'll talk later." I don't mind that Whitney knows what I can do; if you can't trust your drummer, who can you trust? But I don't know her brother that well.

"I'm bored and my feet hurt. Can we go?" he begs.

"I'm pretty beat, too. How about you, Whitney? Wanna bag this and find a nice warm bus home?"

"Yeah, OK. Let's go, as long as you really do mean home and not the Federal Building."

Now that she mentions it ... but there's a big difference between stopping a little pepper spray and containing a bomb. And my performance today wiped me out. "No, the bomb squad can handle it."

Hideo scowls at me. "Duh. It's their job. Why would *you* go there?"

"Right. I wouldn't. It's my job to check for snipers." I make a big show of looking through hand-binoculars at the surrounding buildings. Hideo copies me and even does some convincing video-game-style military chatter. The difference? My binoculars actually work. For one heart-stopping moment, I think I see a rifle poking over a balcony railing, but it's only a camera.

Whitney makes an impatient noise. "Come on, you two; save the world another day."

"That actually sounds exhausting." And in the movies, it always makes a huge mess. "Let's go home." And update my spreadsheet.

30

IN THE MONSTER'S LAIR

On a rainy Saturday, I get on a bus to go face a scary monster. I should be doing homework because I'm still not quite caught up, and the semester is almost over. But I'm the only one who can deal with this situation. This hero gig kind of sucks.

Actually, all this hero talk is mostly a way of motivating myself to get out and do this thing. I put on a brave face for Whitney and Carol Anne, but I'm a lot less sure on my own. If I'm lucky, I'll get there, and there won't be a monster; there'll just be a guy.

But monster or not, he's holed up in his lair. By which I mean an apartment complex on the far side of the freeway. It probably looked nice when it was new. Every unit has a balcony or two, with pretty decorative railings. I'll bet that was a selling point: Outside! Al fresco dining! Container gardening! These things are large enough for maybe two chairs, or a small grill, but not both. A lot of tenants are using them for bicycle storage. But more than a few have dead plants in pots, so maybe container gardening is an actual thing. Just not in January.

I have a choice of elevator or stairs. The elevator's out of order, so stairs it is. I'm glad I'm only going to the second floor because the stairwell stinks — that old-puddle-and-concrete funk plus what I can't help thinking is monster pee. I come out in a featureless carpeted hallway. Behind door number one, crying and screams; behind door number two, screams and laughter; behind door number three, laughter and music; behind door number four, music and explosions and shouting.

What am I doing here? I'm no superhero. Not today. I swallow an anxious queasiness. Behind the fifth door, shouting and a deep rumble. Dragon's snores? I knock before I can change my mind.

I mean, do we really need a bass player?

The shouting cuts off, and a skinny old woman with dyed orange hair opens the chained door. She looks me over through the gap. "Yeah?"

"Um, hi. I'm Barbara? I'm here to see Travis? I called this morning?" God, why am I uptalking? So nervous.

"Huh. Just a sec." She closes the door and the chain rasps and rattles as she slides it out of the socket. Then the door swings open. "I'm Alice. The boy never mentioned a girlfriend."

"Oh, no, I'm not — "

The rumbling cuts off (not a dragon; a bass guitar), and Travis appears behind her. "Barbara!" He's wearing sweatpants and a Dead Bars shirt. His brown hair is damp, shorter than it used to be and curling above his neckline. He's clean shaven now, too. He's no prince, but not a monster, either. Just Travis.

He takes several deep breaths. "OK. Grandma, this is Barbara. Barbara, this is Grandma. She came to stay with us while I'm ... you know." He raises his pant leg to show the ankle monitor. "So I can get to appointments without Mom taking off work all the time."

"And so he doesn't off himself." Alice plants herself on a futon couch and unmutes the TV, which blares some talk show. The futon is covered with a bedsheet, with a pillow and a folded blanket stacked at one end.

Travis is looking at me, blinking at regular intervals like maybe he's counting in between. But he doesn't say anything. I guess it's up to me.

"I called this morning and talked to your mom, but you weren't up yet. Did she tell you I was coming over?"

"I didn't see her before she went to work. Oh." He ducks into the kitchen. "She left a note on the fridge. I didn't see it before ... sorry."

"It's OK." We're both yelling, but Alice doesn't turn down the volume.

"Do you want a can of pop?" He says it like he's reading off a script for how to offer hospitality. "We have orange, root beer, and cola." The blinking speeds up.

"Orange, I guess?" I'm not thirsty, but he's so eager.

Travis returns to the kitchen and comes back with a can of store-brand orange soda for me and root beer for himself. Room temperature.

"Sorry. There wasn't room in the fridge, and nobody made ice."

"Really, it's fine. Who wants a cold drink in winter?" We're still yelling. "Is there somewhere we can talk?"

"Um, my room, I guess?"

"Door open!" Alice calls, like my grandma and Carol Anne's mom. Some teenagers must lead much more interesting lives than mine. Except without the superpowers.

A narrow hallway leads away from the living room and the shouting TV. Open doors show me a small bathroom crammed with too much stuff on not enough counter and two dinky bedrooms. Neither is tidy, but the one we enter looks like a laundry explosion and smells like boys — kind of skunky and oily. Now I'm thankful we have to leave the door open.

I've never been in a boy's room for more than a few minutes. Well, I don't actually know that many boys. I've never even been to Zach's house, and other than that one time when Jackson showed me his costume designs, we always hang out in the family room and watch movies. I wonder if I'm the first girl to visit Travis's room. Yeah, dumb question.

An electric bass and a pair of headphones lie across the bed — a mattress on the floor, heaped with rumpled bedding. The standard double mattress takes up most of the floor, with enough space to walk around it. Along the far wall are a bass amp, and books piled on a cinder-block-and-board bookshelf. Historical maps and rock show posters cover the walls, including one for a long-ago Plague of Turtles gig. Through a sliding glass door, there's one of those tiny balconies. A white plastic chair collects a pool of rain. I imagine Travis sitting out there on nights he can't sleep, hearing a noise, finding a gun ...

Travis flops onto his unmade bed. He does that weird blinking thing again, which spoils the effect of his admittedly pretty blue eyes.

"Is something wrong with your eyes?"

"No. I'm blinking. So I don't look like I'm staring."

"Right. The staring was kind of ... unnerving." So's the blinking, but I hate to say it. He's trying so hard.

"You can sit."

"Where?"

He leaps up and scoops clothes off a desk chair. "Sorry."

I sit down sideways and lean on the back, facing him in a way I hope looks cool and casual. I won't deny I like having something between us, even if it's only a chair back. I open my pop and take a swig. It's sweet and citrusy, and less terrible warm than you might think. "What's up with the maps?"

"I like maps. They show where things are. Historical maps are even better. How things were doesn't change."

"I like that Oregon Trail one. Did you ever play that game?"

"All the time! I even got all my people to Oregon

alive once."

"I hated losing anyone. I used to quit and start over as soon as a character died; I didn't finish too often." I can still feel the frustration, though I haven't played or thought about the game since I was eleven. "But after the first couple of trips, I always remembered to buy salt."

"Yeah!" Travis sits up, engaged in this topic. "Tricky, how you could only get it at the first shop. I used to catch all these fish, and then wonder why they went bad."

"Or bring back three-hundred pounds of bison meat, only to have most of it rot!"

"No, I didn't like to shoot anything. I did the fishing games and brought a ton of bacon. And a banjo."

I smile about the banjo, because I always had one, too. "I guess you still feel that way, huh?"

Travis frowns. "About bacon? Or the banjo?"

"No, um, shooting. Good thing you don't like it, right?" I give him a weak smile because this isn't very funny, but it's too late to not say it.

"Yeah." He's thoughtful, then perks up. "Yeah! I'm not that guy!"

That's a relief. I haven't spoiled both our days. "Maps are cool, but it's not like history stops when you mark it down. One event causes another, and another, until here we are. And someday we'll be someone else's history."

He spends more time thinking about that than it merits. Finally, he looks up at me, staring again. "That really happened, didn't it? Us in front of the school."

"Yeah." I can't hide the shiver that runs through

me. I'm doing better, but some days, that scene is still too fresh. I don't like to use that entrance anymore. That's one reason I'm here — so I can picture us both in a calmer situation. That was Dr. Burke's assignment from our second session. She seems to know her stuff, though I don't think she meant I should visit Travis in person. My imagination wasn't good enough to do it any other way.

"Would you change it, if you could?"

That stops me cold. Would I? Like, go to a different entrance? Or hide and phone for help? Stay home that day and not get involved at all? But then Travis would have been all alone. "Things could have gone a lot worse, so I guess not." I've had nightmares about some of those worse alternatives. We need to change the subject. "You shaved, didn't you?"

"For court and stuff. Lawyer's idea. I got a suit and tie, too."

"A suit. Cool. So, how are you doing?"

"OK, I guess. It's better than the hospital." He looks at me and forgets to blink. "This is gonna sound weird, but when I was in there, it was like you were with me sometimes; like you had my back. So that helped."

"Oh. Weird." I don't want to go into detail about how I could see him, but it's nice to know it did some good. "I'm glad you didn't have to go to juvenile detention. Your mom was pretty worried about that."

"Mom was *sick* about it. I'm not that far from turning eighteen, and I guess I look older than I feel or act or whatever. What if they'd tried me as an adult?" He looks terrified for a moment, then lets out a long breath and relaxes. "So yeah. This is also better than jail, I guess."

Or being dead. I keep that to myself. "You can go out?"

"To doctor appointments and all — I see a shrink, and there's a group class for how to act normal. And court things, to prove I'm going to my appointments. I could go to school, except I was expelled. That's what happens when you take a gun to school. I don't miss school so much, but I'm bored out of my mind. I end up watching way too many online videos. Did you see that one from the King Day march?"

"No. Why?" Now I'm the one who has to remember to blink. Of course there's a video, duh.

"I thought you might have been there."

"We left early. What happened?" Like I don't know already. What was I thinking?

"The guy was filming the police, but he claims he saw somebody flying."

"Flying? Wow. And it's on video?" So much for a secret identity.

"I couldn't see anything, but the image was all glitchy. It's not a finger gun, but I thought of you."

Thank you, Lord, for glitchy videos. "You must be bored. At least you have your grandma for company."

"It's so weird. I hadn't even seen her since Dad took off, but when Mom called her, she came right up. She's kind of an old crank, but she came. She says she'll teach me how to do laundry."

"What a great idea!" OK, that came out way too enthusiastic. "I mean, learning a life skill. Might help with the boredom, too. So, no dad, though?"

"He left when I was seven. Because of me being

such a little weirdo."

"That can't be true."

"No, that's what he said. I was standing right there."

"Well, that sucks." My dad and I have had our moments, but I can't imagine him ever doing or saying a thing like that.

"Before he left, he was trying to teach me to play guitar." He rolls across the bed and reaches to slide the closet open. After a brief search in the back corner, he extracts a tiny guitar. "Six strings were too much for me, so he took off all but two and tried to teach me power chords. I wasn't any good even at just two strings, and then he was gone. I thought he'd come back if I learned to play. I looked up how to put the other strings back on and practiced so much my mom had to make me stop before I hurt my hands. And I still wasn't that good. Better, but not good enough."

"You know it wasn't your fault, right?"

"I know that *now*. But music seemed like something we could share, and even that was wrong."

"I hope he at least left you his record collection."

"He took his stereo and all the vinyl, but he left 247 cassette tapes and a Walkman."

"That's a very ... exact number."

"Counting things calms me down."

I almost ask him how he feels about spreadsheets, but the tapes sound more interesting. "Anything good?"

"Yeah, some. There's a Trollrocket album I really like, and a lot of cool mixtapes."

"Never heard of Trollrocket. What kind of band was that?"

"Sludgy. They have no Web presence at all, and the tape just has the band name handwritten on the label, so that's all I know."

"So maybe this tape is like a collector's item!"

"I don't know, maybe. I've started ripping the ones that still play to digital. Some tape doesn't hold up very well."

"Smart. Tapes don't make up for your dad leaving, but — "

"Oh, and the bass!"

"What about it?"

"He left his bass and amp, too. Mom gave them to me for Christmas when I was twelve. She couldn't afford the Xbox I wanted."

"I hope you weren't disappointed, because that sounds like an awesome gift."

"Yeah. I gave her shit about it at the time, until she told me Dad left them. Once I learned to play some, I was happy. Happier."

"Not the same as having your dad back, though."

Travis sprawls back with his hands behind his head. His shirt pulls up to reveal a few inches of gut. "Maybe we're better off without him. Mom has to work a lot of hours to support us, though."

"What does she do?"

"Nursing assistant, and she tends bar on her nights off."

"That is a lot." Being a grown-up is sounding worse all the time.

"Yeah. She doesn't need my drama."

"Well, somebody needed to see what was happening with you."

"Maybe. I had to get arrested and expelled, but at least now we know some of the things that are wrong with me — depression, anxiety, at least one kind of spectrum. They make pills for most of them."

He points at the desk behind me. Next to the monitor stands a row of prescription bottles. I won't even try to pronounce the names.

"Do they work?"

"I think maybe. Better than pot, anyway. That stuff made me paranoid."

"Why'd you hang out with the stoners then?"

"Only group that would have me."

OK, I'm doing this. I hold out a CD in a paper sleeve. "It's not a pill, but here's something to help with the boredom. This has all the demos Carol Anne and I made, and Zach's recording of the St. Rage set at Maddie's party. Think you can work up bass parts from that?"

"So you meant that?" He beams. "I will absolutely work up bass parts!" He sobers as quickly as he cheered up. "The rest of the girls are OK with it? I don't want to make trouble."

"Travis, I think we can safely say you've already made plenty." He hangs his head and I feel bad for bringing it up, but it's the truth. "The others are ... coming around to the idea; as long as you don't make *more* trouble, it should be OK."

He looks up, a light of hope in his eyes. "Yeah? You think so?"

"Whitney needed the most convincing, but she's almost there. I'll tell her about that P of T poster; it might help."

"You think? 'Cause I have the shirt, too."

"Couldn't hurt to wear it. I didn't expect this, but Storm's reaction was almost encouraging."

Travis shudders. "Storm's scary."

"We've both seen worse." But I don't think either of us wants to think about that.

"Yeah, I guess. You guys start on your EP?"

"Not yet. We were gonna use the set from the Eagles show, but now I'm not sure."

"I saw that set on YouTube. Those are good songs."

Somebody — not us — put up a video of that show. It didn't exactly go viral, but it gave us something to share on our page and has gotten a decent number of hits. At least we have more web presence than Trollrocket.

"Thanks; it's not that. It's just, that set's missing something. Maybe I'll write a new song."

"Don't you have a deadline?"

"We're waiting for you, anyway. One song shouldn't be too much." I hope.

"Let me check this out." He settles the headphones onto his head, plugs the cable into his computer and slides the CD into the drive. After a moment, he smiles and picks up the bass. With the dragon rumbling again, he doesn't hear me when I say goodbye and leave the room.

Alice looks up and mutes the TV. "Good of you to stop by. You're the only friend to visit since Travis came home."

"We're not exactly friends." Oh, nice, Barbara. "I mean, we haven't known each other long."

"You know what he did?"

"Yeah, I was kind of there."

"Oh, you're *that* Barbara! Pretty brave, what you did."

"I didn't think it through. But you're pretty brave, too, to drop everything and come stay with him."

"I was surprised when Sharon called me, but what are grandmothers for? Would have been better to get out of Tucson in summer, but we can't be too choosy."

"And you came all this way to sleep on the couch."

"I wasn't about to kick Sharon out of her room when she works so hard. I don't even want to go into Travis's room." She wrinkles her nose. "So you came by to see how he's doing?"

"That, and we're working on some music together."

"Travis loves his music. Keeps him going."

"Is it true his dad was a musician, too?"

She nods and sighs. "You ever hear of Trollrocket?"

I glance back down the hall. "Not until just now."

"No reason you should have. They must have been the only grunge band in town that didn't get signed to a record deal."

Another piece of the Travis-puzzle falls into place. "Let me guess — Travis's dad was their bass player?"

"Cal was so sure they'd make it." Alice pats the futon beside her. "Have a seat; it's kind of a long story."

I guess I didn't have any other plans today. Homework can wait. I sit.

"The band had enough local success to think they could break out. They recorded one album, but it never got released. From what I heard, the recording process destroyed the band."

This is so not what I need to hear when St. Rage is

planning to record something. "That's too bad. What was the problem?"

"Oh, they were already falling apart. Touring was hard, and nobody had any money. They'd all reached an age where they had to decide — keep on with music or get grown-up jobs. Most of the guys had wives or serious girlfriends by then."

"Cal, too?"

Alice smiles. "He wooed Sharon with mixtapes. They met when her housemate was dating Trollrocket's lead singer. He went on to other things. You might've heard of him."

She says a name I recognize — not Eddie Vedder famous, but up there.

"When the band broke up, Cal didn't want to go through that again. He thought he'd settle down, work a nine-to-five job and be a husband and father. His own dad died in a motorcycle wreck when he was three, so he wanted to give Travis what he didn't have."

"So why'd he leave, then? Was it really because of Travis?"

"Travis was a difficult kid from the start, but I think Cal was unhappy with how everything turned out. He wasn't doing music, and he didn't like his job, and then he had this weird kid who wasn't ... that he couldn't ... well, none of it was what he'd hoped for. I wish he'd get his head straight and come back, but I don't know, after ten years ... "

I don't even know how to respond to that. It's more than I expected to know about my new bass player. I don't know whether it explains something about him, or adds another level of complication. There is one thing, though ...

"Does Travis know any of this about his dad and the band?"

"I doubt it. Sharon doesn't like to talk about those days, so I don't bring it up. Why?"

"Travis has a tape of that Trollrocket album."

"Cal must have kept a copy of the mix. Is it any good?"

"Travis likes it. Don't you think he should know?"

She answers quietly, like she's speaking to herself. "Maybe. What if it made things worse?"

"Worse than what? Bringing a gun to school? Getting arrested? He might have killed himself!"

"That's what I worry about." Alice squints at me. "Barbara, do you believe in Hell?"

"Like, literal lake-of-fire Hell? No, not really. I think it's more of a — "

"I forgot, you kids these days aren't into organized religion."

"Well, actually — "

"I was brought up to believe suicides went straight to Hell. So I worry, if Travis ... you know ... " She puts a finger to her temple, which is way worse for me than if she'd just said the words, but she doesn't know that. "So you don't think he'd have gone to Hell?"

"No. I think he was already there. I'm trying to help him get out."

"Don't hold your breath. I love Travis, but the poor kid's a born loser."

I get why she thinks that, so I'm not going to argue. But I think she's wrong. Bass notes leak out of the back bedroom. Although the bass line is all I can hear, from the tempo I'd guess "Half a Bus Closer to Home." Whatever it is, it sounds like a winner to me.

31

ST. RAGE VS. LEGION OF MORONS

CAROL ANNE

"You guys, this is so cool!" Barbara blasts into rehearsal with more spark than I've seen from her since our Christmas show. "We have a show in February, the Sunday of the holiday weekend!"

I take a break from tuning. "Nice! How'd you swing that?"

"That's the coolest part. They came to us — we got a Facebook message from someone who heard our set at the Eagles show. I don't know if they were there or watched the video later, but they want us to fill out their bill at the Skylark."

"Told you we had to have a band page." Whitney plays a celebratory fill. "What's the other band?"

"Legion of Morons. Must be boys, right?"

Storm arches an impeccably groomed eyebrow. "Legion of Morons? Is that the kind of thing we want to be associated with?"

"But the Skylark's a f ... reaking awesome place to play," Whitney assures her. "The sound's great, and they do all-ages shows. We'll be able to hang out in the venue all night, as long as we stay out of the bar."

I tap a pick against my teeth, thinking. "I've never heard of Legion of Morons."

"Not like we have such a big presence, either. The guy who invited us is ... Tod Something, or maybe Tad?"

"Fuck. It's not Tad Lanier, is it?" Whitney whips out her phone and stabs the screen. "That asshole. He just changed the name. He didn't even change the naming scheme." She shows us a Facebook page for Legion of Morons ... formerly known as Sack o' Hamsters.

"Does it matter?" Barbara asks. "The point is, they want us on their show."

Whitney rubs her sticks together like she's sharpening knives. "You know what? You're right. This is my problem to deal with. The past is the past, and it's time to stop being so fucking immature."

"Including your language?" I hate to remind people of their New Year's resolutions, but ...

"What? Aw, fu ... dge. Well, what are we waiting for? We have a set to rehearse."

WHITNEY

Sunday shows start and end early, so load-in's at six forty-five, and everybody's actually more or less on time, for musicians. It probably helps that we're mostly all high-schoolers without licenses, so our parents have to bring us. Even Storm, the only one in our group with a car, decided to ride with her family this time. Dad parks the station wagon in the lot below the café, next to a white van covered in band stickers and dust.

There's a ramp up to the stage door, as well as an outside entrance to the green room/storage area in the basement below the stage. We're playing second, so I'm about to unload my kit into the basement when a wiry brown-skinned boy in a tank top appears out of the back of the van. "Hang on, I'll give you a hand!"

I don't know him, but he looks vaguely familiar, and not so vaguely hot. Tank top in February seems early, but I'm not complaining. "That's OK, I've got it." I hoist the floor tom from the back of the wagon.

"The opener is a solo act; you can set up onstage." He grabs the kick drum and I get to admire his well-defined biceps. "We met that one time — I'm Ike. Ike Javier."

"Oh, right. Whitney Pratchett."

"I know."

He heads up the ramp, so I follow. My parents and brother are behind me with various drums and bags, so I can't be too obvious, but the view from behind is not bad. When everything is on the stage, I have to organize all the pieces into my familiar array. I don't usually let anyone touch my gear, but Ike's a drummer and seems to know what he's doing. I put him in charge of cymbals while I position toms and snare.

"I'm a Tama man myself, but these are some sweet Ludwigs. The clear shells look so awesome on stage."

"Thanks. They were my uncle's. He wasn't using them much so he handed them down to me. I love their sound."

Ike tightens the hi-hat clutch, positioned so I hardly have to adjust it. "I'm stoked St. Rage wanted to play tonight."

"I was kind of surprised Tad asked us. He and I have ... history."

"You can thank me for that. I nagged him to ask."

"You did? Why?" I get down on the floor to attach the kick-drum pedal — vintage Speed King that lives up to the name.

Ike positions a cymbal stand. "Because you guys are awesome! The best way to hear a band you like is to book a show with them."

"It's nice to meet a guy who can take initiative."

"Yep, when I know what I want, I go after it."

I sit back and raise my head, and he's looking right at me, but then turns away. I think he's blushing. I know I am. I've never flirted at the drums before. It's fun, but maybe time to walk things back a step or two.

"Tad's kind of an a-hole, in case you haven't figured that out yet." It's hard to stick to my resolution when the subject is Tad. This is going to be effing exhausting.

"Yeah, I noticed. Good singer, though." Ike spins down a wingnut on the last cymbal.

"He's come a long way," I admit. "When we started out, he mostly yelled."

"You've got skills yourself."

"Well, I've been playing a long time."

"I think it's cool how you don't have to play loud or show off all the time. You're very musical. Did you have lessons and stuff?"

"Yeah, since I was ten. You?"

"Self-taught. I can't do any really intricate stuff."

I reach into my snare case and pull out a book. "You should try this book of sticking exercises." He reaches for it, but I pull it away. "No, I need that. Get your own copy."

He laughs. "Fine. Hey, I need a smoke. Come outside with me?"

"Yeah, OK. I need to stretch, anyway. But seriously, you smoke?"

"Trying to quit."

"What? When did you start?"

"Middle school. I find it hard to believe you never smoked a cigarette."

"A little weed in my wasted youth, by which I mean ninth grade. But tobacco? Ew."

"Yeah. I just turned eighteen; seems kind of pointless now that I can buy them legally." We go out the back door to the deck overlooking the parking lot. Ike pulls out an e-cig.

"You've got to be kidding. At least a cigarette looks sort of cool."

"I know, right? These things help you cut down and make you look stupid at the same time so you want to get through it quicker."

I lean on the railing and take in the view of the parking lot. "Is that your van?"

"The Hunk o' Junk? Better believe it. Nothing like it for hauling gear, if you don't mind a breakdown every other month."

"Better than relying on the rolling refrigerator there." I indicate my parents' venerable Volvo station wagon. The Skyes' Tesla looks mortified to be in the same parking lot. "Is it any wonder I don't want to learn to drive?"

Ike laughs. "Could be worse." He nods toward the orange PT Cruiser at the other end of the lot.

"Don't diss Barbara's Pumpkinmobile. It came to my rescue at least once."

I go through my stretching routine — not that different from pre-gymnastics. I suspect Ike is checking me out, but he's not rude about it. And hey, I'm checking him out, too. He's in shape, and he's got sultry Latino looks, but with something Asian in the mix. I'm a total hypocrite — I desperately want to ask my least favorite question.

"I'm mostly Filipino," he says before I get my voice working. "How 'bout you?"

"Oh. I ... yeah. I'm half Japanese, half Black, all punk."

Ike smiles big enough to show his teeth, which are gorgeous. "So Whitney, who came up with that name — Plague of Turtles?"

"That was all mine. I had this plush sea turtle in my kick drum as a damper, and a plague of turtles seemed dire and silly at the same time."

"The guys talk about those days all the time."

"They need to get a life."

"It must have been something, though, to keep

going when you went off to different schools. I mean, what's your best memory of middle school?"

I have to chuckle as I admit it. "Plague of Turtles."

Ike grins and sucks his e-cig, which still looks like a pen with a light on it. Even Ike can't make that look cool. "Tad must have been crazy about you then."

"He said that?"

"No, it's more like the way he doesn't say it — like he actively avoids saying your name, but he can't help talking about the band. He says, 'our old drummer.' Seems like there was a lot of chemistry there."

"Oh boy, was there. Bad mix, though. We were — "

"Oil and water?"

"Baking soda and vinegar. That kind of chemistry — lots of excitement and a big mess."

"OK, I can see why you split up. And the band couldn't take it?"

"Well, I couldn't." I flash on how it ended. Maybe angry break-up sex can be good, but I don't recommend it if it's the first time for both parties. Definitely not my smartest decision ever. I shake my head to clear the image. "How many people stay with their eighth-grade project?"

"Tad must have wanted to."

I consider how he keeps re-using the same naming formula. I figured he lacked imagination, but maybe he can't let go. "You guys could do better than Legion of Morons."

"I suppose Legion would be a good name."

"Or Morons, depending." I consider their history. "What about Sack?"

He nods. "Sack could work. I won't tell Tad it was

your idea, though."

"No, he'd hate that."

As he finishes his vape, a beat-up full-size pickup roars into the lot and parks next to the Pumpkinmobile. The door opens and a lanky figure unfolds from the driver's seat.

"Yee-haw!" she yells, waving a cowboy hat.

OK, that's different. Ike and I look at each other and quietly slip back inside to order some food before the show. Ike joins Tad and the others, while I sit with my band and our families. All our parents have decided to come out and be the middle-aged St. Rage fan club, since we're not playing too late and tomorrow's a holiday. The cowgirl joins us too, because, as it turns out, this is Bailey. But my attention is elsewhere.

Dee punches me in the shoulder. "Hey, Nee, is that your new boyfriend?"

"Shut up, Squirt. Ike's a fellow drummer. That's all."

I'm not looking at Dee. Across the way, Ike keeps smiling at me, and Tad keeps scowling at Ike, which kind of makes me want to smile back.

STORM

Whitney's in a good mood. That scares me.

I wanted to play this show, but I was around when Whitney was with Tad so I know what a mess they can make. However, this Ike guy has her smiling and joking around like a regular person. Maybe I can let out the breath I've been holding.

The second surprise of the evening is the arrival of

Barbara's friend Bailey. I gather she came over to visit a brother or somebody over the long weekend, so our show was perfect timing from her perspective. But she won't shut up about the traffic and roads.

"I never saw so many bridges in my life!" she exclaims. "And this place, down in a hole under all those overpasses! I drove past it and had to turn around, and then I almost missed it again!"

"Bailey, do you drink coffee?" I ask, as nicely as I can.

"Oh, hell, no! You'd never shut me up!"

She's wearing a Western-style chamois shirt with pearl snaps and fringe on the yoke. It's a strange look for a rock club, but Barbara admires it — she's weird about fringe — and Bailey unsnaps it and hands it over! She's wearing a black tank top underneath and suddenly looks a lot more punk. Carol Anne stares a beat too long to be polite, especially with Marina sitting right next to her.

"Not for keeps, now, but I'd be honored if you'd wear it onstage."

"You bet!" Barbara puts it on like a jacket over her black shirt with the pink banana. She found some great pink jeans to wear with it, so it was almost an outfit until this fringe thing happened. Sigh. She was going to ruin it with a propeller beanie, anyway.

The third surprise comes when the opening act, The Fabulous Izzy J, turns out to be that same Ike, in his guise as a uke-strumming folkie in a flannel shirt and trucker hat. His songs are fun, and he's got loads of stage charisma. I mean, I could just eat him up, except Whitney's standing next to me, grinning and flirting.

We go on second. The place isn't packed, but it's full-ish. I don't even recognize everybody in the crowd. Our parents are as far as possible from the amps, but they're cheering and having an embarrassingly good time. They all took a pledge not to drink more than one beer. Mom's been good, sticking to soda water. She seems to be hitting it off with Barbara's mom, who's keeping her company on the wagon. Marina is right up front, dancing and making Carol Anne blush. Bailey keeps hollering and waving her hat. Zach and Maddie came out, too, but they've stationed themselves back by the sound booth. Jackson and Justin show up fashionably late in the middle of our set, holding hands and as cute as could be. I blow them a kiss from the stage.

And I'd like to think thanks to my efforts, Barbara moves while she sings. Not a lot, but enough. In fact, when we do the Taylor Swift cover and Bailey shrieks, Barbara gracefully sheds the fringed shirt and tosses it to her. Fringe or no fringe, that's a total rock star move. See? All she needed was a good coach.

32

KILLER ALGEBRA

BARBARA

Best. Show. Ever!

Yes, I realize we've only played three (not counting chamber concerts) and I've felt that way every time, but that's because it's true. This time, though — something magical clicked into place. Probably partly that we were playing a complete, well-rehearsed set. But also, Carol Anne was burning it up. I don't know what got into Whitney, except maybe showing off for her old bandmates, but she brought her A-game. Storm put on ripped jeans and flannel (and still looked like a model).

And Bailey was in the audience. Was I gonna just stand still and sing? I didn't think so.

Afterward, Jackson gives me a big hug. I like that more than I should, but I don't want to make things awkward with Justin. But when we break apart, Justin lifts me off the floor and spins me around. OK, I like this guy. He might be worthy of Jackson.

Bailey greets me with a screech and a crushing squeeze. "You guys are amazing! I almost didn't recognize 'Wildest Dreams,' but it sounded great! And your friends aren't bad, either." She winks and glances meaningfully at Jackson and Justin, who she's been dancing with for most of the set.

"Um, you know they're a couple, right?" I murmur.

"It's kind of obvious!" Her stage whisper is like anyone else's outdoor voice. Jackson guffaws and kisses Justin on the cheek. Justin's ears turn red, but he grins.

"So, Bailey, you wanna do something tomorrow?"

"Maybe in the morning? I have to head home about noon."

"Let's ask Mom if you can come for brunch."

"Ooh, brunch! So elegant!"

Whitney lets Ike help move her drums off, which is out of character for her. And then he lets her help move his drums on. Interesting. I want to ask her about it, but she's watching the sound check with rapt attention. Then my mom joins us, and by the time I look again, Whitney has disappeared.

"Mom, I invited Bailey for brunch. Is that OK?"

"Great idea. Waffles?" Mom hands back my phone, which I gave her for safekeeping. "I think it went off once during your set."

"Weird. Nobody calls me but you." But I check and there's voice mail. I can't hear much over the house music, so I excuse myself and take it outside. Not like Bailey needs me to make introductions; she's already best buds with everyone in the place. Across the parking lot, some unidentifiable couple is making out against a white van in the dark. I turn my back to give them privacy and listen to my message.

"Barbara? It's Travis. Help! Please?"

My first thought is that he's feeling suicidal and wants me to save him again. He left the message at nine and now it's almost ten; is it already too late? Not that there's any fast way to get there from here. I could maybe fly across the parking lot if I needed to, but that doesn't really help. My heart thudding, I call him back. It rings a bunch of times before someone picks up.

"What's the idea, calling this time of night?!"

I recognize that rasp. "Alice? It's Barbara. Sorry, did I wake you?"

"Oh, Barbara. No, I was on the balcony, having a smoke. What do you want?"

"Travis left me a message, and I forgot he doesn't have his own phone. Is he OK?"

"I think so; let me put him on."

I almost pass out from relief.

"Barbara?"

"Travis! I got your message — what's going on?"

"The judge and my shrink and my mom and everybody want me to get my GED."

"That's your emergency?" It's probably a good thing we're not face-to-face, or he would be covered in birdshit. "I agree with them; you weren't that far from graduating. But what does it have to do with me?"

"I looked at a practice test, and there are algebra questions! I don't remember how!"

"So ... you want me to help you study?"

"Yes! You're good at math, right?"

"Yeah, but I can't do much over the phone. I'm not even at home."

Behind me, someone comes out of the club. I turn to see who it is, as he yells across the parking lot. "Ike! We need you onstage."

So I'm staring at the couple by the van when they separate into Ike and Whitney. She gives me a flustered grin as she dashes up the ramp, straightens her lip ring, and follows him inside.

I tune back in to the middle of what Travis is saying. " ... come tomorrow?"

"Tomorrow? Oh, yeah, I'll try, but don't expect me early. Hey, gotta go — the band's starting up."

"You're at a show?" His longing pours out of the phone so my own heart aches.

"Yeah, we played already. It was great." I want to give him something. "But it would have been better with bass."

"I'll see you tomorrow." And he hangs up.

Remember that pile of stuff on my desk from when I emptied my backpack last June? I didn't want to think about it over the summer, and now it's kind of a fixture. After brunch with Bailey, I dig around and find some old algebra quizzes to share with Travis. Buses are on holiday schedule, so it takes a while to get to his place.

He's waiting at the door when I arrive. I find it encouraging that he's still clean shaven.

"Hey, Travis. Why do you look taller?"

He grins and looks at the floor. "Maybe my posture's better. I've been lifting weights — nothing better to do. Those were Dad's, too."

"So let's see what we can do to exercise your brain. Is anything giving you trouble besides algebra?"

I wave to Alice, smoking on the balcony, and follow Travis down the hall. He puts his finger to his lips as we pass his mom's room — she must be napping on this holiday. We tiptoe past and into his room.

"I should be OK on social studies and language arts. Math and science, maybe not."

"I'll try to help, but maybe there's a class you can take online."

"I do better one-on-one, unless it's something I'm already interested in."

His room doesn't smell as bad as last time, and the bed's sort of made. He's making a real effort. He drags in a second chair so we can sit at his computer and go over a practice test. It doesn't seem that hard.

"Maybe I should do this, too. Then I wouldn't have to write the research paper."

That was mostly a joke, but Travis sits back, genuinely shocked. "No way. You need to graduate for real."

"Why, though? Just to walk across the stage and get my diploma?"

"Well, yeah. They're probably gonna give you a medal or something, right?"

"A medal? For what?"

He stares at me. "For the thing. You know. With me."

Right. That thing. "No, they already did that at an all-school assembly."

"You got a medal? Can I see it?"

"Not a medal, a Certificate of Valor somebody printed out on the computer. Then I had to make a speech. It was really embarrassing."

"Wish I'd been there." He considers. "I guess that would've been inappropriate. But you still have to graduate. Because, you know. There's a hat."

Oh my God. He's right. It's the one time in my high school career when my whole class would be wearing hats. The same hat. So would I be invisible again?

"You make a good point, Travis, but that doesn't solve the problem of the research paper."

"What's your topic?"

"I don't have one yet; that's the problem. Got any ideas?"

"I don't know. What about some kind of music thing? Local. Like history of it?"

I'm too stunned to speak right away. Local music ... local bands ... from the past ... where are they now ... "Travis, you're a genius."

"No, genius is an IQ of — "

"One, you don't have to be a literal genius to be a genius, and two, have you thought about teaching? That's exactly the kind of suggestion I needed. So let's see if I can help you now."

We start into the math section. He actually does pretty well on geometry questions.

"It's like maps somehow," he explains.

"How far did you get in algebra?"

"I was repeating Algebra 2 when I got expelled."

"So it hasn't been that long ... "

"It doesn't stick, though! I can't remember anything!"

I let him calm down, and then we review polynomials and solving quadratic equations. I think he's getting it, and the review is good for me, too. After about an hour, he gets out of his chair and collapses face down on the bed.

When he doesn't move for a few minutes, I begin to worry. "Are you all right?"

"My brain is full." The pillow muffles his voice. He rolls over. "What's the point?"

"So you can get a diploma?"

"Yeah. Loser diploma, that suits me."

"Hey, don't knock it. People get into college with that loser diploma; they get jobs. What do you want to do when you grow up?"

"I don't know. I'm not good at anything useful."

"I know that feeling. I'll ask another way: what do you like to do?" At Dr. Burke's suggestion, I've been trying to do this for myself, starting with stuff I'm good at or like to do and coming up with possible careers. It's a pretty weird list, with everything from accountant to minister to singer to spy.

"Play music. Look at maps. Read about explorers and stuff."

"OK, so maybe something with land? Real estate, surveying. Title insurance, like my dad. Or, like, National Parks Service or USGS? Or I wasn't kidding about teaching. You could teach history, or ... "

"I never liked school. Why would I want to teach?"

"That's why! A lot of kids don't like school. What if the teacher knew what it felt like and did a better job?"

"I don't know ... "

"Well, what did you want to be when you were a little kid?"

"I ... I wanted ... to be a real boy."

Whoa. This is more Jackson's area, with his instinct for what people need and how to get it. "Now I'm confused. Aren't you?"

"I have the, um, parts."

"So ... you felt like you should have been a girl?" I try to keep an open mind, and there have been a lot of stories lately, even if I don't completely understand.

"No, I would have been an even worse girl! It always seemed like other kids naturally knew how to do boy things, and it was easy for them. I didn't get it, no matter how hard I tried."

OK, I can relate to that. I'm beginning to realize I'll never be the kind of girl I thought I was supposed to be. "But that doesn't mean you're not a real boy. You're just ... your kind of boy."

"But why couldn't I be normal?"

"Normal's overrated." I keep hoping that's true. "It is probably easier for some people. But you're making an effort. I see how hard you're working to get better, to pass for normal. And hey, at least you haven't died of dysentery!"

That finally gets a smile out of him. "I guess this is better than croaking along the Oregon Trail, surrounded by useless grandfather clocks."

"See? It's all a matter of perspective."

Travis rolls onto his back and stares at the ceiling. "I'm not in an open boat crossing the Southern Ocean in the middle of winter."

"Um. What?"

"Something else that's worse than learning algebra. You know Shackleton?"

"Maybe. Explorer, right? Antarctica?"

He sits up and reaches into his bookcase. "Here, you should read his book. It's about not giving up." Travis thrusts his copy of *South* into my hands.

"Thanks, I'll try to find time to read it. Unless you need it?"

"I've got it up here." He taps his head. "You reminded me."

"And just think — in a few weeks, you get to play bass with a bunch of girls. You'll be a better boy than any of us."

"Oh, God, what if I'm not? I'm such a loser." He deflates again, and here I thought we were getting somewhere.

I kind of want to give him a hug, except we're in his bedroom (door open) and I'm not a hugger, and I remember in time he doesn't like to be touched. Maybe I've already done everything I can for him. It doesn't feel like enough.

33

THE ONLY BOY IN AN ALL-GIRL BAND

CAROL ANNE

If we had to find a new practice space, we could do a lot worse than Maddie's enormous basement. It started out as an offer of a temporary recording studio — somewhere we could leave everything set up over a weekend or two. It was a short step to practicing there so we didn't have to haul the heavy stuff around. That's what we told Maddie's parents. We conveniently left out the part about how we couldn't practice at school anymore. Because our bass player — who we hadn't even practiced with; who we didn't even know was our bass player — brought a gun to school and got himself expelled.

I'm trying to be calm about this because Barbara is my friend and the band is worth the trouble. And apparently Oakley is doing better. But, man. I wish this was already over so we could laugh about it. But it's not over. It's now.

We'll probably go back to practicing on Thursdays after school, but to get everything set up, we're doing this first one on a Saturday. I came over early to hang out with Maddie and set up my effects pedals. I figured Barbara would be here early, too, but Whitney's next to arrive, with a carload of drums and cymbals and stands. She sets up in silence, but I'm picking up a distinct put-out vibe. Understandable — practicing at school was a lot more convenient for her. At least this part of the basement used to be a garage, so it's easily accessible from the driveway. Storm breezes in almost late — always making an entrance. Of course, she doesn't have a lot in the way of gear. She's dressed way down, for her, in a black velour tracksuit and canvas sneakers, minimal makeup, her hair in a simple ponytail.

Finally, Barbara pokes her head in the side door. "Sorry I'm late — Travis's elevator is still broken, so we had to bring his amp down the stairs."

"He's with you?"

"Yeah, his mom had to work today, so we gave him a ride." She looks around at all of us, but maybe especially at Whitney. "He's pretty nervous, so please, try to be nice."

He's nervous? OK, well, that gives us something in

common.

Barbara's dad and Oakley wrestle a bass amp through the door. Steve greets us all, but Oakley races back out without a word, returning with his bass.

"That everything?" Steve asks.

Oakley nods. "Yes. Uh, thanks."

"Let me know if you need a ride home."

Maddie pipes up. "I'm letting Carol Anne leave her amp here. Travis, you're welcome to do that, too."

"Oh! Yes, that would be a big help."

Oakley and I tune up and plug in our axes. "We'll keep the volume down for now, so we can hear the vocals. The PA we're using is pretty rinky-dink."

Oakley nods, but doesn't say anything right away. Finally, he blurts out, "I like your guitars. That's a pretty twelve-string. Is that the kind that's made for girls?"

"If it sounds good, does it matter?"

He turns red but doesn't give up. "What I mean is, it's nice there's a good guitar if your hands are small. Like, it would be good for a kid, too, right? I would've loved it when I was ten."

Now I feel bad about snapping at him. "Do you play guitar, too?"

"Not like you, but yeah. I still have the kid-size acoustic my dad got me."

Barbara claps her hands. "All right, let's warm up with 'Huge Guy.' Travis, you can listen this time, or play if you feel ready. Then I've got a new song I hope we can learn for the record."

A new song? For the record? Sweet mother, that's kind of last minute. I might have to talk some sense into Barbara later.

Oakley takes off his fleece jacket and straps on his bass.

Whitney stares at him. "You better have your shit together." Then she counts it off. "One, two, three, intro!"

Whitney and I play our usual marching thing, but something's different — it sounds deeper, and more supported. Because Oakley is already playing. He stutters as we transition to the verse, and the rave-up is sloppy, but other than that, he's got his part worked out and is in the groove. At least now we know the boy can play.

WHITNEY

I can't believe we're actually doing this. Oakley arrives, and he's exactly the awkward weirdo he always was. He doesn't seem dangerous, but he never did before, either. Who thinks it's a good idea to shut ourselves up in a room with this guy?

I've been in a mellow mood lately because of Ike. Tad even gave us his blessing — by text — which was sweet, if unnecessary. That's probably the only reason I'm still going along with this Oakley scheme. I agreed to give him a try, but I won't need much excuse to boot him out. Barbara says something about learning a new song ... wait, what? Did I miss something?

Oakley takes off his jacket and holy fuck, he's wearing an old Plague of Turtles shirt. It's pretty worn, but I'd recognize that design anywhere, considering I silkscreened about a hundred of the damn things myself.

"You better have your shit together. One, two, three, intro!" Carol Anne and I play our marching riff.

That shirt. I'll bet Barbara put him up to it, to get on my good side. But, wow, he kept it all these years? No, that means nothing — boys never throw a T-shirt away. Still ...

We finish the intro to "Huge Guy" and start into the first verse. It sounds better than usual, like some missing piece has fallen into place. And I know what it is, even though I don't want to admit it. I'm floating on an ocean of bass. Long time since I had a bass with me, and it feels so right. I'll even admit I'm impressed — he came right in, he's got his part worked up, and it sounds good. He's playing with his eyes closed, and he's obviously concentrating. He looks almost like a normal person while he's playing.

I don't mean to smile, but I can't help it, and then Oakley opens his eyes and smiles back. No, this isn't happening. I shut down the grin and keep playing. Damn, though. It feels good.

We get to the end, but the bass line continues for an extra bar before cutting off. Oakley's eyes snap wide open. "Sorry! I miscounted the ending. It won't happen again!"

"Whoa, take a chill pill!" Carol Anne says.

Oakley looks right at her, serious as fuck. "I can't. My dosage is one a day, and I already took it this morning."

"Oh, man, I didn't mean ... so you take actual chill pills?"

"The real name is hard to pronounce: fluoxasomething?"

Storm perks up. "What, fluoxetine? Prozac, right?"

"Yeah, the generic."

"I take the name-brand stuff, but at night. I can't take anything by mouth before about ten in the morning. Makes me barf."

"That would suck. It doesn't keep you up at night?"

"No, I lucked out that way."

Oakley nods, an intense look on his face. "I take it for anxiety. You?"

"Same. Is it working for you?"

"I, uh, think so."

Barbara breaks in. "It's cool that you guys are bonding over your meds, but this is still band practice. Travis, your part sounded good, even if you did muff the ending. Sounds like you've been practicing."

"Yeah, I play along with your demos every day." He gives me a tentative smile. "I like playing with real people, though. Whitney keeps a solid beat."

"Just doing my job. So what's this about a new song? I thought we had the record worked out." Can you tell I'm not in a mood to exchange compliments with Oakley?

"Yeah, me, too. But I don't know, 'Distracted Driver' seems kind of lightweight."

"Oh, and 'Huge Guy' is so serious."

"See, that's the thing. 'Huge Guy' and 'The Drink I Didn't Have Last Night' are both goofy, and then 'Half a Bus' turns heartfelt. Something more in that vein strikes a better balance, I think. So I wrote this new one."

I'm expecting something gooshy and sentimental,

but the song Barbara sings is actually driving and fierce. I don't catch all the words, but I like what I hear —

I'm a loser, but I'm gonna make it look like I'm winning.

We spend the rest of our practice on this song, nailing down the melody and chords and beats. By the end, we can kind of slop through it.

"I really like this one," Carol Anne says. "I agree it belongs on the record, if we think we can learn it that fast. But we've never turned anything around that quickly."

"Let's play it again." I can't believe I said that out loud, but yeah, I like this song.

Oakley nods and smiles at me. This time, I smile back.

STORM

Everybody in this band is in therapy. Well, except for Whitney, but she gets to hit things.

I don't know the details on Barbara, only that she mentioned a counseling appointment once. And who am I to judge? Carol Anne's is more for her parents than for her. They needed help with the idea that their daughter likes girls. I'm like, hey, there's way worse things: Exhibit A, my psycho sister; Exhibit B, Travis Oakley with a gun. So his therapy is court-ordered, and it better be working.

Whitney was the least receptive to our new bass player, but by the day of our first practice with him, I'm ready to back out, too. I mean, I guess I owe Barbara for how she stood up to Heather with me. But this Oakley dude — will he freak out and try to kill us? Or will he be intolerably weird? Either way, by the time he shows and we're ready to start, I'm feeling more tense, not less.

I get through the first part of our practice by pretending he's not there. I play my tambourine and shout out "Mosh pit!" like always. And then Carol Anne makes a flip remark about a chill pill, and before I know it, Oakley and I are having a discussion about the effectiveness of Prozac to treat anxiety. Weirdly, everybody's anxiety level seems to drop.

Then we start learning a new song, even though it's kind of late in the game if we want to record it. But it's a good enough song to keep playing over and over.

"I like it, except where you sing 'We're all losers.' I mean, I have to think about my brand." Wait, did I say that out loud? I guess I'm still one of those girls, at least until graduation. Which can't come soon enough, and this is my senior project, so maybe I should put up with whatever.

"Do you think she should sing 'We're all losers except for Storm, obviously'?" Whitney hits a rim shot. "Doesn't really scan."

"I like it," Carol Anne says. "It could mean all of us in the band, or all of us in high school, or all of us on the planet. I bet everybody feels like a loser sometimes."

"Or some of us, all the time," Oakley mutters.

"Carol Anne gets it." Barbara squeezes Oakley's shoulder. He leans into it for a moment, then twitches away. "What we see on the outside of people doesn't always tell us what's going on inside. Storm, you work awfully hard to protect your — did you actually say brand? — OK, I respect that. The point is not that you *are* a loser, but that you feel like one sometimes. Because you're a human being, and things sometimes go wrong. Right?"

"Whatever. Let's just ... play the song again." I hate it when she's right.

34

LOSER

TRAVIS

St. Rage is recording in Maddie Gowan's basement, and I am their bass player. Yeah, I can't believe it either.

Playing music, I feel almost normal; playing with other people, almost happy. And with friends? Well. I don't know whether they're my friends exactly, but they haven't kicked me out yet. I take what I can get.

We finished "Huge Guy in the Mosh Pit" and "Half a Bus Closer to Home" last weekend. The girls have been playing those songs for almost a year, and I'd been practicing my part for months, so that session went smoothly. Why wouldn't it?

We were so spoiled. This morning, we're trying to do "The Drink I Didn't Have Last Night Is the Drink I Shoulda Had." It's the shortest of the four songs, but it's taking a lot more time than anybody expected.

Barbara takes off her green cap and runs her hand through her hair. "I don't know, maybe we should go back to how we used to do it."

Carol Anne removes her headphones and takes a swig from a water bottle. "No, I think you were right. These new harmonies will give it a more obvious country feel. I just wish we'd worked them out before today."

"OK, well, let's rehearse it a few more times before we try to record."

"Could I hear you do my part?" Storm asks. "I feel like I know it, but then I can't remember it all when I have to sing."

"Whatever will help. Zach, can you play the rough mix over the speakers?"

Zach Brown is on the project as recording engineer, so at least I'm not the only guy in the room. We all get quiet as we listen to the guitar intro. Barbara mouths the words over her recorded solo verse. Well, I guess we all do. On the chorus she jumps up to the high harmony to demonstrate Storm's part. It's not complicated, and it sounds believably country with the melody. Even Grandma would like it.

"OK, everybody, let's try it together this time."

Zach starts the song over. This time, Barbara sings along with her recorded lead part, with the backing parts "oohing" lightly in harmony over the verse, then switching to words on the chorus.

"I'm a punk rock girl," I sing, as loud as I can in falsetto.

Everybody stops and stares at me. Zach buries his head in his computer keyboard. Whitney laughs helplessly back there behind the drums.

"Travis?" Barbara, at least, is trying not to laugh.

"Oh. By 'everybody,' you meant Storm and Carol Anne."

"I did, but Travis!" Her eyes — they're brown, by the way — look huge, and she's grinning. "I didn't know you could sing. You are hereby enlisted as a backup singer."

"OK, I guess." I've always sung along with the radio and in the shower, to my mom's amusement and eventual annoyance. In front of anyone else, not so much. I don't know what got into me. If it were anyone but Barbara, I'd flat refuse. But it is Barbara. I'll pretty much do whatever she says. "So is there a third part for me, or what?"

"Let's not make it worse than it already is. Sing Storm's part with her."

"You want me to sing about being a punk rock girl?"

Now she does laugh. Can't really hold it against her. "Especially that! Anyway, I try to keep an open mind."

I don't want to take too much credit, but after that, we finish recording the backing vocals in about ten minutes. We break for pizza, and then back to work. The only song left is the new one, a punk anthem called "Loser."

Whitney counts it off and thumps out a series of straight kick drum hits. Carol Anne comes in with big chords. Then I join in and we fill the basement with sound. We're recording the instrumentals as a band to capture more of a live feel, and it feels great. I can almost imagine we're up on stage somewhere. I lay down my bass lines on top of Whitney's solid beat. Whether or not we're friends, we make a strong rhythm section. She's really focused, but when we have our groove going, she'll throw me a quick smile. It's a privilege to play anywhere near Carol Anne. Storm is too beautiful to look at, and I don't know what to say to her. You can get only so much conversation out of anxiety meds. But I can handle singing with her.

And then there's Barbara.

She doesn't play an instrument, so she's watching and listening while we play. I don't know about the others, but that kind of makes me nervous — more than it would if she were up front singing. During the second take, she wanders to the other end of the room, and I breathe easier.

Zach pastes together the best of both takes into a single backing track. Barbara's back, and she approves of his choices. (But when did Barbara come back? She's like a ninja. She took her hat off; I think that confused me.) The rest of us sit back and listen while she adds the lead vocal.

The song's about not being popular ... and not giving a shit. That's actually the first line, almost verbatim. Barbara shout-sings the opening, then slips into the melody and sings through to the end.

I know I'm a loser,
so why do I feel like I'm winning?
When she gets to the high part in the bridge, her

pure, unaccompanied voice is sort of eerie. Enough of the band track leaks from the headphones that I can tell she's right with it. And when this song is finished, so is the record, a four-song EP we're making for our senior project. Well, *their* senior project.

I regret the reason for it, but being expelled was the best thing to happen to me in years. School was getting me down, and I wasn't going to graduate on time, or at all. Barbara's making me study for the GED so I can maybe go to college. I never planned on college, but I'll take the test for her.

I still have the hat she gave me. I should give it back, but she hasn't asked for it. When I can't sleep and I feel like nobody, or when I wake up from nightmares and feel like a monster, I put on Barbara's dorky, furry hat and remember.

Barbara should have run away, but she didn't. She walked up to me and stopped me doing something ... permanent. She saved my life.

And then she let me be in her band.

I guess they almost broke up over that decision. Bad enough she was bringing a guy into an all-girl band, but that guy happened to be the loser who brought a gun to school.

That I'm here at all says a huge amount about how much the rest of the band respects Barbara.

Once Barbara and Zach are both satisfied with her track, Storm and Carol Anne lay down their backing vocals, and then everybody's ready for a break. Barbara heads into the basement mudroom, and Maddie takes Whitney and Carol Anne upstairs to find other bathrooms, plural, because this house is huge. Well, compared to my apartment, anyway, which isn't saying much. Storm goes outside where the cell reception is better. Good of her to leave the door open; the fresh air wakes me up. I didn't realize how stuffy it was getting in here. No wonder Barbara took her hat off.

I wander over to watch Zach do mysterious things on his computer. "It's cool that you have all this gear." Zach took a Saturday class in sound engineering. I wish I'd done something like that when I had the chance.

"Well, the computer's mine. We all chipped in to rent the rest of it." Zach looks up at me, all puzzled-like. "That's the most I've heard you talk since we started this project, but you never used to shut up. What gives?"

He's got that right. I talk too much or not at all, so lately I've been deliberately going for not at all. "I weird girls out."

"Dude, no offense, but you weird everybody out. Always have. That's maybe the least of your problems."

True, but it doesn't help. "OK, but still ... how do you know what to say to girls?"

"I don't. Huge nerd over here."

"You have a girlfriend. You work with this band."

"Dude, my girlfriend is a bigger nerd than I am. And you're *in* this band."

"Yeah, but mostly I don't talk. I just nod my head and do what I'm told."

"OK, good point. For what it's worth, it seems if you talk to them like people, you'll usually be all right."

"Like I'm people?"

Zach looks at me like I'm a world-champion moron, which I probably am. "Yeah, dude, like everybody's people, including you."

That's gonna be hard. Like he said, I weird people out. I think I'll just play bass and keep my mouth shut.

When everybody comes back, we listen to the rough mix.

Zach looks up from the computer when it's over. "Sounds good to me. Anybody want to redo a part or add anything before I mix and master?"

We all look at Barbara, who flinches, like she's surprised people can see her. "What?"

Carol Anne wraps an arm around Barbara's shoulders. "This is your project."

"It's *our* project."

Whitney grins. "But it's your baby."

Barbara frowns — a thinking frown, not a grouchy frown. I've gotten so I can almost always tell. "I'm fine with my part, but it needs something." She looks right at me. "Travis."

"Um?"

"The backing vocals sound great, but they need more — "

"Balls?" Whitney suggests.

"Depth." Barbara nods decisively. "Zach, do you mind adding one more track?"

"No, that's fine. Anybody else want to fix anything?"

Either they're all happy or everyone else is too tired to do any more. They start to pack up their gear. The amps and drums stay in the basement because we'll be back here Thursday for band practice, but Whitney takes her cymbals with her, and Carol Anne, her guitars. It's not too bad taking my bass on the bus, but the amp — no way.

"OK, then," Barbara says. "Thanks, everybody. It'll be close, but it looks like we'll have this project in by the deadline."

It's close because they waited for me, and they waited for me because Barbara made them wait for me. So I'm not about to complain about staying late to record a part. I'm still nervous about singing, but Barbara coaches me through it. At least I don't have to do more falsetto. It's pretty simple, doubling one or the other of the girls' parts down in my register. When Zach puts it all together, I don't stick out, but Barbara's right — it does sound fuller and deeper.

"You should sing more, Travis. You've got a nice, comfortable baritone, and a killer falsetto."

I'm not used to compliments. I give her a quick smile, and then get busy helping load gear into Zach's mom's car. The air outside is such a relief after the stuffy basement. It smells like flowers. I don't know what kind, whatever blooms in the middle of April.

We've been at this all day and everybody looks exhausted, but in a good way. Barbara puts on her green cap and picks up her backpack. "Maddie, thanks again for the space. See you Monday, everyone."

Except for me. "You walking home? I'll come with you if you want." I spit it out fast before I change my mind.

"I don't need a protector."

"I know. I just ... don't want to go home yet. Unless you don't want me to."

"No, it's fine. Come on, let's go."

Barbara's a fast walker, but I'm taller, which almost

makes up for being out of shape and carrying a bass guitar.

She tips her head back and breathes deeply. "Mm, smell those lilacs!"

So that's what they are. "Yeah, lilacs. Love those."

"Why don't you want to go home?"

"Mom won't be home till late, and the place feels so empty with no one there."

"Your grandma's gone?"

"Yeah, she went back to Tucson as soon as I got the monitor off." I shake my ankle. Sometimes I still feel that thing. "Anyway, I spent enough time in that apartment. It's good to be out."

"I'll bet! I didn't even think of that."

"At least you came to see me." I was on home monitoring for three months, which I guess was a pretty light sentence, considering. But still, three months stuck in a two-bedroom apartment — being out anywhere feels like a big deal. "Good session, huh? I ... I really like that new song."

"Thanks! It's like our theme song, right?"

Before I say something stupid, I figure out that she's talking about the whole band, not her and me. "I still don't think Storm ever felt like a loser."

"You'd be surprised."

She doesn't say any more and I guess it's none of my business. "That shouty thing at the beginning was new, wasn't it?"

"Yeah, I was so inspired by the band track. Does it work?"

"I thought it was great." I crank up my courage to say what I meant to all along. "I'm, um, glad you're not afraid of me walking with you, Barbara."

She glances at me sidelong. "I haven't been afraid of you in a long time."

"Oh. Were you, back then?" She'll know what I mean.

"Yeah, but mostly I was just so pissed!" She turns to me with a frown — the thinking kind, I hope. "Were *you* afraid of *me*?"

"Totally." I don't even have to think about it. "Still am. Superpowers, jeez!"

She chuckles. "I'm seeing someone about that."

"What, like for training?"

She shakes her head. "Anger management. I could really hurt someone, you know? And those poor birds — all that crap has to come from somewhere, right? I'm learning to control it; I don't want to hurt anyone or anything. But if I can do some good ... "

"Yeah. I know what you mean." Something has been puzzling me for a while, but this is the first time I've felt comfortable saying it aloud. "There must be a lot of people who have them. Or not a lot, but more than just you. Right?"

"Wow, that'd be a thing, wouldn't it? A whole Rage Brigade or whatever."

"Yeah! Your people!"

"I don't know. When I look online, all I find is nutcase vigilantes with homemade weapons and silly costumes. Anyway, I feel like I've found my people already." She hums a few bars of "Loser."

We walk along in silence again, but it's nice. Is this talking like we're people? Because I think I feel like people.

Barbara is the first to speak up again. "You can stay for dinner, but then I have a lot of homework."

"On a Saturday night?"

"I have one week to turn an eight-page draft into a finished twelve-page paper. It'll be a pull, but it's a graduation requirement and the deadline is non-negotiable."

"Yuck. There's another reason to be glad I'm expelled."

"It could be worse. At least I have an interesting topic."

"Yeah? What?"

Barbara chuckles. "I took your suggestion — it's about local bands who made some kind of splash, then disappeared for a long time but were influential or something later. I have a section on the Sonics and one on Sleater-Kinney."

Now she's speaking my language. "Oh, yeah, there's tons of articles and interviews with both of them."

"Those parts are pretty much finished, but I want to do a third section on Trollrocket. You were right, there's not much out there."

I nod in agreement. "You should talk to my dad."

"Yeah, I interviewed him by email — " She freezes, like she's spilled a big secret.

"You already knew he was the bass player?" I'm proud and hurt at once. Cool that she knows, but I wanted to tell her. "How did you find out?"

"Your grandma mentioned it. She thought you didn't know."

"I didn't, until I put that album up on YouTube. It got a ton of hits! I just wanted to share it, you know?

And see if anybody else knew about them. Then my dad called."

"Uh-oh. Was he mad?"

"Maybe, at first. He wanted to know what I thought I was doing. We talked for a long time."

"OK. And ... ?"

I sigh. "It's not like he's coming back or anything, but, you know, at least he remembers I exist. And because of how well it did online, they might finally release the album officially."

"Then they should give you producer credit."

That's a typical Barbara declaration. She has strong opinions about justice, even or maybe especially about little things. But producer credit; I like the sound of that.

She's still talking. "By the way, thanks for finishing my paper for me. I still have to write it down, but that's the easy part."

"No problem. But if you have to work, I don't need to hang around."

"Mom will insist. I think she's making lasagna."

"That sounds amazing! My mom hardly ever has time to cook. But are you sure she'll let me?"

"Oh, yeah. To her, you're this tragic case that I heroically pulled back from the brink, so we're kind of responsible for you now."

"Wow." Tragic? No. Pathetic? Absolutely. "That's really ... that's just ... wow. I'm surprised she wants you around me at all."

"Mom's all about grace and second chances."

So now I know where Barbara gets it. "Is that like a church thing?"

"Yeah. I mean, I guess so? I'm bad at talking about it! At ours, it is. Do ... do you ever go?"

"With my grandma — the dead one, not the Tucson one — sometimes, when I was little and she wasn't dead. I liked how it was everybody together, and the singing. But I made people ... uncomfortable. Well, no, I kind of drove them nuts. I didn't know how to act and I was such a little weirdo."

"Come to ours sometime — we could use you in the choir, and they're very accepting of us weirdos."

"You're not a weirdo, Barbara."

"Um, superpowers? Weirdo."

OK, she has a point. "Does your mom know about the superpowers?"

"Are you kidding? The first rule of superpowers is you never tell the parents about superpowers. They think I'm in therapy for stress and social anxiety. And some lingering trauma. Which is all true, but ... "

I stop in the middle of the sidewalk. "You have nightmares, too?"

She stops, too, and faces me. "Not as often now."

"Do I ... shoot people?"

"Sometimes. The worst one is where I shoot you, and then wake up before I know if you're all right." We're passing the reservoir, and Barbara pauses next to a fence post that's shinier than the rest. "This is the spot, isn't it? Where Otis wrecked his brother's truck?"

"And you punched me in the nose." I consider that. "Which I totally deserved."

"A lot can change in a year." She plops down on the grass and leans against the fence.

I welcome the excuse to set my bass down. "Otis

was so stoned. He shouldn't have been driving, even if he'd had permission to take the truck." I sit next to her, taking care to leave what I hope is the right amount of space. My therapist talks a lot about boundaries. I don't touch people because I don't like to be touched, but I tend to get too close because I don't have a clue.

"Why didn't you stop him? Or were you stoned, too?"

"No, I'd already quit weed by then. Doesn't matter — Otis never listened to me."

"I was walking home from our first real band practice — never would have guessed I'd invite you to join us."

"Boy, me neither! I'm glad you did, though — it's saving my life." That maybe sounds too serious, so I move on before she can comment. "Will you keep the band going after graduation?"

"Over the summer, anyway. Now that we finally have a bass player, it would stink to split up before we get to play out, so Maddie's trying to line up some shows. But everybody's scattering in the fall. I'm the only one staying in town."

"I'll be here," I remind her.

"God, I'm sorry, Travis. I didn't mean it like that. It's just, it took me so long to put this group together. I guess I sort of thought we'd all go to community college together and be a band forever."

"Why aren't you going away somewhere? I thought you were good in school."

"I'm good *at* school, but I don't know what I want to do next. Music? Engineering? Religion? Accounting?"

Accounting? I guess I don't know Barbara that well. "You're good at songs."

"Yeah, but can you major in that? Make a living at it? I suspect I'll need a day job. What, though? I don't want to spend big tuition money when I don't have a clue." She sighs. "I won't miss high school, but I wish we had more time. Why didn't I start this group years ago? We could have been doing this all along!"

"Yeah, but, well, what if you hadn't done it yet?"

She stares at me intently, which makes me nervous because who knows — maybe laser eyes. She blinks and turns away. "Thank you, Travis. You're right. That would have been so much worse."

"I'll go to community college with you, Barbara." When did I make that decision? But now it's made. Maybe they have audio engineering ...

"Get that GED then." She digs into her backpack and pulls out a granola bar. "Want some?"

"That's OK, I had two pieces of that pizza at lunch."

"Pizza. Did I eat any? 'Cause I'm starving."

"Maybe half a piece? Then you went all record producer with Zach and never finished."

She laughs, just one squawk, but it makes my heart kind of fizz. "I can't believe I'm turning into that person who has to be reminded to eat. Here, have some so I'm not eating alone. These are so good." She breaks off a piece of the granola bar and holds it out.

I take it to be nice, because who gets excited about a granola bar? But ... "Oh, my God, that's amazing! It tastes exactly like canned chocolate frosting!"

"I know, right? Storm turned me on to these. I don't know who came up with the formula, but it's perfect!"

She takes another bite and smiles blissfully.

"That was my favorite food when I was ten. I once ate an entire can by myself."

"Ew. How sick were you afterwards?"

"Not sick at all, but the sugar rush was epic." We're both laughing, and I feel great, for a change. "So, prom must be coming up, huh? Is everybody going?"

"All but me. Not my scene, you know?"

"Yeah, not mine either. If I could go." I'm secretly glad she doesn't have a date, but I'm not saying that out loud. No way.

"Ooh, idea!" Barbara gets a gleam in her eye. "We should get all dressed up on prom night and go do something else!"

"Like what?"

"I don't know, something fun. I'll find out when prom is, you pick the activity. How does that sound?"

"Good, I guess. So is this like a date?"

"No, I can't date."

"Aren't you almost eighteen?"

"This isn't a parental thing. Maybe it's more like I *shouldn't* date; you know, because of the superpowers."

I nod. "Oh, right. Because your enemies might try to get to you through your boyfriend."

She laughs and laughs, which is so great. Can you be in love with a laugh? "I don't have any enemies except maybe Zach Morton and a few bad drivers. But I probably shouldn't have a boyfriend until I'm sure I won't drown him in birdshit if he makes me mad."

"But it's OK for us to go out and do something?"

"Sure. Remember what you said about doing something you like with people who like you? Even us weirdos get to have fun with our friends." She grins.

I'm her friend? That's the best news I've heard in a long time. I'll take it.

Barbara stands, then grabs my hand to help me up. A tingling pain zings up my arm, like that time I stuck a key in the electrical outlet. That sensation is why I don't like to be touched. But I'm kind of sorry when she lets go.

35

RELEASE

BARBARA

I must be dreaming. Here we are, back in Maddie's basement, deja vu all over again. We've got the Mylar streamers and Christmas lights. Carol Anne and Whitney are setting up drums, amps and monitors, with able assistance from Jackson, Justin, and Whitney's friend Ike. Because I'm such a glamorous rock star, I'm on the floor, taping down cables. I don't mind because the person most likely to trip is me. Zach's at the soundboard. Maddie's mom is behind the bar, once again loaded with snacks, bottled water, and cans of pop. Lesson learned: no open punch bowl this time. Maddie's dad is at the door, ready to check tickets and student IDs and bar anyone who seems inebriated or otherwise ready to make trouble. Other parents are upstairs in case anyone comes to that door.

Oh, the other big difference? We're not the entertainment this time; well, we are, but this is our show. We did a presentation about our EP project at school, but this is the official release.

If anyone thinks we chose an easy senior project ... St. Rage would like to introduce you to some birdshit. Even with the three songs we already knew well, the recording sessions were intense. Partly my fault, bringing in Travis *and* a new song, but I think it was worth it. The band stepped up to the challenge. Not only did we finish on time (so we can graduate — yay!!!), we made a kickass record.

Uh-oh. Speaking of Travis, Maddie's dad is giving him a hard time at the door because he doesn't have a student ID.

"It's OK, Mr. G; Travis is with the band." I jump up and hurry over there to make things right. "I guess you didn't meet him when we were recording."

"The instrument case should have been a clue. Come on in."

Travis has his bass in one hand and a manila envelope in the other. He glances at me and looks away, red-faced. Yeah, we're back to being awkward(er) since our non-prom non-date. It might have been better if we'd had a bad time. The problem is, we had fun. He decided we should go to the free swing dance at the Armory, where they have live music and a dance lesson. Not what I was expecting that night, but way better than a school dance with a DJ. I wore Grandma's prom dress, he wore his court suit and a clip-on tie, so we looked right, even if neither of us is a good dancer. Especially that kind, where you have to touch. Travis pulled his sleeve over his hand so we weren't skin-to-skin, and our moves improved as the night went on. We had a great time, so what's the problem?

This: I think he likes me, as in *like*, which I probably should have figured out a long time ago. And I don't know how I feel; it's too tangled. Probably a good thing I made it clear I shouldn't date. Still awkward. But he's our bass player, so ...

I follow him over to where he's setting up. "Hey, Travis, I got you something."

He starts and turns, staring first and then blinking in that careful way. "Oh. Hey. You did?"

"Yeah, yesterday we all picked up our caps and gowns for graduation. I went over to Display & Costume so you'd have something, too." I pull the cardboard-and-tissue-paper mortarboard from a shopping bag and hand it to him. "Here, let me hold that."

Speaking of deja vu ... Travis gives me what he's holding — that envelope, which is a lot less scary than a gun. He puts the cap on and fiddles with the tassel. "This is dorkier than that furry one. Why do I need this?"

"Because that's our stage outfit tonight."

"I thought we agreed on T-shirt and shorts." He plucks at one of the pocket flaps on his cargo shorts.

"That was before we knew we'd have our caps and

gowns in time. And we are wearing shorts." Storm was right, by the way. The thrift stores are full of last summer's lace shorts. I tried on a pair but didn't buy them. I went for a sturdy denim pair with functional pockets. Jewelled sandals, on the other hand, seemed like just the thing for tonight, and for graduation. You know, since I don't have to walk a mile in them. And they go great with my gold nail polish. "Besides, if you're taking the GED soon, that's a kind of graduation, right?"

He smiles, more at ease now. "Look in the envelope."

I slide a single sheet out. "Oh. My. God." It's his GED certificate, dated yesterday. "Dude, you did it! You graduated!" My throat tightens and I have to blink away a tear. "Congratulations."

"They blew bubbles for me. No hat, though, so ... thanks." He touches the top of his cheap mortarboard and it slides over his eyes.

"Sorry. Even the real ones don't fit so well. Storm brought a ton of hairpins."

"So, do you think people will come? Like, do they know I'm gonna be here?"

"Yeah. When we presented our project, we announced that there'd be a release party and whoever was interested should see Jackson for details and tickets."

"Why Jackson and not you?"

"Because Jackson is a billion times better with people than I am. He already knows everybody. And there was a lot of interest, but it seemed only fair to be open about how you'd be here. If nobody else comes, we'll play for Whitney's friends and our parents. It'll be OK, no matter what — making music with friends, right?"

"Right. Um, if people do come, can I introduce 'Loser'?"

He wants to talk in front of people? But I did write the song for him. "OK, if you really want to. Sure."

I let him get back to setting up while I return the gaff tape to Zach. I can't stand still. I don't think I'll be this excited even at actual graduation. This is the celebration; that's the beginning of the end.

Zach looks up from the board and grins as he takes the roll of tape. "Hey, Barbara. Ready for this?"

"Can't wait! Have everything you need?"

"I think so, as long as the opening act doesn't need more than four microphones. I'll DI the keyboard through the PA ... "

And he loses me with the alphabet soup of engineer talk, but that's OK. As long as he knows what he's doing, I can nod and smile with the best of them. At the merch table (which I love being able to say) Maddie fans out stickers. Maybe someday we'll have T-shirts, too.

"Barbara, did you say there's a poster? Mom says it's OK to put it up if you use poster putty. I think she brought some down."

"Great, I'll ask her."

Mrs. G greets me with a big smile. "Barbara! It's your big night!"

"That's what they say. Maddie said something about poster putty?"

"Right here." She hands over the package. "So,

what's next for you?"

"Learning to drive, battling evil and injustice ... the usual." We share a laugh over that ridiculous notion. Seriously, me behind the wheel? That's scarier than superpowers. "And I have a temp job in my dad's office this summer — scanning documents, shredding stuff, data entry — you know, whatever."

"Good experience. But what about after the summer? College? Work?"

"Community college. I don't really know what I want to do, so I'll get some of the basics out of the way on the cheap."

"Smart. We're lucky Maddie got some good scholarships."

"You must be proud of her — valedictorian, going to MIT ... "

Mrs. G struggles to smile. "We are. It's so far away, though."

"That's what Skype is for, right?"

"I keep telling myself exactly that." Big sigh. "The one I really feel sorry for is Zach."

"Zach who got a full-ride scholarship to Stanford? I think he's doing OK."

"But they're so good for each other, and they'll be on opposite coasts."

"If two geniuses want to be together, they'll figure something out."

"Easy for you to talk; it's not your sweetheart thousands of miles away."

"Yeah, maybe it's a good thing I don't have one." It's bad enough to think of all my friends except Travis moving away, though it's exciting to imagine the cool stuff they're going to learn — engineering, computer science, costume design, circus arts, and who knows what else? How did they get so ambitious? Meanwhile, here I'll be, taking general ed. classes and looking out for opportunities to use my superpowers. Maybe I'll take on a sidekick. "Hey, thanks for the putty — I need to hang a poster."

We blew up the EP cover art to hang behind the band. It's a photo Storm took of the sign at the storage place that gave me our band name in the first place. They'd replaced the burned-out bulb by then so she had to Photoshop the O out. Then she kept going and made the image all dark and arty. She acted like it was no big deal, but I think it's great. If the circus thing doesn't work out, she should think about photography or graphic design.

It's showtime! And people came! Mostly seniors (not as many as after Homecoming), and a good turnout of younger students, too. And I'm pretty sure the entire chamber music club. I was telling Travis the truth, that if no one showed up we'd still play, but this is better. Maddie's basement is comfortably full by the time the opening act goes on.

"Hey, everybody! Thanks for coming out! We've had a bunch of different names, most recently Legion of Morons." Tad waits out the smattering of applause. "After tonight, we're changing direction with a whole new name, but for tonight only we are ... (Boy)Friends of Whitney P!"

Ike takes over the intro. "In case the parentheses were unclear, we're all her friends, but only one of us is her boyfriend. 1 2 3 4!"

Tad, Ike, and the gang throw themselves into a loud, energetic set. Right up front, Whitney playfully slams into Travis, who gently bumps her back — a scene I couldn't have imagined a couple of months ago. And I'm right to put my trust in Zach; he's making the band sound great. The crowd seems into it, and newcomers keep joining them.

"Thanks, guys! We were (Boy)Friends of Whitney P, but after this we'll be known as The Greebles! Be sure to stick around for St. Rage, and buy their EP. You know it's good because Whitney's playing on it."

As the crowd yells for them, we sneak out to the laundry room to get ready. While Storm's securing my mortarboard with hairpins, her shorts pull up to reveal a colorful mark on her thigh.

"Storm, did you bruise your leg again?"

"Birthday tattoo." She rolls the shorts leg up so we can see the design: a tambourine with *ST RAGE* in the middle. "I can't wait for high school to end, but I'm keeping this one thing."

"Cool." I don't think of myself as a tattoo person, but I could almost go for something like that.

Carol Anne puts her graduation gown on over her pink pedal-pushers. "Zipped or not?"

"Not," Whitney says before anyone else can express an opinion. "It's already fucking hot in there." She kept up her resolution longer than any of us expected, but it was no surprise when she started dropping f-bombs again. She's so cheerful about it, though. Must be love. The real surprise is her hair. She's growing it out, so instead of spikes she has curls. Still green, but curls.

"Travis is lucky he doesn't have to wear a gown. He

already has his diploma." I offer him a fist and we bump. He can tolerate that much touching.

"Dude." Whitney punches him in the shoulder and he pretends to fall over onto the washing machine.

"Aw, Travis, that's great! Congratulations!" Storm plants a kiss on his cheek as he stands back up, and he turns red enough to almost hide the lipstick smudge. But he doesn't wipe it off.

"Proud of you, Travis." Carol Anne takes off her glasses and dries them on her gown. "So, are we ready?"

"Let's go put on a show!"

Zach cues up a recording of "Pomp and Circumstance" for our entrance. We learned something from the Eagles show: shared drums and amps is the way to go, so there's no need to reset the stage. We go on, tune up quickly, and dive right into "Something of Mine." We continue without a break to "Distracted Driver" and "Wildest Dreams."

Now I'm ready to talk. "Thanks, guys! We are St. Rage, and one of our wildest dreams is coming true. We are thrilled to release our first EP! This was our senior project, so not only do we get to rock out, we get to graduate. That's kind of like the school releasing us!" All the seniors in the room roar in response to that. Once they've settled down, I go on with my speech. "But this project couldn't have happened without a lot of work from a lot of people. Huge thanks are due to Mr. Zach Brown, who recorded and mixed and made us sound amazing. Maddie Gowan not only provided practice and recording space, she took care of a ton of administrative and technical stuff. She's so good, she's officially our manager now. Shout-out to Mr. P's after-school chamber music club for making us feel welcome." A healthy cheer from the chamber players. "Everybody up here had a hand in arranging and performing the songs, and writing the liner notes. Storm Skye is responsible for the incredible artwork. And we wouldn't even be here if Jackson Durand hadn't given me what I needed—a hat on my head and the courage to start a band with these talented folks." Jackson, right up front, turns around and takes a deep bow. "The record is available as a download for $5, but if you buy it tonight, you get a limited-edition cassette with the download code for only $4, so be sure to see Marina and Maddie at the merch table before you leave. And now, let's play the songs!"

We start with "Huge Guy," and the entire chamber music club gets right up front and starts a mosh pit. Then comes "The Drink I Didn't Have Last Night," followed by "Half a Bus."

Even while I sing, I can't stop smiling. These three songs — the first we learned — are so much a part of my friendships in the band. It's really something to see all the others wearing the same hat as me. I don't know how I'll feel on graduation night, with our whole class wearing it. It'll be OK to be invisible, I guess. Tonight I feel *seen* enough to last for months.

We pause before the last song. "You might have noticed our token guy up here on bass. This wasn't his senior project because of ... an unfortunate incident back in December. Bringing him on board was an act of faith for us and for him. We're pretty pleased with how it all turned out and hope you agree. Before we play our last song of the night, he has something he'd like to say. Travis?"

He steps up to his mic, a nervous smile on his face. "Hey, um, thanks for coming out. It says a lot about these girls that you showed up even knowing I'd be here. Everybody probably knows I got expelled, and why. A few months back, on the worst day of my life, I made a really shitty decision — sorry, Maddie's parents, can I say shitty? — OK, whatever. It was. Shitty, I mean. The decision. I did something awful just to see what would happen, and I found out. So I want to say I'm sorry for trying to share my worst day with all of you." He pauses so long, I figure he's finished. Then he draws a ragged breath and continues. "But that worst day was the beginning of things getting better, because of Barbara and St. Rage. I've always been a loser. But because of these amazing girls ... " Travis closes his eyes and breathes for a while, then opens them and looks at all of us. "No, these amazing *women* ... well, *people* ... I'm starting to feel like maybe I could be less of a loser. Because of Barbara, I got my GED, and I'm going to college. Because of this band, I get to grow up and be a real person, which is kind of like a winner. So, thanks."

A few people clap, and then a few more, until there's a healthy ovation going. Is it for Travis? For us? I give Carol Anne and Whitney the count, and the intro to "Loser" cuts through everything. I shout out my opening lines with all my heart.

This is a song about not being popular
And not giving a shit!

It's the last song, which means this show is almost

over. Next week is graduation, and high school will be over. After the summer, we'll scatter, so maybe the band will be over, at least for a while. I still wish I'd started it sooner. But, yeah — like Travis said, what if I hadn't started it yet? Besides, what's the other name for graduation, the one they put on the formal announcements? Commencement ... not the end; the beginning, a brand new start. I don't know what's coming, but I can hardly wait to find out.

What's next? And why do I feel like I'm winning?

THE END

Bonus Tracks

St. Rage may be a fictional band, but the songs are real!
Find recordings and lyrics at
https://strage2.bandcamp.com/

Are you reading with a book club? Find discussion
questions at
https://kareneisenbreywriter.com/my-books/the-
gospel-according-to-st-rage/

Find more info on Karen's books and short fiction,
follow her band-name blog, and sign up for her
quarterly newsletter at
https://kareneisenbreywriter.com

About the Author

Karen Eisenbrey lives in Seattle, WA, where she leads a quiet, orderly life and invents stories to make up for it. Although she intended to be a writer from an early age, until her mid-30s she had nothing to say. A little bit of free time and a vivid dream about a wizard changed all that. Karen writes fantasy and science fiction novels, as well as short fiction in a variety of genres and the occasional song or poem if it insists. She also sings in a church choir and plays drums in a garage band. She shares her life with her husband, two young adult sons, and two mature adult cats.

Special Thanks

... to Benjamin Gorman for starting a publishing company that so perfectly fits my writing; and to Kelleen Cummings for astute, on-the-nose editing.

... to the whole Not A Pipe family of authors for their support, encouragement, and example.

... to the late, lamented Pankhearst Collective, without whom Barbara and her stories would not exist.

... to Angelika, Keith, Nan, and Yvonne, my invaluable beta readers.

... to Amy and Tim, my writing group that willingly listens to chapters out of order, some of them more than once.

... to the Seattle bar bands who made a middle-aged drummergirl feel welcome, and especially to those who agreed to appear in the book: Ne'erdowells; Your Mother Should Know; and Dead Bars, who reminded the author what it felt like to be seventeen.

... to my sons, who were teenagers when this project got underway. Isaac named Justin Hornbaker, gave

Jackson his secret hobby, and suggested all the best superpowers. John gets credit for Sack o' Hamsters and Legion of Morons.

... to Neal Kosaly-Meyer and Your Mother Should Know for bringing Barbara's songs to life.

... to my parents for letting me keep my drums in the living room, for letting us take over the stereo with our loud music, and for always believing in me.

... to Keith Eisenbrey, my example for doing the creative work that needs to be done in spite of everything else. He has read countless drafts (of this and other projects), listened to me fuss over ideas, welcomed the host of fictional people who live in my head, and kept a roof over our heads all these years. I couldn't do any of it without him.

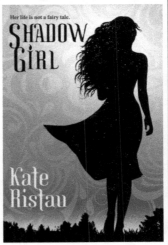

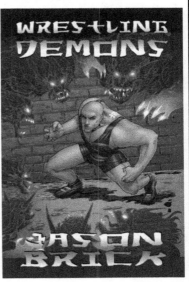

CPSIA information can be obtained
at www.ICGtesting.com
Printed in the USA
FSHW020937190420
69352FS